MISTLE CHILD

Also by Ari Berk

Death Watch

MISTLE CHILD

✦┼ THE ┼✦ UNDERTAKEN ┼✦ TRILOGY ┼✦

✦┼✦

ARI BERK

✦┼✦

SIMON & SCHUSTER BFYR

New York London Toronto Sydney New Delhi

SIMON & SCHUSTER BFYR

An imprint of Simon & Schuster Children's Publishing Division
1230 Avenue of the Americas, New York, New York 10020
This book is a work of fiction. Any references to historical events, real people, or real places are used fictitiously. Other names, characters, places, and events are products of the author's imagination, and any resemblance to actual events or places or persons, living or dead, is entirely coincidental.
For information about special discounts for bulk purchases, please contact Simon & Schuster Special Sales at 1-866-506-1949 or business@simonandschuster.com.
The Simon & Schuster Speakers Bureau can bring authors to your live event. For more information or to book an event, contact the Simon & Schuster Speakers Bureau at 1-866-248-3049 or visit our website at www.simonspeakers.com.
Book design by Laurent Linn
Map illustration by Drew Willis
The text for this book is set in Minister Std.
Manufactured in the United States of America
10 9 8 7 6 5 4 3 2 1
Library of Congress Cataloging-in-Publication Data
Berk, Ari.
Mistle child / Ari Berk.—1st ed.
p. cm.—(The Undertaken trilogy ; bk. 2)
Summary: As the only living resident of Arvale Manor, Silas must seek to understand the past and put an ancient wrong to right, as he discovers that even a house of ghosts can be haunted by its past.
ISBN 978-1-4169-9117-5 (hardcover)
ISBN 978-1-4424-3916-0 (eBook)
[1. Fantasy. 2. Ghosts—Fiction. 3. Families—Fiction.] I. Title.
PZ7.B452293Mi 2013
[Fic]—dc23
2012002977

For Tracy Ford
Amicitia Numquam Moritur

CONTENTS

Here is the book of thy Descent . . .
Here begin the Terrors.
Here begin the Miracles.

—*Perlesvaus*, 1225

There the patient houses grow
While through the rooms the flesh must flow.
Mothers', daughters', fathers', sons',
On and on the river runs . . .

—From "A Devon Signpost" by Jacquetta Hawkes

Thus he arrived before a great castle,
on whose façade were carved the words:
I belong to no one and to all.
Before entering you were already here.
When you leave you shall remain.

—From *Jacques Le Fataliste* (1773) by Diderot

PROLOGUE

"BRING HOME THE CHILD . . . ," she said through her sobs. "Little soul, by swift wing fly homeward to me." Maud Umber spoke desperately, her eyes spilling over with tears. She looked as though she had been crying for a thousand years.

She could move freely at most times through the whole of the house, though she often allowed her losses to hold her here, in the zone of the tears of fire, and within her private chapel. This was her own place, a casket for her grief. Here, alone in the chapel, Maud Umber gave free rein to her sorrow.

She stood in a long woolen gown, limned with flickering, melancholic fire, looking out over the twilight salt marshes. The deep casement of the window was used as an altar and was thick with wax from the centuries of candles left burning there. Little blue flames flowed and leapt across the surface of her hands and fingers as she lit another candle. She stared at a small, gilded statue of a woman who sat on a throne with a small child in her lap.

Maud closed her eyes and wrung her hands in front of her heart in desperate supplication.

"Almighty and all merciful Queen, to whom all of this world fleeth for succor, Flower of Flowers, help and relieve my mighty misery. Lady of Heaven and Mother of the Stars, Thou who guardest little children in life and in the hour of their death, and hast prepared for them, *and their mothers,* a spacious place, even in the angelic abodes brightly radiant which befit their purity, wherein the souls of the righteous dwell, Thou, Cause of Our Joy, who makest a way for all the mothers of the world: Do Thou take pity, and restore my child to me . . . to my arms. Let a mother's prayer be answered, I beg You, Holy Mother, Advocate of Eve. Bring home the child. Please, Mother of Heaven, light the way for my child to come home again so that we may make our way to Your side. Bring home the child. BRING HOME THE CHILD. . . ."

The prayer became a scream woven with every kind of sorrow and longing and misery. It was the cry of a soul torn into portions of unfathomable grief. She screamed until there were no more screams left in her. She dropped to the floor, looking up at the carved beams of the ceiling and the thick, impervious stone of the walls.

Shadows hung all about her, cast from the candles and from the preternatural glow rising from her form. Her chest heaved as she turned to look at the fluttering tapers. Suddenly, beyond the window's frame, something flew upward from the earth and filled the air of the distant sky. Flocks of small birds were circling over the salt marshes, joined in their flight by the night herons. Something was happening. That place was changing. She rose from the floor and walked quickly to a bronze mirror hanging next to the hearth. She breathed across its surface and whispered, "Mother of Heaven, *who* hath caused this?" An image rose.

A young man, a scion of her own house, blood-kin, stood before the salt marshes where nested the souls of the mothers of the lost. She knew that place well and had at various times looked out over the water, seeking solace with those weeping souls who had also lost their children, but whom she could never join. Now the once heavy, miserable air of the marshes was light with birdsong. Small birds. Children. The spirits of children filled the air. And below them stood a young man. It was the son of Amos Umber, and he had brought the lost children to the Bowers of the Night Herons where the mothers of loss had long been waiting to be free of their sorrows, to have their hearts restored to them, to find their children, any children, to whom they could give comfort, and so know peace.

Maud Umber's heart leapt and the flames that traced her body stilled and nearly went out. So, the child of Amos Umber held within his hands the rare power to bring lost children home. She went to the door of the small ancient chapel, stepped across the threshold, and ascended one of the high towers of the house. Without any consideration, without a care for the consequences, she raised her arms and spoke the words of summoning.

"Let name call out to name! Scion of the house of Umber, come home! Your family calls you. Take up the mantle that is yours by rite and right. By threshold and Door Doom, by Limbus and mansion, by hall, by chamber, by lintel and post: Child of Amos Umber, come, now, by the ancient way, to the house of your kin!"

She prayed he would come, for fascination with the house, with the ancestral manor, if nothing else. And once he arrived, he would take his place as Janus and would help her. He would restore her losses. He was obligated to his relations.

A deep brazen trumpet sounded. Long and low came the ancient carnyx-call from some high place among the range of battlements. Then, from atop the long-abandoned clock tower, a decorative figure carved of limestone stirred, shifting from steadfast rock to undulating fabric just below the huge, unmoving dial. Tall and hooded, the figure slowly bent forward and set down its mighty scythe by the foot of the clock's face, then stretched its hands, each finger a thick, sharp-tipped bone that clicked and scraped against its neighbor.

Again, the trumpet cried out in metallic staccato notes that lengthened and deepened the longer they were held— *SilAAAAAs, SilAAAAAs, SilAAAAAs*. The blasts pierced and shattered the freezing air.

The messenger pulled back its hood to reveal a skull, no longer of pitted, greening limestone, but dark, smooth bone, polished now like obsidian. From below the shelf of stone where it stood, a wind blew up the tower and roused the tattered hangings from its flowing robes into the semblance of wings. Then, as though the wind had caught in the billowing garment, it rose into the air and flew from that high place to deliver its invitation. Its eyes flared like embers leaping to flame as it flew along the lychway. When it came before the gates, the messenger unhinged its jaw and let forth a sound like the cry of a thousand night birds. The gates opened, and in this way, the messenger passed into the town of Lichport.

It floated silently down Fort Street, unseen, except by one venerable corpse sitting watch in a high window of its crumbling house.

The messenger passed from shadow to shadow along the leaning and abandoned buildings, swiftly making its way closer and closer to its destination. A few moments later, the messenger stood on the porch of Silas Umber's house. Without pausing, it drew its long finger up and down across the surface of the door, tracing out six letters in flame, burning the lines deeply into the surface of the wood . . .

ARVALE

LEDGER

Sanctify unto me all the
firstborn . . . both of man and
of beast: it is mine.

—Exodus, 13:2. Marginalia of Amos Umber

CHAPTER 1

LIGHTHOUSE

NIGHTMARE TIME.

From the ruined lighthouse clinging to the rocks stacked high above the sea, a gray ghost-light swept out over Lichport.

Every evening, for over a week, on the very edge of town, the miasmic beam shone down from that tower. Grim weather descended with that light: furious winds and buffeting rain. And when the storm rose into a gale and screamed from the cliffs and whipped the surf into flying sheets of foam, that's when the bad dreams began. It was mostly in the Narrows, where folks lived closest to the lighthouse; they would wake, terrified, from awful dreams of drowning and shipwrecks and muted voices crying through slowly rising bubbles far beneath the surface of the sea. Even in the upper part of town, people were affected.

But not Silas Umber, the Undertaker of Lichport. He wasn't sleeping anyway. Not since a few nights ago, when someone burned the name of the old Umber family estate into his front door. Silas had spent the rest of that night pulling books and records from the shelves of his study, anything he could find that would tell him more about the house called Arvale. He had a large pile of these on his desk, awaiting his attention. But the lighthouse would have to come first. People were talking. Letters requesting help had been coming in every day since it started. Nights were bad for the rest of the folk in Lichport, and Silas knew they expected him to end the trouble.

Mrs. Bowe, who lived in the house attached to his, woke screaming six days ago and hadn't had a good night's rest since. Silas's mother called him two days before to say the dreams were so bad that she had resorted to only napping in a chair during daylight hours. Silas had spent several evenings at his mother's house across town, playing cards with her from midnight until morning because he was worried she'd go back to drinking to calm her nerves. Things had eased a little between them. They were talking *to* each other now, not *at* each other. He knew his mother was proud of him in her way. She still had trouble saying it, Silas could tell, but things were better. She had come to his dad's wake and had begun talking about Amos civilly. Silas had even invited his mother to move in with him once more. And although she declined, saying again the house on Temple Street was *her place* now, and the only way she was leaving was *feet first*, she took her son's hand warmly and kissed his cheek for having asked.

But the nightmares were fraying the edges of everything.

Now Silas looked out from a high window in his house. In his hand, the death watch was silent, its ticking stilled by his thumb against the dial. Silas could see, clear with the ghost-sight the watch bestowed, the beams of sickly gray light turning out from the lighthouse and falling like a pall over land and sea.

At first, Silas thought the light might have been one of the occasional phantasmal glimmerings seen near the ocean. These were not uncommon, and while they might be related to sunken ships, or some poor soul lost beneath the waves, no ghost ever manifested, and the lights would usually vanish almost as soon as they appeared. But this was different, and people in town, *his* town, were suffering.

Enough, he said to himself. *Enough*.

He opened the enormous funereal ledger that contained

everything his father and the other Undertakers of his family knew about ghost lore and death rites. Scrawled throughout the book and upon its margins were the notes, instructions, and gleanings of his ancestors, those previous Undertakers who, like him, sought to bring Peace to the unsettled dead.

The ghost of the lighthouse had been known to his father, but only through secondhand accounts. Silas had read an entry in his father's handwriting that explained that the ghost of the lighthouse would never appear to him, though he had tried to speak to the spirit on more than one occasion. For several days, and as the nightmares continued to run like wild things through the town, Silas read and read, making an especial study of the lighthouse and its sad history. He devoured newspaper accounts, memoirs, notes, rumors: everything he could find in the ledger and in the large collection of books on local history that spilled from the shelves of his father's home library.

When he had learned all he could on the subject of the lighthouse and its last occupant, Silas set out for the cliffs, a little before dark. In the months since his father's death, he had diligently applied himself to Undertaking, reading widely, and practicing the arcane rites he'd read about in the ledger when and where he could. And while Silas wasn't even sure if he'd be able to help, he was resolved to try. In his mind Silas carried a name, held it like a talisman with which he might be able to settle the dead within that spindle of brick perched upon the rocks. He prayed the name would be enough.

The sky was pouring down pitch as Silas walked quickly along the cliff toward the old lighthouse. He wore an oilskin cape over his father's jacket and held a small lantern. As he approached the high tower, he reached into his jacket pocket and took hold of the death watch, that ancient timepiece that when stopped, compelled the dead to become visible to the living. Silas drew no comfort from how quickly the silver warmed in his hand. It was as if the death watch wanted to be held and used. It made Silas feel uneasy.

Before even reaching the door, before stopping the hand of the death watch, he could sense the past of the place weighing down on him, more and more with every step, pulling at his feet as though the earth itself were trying to hold him back. He picked up his pace and when he reached the door, he took out a large iron key lent to him by Mother Peale, who had taken it upon herself to keep an eye on the place many years ago. She had been only too happy to hear that Silas would try his hand at bringing Peace to that haunted tower.

"You take this key and do what you can, Silas Umber," Mother Peale had said. "You know we're all for you, no matter what happens. And remember, if you don't come back, your funeral is paid for by the townsfolk, as is customary, so don't you worry. It's all taken care of should it come to that." Mother Peale had smiled and winked at Silas then, to rouse his good humor. Silas had smiled back, but hadn't found it terribly funny.

At first, the key wouldn't turn in the lock. Silas twisted it back and forth, worried that it might break. Finally, the rust gave way and the lock turned, but when Silas pushed the door, it wouldn't budge. He shoved it, then struck it with his fist as though the door might fly open by the sheer force of his rising aggravation. Finally, in anger, Silas threw his full weight at the door, hitting it hard with his shoulder, and the door relented. A damp, salty smell flowed out from the darkness beyond the doorway as he stumbled inside. He held up the lantern, its weak light barely making an entrance into the inky black of the room, and then closed the door behind him. He walked to the center of the room, set the lantern on a small uneven table, and took the death watch from his pocket. Opening the jaw of the small silver skull, he brought his thumb down hard on the dial. He could feel the watch's little heartbeat slow and then stop. Silas closed his eyes, drew in a breath, and opened them again.

Where only a moment ago there had been an abandoned room with a few pieces of rotted and broken furniture, now a new scene glimmered before him. A wood-burning stove glowed on the far side of the room and a few toys lay scattered on the rug. In the middle of the room, a table was set with a cloth and candles. A hutch against the wall bore dishes and mugs. Here was a comfortable family home.

A sudden movement caught Silas's eyes. A shadow was drawing away from the wall. Slowly it lengthened out across the floor, and began to rise and take shape. The shadow moved against the light to place itself in a chair across the room from Silas. There, now, smiling faintly, was a young man, perhaps in his twenties. His body gave off a gray ineffectual light, as though he were a candle seen on the screen in an early film.

"Good evening," said Silas to the ghost, breathing slowly, steadying himself.

"Is it evening? I hadn't noticed," the ghost replied absently.

"Almost. I am looking for the keeper of this lighthouse. Is that you?"

The ghost looked away. "No. That is my father."

"May I speak with him?"

"I am afraid not, sir. He's not here at present."

"May I ask where he is?" Silas inquired.

"My father's not here. Just me now. The son."

Silas was surprised. He knew that the lighthouse keeper's son, who had died with his mother in a shipwreck, had been an infant.

So who was this? Was there another son? Had the records he'd consulted been incomplete? There was something in the ghost's voice—a knowing hesitancy—that made Silas uneasy.

"I need to speak with your father," Silas said again, this time putting some iron into the words.

The ghost began to shake. He looked at Silas, then toward the window.

"I think I know you. . . . I've seen you, sitting out there, with a girl." The ghost smiled wanly then. "You were with a strange girl. Her skin was like the moon—"

"I don't remember," Silas said. While he couldn't recall the particulars, he knew the ghost was right. He'd been there with a girl. What was her name? No. He didn't want to start on this topic. Not now. Memories of her . . . of the girl . . . made his heart ache, and he hadn't come to the lighthouse to talk about his own losses. "But," he said instead, "I am pleased to meet you. I am Silas Umber. I am the Undertaker. I am here to help you."

"I am Daniel. Daniel Downing." As the ghost spoke the name, he seemed to dim and lose the definition of his form. His edges blurred.

Now Silas was confused. Daniel had indeed been the lighthouse keeper's son, the very son who had died out upon the reef with his mother when their ship struck the rocks. Thus far, Silas's experience had been that ghosts appeared as they were at the time of their passing, or as they had been at some especial point during their life. Ghosts only had full knowledge of what they had been and what they had done during their lifetime. So how could a child appear as the man he had never become?

"Now, if you please. I would like to speak with your father."

The ghost looked down at the floor and shook his head.

"He's not here. I told you."

"Are you sure?"

The ghost looked up, his eyes rheumy and unfocused. "It's time to light the lamp," he whispered.

"All right," Silas said, trying to encourage him. "Let's have some more light."

But the ghost looked frightened and only repeated, "Time to light the lamp." The ghost began to open and close his hands as though he were giving some kind of frantic semaphore to the floorboards. "It's getting dark."

"It is. Night is coming."

"Oh, God," said the ghost.

"You don't want to light the lamp? May I help?"

"I do. I must. It's just that . . . the light affects me badly . . . my head."

"Let's climb up together. I will help you."

"All right," said the ghost passively. The color of his form deepened and darkened, becoming more present, the buttons on his clothes coming into focus, and he added, "If you like, I can show you the spot where my father jumped."

"Thank you," replied Silas, his nerves prickling at the ghost's mention of the suicide. "That will be fine."

They climbed the steep stairs of the lighthouse together. When they reached the uppermost chamber, the great lamp of the tower burst into spectral flame and began to turn, casting its grim light over the sea and land and the tower itself. As the beam passed through the ghost, Silas could see another aspect, another face, hiding just below the glimmering ashen surface of the ghost's skin. It was older, but not vastly different from the one Silas had seen only a moment ago. When the beam swung away, the older face vanished, and the young man was there again.

"Let me show you where he jumped, Silas Umber. Just here.

You see, the rail is not so high. Just here, the waters below are churning and churning. They never stop. How restless the sea is . . . that's where you'll find him. Down there."

Silas tried to turn away from the rail, tried to focus on something, anything other than the dizzying descent and the noise of the waters crashing on the rocks. He looked at the lamp room and found it changed. The piercing light now seemed to pass through the solid walls of the building. And just as the death watch had altered the appearance of the room below, now the beam illuminated a space different from the one Silas had first seen; the room appeared in the full flush of its heyday long ago, long before the lighthouse was abandoned. This spectral effect was taxing on Silas's eyes and the repeating flash of past, present, past, present made him dizzy and disoriented. He knew the spectral effect was a warning, but Silas could not yet perceive which way lay hidden rocks and which way the safe harbor. To steady himself, he ran his own name through his mind: *I am Silas Umber, Silas Umber, Silas Umber*. As he did, he remembered what it was he came to do, and his face flushed with resolve. By speaking his name, by saying the word "Umber," he could sense his father's steadying presence. Silas stood up straight and pushed back his shoulders, feeling, in his blood, that a part of his father was always with him.

The ghost stood at the rail, looking out at the sea.

Silas stepped close to the ghost and said, "I believe I know who you are. You are J—" But before Silas could continue, the ghost began crying out in a rapid circle of words.

"Gone . . . all gone. I have nothing now. No one. All my fault. Now all is lost. All is lost. All is lost. . . ." And like the rising of a sudden gust, the ghost lifted quickly into the air above the railing, his eyes darkening, their sockets becoming black and empty.

Over and over and over like a prayer, Silas called out the

ghost's true name. "Joseph Downing! Wait! Joseph Downing, be still!

The ghost stood upon the cold air, holding himself in the posture of an angry child, fists thrust up over his ears.

"No!" cried the ghost. "My father is below! I am his son. This is my home."

Standing his ground, Silas shouted back. "You are Joseph Downing! Hear these, my words! You are Joseph Downing, the keeper of this light—"

The ghost fell upon Silas, trying to push him from the tower, his blurring form buffeting Silas with a freezing blast of air. The great wind took Silas off guard, raised him up off his feet, and made him lose his balance. He fell forward, nearly over the rail. Looking down, Silas wove his arms through the railing and held it fast. Silas looked up. The ghost was hanging in the air before him out beyond the protective rail. And all the while, the dark light continued to go around, washing the world in successive veils of its dismal nightmare-light.

When the lamp beam poured over Silas, his own name began to unravel. In that light, he heard only the call of the waiting rocks below and the deadly churning of waters. He arms loosened on the rails. He stood at the edge of the tower as the ghost swayed back and forth against the backdrop of the black sky, crying with a throat of storm, crying shards of a lie, a tale grown twisted and false.

"My father is lost. He is lost down there!" The ghost turned in the air, thrusting a finger toward the rocks and sea. "Even now. Lost among the waters. Dark places. Below the kelp. Cold. Cold. Cold. My father is—"

But Silas cut him off. "Joseph Downing, enough!" he said.

"I am Daniel Downing," the ghost moaned piteously, desperately, hiding in the name. "I am the son—"

"Enough! Here is your story and your name!"

And while the ghost continued to sob, Silas told the ghost its own sad tale.

"Their ship was coming back to Lichport, returning from up the coast, where they'd been visiting family. Your wife. Your child. They were coming home. All day you'd been waiting, but how were you to know the ship had been delayed? Only two days, due to bad weather. But when the ship did not come in, you waited. All night you waited up on this tower, straining to see through the night. Hoping to see the silhouette of their ship against the moonlit sea. But the ship did not come. The next day, twilight found you still up on the tower, sitting, watching. And as the day ebbed, so did you, and for only an instant, you told yourself, 'I'll close my eyes.'"

The ghost stood frozen on the air, his eyes wide and fixed on Silas. He muttered, "I did not sleep. Only rested. I did not sleep. . . ."

"Nor has anyone in this town slept. We have all kept vigil with you. But Joseph, that night, you did sleep, and evening stole in and the lantern had not been lit, and so when their ship approached, there was no candle to guide it home. The ship struck the reef and all aboard were lost to the sea. Your wife. Your child. Both lost. On this very night, long, long ago."

The ghost wavered and began to dissolve, falling away into his own misery and shame, but Silas spoke again. "Wait, Joseph Downing, one moment more."

The edges of the ghost's form sharpened and took hold of the air again.

"Now, Joseph Downing, tell me what happened next. Speak."

Slowly, the ghost began to move his mouth, then the words came.

"A boy from town told me what had happened. Everyone knew there had been no light. My son and wife were gone, gone below, and . . . " The ghost's voice began to waver.

"Go on, Joseph. It's all right now. There is nothing left to lose but your own good self. Speak your name and tell me what happened."

"I am . . . I am Joseph Downing. Yes. That is my name. And when I learned what had become of them, I tried to put myself low, to be with them in the sea. I jumped from the lighthouse! But, oh, I fell upon the rocks, there! Oh, God . . . even in death I was denied them. . . ." The ghost pointed to where Silas was now standing. Silas looked toward the railing, but when he looked back, the ghost was standing by the lamp room and had started walking toward him.

"Wait! Joseph! Abide!"

The ghost's eyes had become flat, black stones. He walked past Silas and through the railing and fell like a thing of substance down into darkness.

Silas stood by the rail, looking down, unsure of what had happened. Was it over? The ghost had said his own name. Had it been enough? He must not assume. He straightened his back and called out over the water. It felt unfinished. Should he summon the ghost back, compel him to return? But Silas thought about the ghost and his family, his wife and child, lost in the waters. Perhaps there was something he could do for them all.

"Who will come for this weary soul?" Silas intoned. "Who shall abide with Joseph Downing and keep him?" Silas closed his eyes. With his words, Silas sent his mind's eye out into the sea, searching along the bottom for the bones of those who had been lost so long ago. And as he'd learned from his father's writings, he imagined his words stirring the remains, sinking into them and waking, gently waking, those who had waited to find the Peace their awful deaths had kept from them. *Mother and child*, Silas said to himself. *Come, now, for here is restoration. Mother and child, bring peace to this lost soul. Mother and child, carry him to peace. . . .*

Silas closed his eyes and tried to feel the words flowing out across the sea, though a small voice in the back of his mind held back and whispered to him, *It is wrong to summon the dead.*

But he pushed back against his fear and silenced it, and out beyond the reef, two small lights appeared, growing larger and brighter as they came over the water, drawing close to the rocks below the lighthouse. As he looked down over the thin rail, Silas could see the form of a woman holding a child and standing above the waves. Below the surface of the sea, another light stirred and slowly rose to join the woman and child. As he emerged from the water, the ghost of the lighthouse keeper stood beside his family. From the high tower, Silas shouted down, "Peace be with you and Peace be upon you all, until—" But the ghosts had already vanished. The grim, gray candle of the lighthouse lantern was extinguished, and darkness descended upon the waters. Silas was hopeful, but unsure. He might have given them the waters of Lethe that would bring forgetting and dissolution to the dead. That would have been best in this case, he couldn't help thinking. At least they were all together now. But where? At the bottom of the sea? Wasn't that still lost? He wished his father were there to ask. There were complexities to the Undertaking that were still unclear to him. But, the spectral beam cast by the lighthouse lamp had gone out, and the ghosts were together. It would have to be enough.

Silas came down from the tower and left the lighthouse, locking the door behind him. Worried that the ghost might return, he put his open palm upon the door and said resolutely, "This place is Peace-bound. May no malediction come to be set upon these stones. May no malicious spirit nor wandering ghost harbor or be bound here from this day forward until the breaking of the world." And a shudder passed through Silas, through the bricks and mortar of the lighthouse, flowing through the rocks of the cliff and down into the sea, and it was done.

CHAPTER 2

EARTH TO EARTH

THE LIGHTHOUSE TOWER WAS DARK. Silas released the dial of the death watch and felt the now familiar tightening in his stomach and quickening of his breath as the hand returned to its circular course about the dial. The beat of his heart picked up its pace, as if it, too, had been stopped with the watch and suddenly been started again. Silas gasped at the sensation, then slowed his breathing, calmed himself, and began walking back toward Lichport. He paused, realizing the death watch was still in his hand. It took an act of will to drop the watch into his pocket, but once he did so, he walked more quickly. He could feel the exhaustion in his bones, and his shoulder still ached, but he didn't want to go home. The clean night air felt good in his lungs and his mind was restless.

A name was going around and around in his head and he needed to know more about it. Since the night it had been mysteriously engraved into his front door, and he had pulled book after book from his father's library, his mind had turned the name over and over in a vexing loop. ARVALE. Each time he said it, whether aloud or in his mind, he felt something pull at him, as though the very word exerted a kind of gravity.

He needed more than mere historical information; he wanted to find out what the *appearance* of the name meant. Who had carved this in the door, and why now? Asking Mrs. Bowe was out

"And we, your friends, are most glad for it. Indeed, you have made great strides these last months. Many folks are sleeping easier now that you have woken to your calling," she said, wrapping her arm and her shawl around his shoulders. "Still, for you to be wandering about so late and not home with your nose in a book . . . I wonder if there isn't something consternating you, Silas? Or perhaps you have been out on business?"

He nodded. "I am just coming home from work."

"Yes, you have the look about you of a man who has been keeping grim company. May I inquire . . . ?"

"The keeper of the lighthouse."

"And?"

"I believe he is at last at rest."

"Well, well . . . ," said Mother Peale with real surprise, "that is fine news indeed. That place threw a particular pall over the Narrows and no mistake, though all in Lichport suffered when it cast its light about. I am glad to hear your work went well. Maybe there will be a good night's sleep waiting for me at home."

Silas shook his head briefly but was soon still again. He did not look at Mother Peale, but instead down at the earth of Mr. Peale's grave.

"But there is more to your tale, I think."

Silas told her about his front door.

Mother Peale hesitated for a moment, then nodded. She was at least familiar with the name Arvale. "Have you told this to Mrs. Bowe?" she asked.

"No," answered Silas more emphatically than he meant. "She doesn't enter my house by the front door, so she hasn't seen it. I think it would make her nervous. She would know something about it—it's a kind of invitation, I think—and she'd just tell me all the reasons I shouldn't accept it. She would tell me, and keep telling me, why I should try not to seek out trouble. My work worries her."

"Your work worries everyone, Silas, because it concerns the whole town, especially when things go bad. I'm not sure you're being fair to Mrs. Bowe, child. She has been your good friend since you arrived here."

"I know, it's just that sometimes . . . let's just say I can take care of myself."

"Well, now. It so happens I must beg to disagree with you. I believe a man in your position should cherish his connections. Do not make an island of yourself, Silas Umber. Not now. Do not forget that your profession is a community service, for the dead *and* the living."

"Maybe we could change the subject? Just for the time being," said Silas, shifting his weight on the stool.

"As you wish," said Mother Peale. "How have your dreams been, since taking up your father's work?"

"Nothing to speak of," he said quickly, trying to cover the lie. While he hadn't had any dreams recently, that was because he hadn't been sleeping. But before that he'd had some dreams, all right. Terrible, most of them. But he was tired of doing nothing but worrying the women in his life, so he said nothing.

"No nightmares? Nothing strange?"

Silas didn't answer.

"I see. Well, all right, then, young master. Keep your own counsel if it pleases you."

Silas could see she was willing to let the matter go, but he could read her sincere desire to help him, so he relented. "Mother Peale, how could I tell the difference? Everything in my life is strange in one way or another. Sometimes I dream I'm drowning. Two weeks ago, when that warmer wind came in, I thought I could feel someone watching me in my dream. I mean, someone not actually of the dream, but present just at the edges of it, looking in at me, watching from around a corner. But when I wake, it's a blur. Whenever I try to remember the details, I get sleepy and my mind wanders to something else, and before I know it, I can't remember what it was I was trying to remember."

"Best not to make too much of it," Mother Peale said, though her eyes went small and her brow formed furrows of concern.

It was getting to the part of the night when morning just begins to rouse itself, but darkness is still deep and the air is very cold. The sky was completely clear now and the bright congregation of stars looked down and gossiped among themselves.

"I guess I'll head up the hill to visit my dad," said Silas, rising from his seat and returning the wooden stool to the hollow of the tree.

"Just a moment." Mother Peale reached for Silas's hand, grasped it, and pulled herself up from her seat. "Is it your intention, then, to pay a call at . . . *that place*?"

"You mean Arvale? Yes, that's my plan. I believe I have been summoned."

"Perhaps, but, Silas, it is your choice and yours alone whether you answer that summons now, later, or never."

"Mother Peale," Silas said with a sigh, thinking she was trying to talk him out of it, "I am going very soon. I think it is somehow required of me, and honestly, I'm curious."

"So be it. But, Undertaker of Lichport, if you are leaving us for a time, allow me a moment to make preparations."

"Leaving?" Silas asked. "Why do you say it like that? I'm not leaving Lichport."

"Silas, every great house is its own world. If you are going *there*, you are leaving *here*, one way or another. Distance has nothing to do with it. Now, let me give you something."

Reaching down, she pushed her fingers into the cold ground, took a handful of earth from her husband's grave, and put it in a pocket of her dress. She picked up another handful of grave dirt and put it in the front pocket of Silas's jacket.

He looked at her questioningly.

"Oh, dear! Have you learned nothing from your father's many notes in this town's great book? You see, there is always something we may learn from our friends when we keep good company. Grave dirt can be very helpful in a pinch, for it is said, and said truly, that if that stuff is thrown upon a ghost, it shall then become quiet and easy and perhaps even wait upon command or be banished, for a time. Though, it is also said that any banished in this way will surely return, and not so happy as when they left. And besides, it's always best to carry a little bit of home with you wheree'r you roam! I'll sleep better knowing you have it, Silas."

Mother Peale patted the pocket in her apron filled with earth. "There, now. Go where you like. I shall be able to keep things quiet in your absence for a short time, if absolutely necessary."

Silas was relieved that she'd put the dirt into the empty pocket and not the one holding the death watch. "But I am not leaving you. I am going to visit my father's grave, an errand of but a moment. In a day or so, after a little more research, I will walk to a house on the far side of town and be back before dark in all likelihood."

"Silas! I took you for a learned man!" exclaimed Mother Peale. "That house, well . . . it's neither here nor there. That is what folks say of it. Neither here nor there. It is a queer place, if you don't mind my saying so. And as I've told you, where you think it is has very little to do with it."

"Do you mean to suggest that there is something strange about my family and their habitations, Mother Peale?" Silas said in mock surprise.

But Mother Peale grew serious and concern flushed her cheeks. "I only mean to say, a visit *there* may take longer than you think, and I pray that when you return, I shall still be here to welcome you."

All humor had left her voice, and her words made Silas nervous. Her tone reminded him just how little he really knew about the world that he'd entered, all his put-on confidence aside. Below, somewhere near the bottom of the hill, a dog howled and Silas jumped. "What the hell was that?"

"What the hell, indeed," replied Mother Peale, unshaken by the wild night call. "That is surely the black dog. Have you not heard it before, Silas? It is often here, upon the hill, when someone is about to die."

"I've never heard that sound before, Mother Peale. Do you mean someone is going to die . . . now?"

"Soon, I expect," she said, looking up as another low howl broke the surface of the night. "I wouldn't let it worry you, Silas, unless you actually *see* the black dog. That is a grim omen to be sure."

Silas kept looking back over his shoulder with a worried expression.

"You don't like dogs?" Mother Peale asked wryly.

"I don't feel one way or other about them. But *that* dog sounds . . . very large."

"My mother told us as children not to trust a great black dog if we met him on the road. 'That'll be the Shuck, and no mistake!' my mother told me. Road hounds are an odd sort. Wanderers. Though the ones you see in cemeteries are just as strange by my reckoning."

"Have you seen a dog here before, on the Beacon?"

"Oh, yes. And elsewhere besides. I saw a black dog just before you came to Lichport. I thought it boded ill for your arrival, but then, it was your uncle that was taken, so that was all right, wasn't it? Oh, aye, I've seen one here on the Beacon before. Just after a funeral, that was years and years ago, but I can still see its ember-eyes and feel its cold breath on my hand. My mother told me that once, folks would make sacrifices to the dead, to keep 'em peaceable just after their dying time. And those offerings were given at the burial plots. But times changed and folk weren't as keen to leave all them good victuals and finery about just to rot or get stolen. No one likes waste. So, it became the custom to leave a guardian to watch over the burial places between funerals. The spirit of the last one buried had to remain until the next person died and was buried, then it would be their turn to keep lookout. Well, that was all right for a time, but the dead can be a restless lot, eager to be about their business if they can. So then the dogs were left. A dog, usually black, was buried near the more recent grave and the dog's ghost took up the watch. Usually it was all right, and that dog stayed put and watched over the dead."

Silas's eyes were fixed on Mother Peale.

"Other times, when the burial plots were left lonesome too long, abandoned by the kin of the dead, them dogs took to wandering themselves. Who can say what they are, really. Mind you, I'm not sure they are truly dogs at all, but whatever they be, they have *the know of a dog*," she said. As if to put a period at the end of her story, the dog howled again somewhere down the Beacon. Mother Peale rose slowly from her seat.

"Well, this evening's chat and the night air have indeed cleared my head. I shall take my leave of you. I am ready for bed!" said Mother Peale. "Dear Mr. Umber, I wish you well upon your travels." She hugged him quickly but hard, then began to slowly make her way down the hill, her lantern growing smaller and smaller in the distance.

Silas was nervous now and kept looking back over his shoulder, but continued up the hill and easily found his father's grave. The small mound had settled a lot already in the months since Amos Umber had been buried. Silas his put his hand upon it. The earth of the grave was cold.

As much as he usually loved being on the Beacon, Silas now felt impatient. After his talk with Mother Peale, he was eager to set his feet forward on their road. He also sensed he was being watched. He looked around the hill, hoping to see the sexton, that kindly spirit who was often here keeping watch over his "flock." But there was only the cold wind tearing dry leaves from the ground and casting them up into the sky. Then something else stirred the air. He paused, not sure he wanted to turn around. Silas could hear breathing, something or someone panting just behind him. He tightened his fists and whipped about. Sitting next to his father's grave was the biggest dog he'd ever seen. Silas wasn't sure what breed it was, maybe part Labrador, but it was shaggier, larger, and wilder. Its head was massive, and Silas could see that it would come up to his chest. There was a light in the dog's eyes, and Silas was not at first sure whether he looked at an animal of this world or some other. The dog looked at Silas, its tongue lolling to one side. It was wagging its tail.

"Good evening, hound of hell," said Silas, trying to speak in a high, happy tone, though his heart was tight in his chest. "Are you a good puppy, or . . . something else?"

The dog rose up on its massive paws and walked over to Silas, looking at him expectantly. Silas stepped back, feeling the earth shift below his feet. He reached behind him to steady himself on a tombstone, looking away for only an instant. When he looked again, the dog had vanished.

Silas sat down hard on the ground next to his dad's grave and remained there for many moments. It had been a long, strange night. His mind began to turn toward home. Mother Peale's words and the dog's appearance had shaken him, and now the whole evening, lighthouse and Beacon both, felt like one long troublesome dream. He didn't like feeling anxious. He'd spent a lot of time in the last months trying to focus on his work, trying to take charge, trying not to remember how much he still had to learn.

He put his hand on his dad's gravestone and pulled himself up, then arched his back and stretched. Sleep was the only thing for it. He put his hand in his jacket pocket and grabbed the handful of grave earth in case he should meet the dog, or anything else on his way home.

When Silas reached the bottom of the Beacon, he turned up Main Street. Nothing troubled his homeward journey. When he reached his front porch, he found a basket of eggs, several glass bottles of fresh milk, and a cheese—gifts from folks who had already heard, or sensed, that he had worked that night at the lighthouse, or perhaps from one of the families he'd helped earlier in the week. His heart was warmed momentarily by the kindness of these "payments." But as Silas went to open the front door with his key, his eyes were held by the deeply engraved letters. He paused there on the threshold, worry rising in him again. Back at the Beacon, he could still hear the black dog's howl, leaping now to greet the dawn.

CHAPTER 3

BOOKKEEPING

TIRED THOUGH HE WAS, the memory of the dog's baying kept Silas from sleep. He tried to doze in a chair by the fireplace in his study, but too many questions flooded his mind. After an hour, he rose and turned to his books.

On the same desk once used by his father, the great funereal ledger of the Undertakers of Lichport lay open, and dozens of volumes containing references to Arvale were stacked about it like crooked towers. Most of the books had been marked with small slips of yellowed paper. This was how Silas liked to read while he was researching something: opening many books at a time, letting his eyes flow from page to page, catching words, phrases, and passages in quick succession. The method was more intuitive than critical, but it allowed the texts to flow into one another, no longer masses of individual references, but one massive volume on precisely whatever it was he was trying to find.

There were no books entirely dedicated to the subject of Arvale house. But there were references to "Arvale" throughout many different volumes and in numerous entries in the ledger. Silas began making a list.

Toward the end of the ledger, Silas found a page of book titles in his father's handwriting. None of these works was in his library, but it was clear that at some time his father had taken up a study of Arvale just as Silas was doing now. The list was headed with the words "Relating to, or with references of, A R V A L E." Silas noted with interest titles such as *Spectral Domestic Topography: Visions, Encounters, and Displacements*; and *Manes Intus, Manes Foris: Being a Practical Examination of Internal and External Spirits and Demons*. At the end of the list of titles were more notes in his father's handwriting. One read:

WHERE WE HAVE ENACTED OUR ABYSMAL RITES, THERE SHALL WE PAY THE PUNISHMENTS FOR THEM, FOR SO LONG AS THE DOOM IS PREDICATED ON JUDGMENT AND BANISHMENT, SO SHALL ALL THE FAMILY BE LIKEWISE HELD AND JUDGED. SO THE HALLS AND GALLERIES AND CHAMBERS OF ARVALE SHALL BE A PRISON-HOUSE BECAUSE WE THINK, IN OUR ARROGANCE AND OUR GOETIC POWER, THAT WE ARE ABOVE THE MORE ANCIENT MAGICS OF SYMPATHY AND KINDNESS. THE CALL TO THE HOUSE MUST BE HEEDED, BUT AS TO WHETHER THE UNDERTAKER SHALL SUBMIT TO THE "OBLIGATIONS AND TRADITIONS" OF THE HOUSE AND ITS PERILOUS THRESHOLD, THIS IS A CHOICE EACH MUST MAKE IN HIS OWN TIME. EITHER WAY, THERE IS A PRICE TO BE PAID.

Throughout the ledger and in other books, Silas found the word "Arvale" written on many earlier bookmarks. Within the ledger, they highlighted inscriptions of varying length, most copied out from other works, other authors' attempts to offer some insight into the place, or into the *condition*, that was Arvale. Some of the marginalia were authored and included an Undertaker's name; other commentators preferred to remain anonymous. It seemed most of the authored posts had been made by a distant relative, Jonas Umber.

The entire heaven is divided into societies
. . . and every spirit . . . is taken to the
society where his love is; and when he
arrives there he is, as it were, at home,
and in the house where he was born.

—Copied by Jonas Umber from Swedenborg's
Heaven and Hell

The greatest throngs of the dead appear, as
Gervase hath writ "Confinibus et Amicis"
to "friends and relatives." But so long as
they remain in the lands of confinement
or punishment, those places that border
and share so wide a frontier with our
world, they may, of their own power, or
divine dispensation, appear in the dreams
and visions of their living relatives in the
semblance of their living bodies. Yet, when
their allotted hour comes and they either

cast off their cares or are freed of them by
the goodlie actions of their kin or Pelter,
they are gone from all the spheres and shalle
present themselves to us no more.

—J. Umber

And so we must find that the dead, by
preference and when able, will congregate
about their kin, about their descendants, in
whom they place their hopes not merely for the
future of the family's honor and estates, but
for their rescue from the shadowlands or other
purgatorial entrapments that only memory
and the honoring of their names may effect.

All must attend the house and its springs,
for where else may the waters of forgetting and
the waters of memory be found? For Arvale
is the very font of Lethe . . . the source of the
Undertaker's power to bring forgetfulness to
the dead. That other spring, which some call
Memory's Cauldron, it bubbles up through the
earth there too, though its waters are not for the
nourishment of all. . . .

The entries became briefer, mostly quotes, many in his father's hand, marked "Arv./Damnable Mansion." Some had been scrawled and even amended in ways that seemed to suggest his dad's anger or frustration.

From Rushworth's *Historical Collections*:

I have neither eye to see, nor tongue to speak here, but as The House is pleased to direct me.

From the Book of Psalms:

And yet they think that their houses shall continue for ever: and that their dwelling-places shall endure from one generation to another. . . .

From Milton:

Yet some there be that by due steps aspire to lay their ~~just~~ hands on that "golden" key that opes the palace of eternity.

As Silas read, he came to understand that the house of Arvale might hold more in common with the shadowlands than even the oldest homes of Lichport. Recent accounts that referred to Arvale seemed increasingly philosophical and speculative, less about its architectural prominence and more about the nature of its existence. He began to sense that his summons was no mere invitation to supper. He also wondered very seriously about what he might learn there. Every shadowland he'd visited taught him something new about his work, and sometimes at great cost. What might such an ancient place teach him about the landscapes of the past and the habitations of the dead? Would he meet people there who knew more about the Undertaking than he did? The thought both excited and worried him.

Whatever else it might be, Arvale was clearly the ancestral estate of his ancient family, and though every Undertaker journeyed there at some point, some even visiting many times over their careers, no one who left a record of their visit in the ledger seemed to think of the journey to Arvale as a homecoming. Arvale was an obligation, one of many dangerous responsiblities that, as he read Amos's final entry on the house in the ledger, he now knew he was required to undertake. . . .

BUT THE SUMMONS IS A KIND OF
BINDING THAT WORKS THROUGH BOTH
BLOOD AND BLOODLINE, AND IT MUST
BE HEEDED, NO MATTER WHAT COMES.
FOR SHOULD THE SUMMONS BE
IGNORED, MADNESS AND DEATH FOLLOW
LIKE FURIOUS HOUNDS, AND THE HOUSE
OF ANCESTORS BECOMES A PLACE
OF PERDITION AND DEMISE, AND SO I
HAVE GONE TO THAT STRANGE AND
LONG-ENDURING HOUSE AGAINST MY
WILL BUT IN PRESERVATION OF MY
LIFE,
AND ONCE, MY SON'S.

CHAPTER 4

REGRETS

MRS. BOWE SAT IN HER CANDLELIT PARLOR and heard the front door at Silas's house. She waited, but he didn't call from the hallway, or come over for a cup of tea before bed, or even knock to see if she was still up, as were once his customs.

She was a little hurt by this. It was not the first time it had happened. Since Amos's funeral, Mrs. Bowe assumed, Silas had wanted to feel more self-sufficient. So she tried to convince herself Silas's behavior was normal. Well, as normal as the behavior of a young man could be, considering he spent much of his time talking with the dead. *This must be what it's like for every parent when their child prepares to leave the nest,* she thought. True, he'd avoided her a little over the last month or so, but he was still hurting and trying to adjust. Anyone could understand that. He was also turning into an adult. If she thought about it calmly, it was all completely understandable. He'd been busy. He was settling in. It had been only two months since the discovery of his father's death; Silas was adjusting to a new life. No matter that she and Silas used to share a meal nearly every day.

But it was *all completely normal*, she said to herself. *Normal. Normal.*

Mrs. Bowe didn't believe it for a minute. She went about the room, pinching out the candles. Of course Silas could feel her intrusion into his life. She had interfered in his infatuation with the girl from the millpond, and while Silas didn't know the particulars of what she'd done, Mrs. Bowe guessed he could feel her involvement. His senses were sharpening every day and she even wondered if he might have a bit of the Sight, as her people called it. He was discerning, that much was certain. So she was fairly sure that Silas could sense, at some level, that she had played a role in banishing his paramour. He knew it, all right. But she couldn't bring herself to stop trying to protect him. Every few days, she checked to see if the binding she'd put on the millpond was holding. Even now, as she looked into her crystal, Mrs. Bowe could see water on the surface of the pond. It might have been merely the weather, for wasn't the day a little above freezing? But she was worried her spell was too dependent on the ice, and if the weather got even a bit warmer, so much the worse. The ice would melt and her binding would ebb away from the water and then the girl's spirit would rise and it would all begin again. *I am only looking out for what's best for him,* she told herself, and that much was true, no matter what Silas came to think of her. *Let him be angry with me, at least he'll be safe. In time, he'll see what I've done was best for all.* There was no choice. If the ghost girl rose again, she could lead him wherever she wanted. All the way to hell, like in the story of Orpheus she'd foolishly told Silas. All the way to hell. And then what wouldn't he do to bring her back to the upper world? Just thinking it put a chill in her blood.

Mrs. Bowe sat back down, trying to breathe slowly and get control of herself. Her anxieties were beginning to roll up into a boil.

She had made her decision and would keep to it. She'd started as she'd meant to go on. She knew her spell couldn't last, but she also had an idea for strengthening it. She would need Mother Peale. Now, that would pose no problem, for while it was still difficult stepping out the front door, she had found her footing in the world again and would not return to being prisoner in her own house. So she would walk to the Narrows the next day. But they'd still need another. And the closer the woman was to Silas, the better. Blood-kin: Yes, the mother would be essential. She needed Dolores Umber's help, although that might be a little harder to obtain. She took out pen and paper and carefully wrote to inform Dolores that she would, on the following day, be receiving company. She sent the note via a neighbor's child who agreed to run the letter over to the house on Temple Street for a quarter. When Dolores's reply came back, Mrs. Bowe then sent word to Mother Peale that she'd come for her at three fifteen the next day and they would go visit Dolores together.

Silas's side of the house was still quiet when Mrs. Bowe left her home.

She made her way quickly down into the Narrows, slowing frequently to look back over her shoulder for she knew not what. She drew her shawl up over her head and kept walking toward the market where she'd meet Mother Peale.

Mrs. Bowe approached the mercantile run by the Peale family, and saw Mother Peale waiting for her by the door. The two set off, walking purposefully toward Temple Street. It was a bright day and the two women walked, talking intensely, under the low winter shadows of the old, high trees on Prince Street.

"It is just as it was with Amos," said Mrs. Bowe in a tone of plain fact.

Mother Peale nodded. "But I would have thought . . . I mean, wouldn't Amos have made some provision, put some protection over his son? Or, now that Silas is the Undertaker, surely he might—"

"Sure as sin, her curse is on him! The boy is ensorcelled by her. Amos's solution was taking his family from Lichport to Saltsbridge, and that is hardly an option now, is it?" said Mrs. Bowe.

Mrs. Bowe told Mother Peale about what she'd done, explained each particular part of the spell that had been binding the girl's ghost to the waters of the millpond: She described how the bees had brought tiny droplets of the pond water to her, how she'd bound the ghost to the pond with strong words, brought the ice down over the pond to hold fast the curse. And she told Mother Peale that she didn't think the curse would last for much longer. "I am only one person. The drowned girl is very old. Very strong. And Silas's connection with her makes it harder to hold her down. I tried to see to that, so the binding has affected him, too. He remembers very little about her. When he tries to recall more, it falls away from him. That is just as well, for the more he tries to summon her name, the harder it is to keep her put down."

Mother Peale shook her head. This was an awful business.

"Mrs. Bowe, even as she is, if the boy has feelings for this girl, he might . . . *change* her. He might *help* her. In any event, if he had no feelings for her at all, surely he would want to settle her business himself. We should leave it to him. Dealing with the dead, any of the dead, is his job, and I can tell you he takes it mighty serious now. He wouldn't want anyone, not even so good a friend as you, meddling in his work."

"You're not suggesting I should have let this business between them continue?" Mrs. Bowe said. "You *know* what she is, and what he may become, and where this might lead!"

"Aye, I know. You have acted only out of care for the boy. I am just saying that holding something like her down, well, it's not easy. And you're right, as it stands, she won't be kept much longer.

When she rises she again, it will be worse, I suspect. I am torn, Elleree Bowe. I'll say this: The boy has spent a lot of time dredging up his own secrets, things he's borne a long time, and he's done a fine job of making his life a good bit better. And now here you come, trying to hide something from him. Something he's made his own business. Something private. I don't like it. Still, now, something must be done. You've seen to that."

Mrs. Bowe heard but pushed past Mother Peale's words.

"So we are in agreement, then?"

Mother Peale wore a pained expression on her face. She didn't like any of the options. "All right, Mrs. Bowe. I will do what I can and stand with you. Come what may. And I agree, three is always best. It must be three. But the boy's mother . . . that will take some pretty talk."

As they arrived at the corner of Temple Street and Charles Umber's old house came into view, Mrs. Bowe felt her knees buckle. Mother Peale held her up with strong arms and Mrs. Bowe breathed deeply, striving to regain control as they approached the stairs of the front porch. Though many of Uncle's things still lay inside, the north wing had been locked and the entire house had been Peace Bound. Its terrible, long midnight had passed, and now it was merely the home of Dolores Umber. Mrs. Bowe told herself that, over and over: *Only a house. Only a house. It is only a house . . .*

CHAPTER 5

LET THEM DREAM

DOLORES HAD RECEIVED A HASTILY WRITTEN NOTE on poor quality paper saying that Mrs. Bowe and Mother Peale would like to pay her a visit, and she had replied by return messenger, "Please do come tomorrow at four," although she was uneasy about them coming by. At least if they arrived late in the afternoon, they could be given tea and sent on their way. No one would expect to stay for supper. She wondered why they wanted to see her. Were they worried about her house? Had some business been left unfinished? Was there something more to clean up in the north wing? Or, had they all become unspoken friends since the . . . unpleasantness? Now she'd have to think about her words before she spoke them, and sound polite and formal, and she was already tired today. Make no mistake, she liked playing Lady of the House, it was just that some days it was easier than others.

Dolores picked up her yarn basket and put it in a cupboard by the fireplace. She had taken up knitting again. The last time she had so much as looked at a ball of wool was just before Silas was born. Now it brought her comfort. She found it soothing. Maybe it was the regularity, the predictability of it. One stitch after another . . . on and on. You could almost see the future in the stitches. Stick to the pattern and you always knew what you were going to get: a sock, a sweater, a scarf. There was certainty in needlework, and she needed more of that in her life. Still, Dolores felt that having the knitting basket by her chair would make her look too domestic in front of company. She had been making a scarf for Silas. She liked the idea of him wearing something she'd made for him. Like a mother's blessing around his neck wherever he went. The days were still cold enough to need one.

She walked slowly through the reception rooms at the front of her house. Everything was in place and the small table in the parlor was set for tea. After "the incident," many of the peculiar objects in the house had been moved to the attic. Less to dust, and most of those carved things and old fossils and statuary unsettled her. She kept out most of the Roman and Egyptian pieces, finding them stately, and the odd stuffed hippo-lion was simply too heavy to move. So the "Ammit," as Silas had called it, was still at the foot of the staircase, standing guard. Now, the silver—that stayed too. Every stick of it. She had hired some girls from the market to come by and do the polishing. Then, she had thought it best to keep them on, a few days a week, to do a little light cleaning and sometimes a bit of cooking. One girl would have been sufficient, but no one in town wanted to work in Charles Umber's house by herself, so it was two or nothing. Having the extra help felt good. She liked hearing the sounds of people working around her. It made the house feel more alive somehow. She could pay for it now, so why not? Why begrudge herself a little pleasure in life? And the way all that silver shone from the table and the hutch and the top of the buffet! It made the whole house feel clean and grand. For Dolores, the silver bowls, candlesticks, and cutlery changed the very quality of the air.

She heard the knock at the front door and waited for one of the girls to come from the kitchen to answer it. Mother Peale and Mrs. Bowe were shown into the parlor and they were invited to sit down on recently reupholstered chairs.

"Well, ladies," said Dolores, "to what do I owe this honor?" She managed a small smile, but there was something about the three of them together in the same room that made Dolores feel distinctly tense.

"We've come about Silas. Not to worry you, but—"

Perhaps mindful of the bad blood between Dolores and Mrs. Bowe, Mother Peale interrupted.

"Begging your pardon, but why mince words? Dolores, we've come to you, in the ancient manner, for the benefit of kin. Silas needs your help and we come on his behalf. We ask that you go with us to the millpond, and there speak some certain words that will ensure his safety."

Dolores's already small smile pulled very tight and nearly vanished for an instant before she said sarcastically, "'Ancient manner'? 'Certain words'? Ladies, if I didn't know better, I would think you are speaking of witchcraft. Really . . . it's so unfashionable." She tried to make herself laugh a little at saying it out loud, but she could only manage to clear her throat.

Mother Peale straightened her back and struck her cane hard on the floorboards in disgust. "Witchcraft, some may call it," she chided. "I call it simply a woman's work. The work that may set the tilted world to rights again. Our daily bread, I call it."

"All right, Mother Peale, I am sure Dolores didn't mean anything by it," Mrs. Bowe said, softening her tone. "All we are asking for is—"

Dolores closed her eyes briefly and waved her hand in the air as if brushing away a fly. "Be assured I meant precisely what I said. If you think I am going out during the dinner hour to stand around the pond with a candle, singing old songs with you two, I fear you have come in vain. Ladies, good day." She reached over to the table for the little silver servant's bell.

"Dolores Umber, you can sit in this house and play Lady Muck all you like, but I am telling you, Silas needs you. You don't have to like what he does, or what Amos did, but you know the real dangers of that work and you must help if you can," said Mrs. Bowe tartly.

"Dolores," said Mother Peale more softly, "you are his mother. Surely for that and no other reason you will consider helping us help Silas?"

"So, you would speak to me of a mother's sacred duty? And Mrs. Bowe, you of all people who yourself spurned a more ordinary life? Who couldn't be bothered to take a man and get married and have children of your own? Ladies, I need no lessons in mothering, thank you." But her expression was already changing to one of concern. What was happening to Silas? What had he gotten himself into?

"All right, all right!" said Mother Peale, trying to calm the rising temper of the room. "You can help him or not. I am not entirely delighted by these doings, Dolores, I assure you. If you don't wish to help, Mrs. Bowe and I can speak the words right enough, but, Dolores, having you there, having your voice joined with ours, it will help him, I promise you. If we stand together."

Dolores's mind was turning over and over on itself. She looked at the two women. Here was Old Lichport, already trying to kick down her door with its talk of witchcraft! She wanted no part of it, even though such things were woven right through her family. She was about to ask them both to leave, but she considered: For them both to come, and to this house, whatever was happening must be serious. She knew neither woman was especially fond of her, but Dolores knew they loved her son. And so did she. Things had been better. Hadn't Silas sat through those long nights with her recently when sleep was so scarce? She imagined that if she said no to them, it would come out eventually that Dolores Umber was the kind of mother who wouldn't stand up for her boy. She was not that kind of mother. She was trying so hard to . . . *All right,* she told herself. *Let's get it over with.*

"Ladies. I understand. I do not approve of your methods, but there is nothing I wouldn't do to help my son. I will come."

Resolved, Dolores rang the little bell. Mother Peale looked at Mrs. Bowe and rose to go. A young woman wearing an apron came in from the kitchen and stood at the door waiting for instructions.

"Please set the table. We will have a little something to eat, nothing too fancy, and then, I'll need my heavy coat. I will be going out this evening with these two old, dear friends of my son's."

By the time they'd talked a bit more and eaten, it was long after sunset. Only the thinnest wisps of fire hung in the indigo sky as the three women slowly walked through town to the millpond.

Mrs. Bowe looked relieved that Dolores had come. She said, "Shall we go over the particulars once more?"

"Please, Mrs. Bowe. I may not be Lichport-y enough for you, and I may have left this town once—and gladly, too, I might add— but I ask you to remember that mine is an ancient family. I know all the witch-runes and curse-signs like any daughter of Lichport. Just because I've turned away from such relics, such distractions, doesn't mean I've forgotten the sewers of lore that flow under these streets. I know how to get what I want, same as any woman. I know the routine, I promise you. You will speak some hoary, primitive poetry. We will bend our collective wills toward the place of binding. Mother Peale will make some knots in a piece of filthy rope or some such bit of arts and crafts, and I will set my ungloved hand to the ice to trace some peasant's sigil and ruin my manicure. I assure you I have not forgotten the *particulars*."

The millpond was still frozen. At the edges, tall weeds, brown now, stood cold and unbending in the light breeze, their stalks sunk down into the ice.

As Dolores approached the pond behind Mrs. Bowe and Mother Peale, she said in an annoyed voice, "I'll catch my death out here!"

"Don't say such things when the veil has grown so thin!" snapped Mother Peale.

Then with no more than a nod, the three women stood abreast at the edge of the millpond.

Mrs. Bowe closed her eyes and inclined her head.

"She's still down there."

"Good," said Mother Peale. "Let's begin."

The three women joined hands. The words were simple and quickly became a chant. "She shall not rise. She is bound to this place. She shall not rise. . . ."

Then Mrs. Bowe added other words. The boundaries of the spell closed in and the power of the binding grew tight and firm, like the twisting of a rope.

"She shall not rise. There shall be no dreams. He shall not dream. He shall forget her name. He shall not dream of the waters. No dreams . . . ," Mrs. Bowe intoned as Mother Peale let go of Dolores's hand and drew out a length of cord into which she began tying knot after knot to hold the spell. "There shall be no dreams. He shall not dream. . . ."

But the words died on Dolores's lips. Those words would bind her son as well. No dreams. He would not dream, that's what they were saying.

"Stop," said Dolores.

"Do not interrupt!" barked Mother Peale.

Mrs. Bowe raised her voice and kept right on intoning those words. "She shall not rise. He shall not dream. She shall not rise. He shall not dream." And Dolores knew it was wrong. They couldn't take her son's dreams from him. Life could deal you a miserable hand, but you could dream of something more, something better. Sometimes dreams were all a person had. She knew that better than anyone. So she waited until the two women looked at her and nodded that it was almost over. Dolores removed her glove. The freezing air stung her skin. She knelt in the hard, icy mud, and drew a glyph with her fingertip, splintering, as she had predicted, the end of her painted nail. As she had traced the sigil, she said out loud, "You shall not rise to harm my son! You shall not rise—" And then, deep below her breath, she whispered, "But he shall dream whatever he wishes to dream. In his dreams he shall be free."

Mrs. Bowe and Mother Peale did not hear Dolores's final words, but instantly, the ice cracked with a sound like thunder, and water oozed up, flooding out onto the frozen surfaces. Dolores fell back from the edge of the pond as Mrs. Bowe and Mother Peale stepped forward and pulled her up, the three joining hands once more. In one voice, they called out, "Child of the waters, we bind you to your bones. Do not rise! Do not stir! Drink lonesome water and remain below. Sink down! Sink down! We bind you to your bones. We three bind you. By ice, we bind you. By cold, we bind you. By the wills of the Wailing Woman and the Mother of the Narrows and the blood-kin of your paramour, we bind you! By the will of Three, you are bound!"

And the wind rose into a blast, and the green water froze thick and hard again across the pond.

The air grew still. Dolores was trying to catch her breath. Mrs. Bowe took a piece of wool tartan she'd been wearing as a shawl and spread it on the cold ground and the three sat down together, breathing hard. Mother Peale took out a tinderbox and built a small fire to keep them warm while they waited and recovered themselves. It might have been nearly dawn by the time they began making their way home.

Mother Peale looked at Dolores, then at Mrs. Bowe, with concern coloring her face.

"It will be all right," said Mrs. Bowe.

Mother Peale hoped those words were true, but the wind had changed direction, coming in hard now from the north, and she wasn't so sure.

Their words would hold. All their words would hold. But because of Dolores's whispers, down below, at the dark cold bottom of the pond, Beatrice slept, but began to dream again, sending her sunken mind out beyond the boundaries of her watery prison house. And Silas wanted to dream of her. His mind called to her through the lashings of the binding spell. While she could not rise, and his waking memory would remain a blur, in sleep she would find him.

CHAPTER 6

WORDS

THE SUN WAS COMING UP and Silas hadn't slept all night. He stood on the porch of Mrs. Bowe's house, waiting. She hadn't come home last night. That had never happened once during his time living next door to her. Most days, Silas could tell the time by what was occurring next door. Specific kitchen sounds and smells signaled breakfast, lunch, teatime, and dinner. Regular. The sound of music and dancing almost always came on around eleven p.m. Humming came from the garden in the early morning and often an hour before dusk.

Watching the street, Silas could feel in his gut that something was going on and secrets were being kept from him. While Mrs. Bowe did regularly leave the house now, it still felt wrong for her not to be in at night. At least she might have told him where she'd gone. Usually, when he left to work, he would tell her his destinations, just in case anything were to happen. But now his fretting made him feel like a hypocrite because he'd barely spoken a word to her all week. The worst part was, he suspected that her absence had something to do with him. There was a ringing in his ears, and he convinced himself it meant someone was out there, someplace in Lichport, saying his name. And Silas didn't like secrets. So here he was, his mind full of assumptions, standing watch on Mrs. Bowe's front porch, waiting to question her the instant she came home.

It was cold in the open air, and Silas pulled his jacket collar up to lessen the biting wind on his neck. He could hear a dog barking somewhere off by the park near Cedar Street. He was thinking about going back into the house when suddenly he saw Mrs. Bowe, Mother Peale, and his mom come out from behind some buildings and emerge onto Main Street. Silas watched as the three of them paused at the intersection of Main and Fairview, Mother Peale continued south toward Temple Street with his mother and out of sight. Mrs. Bowe stood watching the other two for a moment, before she turned back to Main and walked toward home, where he was waiting for her.

Silas was expressionless, blocking the threshold as Mrs. Bowe ascended the steps from the street to the front door of her house. She looked at him and said, "Good morning, Silas," as though everything were perfectly normal.

"Good morning?" Silas said. "You're gone all night and all you've got for me is 'good morning'?" But he heard the sharpness in his tone, and spoke more softly, adding, "I mean, I was worried about you. I don't like thinking about you wandering around all night and no one knowing where you are. You've never been gone all night before—"

"Silas, please! I am delighted to learn of your concern for me, but let me get inside. I'm cold."

Quietly, Silas moved to one side, then followed Mrs. Bowe in and closed the door. But annoyance was rising in him again. Why was she being so coy? And why was she with his mother? What could the two of them possibly have to talk about? He suddenly and very keenly felt that awkward place inside him that was filled with question marks: a name he couldn't quite remember, a night when he could smell Mrs. Bowe's perfume on the wind just before . . . when . . . when something awful had happened.

Without waiting for her to take off her coat, or for any explanation, Silas started in on her once more.

"I know you've done something again. Why were you out all night with my mother? What's happened to—" He stumbled in his mind, trying to dredge up a name. It was just below the surface. He could nearly grasp it, but then it slipped away again into the murky water and his face twisted in frustration. "What's happened to *her*? Why can't I remember what's happened? What have you done?"

She looked down, away from his stare, to pull at the tips of her gloves. "I don't know what you're talking about, Silas, and please, lower your voice, I am *right* here."

"You've done something. I can feel it in my mind, like you're pushing me away from something I want. What did you do? Why were you with Mother Peale and *my mom*? Tell me now!"

"Silas, I am your friend, I've only been—"

"Just tell me what you've done; then we can talk about our friendship," he said low in his throat, almost a growl. He hadn't planned on getting this upset with her, but now his face was flushed. She was treating him like a child and he couldn't hold his anger down any more.

Mrs. Bowe took her handkerchief from her sleeve and dabbed at her eyes. She turned away from him, saying, "I can't believe you would take such a tone with me. Please just—"

But Silas spat his words at her before he could stop himself.

"Mrs. Bowe," he intoned, lowering his head, keeping his eyes locked on hers like an animal about to fall upon its prey, "speak!"

Below his words pulsed the tone of command, the same tone an Undertaker might use to banish or summon. That power in his voice grabbed hold of her. Before she could recover, she turned so quickly that the neat bun on the top of her head unwound, spilled about her shoulders, and hung down in front of her face. She paused and slowly brushed the hair aside. In her eyes was a fire Silas had not seen since she'd come to rescue him from his Uncle's. Her back went rigid. She put her face directly in front of his and said, "Silas Umber, do not presume to command me, not in my own house, not ever!" Her tone was so severe, so shot through with cold anger, that Silas took a step back. But his frustration flared again, and he said tersely, "Then let me ask you more politely, since you're feeling fragile: Kindly stay out of my business, Mrs. Bowe. You have done something to me and to . . . *her*." Already her name had sunk so far down in his mind that he knew he'd never reach it. "I can feel your hand in this, tonight. Even before tonight, I heard your voice just before she disappeared." His anger was like flying dust in the air between them and it stung both their eyes. "Mrs. Bowe, until you fix this, whatever it is you've done, I can't forgive you. I won't. Until you've undone whatever your meddling has made, I want you to stay away from me." He walked toward the door leading to the hallway between their houses. "It should be easy to avoid me. I am visiting an estate on the north side of town, on family business, and may be a day or two. If you want us to continue being friends, fix this by the time I get back, or I'll find a way to fix it myself."

She closed her eyes and breathed in slowly for a moment, waiting, expressionless. When Mrs. Bowe opened her eyes, she looked pained, as if she'd been frightened of something she'd seen, and been hurt by his words. Her shoulders drew back as if she were going to begin ranting at him, but then she removed her coat and draped it slowly over the carved newel post of the banister. Taking the first three steps, she looked down at Silas in the foyer and spoke slowly and formally.

"Silas Umber, there are some things that shall not go with you when you leave Lichport. The ledger must remain in your house."

"I am not *leaving* Lichport!" he insisted.

"The fact that you say this tells me you are not ready to make this journey. It is too soon. You are not bound to answer this call, Silas. Not now. Not yet. Is this some whim born of your reading? It is customary to wait until a messenger calls for you."

"If you are referring to the word carved into the door of my house, yes, I think the messenger has already come and gone."

Mrs. Bowe paled visibly. "You are not prepared for this. You know almost nothing of the world that awaits you."

"You're right," Silas said.

"Good! Bless you for seeing some reason anyway."

"I mean that you're correct, I don't know enough about this place to go there directly just yet. I should make a stop or two to make inquiries, as is customary." He was serious, but the sarcasm dripped from his words.

Silas could tell that Mrs. Bowe knew exactly what he meant. He was goading her now. He assumed she would not approve of his returning to the house of the Sewing Circle. She turned and climbed the stairs without a word, but when she reached the landing, she looked back down and said quietly, sincerely, "I wish you luck upon your journey." But the flush rose again to her face and she wrung her hands in abject frustration. "Worse and worse. That is how you'll make things if you continue on in this reckless manner. Beginnings are delicate things, Silas Umber, yours especially. You have taken only the merest step upon your path. Child, learn to walk before you run."

Silas started to speak but remained silent, letting her stinging words claim precedent in the air. He knew that Mrs. Bowe thought of him as a child, despite everything they'd been through and everything he'd done. He turned and strode out of the foyer, and when he reached the end of the hallway that connected their two houses, he stepped across the threshold and firmly shut the door. And for the first time since he'd begun living next to her, Silas locked the door behind him.

CHAPTER 7

ANGLE OF APPROACH

SILAS WENT INTO HIS STUDY and finished checking the contents of his satchel. He didn't know what he might need, if anything, for a short visit. He had his jacket and the death watch already. While he chose to obey Mrs. Bowe's direction to leave the heavy ledger behind, he made sure the small *Book of Cerements* from the ledger's back cover was still in his bag from his recent visit to the lighthouse. He had added much to its pages in the past months. He would bring with him the rest of the contents of the "work" bag—the crystal vial, a small silver bell, an iron knife, some old keys, a can opener—that his dad had used in his time as Undertaker. He didn't know what all of them were for, but it felt wrong to take them out. Around his neck was the pendant his father had given him bearing the head of the god Janus. From the closet he retrieved a pair of gloves and an old, ill-fitting, moth-eaten overcoat to keep off the cold, even though the town map showed it was only a short walk past Fort Street to the entrance of the Arvale estate.

He would make two stops first, and then see what was waiting for him beyond the gates.

The downstairs parlor of the mansion of the Sewing Circle was lit with candles. They were expecting him. Silas found this unsettling. In truth, everything about the three made him uncomfortable: the mystery of them, the weight of their knowledge that gave an edge to every word they spoke, and how they always seemed to know so much more than they ever told him. They made him feel small, and Silas didn't like it. Still, he needed them, needed their insight, and he wanted to look upon the tapestry, their great work, to "see what may be seen," as they might say.

Silas entered the large beamed chamber at the top of the long staircase. He did not immediately see the three ladies, but he could hear the clicking of their bone needles and the low hum of the spinning wheel, ever turning. As Silas stepped closer to a familiar corner of the tapestry, he noticed three figures embroidered at the edge at the Millpond, one with a walking stick, one with a shawl, and one he knew, just from the proud angle of the neck, representing his mother. Silas felt his anger stir again, annoyed even at the symbolic depiction of others meddling in his business.

"You have strong women in your life. Strong women who care deeply for your safety," three voices spoke in chorus as they stepped out of the long shadows of the room. The women wore tight-fighting gray gowns that spilled onto the floor in tendrils and wisps of fraying fabric. Their sleeves came to points over the backs of their white hands, and it was hard to tell where their fingers ended and their sharp bone needles began.

Silas kept looking at the tapestry, trying to be nonchalant. "I can take care of myself."

"Truly? Then why do you keep coming back here to visit us?" asked the first of the three pointedly. "Are you so addicted to the wonders of the textile arts? Do you adore the sound of our voices?"

"Is it love?" asked the second, her voice trailing off in a little laugh.

Their warm banter putting him briefly more at ease, Silas

said, "Indeed, it must be the pleasure of your company."

"That is well. That is most well. We like admirers," the three said together.

"But," Silas began, "now that I'm here . . ."

"Here it comes," said the first of the three a little wearily. "All right, then. How may we help you? You know how we live for your little queries."

"I am looking to learn something about a house once owned by my family."

"Oh, yes?" said the second knowingly. "And what house would that be? The Umbers have made homes in many houses."

"Arvale."

At the speaking of that name, the three began to laugh. "He means *the* house. He has eyes but sees nothing!" They stepped back, behind him, farther away from the tapestry.

"Silas Umber, look again."

"What am I supposed to be seeing?"

"It's already before you. Right there. Close your eyes and look again, squint if you must, tilt your head. The angle of approach is everything." Silas backed up and turned his head one way, then another. Slowly, by half-closing his eyes, he began to discern elements of the tapestry he hadn't noticed a moment before. Nothing had changed. Not a stitch had been added or subtracted, but he could see that some buildings, taken together as a whole, formed parts of a greater structure. The more he studied the tapestry, the farther back he stood, the more of this other building he could discern. It seemed at once both isolated and connected to everything else in the weaving.

Silas noticed that the ladies now stood with him on both sides, one to his left, two to his right. They were admiring their work.

His mind bubbled with so many questions that he could

draw forth only the most obvious. He had accounts of the house's history, and had found references by his father and other Undertakers that suggested Arvale's significance, but many of the pieces didn't seem to fit together. Silas could tell by their smiles that the ladies knew much more about Arvale than he did.

"Can you tell me what I'll find when I arrive at this place?"

"You know we cannot. That depends very much on you and why you are going. You know this already."

"It is a family visit," Silas said hesitantly. He didn't want to tell them he had been invited, that the name of the house had been carved into his front door. He wanted to know what they knew.

The first of the three reached over, and with a long, pale, pointed finger, she gently tapped Silas's chest in the very place where his pendant lay under his shirt. She smiled as she withdrew her hand. "You're going for more than a Sunday dinner, I warrant."

Silas avoided her comment and continued.

"I mean, will the place look like that?" He gestured at the tapestry.

"Perhaps it will. At some other time, for someone else, perhaps only a ruin."

"For me?"

"Much more than that, I suspect. If you can get past the gates, it is very likely that a fine supper and many more familial curiosities await you. Onerous obligations, too. Isn't family funny like that?"

"Will I be welcome there?"

"Oh, that is certain, for you're family—" said the third before being cut off by the second.

"Though it's always wise to have a care, yes, even with kin. Especially with a clan so large and old as yours. The values of one age do not always hold true for another. And family secrets can be so curious, can't they? Who knows what skeletons you'll find in the closets, or what dark, forgotten caskets lie strewn in the basement? Oh, the things we fill our houses with! Remember who you are and what your father has taught—"

"Enough!" said the first. "Let him see what he shall see."

Silas could tell they were weary with being questioned and were becoming annoyed. There were no particularly terrible portents; that was a comfort. But they had begun teasing him and arguing among themselves, which usually meant it was a good time to go.

"I thank you, ladies. With your blessing, I'll take my leave."

"Isn't he clever?" the third said, looking at the first, who nodded in agreement. "Very well."

The three raised their bone-white hands with their palms open toward Silas and bowed their heads. On the air between them flowed a low chorus of indiscernibly ancient words that fell upon Silas like a breeze scented with the perfume of lavender and rosemary and the salt tang of the sea. Then the three said, "With our blessing, then."

Silas walked toward the stairs.

"And Silas, dear?" said the first.

He paused at the landing. "Yes? Most fateful and reverend ladies."

The second leaned over to the third and whispered dreamily, "I love it when he talks like that, *really* I do."

Ignoring the other two, the first of the three continued, "See you on the other side."

"You are going to Arvale too?" Silas asked with surprise.

"Not exactly. Simply, we have sometimes been there before, or rather, we have been places that were once connected to what that place has now become." They gestured once more toward the weaving. "That house and its domains are very old indeed, and share more than one frontier with our own . . . *sphere of influence.* Perhaps we shall pass one another in the halls, if you can stand the presence of even *more* old women meddling in your life. Yes, yes. We may see you on the other side of the gate, though we may not be as you are used to seeing us. Who can say? For *over there,* we often appear as we were, not as we are."

"Ladies, I beg you. Can you speak more plainly?"

"Simply then, because you're so polite: We used to travel a lot, in our earlier, more fashionable days. We were older then, and perhaps a little wiser, never staying too long in one place. We used to keep a little pied-à-terre at Arvale. The light was always so good and the views are still accounted very fine. Depending on when you arrive, you may find us in residence."

"I am going today—"

The third shook her head.

"He really doesn't get it, does he?"

"Ladies, do you mean that you're *already* there, or that you're—"

"It is as we've said: We are who we were, and for that matter, so are you."

Impatient with explication, the three faded back into the dark interior of the room to resume their needlework, but continued talking softly, almost mockingly as they spoke over Silas. "Just you hurry to the gate! So many things to be found! Lost and found both! Such marvels await you beyond the gate. We promise, Little Bird, we promise! You hurry to the gate and see!"

At Silas's departure, the ladies of the Sewing Circle turned back to look upon their handiwork.

"It's all redundancy! The same designs here and here and

here! I like it not," said the third, already beginning to pick and fuss at the worn threads.

"*Patterns* are our business," said the first. "What has happened shall happen again. Look here!" she said, pointing to a tree worked out in very old, faded, green silk. Among its roots were stitched tiny bones and little leaves. "Loss shall call out to loss down through the ages."

"But we cannot lose him now," said the third.

"True enough," replied the second.

The third drew forth her needle and quickly embroidered the outline of a comet above the tree.

"What are you doing?" asked the first and second.

"Signs and portents," said the third, not looking up from her work. "Signs and portents. How else will he find the Mistle Child and come home to us?"

"His path is set. You may not change it, nor add what is yet to come."

"This little part has happened already, long ago. I am merely catching up with some unfinished work," said the third.

The first and second nodded, and drawing out their needles and thread, joined their sister at the tapestry.

LEDGER

Of all the omens from the old Northern Lore,
the Washer at the Ford was the most harrowing.
She would be found in the rivers or streams,
cleaning the blood from the garments of some
family member or other destined to die. But her
appearances were various, for, on rare occasion,
she might grant wishes or settle blessings upon
those who were making errand to ill places for
the sake of ancestral obligation.

—FROM *PRIMITIVE AND PAGAN—AN ACCOUNT OF
ENDURING NORTHERN CUSTOMS* BY RICHARD UMBER

CHAPTER 8

WASHING DAY

THE PATH TO ARVALE stood at the very end of Fort Street. So Silas had decided to visit his great-grandfather before taking the short walk to the gates.

As he approached the stream that separated Fort Street from the town, bare trees and sharp-tipped reeds stood their ground against the cold wind. Silas saw a familiar figure standing in the midst of the water.

"Mrs. Gray?"

"Aye, Master Umber."

"May I ask what you're doing in the stream?"

"This is the old Washing Place. Farther on in both directions the stream is deeper than it looks. Folks used to come here to cross and for washing, for it is very low just here, and the crossing is less hazardous." She stood in water up to her thighs and the cold stream swirled her apron about her in spirals and eddies of trailing, threadbare calico.

"Are you no longer working at my mother's house?"

"Aye. I am. But the house's needs are few, now that neither you nor your uncle is in residence. I gave the place a good going-over after his departure. All's well there, I think. Your mother has taken on other help, so really, she has little need of me most days. But don't worry, young master. I've been looking out for her. She is as well as might be expected. Perhaps a little better."

"Thank you, Mrs. Gray. I can't tell you how much I appreciate your help. I know my mother is glad for it too."

"Aye, but she don't say, do she?" Mrs. Gray smiled. "No matter. I know she values good work, even if she's not the type to say 'thank you.'"

Mrs. Gray moved slowly through the water, appearing to glide as she got closer to the shore. "Will you be coming across?" she said, extending a hand.

Something in the gesture made Silas shudder, and he took a step back. "Oh, thank you, Mrs. Gray. But, if it's all the same to you, I'll use the bridge."

"Suit yourself, Master Umber. To each his own way."

Silas saw something half-hidden behind her in the water and moved forward again, closer to the water's edge.

"Is that one of my shirts?"

"Aye. I'll be finished with it soon, I hope."

"Did I leave that at my mother's? Why are you washing it? And why here?" Silas asked, though he knew he hadn't left it. He had worn that shirt within the last week.

"Bloody stains! It's the very devil to get them out! I used to wash all the clothes of the family and don't mind this sort of work. And the water of the stream is most suitable. Don't worry, Master Umber! I shall not cease, I shall not. Not till all be clean. Not till all be washed clean of their earthly troubles."

Silas didn't want to ask more. He was strangely positive that he didn't want that shirt back, ever. He decided to think of it as an offering. To the stream or Mrs. Gray, he wasn't exactly certain. Looking at the old woman standing in the black water, he said, "Are you sure you won't let me help you out, Mrs. Gray? You must be freezing."

"Nay," she replied as she swung the wet shirt against a rock.

"We both have our chores; you to yours, me to mine, Master Umber. Besides, there's worse things than a bit of cold."

Silas said farewell to Mrs. Gray and crossed the bridge onto Fort Street, moving into the shadows cast down by a low winter sun behind the trees growing tall and wild there. Spiky bushes rose up from enormous cracks in the pavement, and high brown weeds and gray ropey vines ran with abandon from the gardens of the dilapidated mansions out into the street. Even now, with most of the trees bare as bones, Silas wondered how long it would be until everything on Fort Street was covered in green, hidden below broad leaves and aspiring creepers. Up ahead, he saw the gate to his great-grandfather's house, the path still clear from his many visits. But as he walked across his great-grandfather's yard, Silas could see how the vines and shrubs were merely waiting for the spring. The winter-paused plants were poised, ready to renew their assault on the house where his great-grandfather had lived and died and yet endured.

LEDGER

It is their particular and willful insistence
on continuation that is most unnatural and
abhorrent. The Restless make a mockery of
the living, pretending to take part in life's minor
and major scenes and acts. They pay no heed
to death and so bring down the wrath of Mors
upon every family or dynasty in which they
endure. And so we must work the Doom
against them though they be kin and our love for
them be true and enduring. Only the Doom
may dissolve both stubborn flesh and wandering
spirit both without prejudice or preference. There
is no other way. "Earth to Earth" must be the
motto of all, or else all is lost.

—MARGINALIA OF JONAS UMBER

AT THAT TIME THE PHARAOH POSSESSED A SCARAB OF DARK BLUE STONE THAT ALLOWED HIM TO WALK WHERE HE WOULD, UNHARMED, IN THE MANNER OF ANUBIS, THROUGHOUT THE TWO LANDS. AND, WHEN HE WISHED, THE DOORS OF THE LAND OF THE WEST WERE ALSO OPEN TO HIM. WITH THE SCARAB'S ENCHANTMENT, HE WENT FORTH WITHOUT FEAR AMONG THE LIVING, THE DEAD, AND THE EVER-LIVING. EVEN THE FEARFUL DEMONS WHO HAUNT THE PLAINS OF CAANAN AND THE LANDS OF THE SONS OF AMMON COULD BE STRUCK DOWN SHOULD PHARAOH RAISE HIS HAND AGAINST THEM AND UTTER THE WORDS INSCRIBED UPON THE STONE. AND OF HIS TRAVELS, PERFECT MEMORY WAS GRANTED ALSO BY THE MIGHT OF THIS STONE ALWAYS.

—FROM THE *EGYPTIAN COFFIN TEXTS, SUPPLEMENTAL SCROLL VI*, TRANSLATED BY AMOS UMBER

CHAPTER 9

MAN OF THE HOUSE

SILAS ENTERED HIS GREAT-GRANDFATHER'S MANSION and crossed the tiled foyer to the stairs, preparing to make his way up to the usual audience chamber on the second floor. But he heard movement somewhere on the ground floor, and paused.

"Hello?" Silas called down the hall.

"In here, boy-o! Right on time. I've been expecting you!" his great-grandfather's voice rasped from some unseen room deeper in the house.

Silas wandered down the back hall leading toward the kitchen.

"In here!" his great-grandfather called out again, and Silas walked through a butler's pantry into what must have once been a very grand dining room. The dusty mahogany table was at least thirty feet long, and tall candles burned in silver candelabras along its length.

The corpse of Augustus Howesman, sat at the head of the table in an elaborately carved high-backed chair. Before him, several tarnished silver trays were piled with fruit and cheese and cold meats. Two glasses stood brimming with wine, and an ornate silver ewer promised more.

Silas's mouth hung open in surprise.

The corpse noticed his expression, smiled, and said, "What? I shopped." Clearly pleased with himself, he beckoned for Silas to come down and join him.

"How did you know I was coming?" Silas asked.

"Call it a hunch," replied his great-grandfather, slowly closing and opening one eye in what might have been a wink.

"You made supper?"

"I have prepared a little something for you."

"You've got to be kidding me," Silas exclaimed, clearly impressed.

"Well, good help has always been hard to find, and in these savage times, a man must fend for himself. I've been feeling a little more spry lately and rather enjoyed my walk to the store. So, I remain the deathless lord of winter, but I still have a bit of spring in my step, as you can see. Besides, you're looking thin."

Silas sat down at the table next to his great-grandfather and filled his plate with food.

"What may I get you?" he asked his great-grandfather.

"Oh, Silas, nothing at all. Thank you."

"Sorry, I wasn't sure—"

"No, no. I don't eat. But I can draw a kind of pleasure from food, a sort of sustenance. The offerings and little sacrifices folks used to leave on the porches were always such a boon. So the glass of wine and these victuals serve me in their way. I like being close to them and feel more vigorous for it. And watching you eat, well, that brings me a particular joy."

"I didn't know, or I would have brought you something on my other visits."

"Not necessary," his great-grandfather said, and the corpse put his large hand on Silas's shoulder and patted it tenderly. "The company of loving kin is itself a form of manna. The best sort, I think. I am sure your frequent visits are responsible for my recent invigoration. Why, it only took me most of the day to walk to the store and back. Slow and steady wins the race, eh? Tell me, how is your mother? She comes sometimes. My granddaughter is still a little formal, and doesn't like to make eye contact, but she talks more."

"I think my mom is getting reacquainted with Lichport, in her own way. But it's been hard. She spent a long time trying not to think about it. But it's getting better, slowly, and between the two of us, things have been improving too," Silas said.

"I suspect that big house she's living in is helping her adjust." Augustus Howesman laughed.

"It's more than that, she . . . well, she just seems relaxed."

"You needn't explain, grandson. We are a family accustomed to a certain degree of luxury. Frankly, I never understood how my granddaughter ever thought she could be happy in Saltsbridge."

"She wasn't happy there at all," agreed Silas.

"No, I don't suspect she was. But that's all in the past, is it not? And here we all are, a family again." A small, satisfied smile spread briefly across Augustus Howesman's taut face. "But grandson," he continued, his smile vanishing, "there is a look in your eyes that tells me this is not the usual visit made for the sake of sharing family gossip. Indeed, I believe I know something about why you're here. Message from the Big House, eh?"

"How did you know?"

"I saw the messenger come from Arvale. Came right down the street in front of my house. So far as I know, that messenger only carries word to one person: the Undertaker."

"Who was it? I never saw who brought it."

"You should be glad of that, for the messenger is not so much a *who* as a *what*, in my estimation."

"I'll take your word for it."

"Best get used to such things, grandson. Your acceptance of your father's mantle, has, I suspect, opened certain doors in the world. Best accustom yourself to wonders, I think, eh?"

Nodding, Silas began eating with gusto.

"What is it about the presence of the dead that gives the living such an appetite, I wonder?"

"Confirmation of life?" Silas guessed.

"Maybe so," said the corpse.

Silas was glad to be here and pleased to see his great-grandfather looking so content. But then Silas imagined the old man rambling about the large house by himself.

"Are you sure you're not too lonely here? Maybe when I get back, you could come and live with me. My place is pretty big. I worry that this street, this house—I mean, it's great, but it's seen better days. With me, you could have your own room, you could have the whole upstairs at my place if you like, a long corridor to pace up and down with a good view of the park. You could have all the privacy you want, but then we could visit whenever we liked."

"Silas, that is surely about the kindest offer anyone's ever made me. Truly. How fortunate I am to have you as a grandchild. But this is my place. My own place. I built this house for my family and added to it as need and fashion required. It may well be that I am what I am because of where I am. Building a world about yourself may be a kind of attempt at immortality, a sort of spell. Might be what's slowed the process down for me. It's worth considering, boy-o, that some places are, or become over time, more important than others. Maybe certain plots are natural thresholds that just need watching. Maybe that's why I'm here, because this place needs me on the lookout. And I have seen things, Silas, living on this street. Wonders and terrors both. Things so terrible that I shall not speak of them with night drawn in. Old things. Things that don't seem to have a place in the natural order of the world.

Things probably coming out of, or called toward, the stones of that house."

And the corpse leaned back, raised his arm, and pointed away behind him toward Arvale.

"Those stones, brought over so long ago from across the sea—who knows from where before that, or what kind of houses or structures they might have been a part of before they were disassembled and brought here. Temple or tomb? Castle or barrow? I can tell you this: that house, however it remains or appears to you, is an old, old place. Lived in, died in, over and over again."

The corpse's words were beginning to weigh on him. Silas felt, truly felt for the first time, that everyone was right and he was a child and he had no idea what he was doing. From his honest ignorance, fear began to flow.

"Will you go with me tomorrow?" he asked his great-grandfather.

"Silas," the corpse said tenderly, "I don't think I could enter beyond the gates unless I was invited." He continued with a wan smile. "It's a *very* exclusive crowd up there, my boy. Not sure even I'd pass muster."

"Why not? You, great-grandfather, are a unique individual."

Augustus Howesman nodded his assent.

"Very true, but for one thing, my name's not 'Umber.' Even now, that house's front door stands wide for you because of who you are. It's the house of your kin, your ancestral mansion. Anyone you meet there, good, bad, or in between, they are more than likely part of your family. Besides, your father told me to give that place a wide berth, and so I have, and so I shall as long as I have a choice in the matter. Though it will be my honor to walk you to the gate. Besides, it is there I may be of some assistance, and it will delight me to help you, even in that small way."

"How do you mean?"

"Only the dead and recognized kin can pass through those gates. You have not been received at the house, so are not yet "recognized" and may not yet be able to open them yourself. I, however, being . . . as I am . . . may open the gate for you if it is required, because the road to that house is a lychway and it cannot bar the way of the dead. Not ever. That's Old Law. I helped your father several times, actually. He could never open it by himself. I expect he wasn't very popular up at the big house. He did have his own way of doing things. Untraditional, he was."

The corpse looked down at his hand and said, "That reminds me, there is something I wish to give you, Silas."

"Sir, you have given me too much already. Really."

"I shall brook no refusals. I would like you to have this." His great-grandfather was already twisting and turning the great ring on his finger so severely that Silas thought the finger might come off with the ring. At last it worked free and the old man handed it to Silas. The ring gleamed bright blue and gold against the dark skin of his great-grandfather's corpse-hand.

"Folk from this street and others have gone past the gates to Arvale. I have heard the call of the mighty trumpet from beyond the gates and watched their departure. Those like me who pass beyond those gates do not return. Your father told me never to heed that trumpet, even should I hear within its call the sound of my own name. He told me that in times past, folks like me were feared by the living, even by their own families. He told me how there yet endured, in some prejudiced corners of the world, pockets of those who might still bear the old hatred toward, well, toward people like myself. Then he gave me this ring and said it would keep me safe down through the years. And so it has."

"I can't take that."

"Of course you can," his great-grandfather said. He reached

over, opened Silas's hand, and slipped the ring onto his middle finger. "That is well, most well. Besides, if you are in residence over there, what have I to fear? More to the point, if you are the one going to Arvale, maybe you could use a little more protection. Besides, I've never felt better a day in my death."

Silas laughed lightly, and looked closely at the large sapphire. He could see that it was actually carved. Lightly engraved lines passed over its surface and shaped it into a beetle, a scarab, the kind the pharaohs wore in ancient Egypt. The bottom of the gem was not covered over by the mount—perhaps so that when worn, the stone would always be touching the skin of the wearer—and on it, tiny, intricate hieroglyphs had been inscribed. The heavy gold setting looked medieval. It was some kind of relic, Silas guessed, a precious object handed down over and over again, treasured through time. Who else had worn this ring? he wondered.

"Your father said it would keep my mind clear. Now you take it and keep it. Do not take it off no matter who may ask it of you. I feel strongly about this, so indulge me. Wear it in memory of me and your father. Let it be a reminder to keep your wits about you and not to do anything stupid that might embarrass your remaining relatives."

"All right, then, I will wear it. It will be like a part of you is going with me."

At the top of the glass in the windows at the end of the dining room, the stars had risen. Augustus Howesman got up from his chair.

"Silas, it's late. Why don't you stay here tonight and we'll make a fresh start in the morning? I don't like the idea of you going through those gates at night. No sense in going all the way home to sleep just to turn around and come back again. There are many rooms along the upstairs corridor, and most of the ones on the inside wall are serviceable if you don't mind a little dust."

"All right. We'll leave in the morning, then."

"Silas, you may recall I don't really sleep. So should you hear any noises in the night, it will just be me, stretching my legs."

"All right. Good night, great-grandfather," Silas said, taking a candle from the table to find his way to a room upstairs. And as he climbed the steps, he realized quite suddenly that the idea of hearing his great-grandfather's corpse shuffle about the house in the middle of the night brought him nothing but comfort.

Ledger

It is right it should be so:
Man was made for joy and woe;
And when this we rightly know
Through the world we safely go.

—from William Blake, "Auguries of Innocence,"
Transcribed by Amos Umber

CHAPTER 10

HIGHWAY

"SILAS? WAKE UP, SON!"

Silas opened his eyes. His great-grandfather was standing over him, holding him by the shoulders. A low light was crawling through the window.

Tears stung Silas's eyes and his throat hurt. His body was glazed in sweat and his hair was soaked. He sat up, rubbing his neck.

"What has happened?" his great-grandfather asked.

"I don't know. . . ." Silas struggled to find the words. "There was water in my throat. Someone was holding me under the water. I could feel their hands grasping my legs. At first it was okay, they were holding me, and it felt warm, but then I couldn't breathe and the hands were like claws and they wouldn't let go. There was light above me, but I couldn't reach it and the light kept pulling back farther and farther, or maybe I was sinking. I tried to call for help, but none came, the water filled my throat. I couldn't cry out."

"Well, you certainly did. Sounded like bloody murder in here. Who was holding you down?"

"I can't remember. I'm okay. Don't worry. I'm okay now."

"I've brought a basin. Why don't you wash up and I'll meet you across the hall in a few minutes."

"Yeah, that's fine."

Silas looked into the bowl of water, but couldn't bring himself to splash any on his face. When he crossed the hall into his great-grandfather's room, the room in which they'd first met, Silas saw an open cedar chest and a large old-fashioned coat laid out over a chair.

"You should wear something a little more formal, I think. Something bespeaking your rank and station. This coat was mine, in my youth. Smells a bit of mothballs but that will shake out, I think."

In his large, dark hands, the corpse held up a black mourning coat, long with a high velvet collar. Silas pulled the coat on awkwardly over his dad's sports jacket, which he always wore when going out.

"No matter," said his great-grandfather, "it looks more interesting this way. You are a man who bestrides the very ages of fashion! You'll be glad of another coat; I think it's rather cold outside, is it not? Might be colder where you're going. You never know."

The coat was voluminous—not too big, just made with a great deal of fabric—and when Silas turned quickly, the bottom of the coat followed him a second or two slower. It was a little like wearing a cape, and Silas admitted to himself that the eccentricity of his outfit really appealed to him. He also liked feeling wrapped in the layers of his family. Great-grandfather, then father, then himself on the inside, protected from the elements by layers of kin.

"Yes. That suits you very well indeed. You are a Howesman as well as an Umber, and should look respectable. If there is nothing else you require, let's get started toward the gates. I find that when walking, things are always a little farther away than you think."

They emerged from the house into a gray morning. The sun

had not yet pushed its way through the low clouds. The air was very still, and it nipped at the exposed parts of Silas's skin, his ears especially. He pulled the collar up on his coat so that it lay high and close to his neck. His satchel hung over his shoulder beneath his coat.

Silas strode across the yard to open the gate for his great-grandfather. The corpse walked steadily if not a little slowly, but still much quicker than Silas was expecting.

"You see what a boon your company is? Why, I'll be running soon!"

Silas took his great-grandfather's arm in his, saying, "I am in no rush, I promise."

They turned onto what had once been a sidewalk, now broken by up-thrust roots and saplings into slabs of ruined concrete, jutting this way and that. The middle of the street was a little clearer, so that is where they walked. While at the top of Fort Street a thin path through the tall weeds had been trod down by Silas's frequent visits, the street past his great-grandfather's house was still very much a wilderness, even in winter. The farther they walked down Fort Street, the denser the undergrowth became. Branches pale as bone, some sharp with thorns or brittle vines, others grown thick and interwoven with their neighbors, made passage slow and difficult. Still, Silas was unbothered as he sought the easiest ways through, helping his great-grandfather step over fallen branches and pull the clinging vines from around his occasionally dragging feet.

His great-grandfather looked at Silas's face, confident, stoic, and asked, "Aren't you scared at all, Silas? I like a bit of bravado, you know, when confronting the unknown, but your calm is spooking me."

"Sir, as long as I've lived, I've felt there are two of me. I walk about and there's one of me doing things, just living in the moment. But then somewhere there's another me that I can't seem to find, though occasionally, that other me feels really close, almost breathing down my neck. I find the rift a little distracting, and maybe that makes it harder to get scared. But I do get frightened sometimes, truly."

"Could be several things, you know, that 'other' you. Might be your ancestors. I can certainly feel mine sometimes, that long ancestral road stretching out behind you. Though just at the moment, yours is *both* before you and behind you. Arvale ahead, Lichport back there. That feeling could be your kin, for your ancestors are, when you get right down to it, another you. Often they rally around you, stand by you."

Silas remembered the group of spectral women that had gathered around his mother while she and Uncle lived in the house on Temple Street.

"But, when folks don't honor and remember their departed kin, those folk of the past stay hid in the shadows. When you keep them in your heart, they fly to you and then you're whole and in that house where your love is. You are one person, but you're never alone."

"I'm sure that's part of it." But Silas knew there was more to it, something not as nice.

"Of course," his great-grandfather continued, "it could just be your death following you around like some old dog. Waiting."

"Now you're trying to frighten me."

"Lord, no, son. But I'm sure you know this already. Everyone has his very own death."

"You mean the 'fetch'?" Silas said.

His great-grandfather nodded.

"C'mon. Really? Do you think there's one following me? Right now?" Silas said tentatively. Something in his great-grandfather's tone told him that the old man already knew the answer.

"I expect that you do. Would you like me to look and see what may be seen?"

"No. No thank you. But, have you ever seen yours?"

"Yes. I think I have, but only recently. It's hard to say with certainty." And his great-grandfather paused in the road and looked at Silas with such affection and sadness that Silas said, "Maybe we'll just change the subject."

"Perhaps that would be best."

They emerged from the overgrowth into a cleared space before the gates. It was as if the trees and bushes, even having grown so bold, pushing through concrete and cobblestone, street and sidewalk, had, upon reaching the gate, become suddenly fearful and retreated. The wild plants kept their distance. Now Silas could see the gates clearly and for the first time.

The massive iron gates stood more than two stories tall. They were covered in decorative metalwork in carefully wrought, sharp-toothed shapes of animals: lions, tigers, birds, serpents, and wilder things sprung from the considerable imagination of the blacksmith. To each side, elaborate castellated stone piers held the enormous hinges. Next to the piers, decorative lodges built to look like classical tombs joined the gates to the high stone wall that ran off to the left and right, an endless ribbon of dressed stones disappearing in the distance, perhaps encircling the whole of the estate and its environs.

As he put his hand on one of the thick iron bars, the usually warm pendant at his chest went ice cold. He felt dizzy until he drew his hand away.

"As I thought," said his great-grandfather. "Stand down,

grandson, and let the old pater be of some assistance."

Augustus Howesman slowly straightened his spine, tilted his head back, opened his mouth, and wailed so loudly that Silas was nearly knocked off his feet. The sound vibrated on the air and Silas could feel it humming in the midst of his very bones. Then, as quickly as the cry went up, it fell back down, lower and lower into the corpse's throat.

Almost at the moment the cry subsided, the gates began to tremble on their massive hinges. In the middle, a space opened, wider and wider, and Silas and his great-grandfather stepped back to avoid being hit by the gates as they swung out toward them.

The path to Arvale lay open.

Both men leaned forward, looking for they knew not what.

"I see only mist. Silas, can you make anything out?"

Silas took a small step forward and said, "A great avenue of trees, the largest I've ever seen. Trunks wide as my house. They must be really old. Cedars, I think."

His great-grandfather stepped up even with Silas, leaned in close, and whispered, "Now hold fast a moment. If it's like it was for your father, they'll return the call."

A horn blasted from somewhere far beyond the trees. Deep and round was its call and the gates shook with the sound of it. Silas and his great-grandfather looked at each other. Here was no shrill, modern trumpet, but a sound instead like some giant-blown saga-horn, calling out its bellowing welcome from the mead hall of an ancient northern legend.

His great-grandfather looked nervous, but he quickly conjured calm back to his face. The corpse put his arms around Silas and held him for many minutes, while that mighty horn sounded again and again, reverberating in both their ears.

Augustus Howesman stepped back, but kept his hands on

Silas's shoulders. "Grandson, I think it's time you got on your way. That horn sets my teeth on edge, I swear! Silas? Have a care, my boy, and come back to me."

"I will, sir. I promise."

And without another word, Silas walked away from his great-grandfather and through the tall gates and into the land beyond. Behind him, the gates shut with a crash. When he turned and looked through the bars, back at where he'd come from, he could no longer see his great-grandfather or any other familiar thing.

CHAPTER 11

OLD STRAIGHT TRACK

THERE WAS ONLY THE ROAD.

Silas walked and walked, unsure of the time or of how long he'd been traveling. He knew he'd passed through the gates at late morning. Was it dusk now? The sky had grown darker, and the land was now aglow with a golden, lingering light.

The road wound its way through the wood. Great trees formed into lines, flanking the road on both sides, casting wide shadows across the path. So large were these cedars, oaks, ash trees, and birches, that each looked as though it might have been planted on the first morning of the world. Their high limbs formed a canopy over Silas as he walked. When he looked up, stars seemed to descend from among the branches, and the air before him was suddenly alight with small white moths that flittered about the path, but parted like a tattered veil as he approached.

Farther on, the lines of trees became intermixed with slabs of stone, growing up from among the roots and boles. Long slim fingers of rock, crude gravestones, small tombs, carved granite sarcophagi . . . crawling up from the soft soil, crowding out the trees. Worn hexagonal stones paved the road, pushing up through the moss and leaf-mold. The path ascended and went over a small hill. What lay on the other side of the rise stopped Silas in mid-stride.

All along the roadway, a forest of monuments towered

before him in mad Piranesian splendor. It was as if all the funeral structures of the world, from the earliest grave mounds to the most elaborate Roman tombs to delicately carved gothic mausoleums, had all been broken apart and erected here to form canyon walls rising above the avenue.

Among the tombs were massive carved busts rendered in marble, jade, jet, chalcedony, and quartz. Many of the faces felt familiar, bore what his mother might have called the "Umber look." These adorned the tops of decorative columns, plinths, and pediments. Other pedestals bore skulls, some in their natural bleached state, others adorned with precious stones. In front of some of the older-looking tombs stood figures of tall youths in the Attic style, their plaited hair carved close to their heads, eyes blank, arms held straight down at their sides. Near these were tall fluted columns, on top of which perched stylized marble griffins, those ancient composite creatures once known as guardians of gold and the dead.

Higher and higher up the carvings climbed into the air, stacked precipitously like blocks from a titan's toy box. Near the top were stone rotundas, surrounded by columns, positioned atop one another like layers of a wedding cake. They stood upon a thick marble base holding engraved slabs that might have borne the names of some ancestral Umbers in a far distant land.

Along the strata of awkward terraces, small trees clung to the cracked stone of the monuments, their snaking trunks bending this way and that around the columns, parapets, and elaborate carvings, striving up and up even as their roots pried loose bits of the masonry that supported them. Below those verdant vandals—strewn across the road where they'd fallen from the memorial battlements—were pieces of statues, broken pediments, and cracked chunks of dislodged decorative brick.

Cautiously fascinated, Silas ventured within some of the lower monuments. Many along the roadway, perhaps a reflection of the great Via Appia of ancient Rome, were decorated in the Roman fashion. Inside, Silas saw murals and carved marble portraits configured in various activities—hunting, playing games, drinking. One depicted a family eating before the deceased as the corpse held up a curved cup in a triumphant gesture. The sculptures of his surviving wife and child cast their eyes down upon the somber offering table, less enthusiastic about the funeral feast.

One after another, Silas explored the burial houses and tenements of the dead. Some bore readable inscriptions, brief, runic lines delineating thousands of individual lives. All remembered. All recorded. Yet in none of them did he encounter the dead themselves. Not a resident ghost in a single grave. Where *was* everyone?

As Silas walked toward a row of primitive-looking rock-cut tombs, he heard someone clear his throat.

From a small Etruscan mausoleum just ahead, a little light danced out onto the avenue and a tentative voice spoke.

"Are you Silas Umber, sir?"

"I am," Silas said hesitantly, peering ahead, trying to see who was speaking.

"Good evening, sir. I am to take you to the house."

A young man about Silas's age stepped out from an ornate doorway holding a lantern. He was dressed in a very antique fashion, wearing breeches, a yoke-necked shirt, a vest, and a long wool coat. His long dark hair was tied at the back with a bit of leather cord.

Silas walked forward and then extended his hand. "I am Silas Umber. Pleased to meet you."

The young man did not reach for Silas's hand or immediately

respond. He stood expectantly as though he was far off and Silas's words had not yet reached him. But then he smiled suddenly, and replied, "Thank you, sir. I am to bring you to the house and make sure you don't get lost, sir."

"There is no need to be so formal. What's your name?"

"Lawrence, sir. Um. Lawrence."

"Do you have a last name, 'Lawrence Sir'?" Silas smiled as he spoke.

"Umber. But you can call me Lars. If you like."

"Really? Then we are kin, Lars Umber!" Without thinking, Silas took Lars's hand this time and shook it, then looked at Lars in surprise. There was a feeling, a warmth, to the skin that was in no way preternatural. Silas knew what a ghost felt like, particularly its presence, and Lars was not a ghost. But his clothes were centuries out of fashion, so what was going on? Silas had assumed he was going to a house that would not be occupied by any living relatives. Now he wasn't at all sure what lay ahead.

Obviously made uncomfortable by Silas's tightening grip and the odd way he was being looked at, Lars drew back his hand and turned to the path. Lars held up the lantern and put his other hand in his pocket.

"Have a care, Silas. The ground is very uneven here."

The two young men began making their way forward. The stones of the path were cracked and broken, some of the hexagonal tiles standing up along their fractured edges at all angles. Picking his way along, content to follow but still curious, Silas asked "Lars? How did you come to Arvale? In what year?"

"Not so long ago. I have only served at the house a short time. I came last year. Seventeen fifty-five, that was."

Silas only nodded. This was mysterious and unfamiliar, but also a little exhilarating. What did it mean? Silas had just become accustomed to thinking of Lichport as both a world in itself and a crossroads. Now, here was another world waiting just on its edges. And behind this one, how many more? And behind those?

Lars was looking at him expectantly again. Silas wanted to ask Lars more about his situation, but he held back. He knew from his work that it was best to let a person, or place, tell its own story in its own time. So although Silas had never met another living person in the shadowlands and wanted to know more about Lars, he decided to wait and watch a little longer. He nodded to Lars again and said nothing about his suspicions.

"And what do you do at Arvale, may I ask?"

"I serve as footman."

"But you are family. . . ."

"Only a very distant cousin. Besides, this isn't my place. Not really. I only came here by accident, and the folk of the house took me in, and well, things being as they were, I thought I'd stay on, since there was a job and things were bad at home. Leaving was the best thing."

"I totally understand," said Silas. And he did. How many times in the last year had he wanted to hide somewhere? Or run away from his own problems?

The two walked abreast. The high-stacked memorials began to fall away from the roadside, and now, on either side were low round hills, some crowned with circles of stones, or tall single monoliths. Some of the hills were open at their sides like Neolithic tombs, their entrances fitted with limestone or granite slabs that might have at one time been opened or closed to allow the corpses of the dead to complete their journeys by returning to the earthen womb.

The road turned to the left, and Silas and Lars were in the open and could see the towers and high walls of Arvale before them. Silas's stride slowed. He felt shaky and dizzy as he tried to focus on the house. It was as though someone had spun him around and around in a circle and then stopped him very suddenly. The house was so large, so sprawling, so vast in its dimensions, that Silas's perception of distance was thrown awry. He had never seen a place like it, more medieval city than house. From every part rose towers, wings, and galleries, hundreds of chimneys, each with its own unique brick pattern. This was no common mansion or castle. Arvale was a world. A place unique and whole unto itself. Silas stared, trying to compass a complete image of the place. He knew that he was standing on the threshold of some estate of the otherworld. Yet here was neither worldly house, nor some mere misthome of trapped spirits. Here, his people had very deliberately built for themselves an ancestral dominion, a home of permanence, a place in which time could not assail them. This thought gave Silas an idea.

"Lars, let me catch my breath for a moment. You go ahead, I'll be right there."

"All right, but don't leave the road," said Lars, looking a little nervous. "I'll wait for you at the bottom of the hill. It's only a short walk to the house from down there. Don't linger too long."

There are some houses that are best approached with evening drawing in. They benefit from the long shadows that dusk provides, and are lent an air of ancient, somber resplendence by the way the last light of day lingers upon the stonework. Arvale was one of those houses. The coming darkness only made it look larger, for there was no telling where its high walls ended and its long shadows began.

Silas looked out over the mansions and towers of Arvale. All the time he'd been walking, curiosity grew in his mind. He wanted to use the death watch. There was no particular reason he could think of to do it, but this was a place very different from any other, and he wanted to know what further vistas of hidden perspective the death watch might show him. He took it from his pocket and opened the jaw to reveal the dial. But the hand wasn't moving. He held it tighter, but felt nothing. Even the skull-shaped case, always so warm in his hand, was cold. The little wound gears and springs of the death watch had stilled, its tiny mechanical heart beat completely stopped. *No time*, Silas thought. *Or a place outside of time.* Closing the death watch and putting it back in his pocket, eager again for the company, Silas continued down the hill where Lars was waiting for him.

Before them, the house sprawled in architectural, almost chaotic, magnificence. The sheer enormity of Arvale made it impossible for Silas to focus on the house as a whole. It was as if the house had never been conceived as a completed structure, as though no one in its long tenancy had ever even thought about what a "finished" mansion might look like. Silas imagined that every occupant, every branch of the family, understood their obligation: Add to the house. New halls. New battlements, addendum after addendum of stone . . . each age of the world adding its signature to Arvale's long rambling narrative about family and place, and the very definition of endurance. What Silas didn't know was whether the house stood just on the edge of Lichport, or whether, beyond that gate was another land entirely. A land where all the portions of his family, all their various homes and tombs, were woven together into one vast estate of ancestral splendor and experience. Was he still in Lichport or some kind of "Umberland"?

Everywhere Silas looked, there was palimpsest. Layer upon hereditary layer, and as he drew closer to Arvale, the very bricks and angles of the walls—windows, towers, chimneys, cornices, ramparts, gables, finials, domes, friezes, tracery, bastions, and parapets—began to speak to him.

I am the battlement raised in 1260 by Gregory Umber for the protection of his family during the War of the Mount. I did not fail them, I did not fall. My walls are washed in the blood of those who came against us.

We are the conical Persian spires. We are a whimsy born of pride. We say, look here! Are we not a fine family? We hold small chambers for secret meetings and assignations. Once, a young man was stabbed to death here. Then his pride-wounded paramour took her own life. Their corpses were left, and the little room was bricked up. Aren't we a grand family, hiding away our indiscretions in such lovely architectural details?

I am the gargoyle carved with the face of a lion. I watch. I do not sleep. I forget nothing.

We are the panes of glass brought from Venizia by Maria Archimbaldo-Umber on the occasion of her marriage, so she might always sit in the light of her homeland.

I am the sixteenth century chimney with the hollow space for hiding what you will. I have held bastard children, patient lovers, silver and plate, and men of unfashionable collars. Indeed, the bones of a priest still reside in me.

I am the Norman bell tower. I have lost my tongue. I cannot sing. My bell was carried away and across the sea.

We are the towers of the north range. We watch the skies through the cold nights. We hold ourselves aloof and aloft. We are not of that lower sort. We grant perspective and vision for we sit among the stars awaiting signs and portents. Climb our stairs and see. . . .

Silas had wandered right up to the edge of the courtyard without noticing he had caught up to Lars, who was now standing directly before him.

"Silas? Sir?" Lars's voice broke Silas away from his architectural reverie. Silas rubbed his eyes briefly, and the two made their way across the courtyard toward the great door. The house was both rising up before them and sprawling away to the left and right. Silas had never felt smaller, or more insignificant.

Lars paused for a moment and looked at Silas hesitantly.

"Why have you come to Arvale, Silas?"

"I was invited, and so I came. I think many of the men in my family have visited here . . . during their lifetimes. I know my father came to Arvale. Maybe more than once. It's sort of a tradition."

"I don't mean to be rude. It's just that, you're different from the usual sort that comes here. It's a queer house, I know. And we're a queer family. Who doesn't know that? But it's best to just keep going forward and not look back. I was lost when I came here and I wish . . . well . . . I mean it would be best if you—"

"It's okay. I understand. I'll be careful. Thank you, Lars." Silas shook his hand again and Lars nodded his head in seeming relief, but what exactly did he think Silas understood? Who did he think Silas *was*?

Lars ran ahead, perhaps to announce their arrival. Silas's feet crunched across the gravel that covered the ground in front of the house. Below the gravel, long thin slabs of stone were exposed in a few places, the kind sometimes seen lining the floors in the oldest churches. The very walls seemed to be inhaling the air around him, drawing him closer. As he came to the massive stone archway of the porch, the shadows of the house enveloped him completely, cutting him off from the rest of the world.

Standing before the entrance, he looked up. The wall rose straight up into a riot of gargoyles and decorative and perhaps ritualistic carvings. Up and up the carved grotesques could be seen, crouching and squatting upon their perches of dressed stone. The farthest away became insects, tiny creatures living on the back of some architectural leviathan. Dizzy, Silas returned his gaze to the ground. But now all feelings of adventure and excitement at seeing new things flowed out of him. What was one person next to a place like this? It must have taken thousands of years to build such a house, and standing before its walls, he knew his lifetime was just the merest moment, not even a second, in its long and continuing history.

The great doors of Arvale loomed before him, fifty feet tall and worked with riveted ornaments. Across them, wrought in early runes of iron, Silas could read the word DOOM. He wasn't sure what to do next. Should he wait for Lars to open them? Should he knock? He hesitated. The cold air was alive with sounds, and voices emanated from the walls. When he closed his eyes, he could hear them shouting, singing, crying, rising and falling like wisps of music from a radio in another room.

As he stood there, unsure how to proceed, one of the doors silently opened.

Beyond the threshold, shadows moved and gathered. He took a step back and looked over his shoulder at the road home. He stared at the details of the path, pulling them into his memory—the trees that flanked it, the curve of their branches, the swell of the hill—suddenly frantic about being able to remember the way back to Lichport. He would have gazed longer, adding details to his mental map of the return route, but a voice from within the house bid him simply, ominously, "Welcome home."

LEDGER

Wraetlic is thaes wealhstane

—ANONYMOUS MARGINALIA (MEANING "GHOSTLY IS THIS
FAMILIAL STONE") NEXT TO AN ENTRY CONCERNING
HOUSES IN DREAMS

CHAPTER 12

A WORD OF WELCOME

THE MOMENT SILAS UMBER HAD PASSED THROUGH the great gates, a shiver had passed from the cold ground and up into the stones of the manor. As he made his way closer to the house's front door, the residents of Arvale felt that shiver as well, and all of them—whether residing in the lowest catacombs or the highest towers—became immediately aware of the approach of kin. Some woke from misty reveries of their former lives. Others began their long journeys from the outer corridors and distant wall towers to the great hall. A few folk of the house were not pleased, and would remain in quiet corners. But everyone would know of the arrival of the Janus; it was house business.

Maud Umber was hopeful but uneasy. The cleverest of the house's spirits would know what she'd done. She knew Jonas would be waiting for her. She traveled through winding corridors and long passages, unsure of how long her journey would take.

When she arrived in the great hall, a single sharp voice rang across the polished stones of the chamber.

"*Who* is this? *Who* is coming?"

"Silas Umber, Undertaker of Lichport," said Maud, refusing to be cowed, knowing he already knew the answers to his own questions.

"Who has called him? Who has done this thing?" Jonas's voice was edged with indictment and anger.

"I have," Maud said.

Even as Maud softened her tone, the air seemed to bristle as their wills began to push and pull at each other.

"Gods Below, Maud Umber! It was wrong to summon him. You know this. It is too soon," accused Jonas sternly. He was tall, a robust man in gray clothes, standing bedside the monumental crest-carved fireplace. He gazed into the fire. The silver buttons on his long coat turned to mirrors of flame, and his lengthening shadow stretched out across the floor, like a finger pointing at a criminal.

"Your actions have caused more trouble than you know. Sending the Messenger has woken—"

"The house must come before all," replied Maud matter-of-factly.

"I agree. That is why we should have waited, consulted, made appropriate preparations."

"You find him too young?" asked Maud as she leaned forward, her long woolen sleeves draped across the table in front of her. She almost smiled, glad to argue about the boy's merits because it shifted suspicion away from her motives.

"He needs time. The boy is still in mourning."

"Beloved descendant, Jonas Umber, you are right, of course. But always and always it hath been thus: The Undertaker shall not be called forth until he, or *she*"—and she put special emphasis on the this last word—"'has served for at least a score of years,' or 'unless the house have need of him.' I have heard such noises from the sunken mansion—the dark huntsman stirs. And we have troubles concerning so many other matters. . . . Forgive me for letting my love of peace drive my actions. Of course, I should have consulted with you. But what's done is done. And, in truth, the past has haunted me. The father refused the call because we waited too long and allowed him to become too independent, too foolish and sentimental about his work. He became set in his absurd, deluded habits, and now the noble office we've both held has been recast in shame. Without a living Janus our work shall never go apace. And what of that greater business? The Ebony Throne has too long sat empty and in abeyance. Who shall govern from that hallowed seat? Who shall once again command the dead and sit in reverend judgment over them and their estate? Who shall call the dead back once more into the circle of the sun? I am weary of waiting for the honors due to us."

"The Ebony Throne? Are you now some saint to speak of relics? Those days have long since passed. The throne is now only an ancient ornament. Had a king been on that throne, lo these many years, why, we might never have been given leave to establish ourselves as we have, here in this great house, so comfortable in our familiar surroundings. Do you know what might have become of us? Have you considered that?"

"But Jonas, if one of our own sits in that chair, we need never fear dissolution. What once was may be again! If one of our living kin should take up that mantle, all those lost to us might be returned to the folds of their family. The Umber name might once more be—"

Jonas raised his hand and cut Maud short, staring at her hard. He looked into her eyes with that well-honed scrutiny that was the family's particular gift. He was looking not at her, but into her, trying to discern if her motives were not perhaps more personal. The moment she felt the intrusion, she shut her mind to him and sat up straight in her chair with the bearing of a medieval abbess—stern, impenetrable, untouchable.

The contest of wills over, for the moment, Jonas looked back into the fire. "Maud, the Revolution has been fought and lost, the King of the Dead has been overthrown and all his dominions put down into the earth. We live our lives. We die. We remain dead, but we *remain*. All that endures of his kingdom is an empty chair and these endless disputations over useless titles. Even in Kingsport, a town *named for him* during the interregnum when he settled on that shore, they have forgotten him. Death is dead. May he rest in peace, I say. Let this larger matter rest as well. Bring the boy, if you insist, but let it remain a family affair. We have benefited from these events, in our way. We have our work. Now let it be. Leave the old politics where they lie and be content with our lot. Neither should our own hopes or griefs trouble this young man who has already known more sorrow than is warranted, even for an Undertaker."

Maud stood staring at the flames on the hearth, lost in her thoughts.

The air around Jonas darkened and soured. "Maud!" snapped Jonas. "Did you hear me?"

"I have heard you."

Maud knew Jonas already suspected her of bringing the boy for some purpose other than the tradition of the household. But the summons had gone out, the boy was on the threshold, even now. When Amos's son entered Arvale, she knew that Jonas would try to work things in his own way, take the boy under his wing. Jonas would try to school Silas in the customary fashion, if he could. Perhaps to the good. She would need to watch carefully. While the role of Janus carried with it certain authority that might make Silas even more useful to her, she did not want to run the risk of someone else directing the boy's actions too particularly.

"I leave you to welcome him, Maud. I will make what

preparations I can and join you shortly. This is to be done properly or not at all," Jonas said, resigned. He silently turned to leave the hall, but then called out to the waiting air, saying formally, "Let the doors be opened for Silas Umber, Undertaker of Lichport!"

The Black Stone, or Limbus, remains shrouded in obscurity. Legend attests that it once sat at the mouth of a cave located on the shores of Lake Avernus and was taken from that place to Rome during the reign of Claudius. It is held that wherever it lies, below it is made a passage to the vaults and caverns of shadow, those deep cabinets of stone where the forgetful dead must await the breaking of the world.

The Limbus Stone played a brief role in the reconsecration of the Via Appia just after the second Hadean Insurrection, and was then installed within the city walls at the threshold of the Temple of Mors. During the destruction of the temple, both the Limbus Stone and the Ebony Throne, or, as it was sometimes called, the Seat of Mors, were lost. However, by the early first century the stone and the chair had resurfaced and the Hadeo-Morsian rites continued under the auspices of the Umberii, that ancient family of goetic magisters, presently known as Undertakers. Wherever they settled, the Umberii rose to prominence as summoners and banishers of the dead. Whomever in the family showed the greatest aptitude would become Janus, or Watcher at the Threshold, and conveners of the fearful Door Doom. Rarely, one of the Umberii (now, Umber) of exceptional talent might assume the Hadean throne, or Seat of Mors, but this was a dark and terrible calling and most forsook it, despite its promise of true authority over the dead.

Both the Ebony Throne and the Limbus Stone disappeared again during the Plague Times. The stone reappeared in the Western Lands, in the town of Kingsport, during the Interregnum of the King of the Dead and sometime after the The Revolution, it was listed among the hallowed relics of the Umbers of Lichport at their estate called Arvale. The Ebony Throne was never found.

—FROM THE BOOK CONCERNING THE HALLOWS OF THE HOUSE, OR, TREASURES OF THE HOUSE OF UMBER, 1912

CHAPTER 13

THRESHOLD

THE DOOR TO ARVALE STOOD OPEN.

The threshold upon which the door stood was a massive slab of black basalt, worn almost smooth from the passage of time and footfall. As Silas walked over it, he could see faint remains of engraving, still discernible upon the black stone's surface. Figures, perhaps, standing in a circle. Deep striations in the stone may have been lines of early writing. The stone extended beyond the doorway in both directions, at least six feet on each side of the door frame. Silas knelt and passed his hand over the stone. He felt a faint electric tingle spark across his palm and fingers, and then his ring grew uncomfortably warm. He realized he had to exert particular force, as though the ring and the stone opposed each other and could not be brought close together. Rising, Silas stood inside the doorway, unsure whether or not to enter. His hand now felt as though it were on fire, and he wanted nothing more than to step off the stone, but some other force held him back, something more than his apprehension. He closed his eyes and the solid ground fell away from him. He floated above a chasm of cold air and far, far below, a river hurtled madly along its course beneath a vault of rock. He was convinced that should he so much as breathe, he would tumble off the edge of the earth. Yet, a faint voice in him, stirring in his blood, whispered, *You have already fallen into the abyss. Here are the mansions of darkness and of wonders.*

Come in! Come in! We've been waiting for you. Here is where you are meant to be and where you shall remain.

From inside the house, the voice that was in his mind a moment ago now rose to his ears as he stood in the doorway. "Do not stand so long on the Limbus Stone, Silas Umber. It's not healthy. Enter this place and greet your kin!"

He lifted his foot over the threshold with difficulty, like it weighed a hundred pounds, but when he stepped into the house and his eyes adjusted to the dim light, the weight fell off him, the tightness in his shoulders lessened, and the burning in his hand vanished. For an instant, he felt the sensation of dizziness, as though he had stood up too quickly. But as he looked down, the deep blue gem of his ring flashed in his sight and his blurry thoughts quickly sharpened again.

From even his limited experience at the Undertaking, he knew that the dead often had their own agendas and while not always doing so deliberately, they could easily draw you into their world, forcing their perspective on you. Ancestral home or no, he knew he would need to be careful.

Before him stood a majestic hall. Massive beams and decorative carved bosses held the roof aloft. A long table ran almost the whole length of the chamber and at the far end stood an enormous hearth, a fire burning in its open mouth. Despite the fire, there was a chill rising through the flagstones and into Silas's feet.

There was a shadow at the end of the table and as Silas stared at it, the darkness grew more discernible. Soon he could see a tall woman in a rich wool dress with gold embroidery about the neck and hem. She wore a wimple of white cloth that flowed about her like a nimbus. Silas walked to the far end of the room where she stood. Briefly looking at the hearth, he saw words carved deep into the stone of the mantle, but before he could try to translate them, the woman spoke, her voice soft and distant, as though carried by the wind from some far-off place.

"In Vita In Morte Familia Manes."

"In Life . . . in Death—" Silas started to work out the translation.

"Family Remains," said the woman, finishing the line, her voice closer now, more distinct and present. "Silas Umber, Undertaker of Lichport, welcome to this house. Welcome home."

And behind them, at the other end of the hall, the massive doors shut again.

Silas looked back at the doors and his nerves went taut. *I am locked in, entombed. I will never leave this house.* Quickly, to calm himself, he looked back to the woman. She was still smiling, without the least hint of threat or malice. A log in the fire hissed and popped, throwing burning embers out into the room, where they died on the cold flagstones.

She looked at Silas with a raised eyebrow, waiting for him to speak. Eager to break the silence that stood between them, he asked, "Are you a relative of mine?"

"I am, Silas. My name is Maud. And I am an Umber, like you. I think I am one of your great, great, great-aunts. I don't how many 'greats' that would be, going back almost a millennium, but quite a few, I expect."

She was trying to set him at ease.

Silas was not surprised by Maud's confirmation of her age. He knew that sometimes older spirits could retain much autonomy. But they could also be more dangerous if the business of their lives remained unsettled. How many like her were at Arvale? he wondered.

"Are you my oldest relative here?" Silas looked about, and

though he saw no one else, he could begin to feel the presence of others, in the air, below the stones, behind the walls. He was being watched, and listened to.

"No. Some are much, much older than I am. But now I wonder what you might mean by 'oldest'? Many souls have occupied this place longer than I have. There are some very ancient folk, particularly toward the southern range of buildings, and in the catacombs. But it is unlikely you'll see them, or that they'd reach out to you. Such spirits almost become parts of the very air, or they blend back into the land itself after forgetting their own names. But my mind is inherent, become a part of this house, in a sense. Thus, I have remained myself and endured, remembering both who I am and, very often, who I was. I take the long view, and so have been here for many ages, just as you see me now. Others have, over the years, *changed*."

As Maud spoke, Silas could feel the weight of those closed doors, the strength of their hinges. No light escaped the door frame around them, and their solidity made him nervous, reminding him of the massive inscribed door once used by his uncle to trap the ghost of his son in the Camera Obscura. "Do you mean that you are all prisoners of this house? And now I am trapped here too?"

For the briefest instant, a shadow of intense sorrow fell across Maud's face, but then she strode away from Silas, to the front of the hall, and pulled the great doors open.

"You see?" she called back loudly "I am thoroughly autonomous. A modern woman. These doors open and close all the time."

She made a small, forced laugh as she swept her hands along the sides of her medieval attire, trying to look blasé. Silas noticed that she did not, in fact, pass over the stone to go outside. She merely stood by the open door. Was she lying? Could she leave the house at all? Silas ran up to the doors, and holding his breath, walked through them. Once outside the house, he breathed deeply before walking back inside to rejoin Maud. *So,* he thought, *it's possible to leave, at least for now. I am not like them.*

Maud Umber closed the doors again. "Anyway, as much as anyone with such a large family may be considered 'free,' I believe I am. I can come and go as I please for the most part. As can you."

Silas was sure he could sense the presence of a lie, but which part of what she said wasn't true? As they walked back across the chamber to the hearth, Silas noticed that Maud came in and out of focus, rising and dimming in his gaze. It was Silas's experience that this flashing effect, given off by some ghosts, usually meant they were troubled, torn, lacked resolution at their life's end, or longed for something they had lost or wanted terribly and never had. *What is she hiding?* Silas wondered. Though the light continued its queer wavering over her form, Maud's voice remained steady and unaffected. "Indeed, Silas, you are Janus of this house. What door could refuse you if you wished to pass?"

Silas put a hand to his chest where the pendant given to him by his father lay. "What exactly does that mean, 'Janus of this house'? What will I be expected to do?"

"Nothing more than those who came before you," said Maud, looking briefly away from him toward the fireplace. "It is no great secret, but you must allow things to unfold in the accustomed manner. This is a house built upon innumerable hierarchies. It is for others to guide you into the mysteries. We must abide by custom."

All right, Silas thought, *don't tell me.* But he suspected that because it was named for the god of the threshold, of beginnings and endings, that whatever the job entailed might be an elaboration on his work as Undertaker, and might involve the massive doors of the house and the dark stone upon which they stood.

"Then may I ask you a historical question?"

Maud nodded.

"Why isn't the title 'Undertaker' used for it as well? Why use the name of an old Roman god? Why the change?"

"The position holds more than merely the name, I assure you. It is no secret that when the Lamb rose up, when that new god came to drive out the old gods, many hid themselves within some of the ancient families, granting them certain authorities in repayment for continuing the old ways. Thus, the Umbers have played host to the Janus for many centuries. Janus was the older title. Undertaker came later. It is, shall we say, a little less exalted and a little more colloquial."

Fascinated, Silas asked, "So, was some part of the god 'passed down' from generation to generation?"

"In a manner of speaking, yes."

Maud tensed and Silas could see the question made her hesitant. She looked about the hall as if fretful about being overheard. Silas pressed on.

"Is there only one god per family?

Maud's body began to lighten and about the edges of her form, Silas could just discern the textures of the wall behind her, as if she were fraying.

"Usually."

"But might a really old, big family play host to more than one god?"

"That is hard to say," Maud said, lowering her voice to a whisper. "At times, in the history of this house and this family, it has seemed so, yes."

"Are you saying we have . . . other forces at work within our lineage? We hold the door for the dead, I know that. We help them. What else?"

"These are not questions I can answer for you at present—"

"I don't mean to be rude, but are you suggesting I was invited here *not to be told* such things?"

"Silas, those answers lie within you, not me." Maud turned her head away. She was shaking. Her form wavered and blurred upon the air. Was it nervousness or excitement? She seemed to want to say more, but was holding back.

Silas thought he might get away with maybe one more question, but it was hard to control himself. "If I am Janus, Maud, what must I do? How long was my dad Janus? Is it very much like Undertaking? Does it only happen here? Is it connected with the Door Doom that I've read about? Did I become Janus when I passed the gates into Arvale? Will I—"

"You are not Janus yet," an iron voice bellowed, reverberating against the stones of the walls. Silas, startled, stepped back at the sound.

From an archway in the dark paneled wall to the right of the hearth, a man emerged and filled up all the space in front of Silas. Appearing to be perhaps in his late sixties, the ghost was large and solidly built. He wore a long coat and had a cravat wrapped tightly about his thick throat. He spoke formally, as though this were a kind of state occasion.

"Silas, I am Jonas Umber. Be welcome in this house. It would be best if you let us answer your questions in our own way and in our own time. Learning too much at once might be . . . awkward for everyone. Know that you are Janus Presumptive, and there will be some formalities necessary before you may wield that title."

"Thank you, sir," said Silas, taking another step back, a little awed and intimidated at the sudden appearance of his formidable ancestor. He swallowed his curiosity for the moment.

As Undertaker in Lichport, he had some authority. At Arvale, he wasn't sure who was in charge or what exactly was expected of him, so he would accept waiting to see how things fell out, for the time being.

Silas recognized the name of the man in front of him. "I sort of know you. You were once Undertaker of Lichport as I am now. I've read a bunch of your writing in the town's death ledger. You are a very learned man. I'm really honored to meet you."

Jonas looked at Maud, and the stony expression he wore as he entered the hall softened slightly. "He is at least a discerning reader, that much I grant you."

Silas reached out to shake Jonas's hand. The firelight caught Silas's ring, and blue fire danced on his finger. Jonas stared at the ring intently, letting his arm fall absently to his side.

"Silas Umber, where did you get that ring?"

It sounded more like an accusation than a question. Silas looked down, embarrassed at being examined, and pulled his hand back. But not wishing to seem rude, he reluctantly held the ring up to the light so Jonas might see it better. "My great-grandfather gave me this. I believe it was my father who gave it to him."

"That was a generous gift both times. Your great-grandfather, you say? You mean Augustus Howesman? Of course, from your mother's long-lived side of the family," Jonas said with a barely hidden sneer. "Very kind of him to return it to the Umbers. I am pleased that you're wearing it. Such relics should remain in the family."

A cold light came from Jonas Umber's eyes and his brow furrowed as if in intense concentration. Then he put his hands together and looked down at his own bare fingers. "Yes. It is well that you wear the ring your father kept and his father before him." Silas could see that though he continued speaking, Jonas's thoughts were now focused elsewhere. He looked at Silas with an expression of resolve. It was clear that he had set his mind to some action or other. "It was a fine day when your great-grandfather put that ring on your finger. A fine day, indeed. Such a beautiful stone . . . he must miss it terribly. But now, as the ring's keeper, you will always remember his generosity, and his sacrifice."

Jonas's voice had drawn into a low growl and Silas regretted telling him where the ring had come from. He thrust his hand into his coat pocket.

Despite his tone, Jonas smiled broadly, then called into the open doorway from whence he'd entered. A man wearing a herald's surcoat walked quickly into the hall. Jonas leaned over to the herald and whispered something into his ear. Silas couldn't hear what Jones told him, but the man ran off, and a moment later that deep bellowing trumpet sounded again, very similar to the blast Silas had heard at the gate with his great-grandfather.

As the sound faded, Silas noticed that Jonas and Maud were conferring in low tones. Still uncomfortable after the conversation about the ring, he stepped away several paces to give himself some space and appear polite. Acting the part of a guest, he pretended to take an interest in the carvings that adorned the wood paneling on all the walls. Jonas and Maud faded, and their forms became transparent. Silas could tell they were talking, but it was like watching a movie with the sound turned off. When he said their names in his mind, however, and closed his eyes, he could hear portions of what they were saying, as if he'd already heard their conversation a long time ago and was only now remembering. The longer he listened with his eyes closed, the clearer the conversation became.

"Really, Jonas! Your haste . . . zeal . . . unwarranted . . . will regret it . . . fear . . . you harm who he loves, for . . . reason . . . turn away from us."

"Maud . . . must insist . . . let me see to things in my own way. I am trying to help him. You should know . . . and . . . if he passes through the fire, he may yet undo what the father has wrought upon . . ."

The room went quiet, and suddenly self-conscious of his eavesdropping, Silas opened his eyes to see the two ghosts staring at him, their forms filling again with detail and presence.

Perhaps realizing Silas had been trying to hear them, Maud said, "It's all right, child. We were just talking about how everyone here, each in his or her own little way"—and she gave Jonas a sharp look—"is trying to help you . . . to welcome you. Ah! But here is more of the company!"

Lines of relatives began filling the great chamber from the many open doorways that emptied into the hall. Their attire was as various as the architecture of the house. Some wore wool dresses and tunics like Maud's and bore an aged countenance, patient and upright, their faces calm and pale as those of the carved caryatids adorning each side of the fireplace and supporting the mantel. There were some who wore doublets and bell-shaped gowns of rich velvet with collars of ermine or lace, their clothes stitched with patterns of pearls and jewels that glowed and glinted against the dark fabric like stars in their constellations. Some men on the far side of the hall wore open silk jackets revealing richly embroidered waistcoats. Gold buckles glinted from their shoes, and three-cornered hats sat jauntily atop their heads. Their female companions wore dresses so wide that they had to turn slightly to pass through the doorway into the hall. Others wore fitted jackets and dresses of the last century with high starched collars on the men, and the women's dresses gathered up into large bustles, their collars buttoned up tightly against their necks. The ghosts of his relations filled the hall, and the closer Silas gazed, the more varied the clothes became: robes of rich silks, turbans set with gems and feathers. And scattered here and there throughout the hall now, standing a little apart from the others, were people wearing long robes of heavy fabric, with great hoods that, if drawn up, would swallow their heads entirely. Thick gold chains of office hung across their chests and shoulders. They never took their eyes off Silas.

"Here is your family," said Jonas with pride. "In time, you may come to know them all, though it is not likely. Some are more 'present' than others. You will understand what I mean." Slowly, the crowd began to move past Silas. Some bowed slightly, some looked him up and down, one or two turned up their noses, others seemed not to see him at all. Some reached out their hands to him, but as Silas stepped toward them, they fell away from the company, drifting back to their own particular zones of the house, Silas guessed. Most merely spoke quiet words of welcome as they approached, then swiftly vanished.

"There are so many folk filling the hallways and hidden chambers of this mighty house. They are your family, Silas. Every last one of them! This is not nearly all. You'll meet more at the feast. Even the most ancient corners and towers are full-filled with relations. Some have 'retired' and no longer attend family functions because of forgetfulness or willfulness. Others are merely bound up in their own affairs and explorations. A few find that a more predictable schedule suits them, and even helps. So we dine regularly."

Jonas looked around, moving his eyes from one end of the hall to the other, trying to find someone or something.

"What is this? When are we? What season? Where is the contingent from the summer house?" Jonas asked.

"The cousins have not yet appeared. But soon, I think," said Maud. "You remember . . . they no longer enter the house."

"Yes. Then word should be sent to them. All must know Silas is in residence and must know him on sight. I want no misunderstandings or accidents."

"What do you mean?" Silas asked, not liking the word "accidents."

"Some of the family are more territorial than others," replied Jonas, scanning the throng.

"Don't worry," said Maud, answering them both. "I shall keep a good eye on our Silas."

"All right, then." Jonas's voice became a trumpet, filling the great chamber with its call. "Let us embrace our relative, Silas Umber! Let him be welcome here! Let him find peace within this place! Let him rise nobly to his most hallowed office! May the work of the family continue!"

From all about the room, cheers and cries of welcome went up.

"Yes," Jonas continued. "Be welcome, Silas Umber. And may the Door Doom, so long abandoned, now continue in its ancient and accustomed business."

This received a mixed endorsement from the crowd. At the mention of the "Door Doom," many of the relatives began to exit the room, continuing their welcomes to Silas by waving behind them as they departed from the great hall. Jonas bowed to Maud and Silas, saying he'd return later to familiarize Silas with various family affairs and other needful matters. A moment later, Silas and Maud were alone again in the great hall.

"Maud, have I been called to here to fulfill some obligation?

To take part in this Door Doom? I think I'd like to know what is expected of me."

"Silas, as I've said, such matters will be discussed in due course. Patience. Let all things reside in their appointed season. Besides, Jonas is particularly looking forward to discussing it all with you. Let's not deny him the pleasure."

"But I didn't get the impression he was very glad to see me for some reason. Did my coming here upset him?"

"Not at all. I think he was just surprised. You are very young. That is unusual. In Jonas's time, the Undertakers would come to Arvale much later in their lives. But times change, do they not? We are all very happy you have come, I promise you."

Silas was willing to play it their way. He looked about the hall, but Maud pulled his attention back. "You are moving rapidly through the spheres, nephew. You only recently became Undertaker. How goes your work?"

"I think I am doing well. Probably it's best that I just keep pressing on. It's what might happen if I take time to stop and think that worries me."

"You are wise, I think, in that. Alive or dead, I've always preferred an active existence, a daily regimen."

They circled the room and approached the front door.

There was more to this simple conversation than the words they were exchanging. Silas could tell that she wanted things between them to be pleasant and for him to trust her, and he could sense that she had a reason for asking him about his work. She wanted something from him. He didn't like being scrutinized or set up. If she wanted something, she should just say it.

To push the focus from himself, Silas pointed to a cloth-hidden chair, prominently located near the door.

"What's this?"

"Furniture," she replied flatly, moving away, trying to draw him away with her.

Silas didn't move. "Why is it covered?"

"It is an ancient thing. You'll find this house is full of relics."

Maud's tone had grown taut. Silas could tell he'd stumbled on something interesting.

"Everything in this house is old," Silas said, "so why is this particular chair covered?"

"I would like to tell you more about it, but I think, just yet, the others wouldn't approve. Not everyone has as much faith in you as I do. Leave it be for now. You'll see it soon enough, I promise you. There is nothing in this house that can't be yours if you just show a little patience and perhaps a bit of restraint. This is not for you, at this time. Not yet."

But Silas couldn't let it go, now that his curiosity had been aroused. "Why all the secrecy about an old chair?" Maud had already begun walking toward the far end of the hall.

"Now, where has Lars gotten to?" Maud called out, changing the subject, gesturing for Silas to follow her. She drew up a little silver bell that hung from a cord about her waist and shook it. Lars, who had been waiting just beyond the archway, looked in.

"Lars, perhaps it is time to allow our guest to take his rest?"

Lars nodded.

"Yes. A little rest would be much appreciated, " Silas said to Maud very politely. But to himself he thought, *I'm not on my home turf. Family and familiarity are not the same. I am a traveler. I must abide by the local customs and let it be for now.*

Led by Lars, Silas and Maud walked to the arch before the hallway where the stairs could be seen. Cool air came through the archway, and the smell of dust and mold and wood filled his nostrils as he breathed. He wondered how long his family had occupied this house. Then a thought came to him. "Aunt Maud?" Silas tried out the title, which somehow, considering their distance in the family tree, seemed appropriate.

"Yes?" Maud smiled at the cordial, familial term.

"Do any of my more recent relatives reside in this house? Is my grandfather about somewhere?"

"He is not, Silas. He preferred a quiet afterlife, and soon took the waters and went the way of Peace. His last years were difficult, and he wished only for rest. He made the decision himself, and was under no compulsion."

Silas nodded. There was brightness upon her face as she spoke. Her words rang true. Slowly, without looking up, he asked, "Is my father among the company of this house?"

"No," said Maud, looking back at the door. "Your father is not presently within this house. As you know, in life he often insisted on his own way. He was no different in death."

Silas's heart began to race at her words. Could he find his father again, even in death? He had imagined that Amos had simply gone to his rest after a troubled and tragic life. Their last meeting in the bell tower in the Narrows had been calm and loving. There had been no mention of shadowlands or wandering. Now Silas began to feel, with a strange hopefulness, that he and his father might meet again.

"Do you mean he *was* here? Where did he go?"

"He used to come to Arvale regularly until he broke with many of our customs. He was very proud, you see. He made a perfunctory visit after his demise, but followed his own path, leaving us here to . . . our own business. I cannot say where *his* business might have taken him, only that he was, it seemed, under obligations that would not allow him to remain among us."

"When was he here, exactly?" Silas asked, his voice growing

desperate. He could see Maud was becoming uncomfortable again. The details of her face began to darken and blur. She was slowly drifting away from him.

"Silas, the nature of my existence does not lend itself to exactitude where time is concerned. I believe your father was here very recently. He did not enter the house, however. I doubt he ever shall again. He made it very clear that Arvale was *our* place, not his." Maud's voice grew bitter and she looked away from the door as if it hurt her eyes.

Lars shifted impatiently from foot to foot.

"Normally, Silas, those who come to this house must find their own way. But I've had rooms put at your disposal very close to the hall. That way, there will be less chance of getting lost. I hope you will be comfortable. Lars will take you now." She turned to Lars and added, "Please stay close to him, will you?"

Lars nodded in agreement, but did not look Maud in the eyes.

"Rooms? That sounds lovely. Thank you," Silas said. "But I wasn't planning on staying here long enough to require 'rooms.'"

Somewhere past one of the smaller doorways, a light laughter broke out among some lingering members of the family, who hadn't yet faded back into their accustomed regions.

Maud waved her hand dismissively and looked at Silas. "Silas, you may stay as long as you want. You are not a prisoner here. You are free to come and go." She glanced quickly at Lars who, for the briefest instant, looked wistful. "Lars can show you something of the house. Let me say this to you, however. Now that you are here, the traditions of the house must be met. It would be unwise to attempt departure before you have undergone the initiations into your appointed place. By coming here, you are now subject to the laws of this house and certain . . . obligations must now be met."

"Can you just tell me if—"

"It would be better for you to rest before we discuss anything further. You have come a long way, farther than you know. Let us leave any questions for another time. Settle in. Be comforted by the presence of your kin. Prepare yourself."

"For what precisely?"

"Lars!" Maud said, apparently finished with the conversation, pulling him from his wandering thoughts. "Please show Silas to his rooms." She turned back to Silas. "Dinner is at ten, by custom. Return to the hall at that time and you shall know something more of this place and its dependents. Do not be late. A moment beyond the appointed hour and I cannot be responsible for where, or in what company, you may find yourself."

IN MY FATHER'S HOUSE
ARE MANY DWELLING
PLACES:

IF IT WERE NOT SO, I
WOLDE HAVE TOLD YOU:

I GO TO PREPARE A
PLACE FOR YOU.

—JOHN, 14.2 (UNDERLINED IN RED INK ON A PAGE TORN
FROM A COPY OF THE GENEVA BIBLE, 1560)

LARS AND SILAS LEFT THE HALL and climbed a staircase bearing massive carved newel posts in the shapes of standing lions, their paws clawing at the air. When they reached the landing, a short hallway lay before them, lit with candles in bronze sconces. Lars kept saying, as though it were a hope and not a fact, "Almost there, at your rooms! Your rooms should be just ahead. Yes. We are almost to your rooms."

Did he need to repeat it for some special reason? Silas remembered the first time he went into the shadowlands. He had needed to focus his mind on where he wanted to go. Was this the same? Did the house contort and alter its topography to accommodate the travelers of its halls and corridors? If so, what kind of a shadowland was this?

And there was to be a dinner. This made Silas mildly uneasy— it meant there would be food he would be expected to eat. Otherworldly food was often taboo. But this was a complicated matter. In some cases, the injunction against eating was severe, but only because it then bound one to the otherworld in some way. But as an Undertaker, Silas was already bound to the otherworld. Indeed, his job was to traverse it. So for Silas, the rules were different. He had to judge each shadowland individually. In one that he knew of, the Peony Lantern Teahouse, eating meant forgetting, very dangerous even for an Undertaker. Yet here at

Arvale, Silas surmised, eating from the ancestral table represented obligation, respect, and perhaps in some way embodied another aspect of his initiation into the family mysteries.

Just as Silas came to the conclusion that he would eat what was offered to him, he arrived at the end of the hall. The architecture made the breath catch in his throat.

That was *his* door.

He was now, in Arvale, standing before the door to *his* house back home.

As they approached, he could even see the word "ARVALE" scratched into the wood as it had been just before he'd left.

"Here we are!" said Lars with visible relief, oblivious to Silas's mounting confusion.

Silas backed up. "What is this?" he gasped.

"Your rooms," said Lars, unsure of what was wrong.

"My rooms? This is the door to my house. In Lichport."

"Yes?" said Lars. "Yes. We are in Lichport. Well, just at the edge of it. In your family's house. And these are your rooms. Silas? Are you all right? Your face has gone positively white!"

Silas stepped up to the door again and ran his hands over the painted wood. It *was* the door to his house. Here was a patch of chipped paint; he'd picked it away one day waiting on the porch for . . . for someone he couldn't quite recall. The handle of the door was familiarly worn. It was the same door. *Where am I?* he thought with rising panic. *I am in Arvale. I am a part of this house. This is an illusion, an image. The house is showing me that we are connected, that I am a part of this place. That I belong here. Nothing more,* he told himself, trying to soothe his fraying nerves. But Silas still felt somewhere down in his gut that what he was looking at was more spider's web than welcome mat.

Lars was standing behind him, clearly worried by Silas's

abrupt change in mood. Silas composed himself and clapped Lars reassuringly on the arm.

"It's okay, cousin," Silas said to Lars. "Let's go in."

Past the door, the room before him was familiar as well, but only in portions, as though certain pieces of the rooms from his house had fallen into this one, or been laid over it. There was his father's desk, but behind was a paneled wall, much older than the wall of his house back in town. Here were bookshelves with familiar carvings, but these were nearly empty, whereas his shelves at home were spilling with volumes.

"It will feel more homely once we lay a fire," Lars said, moving to the hearth, taking dry wood from a copper bucket and arranging it on the grate. He took out a tinderbox and a moment later small flames licked at the little branches at the bottom of the pile.

Other objects in the room at first seemed new to him, but as he gazed upon them—the medieval chest and table; the large, elaborate Jacobean mantel; the tapestries on the walls— everything began to feel familiar, and a voice in his mind said, *This is your room, Silas. It has always been your room. It always shall be.*

Silas shook his head. "Show me the rest," he said to Lars, trying to focus. In the far corner, a small staircase led to an upper floor. Ascending, Lars showed Silas a bedchamber holding a massive four-poster bed and a smaller but no less elaborate fireplace. On the far side of the room, stairs that were little more than thick stone blocks protruding out of the wall led to yet another floor above.

"Tower room," said Lars. "They must like you. You'll be able to look over the whole front of the estate from here. A room with any kind of view is rare here, most are taken, but a little tower all to yourself must be accounted very fine."

Curious, Silas climbed the stairs and emerged onto the roof, which was surrounded by a low circular wall about three feet high. It was open to the air. Silas looked out over the wall, over the battlements of Arvale. Night had finally come in and he could see lights in the hundreds of windows in other parts of the house. Beyond the forest, there were even tinier glimmers, perhaps from Lichport. There were cries of birds coming from beyond the woods, from what might have been the salt marshes. It was hard to identify now what anything was beyond the estate. Silas's sense of place had been turned upside down. Even if that was Lichport away in the distance, was it *his* Lichport? Or the Lichport Lars knew? In his walk to Arvale, how far had he actually come? He gazed at the lights, willing his vision through night's obscuring veil, trying to see something, anything, familiar. He couldn't, but as he closed his strained eyes, Silas told himself it was *his* Lichport in the distance. It had to be. He needed it to be.

Lars stepped up to Silas's side.

"If I may say, I'm glad you've come to live at Arvale, Silas. There aren't really any other people my age here. I've just been sort of waiting for the right time to go home. Just seemed easier to stay on at Arvale, though it's not really a life, if you take my meaning. But now that you're here—"

"Lars, I'm not staying at Arvale. I was asked to come. It's sort of a family tradition. I won't be here long. I am obligated to this house, in some way, but when that obligation is met, I'm going home. People are waiting for me back home. My mom sometimes needs my help. It's been hard for her lately, and I don't want to leave her alone longer than I have to. I have work waiting there for me too. It's difficult to explain, but I feel like I shouldn't stay away from Lichport too long."

"Oh, I understand," said Lars, retreating. "I mean, I know that on your side of the family, there are duties that I don't understand, could never understand. I'm sorry, I didn't mean to . . ." Lars's words broke off, his face going long and Silas could see that now neither one of them was entirely at ease. Silas felt awkward. He'd only really ever had one friend. In that moment, Silas realized he wasn't very good at making living people feel comfortable. Maybe Lars hadn't noticed—maybe he was a loner too. One thing was certain: Silas needed Lars's help at Arvale and hoped there might be some way, at some point, he could help Lars in return. He looked at Lars and said, "I am really glad you're here. The others, you know they're not like us." But the half-truth tasted ashen in Silas's mouth, for how much did he and Lars truly have in common, really? They were both from Lichport, and must be close in age, but did they share anything more than that? Anything at all?

"I know," Lars replied, looking away at the tiny lights in the distance. "The folk in this house are strange, but I try not to think about it. Everyone is queer in their way, aren't they? It's easier being here if you just go from one moment to the next and don't ask too many questions. It's hard to remember things sometimes too. Hard to remember how long you've been standing somewhere, or how long you've been talking to someone. Hard to know where in the house you are at any one time, though I've gotten better at that." Lars paused and looked down at the earth far below them. "I've stayed only because it never seems just the right moment to go back and, I guess, because the forgetting has become a comfort to me. There are some matters I'd rather not think about."

"I understand. I've felt like that too. Lots of times. Not being able to feel one day slip into the next. Have you never tried to go home?"

"Yes, but I got lost. Took a wrong turn, I guess, and after a long night in the woods, I found myself back at Arvale. I don't suppose I really wanted to go back to Lichport anyway."

Lars looked up, and he seemed embarrassed.

"Lars, it's okay. Really. You can tell me anything you like," Silas said. Then he had an idea. "You know you could come back with me, right? It's not easy going back to where you started. Believe me, Lars, I know. But we could go back to Lichport together and maybe if we help each other, we could both find what we're looking for."

Almost as soon as the words left Silas's mouth, he regretted them. What would he be taking Lars back to? Lars's state of existence remained a point of confusion, but Silas guessed a few things: Lars was not a ghost of the house. He was like him, a living person. This also seemed to imply that the world Lars had once known had long since passed away while Lars lingered, outside of time, at Arvale. Still, maybe there was some way to help him go back home, even if it could never be the Lichport Lars had left.

"Silas, I couldn't go back."

"Everyone has problems at home, Lars. They get better only when you face them."

"It's not just that. Things happened back in Lichport, Silas. Things I don't like remembering, things I can't fix. I'm a coward. I fled and didn't look back, and I know that because of me, *terrible things* happened."

Silas looked at Lars. He was shaking, and had brought his arm up to hide his face.

"It's okay, Lars. Come back with me. I'll help you all I can."

"I can't, Silas," said Lars. He wiped his face and looked up, sniffing. "I can't go back and I can't tell you what happened."

Silas put his arms around Lars's shoulder. "That's fine. But if you change your mind about talking about it, my offer stands. I want to help."

After they returned to the bedchamber below, Lars said he'd come back later to get Silas for dinner, and that he should rest, since it had been such a long walk to Arvale, and that the evening's revels would certainly go very late. Lars descended the stairs and Silas could hear the door close.

Weary, Silas lay upon the bed. As soon as he closed his eyes, a dream caught him all up in its strange, strong arms and held him down. He was sitting at the desk back in his study in Lichport. On the other side of the window, rain threw itself against the glass. On the desk in front of him stood a brimming goblet of greenish water. Mrs. Bowe was standing next to him.

"Let me help you," she said slowly.

"No!" Silas insisted. "I don't need your help."

"Don't be so proud, child! If you're thirsty, Silas, drink!" With that, Mrs. Bowe pushed the goblet over on the desk. Water poured from its mouth, gushing forth out of all proportion like a river through a burst dam. The weedy water quickly covered the floor, and when he looked up, Mrs. Bowe was gone and the door to the study was closed and locked, and the water was rising. A familiar shadow arrayed itself on the floor and stood up from the now swirling waters, growing lithe. Who was it? Silas could almost recall. The room was becoming a whirlpool as Silas leapt on top of the desk. The shadow drew substance from the churning foam and water-weeds and though it had no mouth, it hissed enticingly in a girl's voice. "Speak my name, Silas! Silas, speak my name!" Silas knew there had been a name and that he'd once known it, once breathed its syllables like the very air. But the more he grasped for it in his throat, trying desperately to pull the name up into his mind, the further down it fell inside him, lost again in the lightless dungeon of his fear-twisted guts. All the while, the waters rose, and beneath where the shadow stood, a black, swirling hole pierced the water's surface and drew everything down into its depths. Then, even as the desk was pulled toward the eye of the whirlpool, a bell rang out, and the waters grew quiet and the shadow sank away. There was only the bell, and in its sound, a name clanged and rang; his own name, but no other. He followed it away from the water.

CHAPTER 15

AT TABLE

THE SOUL BELL IN LICHPORT WAS RINGING.

Silas turned his face toward the sound, eyes still closed.

Then a knocking began, somewhere below the carved bed on which he lay, below the floor, in a lower room. Silas opened his eyes. He sat up and heard someone close the door and then come up the stairs to the bedchamber. A feeling of helplessness lingered from his dream, but he was used to that sensation and he fought against it, breathing deeply as he stood up, regaining his center, his inner calm. With every breath, he felt better, more himself, but as he looked around at the queer semi-familiarity of the room, Silas remembered where he was, and his stomach dropped back into a state of queasy, nervous expectation. He needed to eat.

"Time for dinner, cousin Silas." Lars smiled as he got Silas's coat from the chair and held it up for him.

Silas put the coat on over his jacket and pulled his fingers through sleep-tousled hair.

"This will have to do. I'm ready, cousin Lars," said Silas, trying hard to put a good face on his apprehension about what might await him downstairs.

They descended the stairs and made ready to leave, but just before Silas opened the door, he paused, unsure of what was on the other side. He wondered for a moment if he would open the door and look out and onto the Main Street of Lichport. Lars pushed past Silas, opening the door for him. Silas looked out. The dimly lit corridors of Arvale awaited. *Still here,* thought Silas. *Not a dream. Not home.*

Silas followed Lars down the long corridor, the bell ringing all the while. The route they took looked different to Silas from the one they had taken before. Different paneling. Different portraits on the walls, different passages. This was a much longer walk. "Taking the scenic route?" he said to Lars.

"Not at all. This is the most direct path to the great hall."

"But this is certainly not the way we came earlier. . . ."

"True. But it is later now, and that path is no longer available to us."

Silas was also wondering why they weren't seeing anyone else on their long walk to the great hall. Weren't others coming to dinner?

"Where is everyone? I thought the way to dinner would be crowded with so much of the family dining at once?"

"You'll see them in the great hall. That is a place of assembly. If you want to meet others, you'll have to seek them out in their own manses, or rooms."

"But never just around the house?"

"The halls and corridors are filled with voices and shadows, so who can say? But you and I, we're different, aren't we? No one here is interested in me. If you were walking alone, you might have a very different experience."

"No, thank you," said Silas. "I am more than happy with your company! Indeed, though we've known each other only a short time, I'm sure I'd be lost without you, Lars!"

"Truly, you would be lost."

"However did you get used to this place?"

"I told you. I just keep going. I don't stop to ask questions.

Not that anyone would answer my questions anyway. I was hoping *you* might tell *me* a little more about this house."

"Lars, I just got here. . . ."

"But this is your sort of place, isn't it? I mean, as Undertaker."

So he knows something of this business, then, Silas thought. *Why wouldn't he? People in Lichport have always known what an Undertaker was.*

"You don't find it all just too strange, then?" Silas asked, testing him.

"I was born in Lichport, Silas. Very little seems strange to me. What surprises me is your surprise, and you an Undertaker and all!" Lars clapped Silas on the back. "Come along, we're almost there!"

As they approached the great hall, Silas could hear the noise of a gathered company. Loud exclamations, snatches of song, the orchestra of sounds made by plate and glass and silverware. The light coming from the entrance to the great hall was exceedingly bright, and as he approached, Silas covered his eyes to shield them from the glare. Lars took Silas by the other arm and led him through the archway.

The great hall was lit by a thousand golden candles. Silas squinted and looked around, trying to take in the details as they emerged out of the glow. What he saw was more dream than dinner party, more phantasmagoria than family reunion. The harder he looked, the more he recalled the vision his great-grandfather had had when they were searching for his father: the high resplendent hall, the rich tapestries . . . the gathered familial throng. On and on their numbers went. It may have been a trick of the candlelight, but the hall seemed longer than when he first arrived, the front door, nearly a mile away to Silas's distorted vision. All the particulars began to blend into a riot of sensation and color and texture suffused with an inexplicable and intoxicating joy, for in this hall he was no longer one person in isolation, but a part of a continuum, a family, a real family, so very much bigger than himself. The mighty presence of kin made him feel there was only clan, only tribe, only the long line of names stringing back to the first lighting of the world.

The glow of the fire playing off the crystal drinking glasses, shining off the silver settings, glinting off the jewels of the family's rich attire, swirled before his eyes and colored the air of the hall with a prism, as though the entire scene was being viewed through an ancient, iridescent shard of Roman glass.

Maud rose from her chair and walked over, welcoming Silas and Lars into the hall. She showed Silas to a chair on the dais that stood before the fire at the high end of the table. He was to sit between Maud and Jonas. All the other seats were taken. Indeed, some members of the family sat upon the floors and stood about the hall, eating from trenchers they held in their laps and hands.

When Silas saw there was no seat for Lars, he said, a little dreamily, "Aunt Maud, I would like to sit with my cousin Lars, if it's not too much trouble?"

Maud looked as though she was about to complain, but then said, "Silas, you are the guest of honor, so tonight, let it be as you wish." She raised her hand and one of the grooms left the hall and returned at a trot with a chair that he placed between Silas and Jonas. As Silas and Lars sat down, Lars whispered, "You shouldn't have done that. They won't like it."

Silas whispered back, "In large rooms, it's best to keep your friends close. Besides, I'm going to need you to tell me what half this stuff is on the table."

Lars put his hand on Silas's shoulder and said, smiling, "Cousin, it will be a pleasure."

"What's this?" Silas asked more loudly than he'd intended,

pointing at two bowls that had been placed in front of him as soon as he sat down.

Before Lars could answer, Jonas leaned over toward Silas and said, "Spelt and salt, as is fitting."

"Am I supposed to eat that?" questioned Silas.

"Be easy. It is *for you*, but not for you *to eat*. The grain and salt are offerings. This is customary."

"Offerings to *me*?"

"Offerings to the Janus. But very shortly, it will all be one and the same."

More and more food was being brought in, and everywhere, people were piling it onto plates and into bowls. As Lars whispered into Silas's ears the names of foods and drinks and delicacies of every sort, Silas's feeling of inebriation grew, even before his third cup of spiced wine had been emptied. He wondered briefly about the safety of tasting the food at Arvale, the food of the dead, but Lars was eating with gusto, and the very air grew wonderfully heavy with music and familiarity, and all his questions swiftly dissolved. His blood mellowed and slowed, perhaps from the proximity of so many kin, so much consanguinity, as though the house was the one heart beating for all. And the wine was good and the air was warm and filled with voices and all of them spoke his name. It was hard to see where any one voice came from. All mouths were moving at once. Everyone was drinking, singing, and exclaiming, and the bright candlelight played on Silas's vision, making the forms of some folks appear almost transparent. He could see bodies through bodies, every person framed within the form of another.

The table nearly buckled under the weight of laden gold and silver plates. More and more food was brought from outer chambers and the ornate sideboards that stood against the walls.

Everywhere Silas looked there was wonder and distraction, and delicacies of every sort. . . .

A mansion of baked dough, housing live birds with gilt feet. They chirped wildly and then took to the air as the revelers' hungry hands tore chunks from the pastry roof, allowing the birds to escape.

A course of quartered stag, two days in salt, served beside civet hare, stuffed chicken, and a loin of veal.

Pies of every size and shape, all silvered around their edges and gilded at their tops. Some colored with saffron and flavored with cloves.

Platters of cheese in elaborately shaped slices: crowns, skulls, and a pride of curd lions.

On pedestals running the length of the table were perched the gelatin forms of birds, eagles, ravens, swans, and peacocks adorned with their tail feathers. In the midst of the table on the dais was a wine-red gelatin head with two faces that jiggled so that the portraits rippled and their expressions seemed to shift from terror to joy to ambivalence as the molded mouths settled.

"Silas! Look! It's you! In the jelly!" whispered Lars, discreetly but deeply in his cups.

Though his cousin protested, Silas refilled Lars's cup and smiled, but was unsure of the likeness in the gelatin. He tried to stand to examine it more closely, but his own head felt heavy and he fell back into his chair.

Maud stood up, holding her glass high. "Welcome! Welcome, Silas Umber, to the family seat! Be forever welcome here. May the doors of Arvale always be open to you!"

Voices throughout the great hall flew up the cry. "To Silas! To Silas, Janus of the house!"

Jonas stood, and lifting a full glass, shouted, *"Ecce! Nos etiam hic stamus!"*

The crowd cheered at those words. Silas lifted his glass and repeated them, not knowing what he was saying. The family, in one voice, began to chant their ancient motto, each time getting louder and louder until the beams of the hall shook in agreement:

"Ecce! Nos etiam hic stamus!"

"Ecce! Nos etiam hic stamus!"

"Ecce! Nos etiam hic stamus!"

The loud chanting only made Silas's eyes feel heavier and the words of the motto became a charm, lulling him, drawing him down further and further away from himself, out into the mind of the throng.

"Ecce! Nos etiam hic stamus!"

"Behold!" said Maud, translating for Silas. "We are still here!"

And the company continued their revels far into the night. Silas no longer knew the hour, and he didn't care. He was with his kin, and for the moment, most everything else had been driven from his mind. Lars had fallen asleep leaning on Silas's shoulder. And as Silas lolled in his chair, the music continued, drifting down from some gallery high above. The music fell all about them, roaming from the hall out into the corridors and down, down through the unlit lower passages, down into the earth. The golden revel-notes tumbled into the blackest, most forgotten corners of the ancient crypts and catacombs, reminding those incarcerated souls that joy yet remained in some far-removed portion of the world, but not in theirs.

Far below the ground, in the lowest chamber of the sunken mansion, something heard the music and the sounds of the gathered company and began to scream until the stones of its prison shook with a mighty din. But those terrible lamentations did not travel far through the thick, deep clay and so troubled the revelers not at all.

CHAPTER 16

KEYS TO THE KINGDOM

"SILAS? CHILD OF EARTH? IT'S TIME."

When Silas looked up, all the family in the great hall were staring, arrayed in concentric circles around him. Each person held a single candle. Jonas stood next to him, wearing a long gray robe. Three other robed figures stood next to Jonas, their faces concealed, each holding a sword.

Silas stared at the weapons, their long, well-used blades honed to wicked-looking edges.

Jonas's voice rose to a shout as he addressed the members of the family.

"We gather this night to initiate one who wishes to serve as Lord of January and Guardian of the Threshold. Here is one who calls himself worthy—"

Silas began to protest, shaking his head, trying to clear it. "I didn't say anything about being worthy!"

"Silence! Silence!" Maud whispered harshly in his ear. "It has begun!"

Maud's voice pulled tight with desperation. Whatever was about to happen, she didn't want anything stopping it.

But then Maud put her hand on his shoulder and said more softly, "This is what you have come here for, like all the Undertakers before you. It was for this that you were born. Do not let fear be your stumbling block. Take your place upon the Limbus Stone and rouse yourself to the obligation of your blood. Come!"

The great doors were opened and a thin, rising mist snaked about the surface of the dark stone on the threshold.

Without waiting for a signal, the family throng pushed in, moving closer and closer to where Silas stood with Maud by the open doors. Silas did not like being forced to do anything, but as the family edged toward him, he backed up until he realized he'd been moved onto the threshold. Looking down, he saw he was standing on the dark stone. His skin and nerves prickled with apprehension, and again, his hand began to warm uncomfortably. He waited, afraid to move. It was all happening a little too fast, and he didn't know enough about what was expected of him. This was an unpleasant contrast to how he felt at home where he was already respected as the Undertaker. But this ceremony was part of what an Undertaker was supposed to do. This was his next step. Silas stood as straight as possible, wanting to appear ready for whatever was to happen next.

Maud looked hard at Jonas who Silas could see was not entirely pleased with these proceedings. Maybe he didn't think Silas should be Janus. Maybe he wanted to wait. Why? Did he think Silas was too young? Silas knew Jonas did not respect his father. Could it be that Jonas was worried that Silas and Amos were too much alike? Whatever the case, it was clear Maud was the one driving things on. *Why does she want me to be Janus so badly? What is all this to her? The family has had many Januses before me and has been without one for a long time. By her own admission, I am too young. So why does she want me to be Janus now? What does she gain by my going forward?*

Perhaps because he took Silas's distraction and silence for assent, Jonas closed his eyes for an instant, his form growing very sharp and distinct, brighter. Then, resolutely, he spoke the required words. "Here is one who calls himself worthy of this hallowed office. One who shall govern the Door Doom with a will of iron and without prejudice, one who will settle accounts and make worthy judgments, one who will walk the Path of Virgil without fear." Jonas stared at Silas, waiting for a reply.

Silas wasn't sure what to say.

"Silas, you are about to be judged upon the Stone. Are you prepared for the initiation that shall mean life or death? Knowledge or oblivion? Are you willing to abide by whatever may befall you?"

Silas trembled at those words. Now was his chance to back out.

"What do you mean, 'whatever may befall me'? I do not abide!"

"The question has been asked. Silas, now is the time for you to answer in the affirmative," said Maud.

"Wait a minute! You cannot command or compel me to do anything against my will. I get to choose. I am the Undertaker." He sounded desperate, pathetic.

Jonas hesitated, but then, perhaps trying to help him, said with a voice full of both surety and regret, "Yes. You could leave now, leave this house and abandon the obligations of your name." He added, "There would be a cost for such action, but then, in time, you might return."

But Maud was having none of it. She looked Silas in the eyes. "Leave, and you may never return, even in death! You would be an outsider, in all worlds. If you remain, you must accede to custom. 'Silas' does not exist. It is the will of the family that matters now." Maud pushed forward toward the door, stopping just before the threshold, adding, "Your father, if he were here, would expect you to honor your obligations. Even he knew what it was to be, before any other thing, an Umber."

That was the wrong thing to say. Silas's face burned with anger and he turned to face Maud. "What do you know of my father? My dad turned his back on this place and its 'ancient rites,' didn't he?" Below him, the stone seemed to vibrate at his words.

The room was silent. Jonas almost looked relieved at the possibility that Silas might step off the stone and leave the house; he was nodding slowly, as if he might be encouraging Silas to stop the rite. Yet, Silas wanted to know what it was to be Janus, what authority he might yet wield.

"Maud, won't you answer me? No? I am here. I will see this through. Please *don't* push me. And I ask you not to invoke my father's name, particularly when we both know he abandoned many of your so-called 'family obligations.'" Silas touched the pendant under his shirt and said, "I know my father meant for me to be here, but this is starting to feel desperate."

Silas began to step off the stone.

Maud muttered something under her breath, and suddenly the Limbus Stone was covered in swirling smoke that rose up around Silas like binding vines. Maud said sternly, "Do not move! Silas Umber, you have crossed the threshold and entered this house of your own free will. The rites of Janus have begun, and there are only two roads open to you now. There can be no turning back. I understand you are scared. Life and death are both framed in fear. Look beyond your uncertainty! Be strong! You may only step off that stone if you are the Janus of this house. If you refuse or are deemed unworthy, you shall be *sent down*, exiled from the mansions of your family."

Silas looked at the stone under his feet. The warm vapor was crawling up his body and his hands began to shake. He feared whatever might be down there, below the stone. Some kind of Tartarus? A prison? An endless chasm worse than any shadowland? He did not move. Maud's warning worked on him like a spell and seemed somehow fateful and true. She had invoked something with those words, and he could only continue. Silas now knew that he must finish what he'd started. His heart was about to burst as apprehension sent the blood flooding through his veins. It was fear, not pride, that made him want to run, and he knew it now. Whatever Maud or Jonas wanted, whatever he wanted himself, he would not bend to fear. Not again. His father, with his own hand, had once put a pendant around his neck bearing the image of Janus. It must mean his dad had expected this moment to come. He was following a path set out for him from the beginning. This was what needed to happen next and what his father wanted. And, he wondered again, trying to look beyond the rite, if he became Janus, what kind of power might he wield then?

Silas raised his head, looking at Maud and Jonas without expression. From somewhere along the battlements, the ancient horns cried out. The three robed figures stepped forward to wait just inside the doorway. They raised their swords toward Silas's throat, making it impossible for him to move. Looking at the swords, he held up his head, unwilling to bend to the fear. This was where he had to be.

"I will abide by the will of family," Silas said. As he closed his eyes, he saw Maud was smiling.

"Then speak the words," instructed Jonas in a voice tinged with regret.

I don't know the damn words! Silas thought. *I'm just here. I've shown up! Isn't that ever enough?*

Perhaps sensing the pause, Jonas said, "It is enough to state your desire to become Janus. Just say what you are about to do, and that shall suffice."

Very slowly, Silas said, "I have answered the summons. I wish to be Janus. I wish to stand at the threshold. I will sit in the seat of judgment." His mind was swirling like the mist on top on the stone below him and he added again, "I will abide by the will of my family." He knew that in the next instant, those three swords would stab through his body, or sever his head from his neck. But instead of the sound of metal passing through warm flesh, he heard only Jonas's voice briefly again.

"Very well," said Jonas, turning away from the door. "Hearken now to the song of the abyss. . . ."

And those words rose and then dissolved in Silas's ears as he knelt, then lay down upon the Limbus Stone, succumbing to the intoxication of that strange Plutonian ether that swirled to cover his face and flowed into his nostrils.

He could hear nothing but the deep sound of a bellows, as though the earth itself was breathing with titanic lungs.

Silas opened his eyes. He was standing again, perched just before a pit of air and fire. Each way he turned, the vision of the abyss remained before him. Even when he looked up, he was looking down. Maud and Jonas had vanished and he could no longer see the hall of Arvale. No way forward. No way back. Thick ropes of vapor rose from about the edges of that earth-door and wound about his face, piercing his mouth and nose. The fumes were acrid and burned his throat, making him choke and gasp and draw them deeper into his lungs. Silas breathed in, accepting whatever might come. The Limbus Stone had become transparent, an insubstantial veil hanging over the chasm beneath him. *There can be no looking back,* he told himself. Then, without another thought, he stepped forward and could feel himself falling. Down and ever down, Silas fell through the earth, plummeting, piercing flames and shadows.

He closed his eyes again and the scene changed; Silas saw himself walking through a barren country. . . .

◆ ◆ ◆

The ground of the valley was covered in bones, brittle and blasted by the elements. Skulls and long bones, spines, and the tiny bones of the foot and hand, all lay indolent under a dark sky, covering the earth like dry branches on a forest floor.

"Here is life," the youth called out to the bones, and the earth rattled eagerly. The youth raised up his hands. On his right palm was burned the image of a key. On his left, the image of a skull.

A voice spoke. "You are Janus. You watch the door. You help the dead pass to where they must go and no more." The voice rose into a bellow. "Who are you to rouse the dead? Depart this place and leave the dead in peace."

The youth closed his right hand, hiding the key.

"I am Mors," said the youth. "I am Death."

"You are Janus—" the voice began again in the same tone, like a recording.

"I am this and that also," said the youth matter-of-factly. "I am Lord of the Bones. These are my subjects."

"You do not need to do this," said the voice, almost pleading. "The dead shall not complain."

"I am Mors," said the young man again, simply, absolutely. It was a confirmation. "That was the bargain. And I shall abide by my birthright."

"You can turn back. You are Janus of the House of Arvale. You will sit in judgment over the dead. Be content."

"It is not sufficient to judge the dead. I will do what else I can for them."

"Life is not always a gift. Leave the dead in peace."

"Peace is what I shall bring to them."

"Thus spoke every King of the Dead since the making of the world," said the voice with an almost familiar sorrow. "So be it. You shall be Life

137

in Death. Restoration may flow from your hand and you shall judge who shall live and who shall die in the Valley of the Shadows. As you claim it, one day, this land shall be yours."

The youth looked out over the field of bones, feeling the losses of the dead hanging in the air like thick smoke. Then he began to speak, low words and phrases framed in dust and decay, but quickly rising in pitch, growing lighter like the coming of dawn upon the land. The words burned his mouth, and as he spoke them the earth warmed and shuddered. The bones turned where they lay upon the ground and drew together. Tendons slid around them, joining bone to bone. Strands of flesh wove and skin grew like mold over all, and where once a field of scattered bones was seen, now a vista of fallen corpses lay. They did not move. They could not.

Without hesitation, the youth looked to the cardinal directions and said, "Four winds come and fill these forms with breath that they might live." And the corpses gasped and filled with air, breathed, and stood up, a mighty company arrayed from one side of the valley to the other.

The youth looked out upon what he had done, and saw before him an army, risen up from their skeletons, and knew at once that it was Death who ruled the world and no other thing.

The youth turned from the once-dead multitude and looked behind him. Away, beyond the mouth of the valley, crying was heard: the sound of a father weeping for his son, though whether he wept because his child was lost or found, dead or alive, the youth could not discern.

Silas could feel something cold against his cheek. His face was pressed against the Limbus Stone.

A little distance away from him, a voice said, "Who stands here, at the threshold?"

But he knew he wasn't standing. He was lying down. He must

have fallen. Where was he? He couldn't think. His mind had been poured full of mist. He wanted to wave it away, for a wind to blow through his brain and disperse the heavy fog.

The voice spoke again. "Who is here? What has come? Speak your name."

He heard himself whisper the word "Mors" through clenched teeth.

"What? What did he say? What did Silas say?" The voice sounded frightened now.

Yes. I am Silas Umber, Silas thought to himself. *I am the Janus of Arvale.* But in the very furthest corner of his mind, another part of him said quietly, gently, coldly, *You are that, and more besides. You have claimed your birthright. There is no turning back.*

Silas opened his eyes fully and tried to sit up. Pale forms wavered on the air before him, condensing into familiarity. Jonas Umber wore a mask of absolute fright and said, "Say your name again!"

"I am Silas Umber. I am the Janus of this house." Silas was not sure how he could be so certain of it, but in every fiber of his being, he knew those words to be true. He looked at the palms of his hands. Nothing stood out. Now, whatever he was, it was inside him, woven right through the very core of his being.

"That is well," Jonas said, sounding unconvinced. "Be welcome, now and always, in this house, *Silas Umber*, Janus."

From the ghosts in attendance, still filling the corners of the long hall, a cry went up, a cheer that rang for a brief moment until the room went quiet again. They were waiting for something. It wasn't over.

Slowly, Silas stood up. His legs were weak. He looked down at the Limbus Stone nervously, afraid of what he might see. Now it was solid beneath his feet. He thought about the abyss he'd seen in his vision, and as he did so, the stone began to vibrate and *thin*, as though the fabric of its atoms was becoming threadbare.

"Stop," said Jonas. "You must regulate your thoughts. The stone is yours to command. It is a doorway itself and will now open and close at your will."

Silas deliberately imagined a door slamming shut, and in response, the Limbus Stone waxed solid again. Silas stepped off the stone, back into the hall.

Slowly, as though she no longer recognized him, Maud walked toward him with trepidation. "Welcome, Silas Umber, Janus of the Threshold. Your family thanks you. . . ." It looked like she wanted to say more, but she stayed several paces back from him and grew quiet. *What does she think I'll do?* Silas wondered.

"So is that it? It's all done, then? I am now Janus?" Silas asked hopefully.

"For the most part, yes," answered Jonas.

"For the most part?"

"Just one small thing remains," said Jonas, a look of mild concern settling on his brow. "A necessary formality."

Emboldened by the first part of his initiation, Silas said, "Bring it on." As he spoke, the tone of the assembled crowd began to turn. A single word had begun working its way through the multitude, one word, rising to the rafters, shouted over and over as the family devolved into a mob.

"Drink! Drink! Drink!" they chanted, and the beams of the roof and the stones of the floor began to shake in time with their shouts.

"You must descend and drink. You must claim remembrance," said Jonas, who was frowning again. "When you drink from the waters of Eunoe, the Spring of Memory, it will be done. You shall be the Janus of the Threshold, and then we shall see what comes of it. This is no idle task. All the Undertakers in the family have walked upon this path and made their way to the springs, *every one*. Though not every one has returned."

"Is this where the water comes from that brings forgetting to the dead?"

"Yes. Though there are other places in the world where that spring appears as well. Arvale is not its source, just one of many places where it bubbles up through the earth. This is also a place where the Spring of Memory flows and it is from *those* waters that you must drink. Although he eventually turned from his responsibilities, your father tread the path below, and it was on that journey that he drank from one spring, and then filled his flask from the other with which he dispensed forgetting to the dead."

Silas still carried that flask of his father's. It was in his satchel, less than half-full. As Undertaker, he felt it was his responsibility to carry it with him almost everywhere, in case it might be needed to bring the Peace. Now he would be able to refill it.

"Are you ready, Silas?" Jonas asked.

"I believe so," Silas replied.

Jonas leaned in very close to Silas's face, and quickly whispered, "Do not stray from the path."

The cry from the crowds lifted up again, this time chanting "Down! Down! Down!", their words becoming almost a howl. The hollering was getting on his nerves.

"Okay!" he shouted. "Enough! I'm going!"

Jonas and Maud walked Silas to the side of the Great Hall. As Silas turned away from the now hushed mob, he noticed that in the high windows, stars were alight. It was still night and it was starting to feel like morning might never come. At the wall, Jonas drew aside a tapestry to reveal a doorway, old and arched. Maud pulled back the bolt and opened the heavy wooden door. A cold, moldy breeze rushed up into the hall. Beyond the door there were steps, well worn and steep, that swiftly descended into darkness. Not even the light of a candle shone from below.

Above the door, carved deep into the keystone, were the words: DIS MANIBUS SACRUM.

Jonas slowly swept his hand toward the opening in the wall with a hesitant gesture of welcome. "Silas Umber, the catacombs await you. Descend."

Silas took one step down, then two more. He turned to look back up toward the lighted hall, to ask for a lantern, but before he could speak a single word, the door slammed shut. He heard the bolt slide back into the thick stone of the wall, locking it behind him.

From The Book of Cerements

BUT THAT PLACE WHICH BRINGS MOST
WEALTH UNTO THE PLACE, ARE NOT
THE WATERS FROM WITHOUT, BUT
THOSE WATERS WHICH ARE WITHIN.

—TRANSCRIBED BY AMOS UMBER FROM *ENGLISH
HISTORY*, 1671

HE THAT BUILDS A FAIR HOUSE, UPON
AN ILL SEAT, COMMITTETH HIMSELF TO
PRISON.

—TRANSCRIBED BY AMOS UMBER FROM "OF BUILDING"
BY FRANCIS BACON

CHAPTER 17

UNDER THE EARTH I GO

SILAS SAT ON THE THIRD STEP in the chill darkness. He wondered if his father had sat here once, and the thought briefly warmed him. A "necessary formality," Jonas had called this part. If this was where the Undertakers went to refill their supplies of the water of forgetting, then this was merely the first of many visits he might be making to the catacombs. That thought calmed him. A candle would have calmed him more. He wanted to ask for one, but he refused, out of pride, to knock on the door for help. Mostly, he didn't want to fall.

He stood up slowly, unable to see any detail of the stairs, roof, or walls of the steeply descending passage. The air was so still, so close, it sounded like he was breathing into his own ears. He reached up and could just feel the rough stone a little above his head. He took another few steps down, each time letting his foot dangle for a moment before he pointed his toe, letting it slowly find the next step. Holding out his hands to the walls, he continued, trusting he would find each step, or that he would eventually come to solid floor. He pushed from his mind all fears that the stairs might simply lead him to the edge of another abyss.

As he descended, he felt things brush his face in the darkness: spiderwebs, or he imagined fingers of the dead formed from the soft condensing air. The air thickened and soured the farther he went.

After what might have been an hour, or a day, Silas sat down on the steps again, frustrated, unsure how deep into the earth he had already descended. He could feel the weight of soil and rock above and about him. His breath slowed on the still air. He could sense the land and the house pushing down on him. He was suffocating, and knew that if he didn't drown his rising panic in distracting thought, he would run back the way he'd come.

He slowed his breath and tried to remember something about light: strange lights appearing in unexpected places. He'd seen them before. Ghosts could give off such illumination. So could places where the dead gathered. As Undertaker, when helping the dead, often he would see little lights. He remembered how he had called out toward the sea for some spirit to help the ghost of the lighthouse keeper, to help guide the way of that lost soul. He had spoken the words, out over the sea until little candles had risen up—conjured, called—in answer to his heartfelt request. He had assumed those preternatural lanterns were kin, the long lost wife and child of the lighthouse keeper, family helping their own, shining through the darkness for the spirit who could not make a way for himself. Wasn't this house filled with family from its heights to its depths? Why couldn't an Undertaker reach out to his own family and ask for help?

Silas stood in the darkness. He tried to let the words just come, like a prayer, a poem, his next breath. *Just a few good, true words,* he thought. He closed his eyes tightly and rubbed them, like he used to do at bedtime as a child. Immediately, little sprays of color jumped up behind his eyelids. *Yes,* he thought at seeing the colorful phosphenes, *the light is always here, we just forget to see it.* In the ledger there had been pages of instructions to help the Undertaker better traverse the dark roads of the shadowlands. No one text stood out in his memory, but some of the words were there, and Silas began to speak them out loud.

"I consign myself to earth. May ancestral light be about me as I descend. Let the deep places make a way for me. May I go forth in the light of my kin."

And before him and behind him, tiny blue particles wavered, barely bright enough to see the walls on either side.

"May I make my way with the light of my ancestors to guide me," Silas added, his voice rising in excitement, cutting through the heavy air. "May the darkness of the world fall away from me!"

Small orbs of light leapt up, becoming candles of blue fire bobbing in the air before him, brightening his way. He stood there in delighted amazement, watching the flames. He could clearly see the dressed stone of the walls and the worn steps below his feet. He pressed on.

The stairs led him to a large chamber with a floor made of rough stone slabs that slanted even deeper into the earth. The chamber—or perhaps it was a vast tunnel—had smaller passages heading off on each side. Coffins and funeral urns filled niches on all the walls. The deeper into the earth he walked, the older the sculptures became, as if his descent was taking him the through the strata of history. He passed carved tombs, medieval sepulchres, Etruscan sarcophagi, and paintings of animals and spirits made on the undressed stones of the walls with charcoal and pigment sprayed from the mouth and shaped by the curves and angles of ancient hands, like those he'd seen in books about the thirty-thousand year old ancient caves discovered in the cliffs of southwestern France.

Silas paused to peer into a side passage, and saw vaulted chambers. Huge blocks of stone formed the walls, seemingly the work of titans. Massive figures like Atlas, carved of basalt and black quartz, stooped and hunched with the weight of the roof slabs pressing down on them. Here were the very buttresses and foundations of all the earth above. Farther down those passages, high-carved arches were set with tiny white jewels that might have been skulls. Silas remembered the hollow sound of the floor under his Uncle's library and wondered if the house on Temple Street had been built above some lost quarter of this sprawling underground necropolis.

One passage caught his eye. It was fashioned entirely of black marble, with rows of fluted columns running along its length. The opening was covered in cobwebs, and some stones had been stacked at the entrance as if, at some point, the passage had been sealed off. Silas moved a little closer, and with each step he took toward the entrance, the colder he felt. *This is a bad way,* he thought. He pushed the cobwebs aside and looked beyond the broken wall. In the blue light in the distance, he could see a greening metal door. Bands of iron had been riveted it, and molten lead had been poured about its edges. Across the door's surface were scrawled the letters DM. And beyond the impassable door, Silas was sure now, someone was crying. As soft as it was, the sound startled him, and he pulled his head back.

"Hello?"

The crying grew softer.

"Is someone there?"

The crying stopped.

Ignoring Jonas's warning about staying on the path, Silas pulled loose stones from the top of the pile to widen the opening and then crawled into the passage. Slowly he walked up to the sealed door. Its surface was rimed in verdigris, and at its edges, tiny crystals had formed, making the door look like it had risen up out of the rock floor.

"Do you need help?" Silas could see no handle on the door.

He began to reach out to touch its surface, but then drew back his hand. He picked up a rock and tapped the door with it. It made almost no noise, for the door was thick and solid, and the dank air swallowed every sound.

"Is there anyone in there?"

Silence. Not the silence of nothing, but the silence of waiting. Something waiting and holding itself still on the other side.

Locked doors were dangerous, in his experience. They were usually locked for good reasons. This door reminded him of the Camera Obscura at Uncle's, and of the sealed tins of souls at his father's house, each with its tortured occupant. Now Jonas's words about not leaving the path began to pull at him. Silas turned away, crawled out of the passage, and continued on, pulling cobwebs off his hair and clothes as he walked.

The farther he went, the more the walls drew in, closer about him until the once vast passage funneled down to a small chamber with a single door on its far side. In the middle of the room, there was an enormous desk where, Silas was surprised to see, a man sat, wearing a green visor like some old-time accountant. His skin was thin, translucent, and creased, his face like a wrinkled piece of vellum. The man's long robes looked like they had been woven from skeins of dust. The desk was covered in nearly tipping towers of papers and just in front of the man were various stamps, seals, and signet rings. Slowly, like an automaton, the man pulled a document from one pile, stamped it, then put it on another pile. About the table were many tall, pillared candles, and on the very corner of his desk perched the skull of a small child.

Without raising his head, the man at the desk rasped, "Dropping off, or picking up?"

"Um . . . neither, I believe. I am here on my own business," said Silas.

"Well, then, who have we here?" the man asked, looking up. When he saw Silas with the corona of corpse fire about his head, he rose and bowed slightly but reverently, and said, "Begging your pardon, sir. I was trying to get through some of the backlog. How may I help?"

"I'm looking for the springs."

"Oh, 'course you are! How long has it been since the last time?"

"I don't believe I've been here before," answered Silas.

"Of course you have," said the man at the desk. "All the Undertakers come here."

"But this is my first time," Silas tried to explain.

"First time, last time . . . all the same from where I sit."

Silas wondered how long it had been since this man had gotten out. Did he live down here in the catacombs? "I don't mean to be rude, but may I assume, sir, you are not among the living?" Silas knew a ghost when he saw one, but experience had taught him it was always more polite to let others describe themselves first, before making any assumptions.

"If you are alive, sir, then in truth, I *am* among the living."

Silas smiled. "I mean, are you dead? Departed? Like the other folk of this house?"

"As you like," said the keeper of the crypt. "It's just a job. Who's to say what's dead and departed down here in the dark? I am here. So I can't be 'departed,' can I? Besides, nothing so small as life or death need keep us from a friendly chat surrounded by the bones and cerements. Living or dead, it's all family down here, in't? Just one big family reunion, that's what the catacombs are."

"I suppose that's true. May I ask what it is you're doing down here?"

"Keeping the records up-to-date. Someone has to make a

note of who and what comes and goes, and that someone, for the time being, is me."

"It's a family trait, I think," said Silas, thinking of the enormous funereal ledger back in his father's house in Lichport.

"Indeed it is. Whenever something ends, there should always be a reckoning. And now, may I ask who you are?" The man looked at Silas skeptically. "You are kin, are you not?"

"Yes. I am Silas Umber."

"That is very well. Now, if you don't mind, would you please show me the psychopompic token?"

"The *what* token?"

"The *psychopompic token*. Any will suffice. Scepter of Mors? Sandals of Virgil? Wand of Hermes? Ring of Anubis? Cushion of Hypnos? Hadean Clock—"

"Yes! I have that one!" Silas exclaimed, relieved as he fumbled for the death watch in his jacket pocket. When his hand closed upon it, the watch felt hot, almost angry. Silas held it before him on its chain.

"Good, good. All is in order, then."

As Silas returned the death watch to his pocket, he asked, "Will you tell me your name, cousin, so that I may remember you?"

The keeper of the crypt paused, and seemed touched that someone would ask him his name. "Indeed, sir. My name is Jacobus Umber. Very kind of you, indeed." Composing himself again, he added, "But I suspect you're not here for a chat with a distant cousin, so, how may I serve the Lord of the Upper Halls?"

"As I said, I've come to take the waters of the spring."

"Yes. So you have. And you don't know where the springs are? Of course. I may be of some small help, then, for the sake of your kindness. You are almost there in any event. Here is what you must do: Pass below that arch and follow the path down, and you shall come to a low hall. Within it, two springs flow up from the deep earth. Now, the spring on the left side of the hall, bubbling up from among the roots of a white cypress—do not drink even a sip of that spring. You may fill a flask of forgetfulness from it as your fathers and mothers have done before you, for the sake of your Undertaking, but nothing more. If any should fall upon your finger, let it dry in the air! Do not put even a drop into your mouth or all is lost."

"What of the other spring?"

"Yes. The spring you seek is on the right side of the hall, and you will see two guards before it. That spring flows forth from the Lake of Memory, and its water is cold and fresh and splendid. From this spring you must drink your fill, drink until your stomach is heavy and your very lungs feel as though they will burst their bands."

"Thank you, cousin Jacobus!" Silas said, already walking toward the arch.

"Wait!" cried the keeper of the crypt. "I have not said all. These guardians, you must get past them and neither strength of arms nor wit will avail you."

"Then how?"

"You must speak these words and none other: 'I am the Earth Child and the child of the Realm of Stars, this you can see already. I am withering with thirst and shall soon perish. Grant me cold water flowing forth from the Lake of Memory.'"

"That is all?" asked Silas, repeating the words in his mind to memorize them. But as the words rang in his ears, he could feel their power, their antiquity, and how familiar they felt, as though he had said them before.

"Traditional, those words are. Old. Just say 'em. Then they shall give you to drink from that holy spring and then, you know, you'll take your place among the heroes and all that sort of thing."

Silas stared at him.

"Look, are you certain you are ready, little cousin? Drinking from the spring is only a portion of the trials that await you. Those who come down, I am sorry to tell you, often lead lives of trouble. Your path shall never be easy."

"Maybe, but if I don't do what I am supposed to do, who will do it?"

Jacobus Umber smiled at that.

"But perhaps," Silas continued, "you could tell me what is to follow?"

"I am no soothsayer. But if I were a gambling man, I'd bet on miracles. Terrors. Blood-deep never-ending Obligations. Doom. That's all."

"What do you mean 'doom'?"

"I mean, isn't that why you've come? Oh, young master, have they told you nothing upstairs? I pray you've the stomach for what follows."

"Do you mean the Door Doom?"

"I do," Jacobus Umber said, but now he looked nervous, as though speaking those words put something poisonous into the air, "but let's say no more about that. None of my business anyway."

"I know something of it," Silas said. "I know I am doing no more than my ancestors before me have been asked to do."

"Well, that's fine, then. You had better be on your way. They'll be waiting for you back upstairs. I wish you *bonne chance*, cousin." Jacobus Umber blew out the candles at his desk and quickly vanished through a tiny doorway sunk almost invisibly into the wall.

Silas went forward as he was instructed. When he passed

through an arch richly carved with ivy vines on one side and a yew tree on the other, he saw the two springs. It was an unusual sensation for Silas, standing there. The springs represented two choices that were very important in the Undertaking: memory and forgetfulness. For wasn't that the very offer he often made to the dead? To fade, or remain? And now, here he was, standing by the waters that made those choices possible.

By the spring of memory, two stone figures stood guard, tall and imposing, each bearing a bronze spear and a shield adorned with twined serpents. Their long tunics and cuirasses were almost the same color as the rock of the walls behind them. Their helmets—high and crested in the fashion of ancient Macedon—obscured their faces. They did not stir.

Without taking his eyes off the guardians, Silas went first to the spring of forgetfulness. It was surrounded by bottles and flasks and human bones, perhaps left behind by those who drank its waters, and then, forgetting why they'd come, merely sat by the spring and let their lives wind down. Taking one of his own flasks from his satchel, Silas bent over and began to fill it, careful to dip only the flask and not his hand in the waters. When he looked down, he felt dizzy. The surface of the spring was in constant motion as the waters flowed up from the darkness below. As he watched, the ripples all began to swirl in one direction, around and around, appearing to draw down at the spring's center like a small whirlpool. Silas felt his throat go parched. He was thirsty, and the spring was right there in front of him. Its waters would soothe his throat. Before he knew what he was doing, he slowly reached down toward the surface of the spring. Just as his hand was about to dip into the water, someone shouted his name from the archway. His own name struck him like a blow and he sat up. Had it been Jacobus trying to help once more?

Looking about him, regaining his senses, Silas carefully sealed his flask, put it back in his satchel, and backed away from the spring. Even standing a few feet away, the spring exerted a force on him. *To forget everything . . . all of life's problems and pains . . . to instantly forget them . . . the bliss of it if . . .* No. Enough. He quickly turned to the other side of the room and walked toward the spring of memory, drawing another flask from his satchel. At his first step, the guardians stepped forward with frightening speed and raised their spears to point at Silas. Startled, he yelled, "Wait!" But the guardians advanced toward him.

Immediately Silas blurted out the words as he'd been told.

"I am the Earth Child and the child of the Realm of Stars, this you can see already. I am withering with thirst and shall soon perish. Grant me cold water flowing forth from the Lake of Memory."

As he said the words, the wisps of blue fire, the corpse candles, rose and arrayed themselves about his head like a crown of bright, flickering stars.

The guardians raised their spears as though about to attack, but instead laid them upon the cold stone of the earth. From the small altar next to the spring, they lifted a black and red kylix, an ancient two-handed vessel, decorated with large painted almond-shaped eyes. Each guardian delicately held a single handle and in unison, bent toward the spring. They plunged the cup below the surface of the water, stood up, and offered it to Silas.

Slowly, Silas took the vessel. He raised it to his mouth, and began to drink. The cup was nearly full to brimming, and the weight of it against his lips made it hard for him to drink slowly. The water was cold, and it hurt his teeth. As it slid down his throat he felt his limbs go numb. And he was so thirsty, more thirsty than he'd ever been before in his life.

From the first sip, he could suddenly feel and remember every moment in his life when he'd been thirsty, and this made his desire to drink even more desperate. He gulped at the water, hoping he would never reach the end. As more and more of the water of the spring of memory filled him, it loosed the bindings of his mind. He could see, as if from a rooftop, all the parts of his life's pageant now become visible at once.

He saw himself sitting on the porch, a child waiting for his father. Behind that vision, another him, but now a young man, still waiting on the same porch, and again, less than a year ago, walking through Lichport, still looking, still waiting for his dad. All three visions occupied the same space, the same moment, no longer isolated in time. He saw himself with different eyes. He was his father, seeing himself as an infant, as a toddler, as a teenager. He saw his father, kneeling by this same spring. And again, Amos kneeling; this time in the tall grass, crying, clutching an infant that lay motionless in his arms. Then he looked out from the corpse-eyes of his great-grandfather who was standing in front of his house, perhaps even now, watching the street, waiting for his great-grandson to return. He was Jonas Umber, eager for the honors due the family, impatient for the next generation to share in a familial sense of obligation. He was Maud Umber, not the maternal ancestress of noble carriage he'd met, but a soul trapped within a circle of fire kindled from her own terrible longing. He wanted to pause, to better understand her sorrows, but his mind was whirled away to see out through a hundred times a hundred other eyes. All his. All someone else's. All the same. Their lives were within him, once only shadows in the blood, now fed and made substantial by the waters of the spring of memory. All the portions of his life, the moment he called them up, became clear and sharp in his mind's eye, every detail of every memory standing out in stark contrast against the others. And in those visions, one thing remained a constant: Each person was waiting for something to happen. There was even a memory of his recent vision: A figure stood before a valley covered with bones. Was it him? Or his father? Was it actually a memory, or an event not yet come to pass? Silas wondered: Was no one in his family ever content?

As he knelt by the spring and set down the empty vessel, he knew in his very bones and blood that this was what some of his relatives and ancestors had also done. Those who remained, those who endured and hid away from time and the dissolution of their lives, had taken the waters of memory and stayed on in Arvale. An idea leapt to flame in his mind. What if the waters of memory were administered to other ghosts? The dead outside his family? Could they also endure with full recollection of their lives without becoming trapped in the shadowlands? Silas knew some spirits could continue in full knowledge without it, but what of those lost souls whose minds were broken, trapped in their own personal landscapes of guilt and shame and forgetfulness? What if he gave the waters of memory to Beatrice?

Oh, God, he thought. *That is her name.*

And for the first time since the night he lost her, Bea's name and all his memories of her came rushing back into his mind on the rising tide of recall that the waters of memory granted. Looking down onto the spring's reflective surface and within its brightly jeweled depths, he saw her face. Bea's eyes were closed, and mud covered parts of her body. Weeds waved in the currents flowing over her form. Silas closed his eyes.

He saw her walking before him, dancing about the tombstones of the town. He saw her by the Umber cemetery, waiting for him beneath the spilling moon. He saw her eyes holding him . . . her smile . . . her laugh, and in his heart he heard her voice singing as a fast-flowing, glistening stream would sing, if it had a human voice.

Beatrice, he thought, his heart flooding with longing. *I will come back for you.*

Silas rose from the spring and left the chamber without looking back. He made his way back the way he'd come. At the partially blocked passage, he paused once more. The crying had resumed, louder, and Silas could now hear it was a girl's voice. Emboldened by his visit to the spring, determined that no one should be imprisoned or forgotten after seeing Bea's face again, he didn't pause. He went over the low, broken wall, stumbling in the rubble on the other side as he tried to better hear whoever was in distress.

The small blue flames about his head blazed out and illuminated the door. Silas saw again the letters DM carved in to the door's surface and could clearly hear someone weeping beyond. He paused, fear creeping up to him. The door had been deliberately sealed, he reminded himself. Whatever was in there had been imprisoned for a reason. But maybe there were more clues on the door itself. Maybe there was another inscription that would tell more of the mystery.

He leaned forward, and as he put the flat of his palm to the door to support himself for a closer inspection, the seals on the door cracked, its locks slid back, and the door slowly opened toward him slightly. Silas stood there astonished at what his hand apparently had done to the door. He *was* the Janus. He remembered Maud's words, that as Janus, no door could refuse him. Now he knew the truth of it.

But with the door cracked open, he became frightened and his hands started shaking uncontrollably. He couldn't see any movement inside. As he craned to get a better view, the door flew open, knocking him down. At the same moment, a shriek crescendoed within the confines of the chamber and Silas clapped his hands over his ears to keep the piercing wail out of his head. As he struggled to get up, a comet of smoke and flame flew past him and out of the passage, and the awful screaming subsided.

His heart was pounding as he looked up into the once sealed cell. He took one tentative step inside. There were bones in the corner, partially covered in rags, rotten and threadbare, perhaps once a garment. Next to the bones lay the desiccated corpse of an infant. Silas put a hand over his mouth as a small pitiful sound escaped his throat. He stepped closer to the remains. They would have to be buried. He leaned over and saw that what he'd thought was a baby's face was only a doll, a child's plaything, the head carved roughly of wood. Its face was stained and its little dress was rotten with holes. From the position of the bones arranged around it, it looked as though whoever died here had done so while holding the doll. The bones were not very big. *God. Little more than a child. Left here to die. Who could do something like that to a child? But what else might have been imprisoned here?* He quickly realized he knew nothing about what he'd just released and that thought nauseated him.

A disturbing sound rose slowly on the air behind him, like someone moaning in pain—at the bottom of a pit, or the end of a tunnel—the most distressing noise Silas had ever heard. The longer he listened, the more terrified he became. As he turned back to the passage to leave, he heard soft breathing very close to him and as he reached around and tried to close the door once more, an ear-rending scream burst the air near his face, and he fell to the floor.

When Silas regained consciousness, he did not know how long he'd lain on the floor of the passage. He got back on his feet to the sound of ringing in his ears, and began to stagger out of the passage and up the huge vaulted corridor of stone, back the way he'd come. At the top of the stairs leading to the Great Hall, he extended his hand toward the locked door to knock. As soon as his hand touched it, the door opened. Not an accident. Just like the sealed door below in the catacombs.

When he emerged and walked through the archway, Maud was waiting for him.

She turned and called to the far corner of the hall where Jonas sat by the fire, "It is done!"

Rising from a small stool where he'd been waiting by the door, Lars jumped up and grabbed him by the shoulders saying "Silas?" as though he was asking him his name.

"Yes . . . ," Silas answered hesitantly, confused by Lars's agitation.

"Just making sure. I have heard that some who come back don't know their names anymore. You're well. I'm glad!"

Jonas strode across the room, studied Silas's pale face, and laughed. "Did you see a ghost, boy?"

Silas didn't answer. He was scared about what he had done, about opening the locked door in the catacombs, and the sound of that terrible cry was still reverberating in his head. Maybe whatever it was, it would just move on, go home, or fall away from the world.

"You do look a little frightened, child," said Maud with a concerned tone.

"No," Silas said, nervous that his guilt showed. "Just a little in awe."

"That is well. Truly, this house sits on mighty foundations."

But there was a hint of familiarity in Maud's tone he didn't like. Did she know what had happened down there? No matter what she said to him, it felt like a script, like everything he saw or experienced had been planned long in advance. And he now sensed, more than ever since his experience at the spring of memory, that she was acting. From the moment of their first meeting he had felt something of the awful grief in her, but looking at Maud now, she was a mask of deliberate calm. She was hiding something.

"Tell me now about the Door Doom. It's part of my work. I want to know what it entails."

Now Maud looked a little surprised. Jonas stepped forward to answer Silas.

"The Doom is the obligation of this house. It is what is required. As Janus, your assistance is necessary to those that reside in the . . . places of waiting."

"To be free? To be at peace? So it is like my work as Undertaker?"

"In a sense, it is not entirely unlike that work, but there are differences. Everything you need to help them is here, before you. The Doom is part of your work as Janus. It is why the Undertaker returns, in life, periodically to this house. The Door Doom is that ancient and hallowed rite by which those who will not go to their rests are brought to their ending by persuasion. Or rather, by compulsion."

"You mean they are banished? I'm not sure I want to do it that way."

"I understand your reticence. It is an enormous responsibility. But it is the surest way, Silas. Yet 'banished,' I think, is a harsh word. They are not banished, per se. They don't go anywhere else, not really. The matter is considered and when a judgment is made by the Janus, well, then the dead are *seen to* in the accustomed manner. It's all very formal, no emotional outbursts required. I think, compared to your father's 'method' where every ghost gets a hug and a good cry, you'll find this much more efficient and far less melodramatic. In any case, you won't have to spend any time convincing the dead of anything. Your word is law when they stand in the doorway upon the Limbus Stone. Won't that be a relief? Not having to haggle with the dead?"

"The Undertaking is not always easy. Sometimes they don't want to go—"

"Yes. Yes. You know how difficult certain of the dead can be." Jonas closed his eyes for a moment and smiled, as if entertaining a happy memory. "It's better if you see for yourself. I would have thought you would be eager to apply your exceptional gifts."

"Well, yes, it's just that I'm not sure I believe that things have to be exactly as you're saying. I have some experience, you know. I am the Undertaker of Lichport and I've never had to 'pass judgment' on anyone."

Frustrated, Maud broke in, speaking fast. "Yes. You are the Undertaker of Lichport, as you keep saying. No one denies this. But Silas, until you experience *this* tradition, a well-respected rite, how can you know what you believe is best? Try. In experience lies wisdom."

"I don't know." Something felt wrong about what they were saying. Maybe this was why his dad had turned his back on "family ways." But Silas could not deny he was intrigued. So far, as Undertaker, there had been a lot of guesswork, a lot of experimenting and interpreting the words and work of others. Maybe the Door Doom would be something he could learn from and make his own. Even if he didn't take it all to heart, maybe some portion of it could help in his continuing work back home. Wouldn't his dad want him to keep an open mind, to experience things himself and make his own decisions?

Jonas spoke again, calmly. "May I take your sober silence as a hesitant 'yes'? Tomorrow, we shall together convene that most hallowed and ancient rite of the Door Doom. You should return to your rooms and get some sleep."

"I am still feeling a little excited from the evening's events. If it's all the same to you, perhaps I'll sit here in the hall, by the fire, for a bit first?"

"Of course, of course," said Jonas. "Good night, then."

As Jonas and Maud left the hall, Lars went and got large chairs from against the wall and dragged them over to the hearth.

Silas settled in and put his feet on the warm stones in front of the fire.

"I'll fetch some wine," Lars offered and ran from the hall to get it.

A moment later, Silas could hear that same soft crying he'd heard down in the crypt, but it was outside the house now and it rose in pitch to a scream. Someone, very far away, screaming. But almost as soon as it had begun, the distant cry quieted, and the warmth of the fire and his own weariness drew him into sleep.

CHAPTER 18

WOKEN

THIS WAS NOT SLEEP. Silas was walking with Bea along the cliffs near the lighthouse in Lichport. She stopped and turned to Silas and kissed him. He could feel her lips against his and her arms about him. He put his hand on the back of her head, just above her neck, and drew her even closer. He could feel that her hair was wet. She wrapped a leg around his and they fell back together and did not stop falling.

Silas didn't even feel them hit the surface of the sea far below the lighthouse.

He looked up through the water. Lights moved above them. Their limbs were still entwined, and Bea kept kissing him, even though his mouth was open now as they sank down together. She pressed her lips to his neck, his cheek, his eyes.

Silas did not feel them come to rest on the sea bottom. But he could see Beatrice, her face pulled back a little from his. She smiled and he heard her words, bubbling at him through the murky water.

"Welcome home, my love. Welcome home."

Those familiar with our Old
Northern Literature will be well
aware how often the forms of
the dead were believed to be seen
again on earth. And there is an
instance, in the old Sagas, where
not only did shade after shade
revisit the pale glimpses of the
moon, to the long and fearful
disquiet of a neighbor, but where
their often-comings could only
be stopped by formal process of
law; by use of which they were,
however, at last driven away.

—Copied by Amos Umber from *English Gilds*, 1870

I have neither eye to see, nor tongue to speak here, but as the house is pleased to direct me.

—Copied by Jonas Umber from *Rushworth's Historical Collections*, 1721

CHAPTER 19

KNOCK, KNOCK

WHEN SILAS AWOKE, the hall was almost completely dark but for a small candle left on the table, and the embers of the fire dying slowly on the hearth. Lars was still asleep in his chair. Standing to stretch, Silas noticed a pale illumination coming through a doorway on the far side of the hall. Curious, he quietly crossed the room, his passage noted only by the wide-eyed grotesques adorning the beams high above. He walked through the arch, following the line of light down a short hallway until he came to a large open door.

Before him was Arvale's library and his heart leapt to see so many books. Candles were lit on a few of the massive and ornate tables. Someone else was there.

"Welcome, Silas," said Maud in what seemed like feigned surprise, looking up from a table covered in scrolls and thick worn vellum volumes. "The quiet hours I like to spend here, among the genealogies of our ancient family. I can tell you, we are a strange, long-lived lot." She quickly rolled up a scroll she had been looking at and flipped closed the covers of several books.

"I thought you had retired," Silas said.

"Mortui non dormiunt."

"The dead can't . . . ," Silas began, trying to work out the Latin.

"Almost," said Maud. "The dead do not sleep."

Silas nodded and walked over to the table and picked up a small book, idly perusing its contents though he couldn't read them, for the Latin was written in a crabbed hand. He looked at Maud, wondering what she had been reading. His mind was still on that rite that awaited him and he was actually glad of her company. Maybe, without others present, Maud might say more about what was in store for him.

"Strange or not, we are all family. That's what's important, no?" Silas asked.

"Indeed, yes. And that we help one another, when we can," replied Maud.

"I am ready to meet whatever's ahead. I'll do my best." In his mind, Silas kept seeing that crown of corpse lights floating above his head, and it filled him with confidence.

Smiling then, and coming up very close to Silas, Maud said, "*I* know you are ready. You would not have been called if you were not. Silas, it is not so terrible as Jonas makes it sound. He is formal about such things and concerns himself o'ermuch with hierarchy. There's no changing him, I'm afraid. I hope you may see the Door Doom as merely an elaboration of what you already do back in Lichport. The name sounds ominous, and its formality perhaps makes it intimidating, but the idea behind the rite should feel familiar to you."

"Where does the name come from?"

"'Door Doom'? That's a term that originates from the northern branch of the family, those wonderful Saga-folk. "Dura Domr" they called it. It's just a kind of legal gathering, a settling of accounts. The Janus may, at his or her discretion, make use of customs from many times and places. The dead are a various lot. The Janus must be able to treat with any contingency. But the core rite, the one practiced here at Arvale for more than a thousand years, is primarily a northern custom. Oh, there are perhaps a few older, more classical elements . . . truly, some things cannot be improved upon. After a time, should you feel the need to innovate, well, that will be your decision. But now, I think, sticking to tradition is best. Elements and fashions come and go. Every Janus makes adaptations to the extant rite. All that is truly required is your desire to put things in order."

"Of course I want to help. I wouldn't be here otherwise. I want to be like my dad and help the dead and the living both. I don't think I need to be reminded by everyone that sacrifices are required of me. I know it. I promise you."

Maud looked concerned. "Oh, Silas, dear child, I know you only wish to do what's right. I know that should any of this house need your assistance, you would try to help in any way you could. I can sense that in you. We all can, I think."

Her tone was saccharine. Silas began to wonder what she wanted from him. But why wouldn't she come out and just ask? He tried to push the conversation back to where she might tell him something useful.

"Is that where the word 'Janus' comes from? From these 'innovations' of others, someone reaching back to the older, classical strains?"

"Possibly," said Maud, pausing briefly at the non sequitur. "More likely, it is a holdover from those earlier times. The rite became more northern as time went on, but the name 'Janus' endures, perhaps to honor the god of that name, or because the power associated with that ancient title resonated deeply with the ceremony itself. But there have always been such rites. Words to call the dead. Words to banish the dead. These are the oldest formulas known to man and woman. So often what we love becomes what we fear—sometimes through our own fault, because we refuse to honor those who die. Sometimes the dead change, because in life something was kept from them, or they were hateful people, and death merely magnifies the problems they bore in life. You know this from your own work, of course. Or sometimes what we love the most is lost to us and no matter how hard we look, we cannot find it. . . ." Maud trailed off, gazing toward the window. It looked like she was about to cry, but a moment later she raised her head, composed herself, and continued.

"As time went on, people did not wish to negotiate with the dead themselves. Out of fear. Perhaps they forgot the formulas. Either way, certain families came to hold these rites. Those with the Umber name are part of that lineage of folk who kept the old ways. Some say we were chosen. Who knows? Perhaps we chose ourselves. There are other families who do this work. We are not the only ones. But we are surely the oldest, and certain of us feel we are owed some honor on that account. Janus is an important title, but there are other seats from which the dead are judged, and called, and those chairs have been empty for a long time. Surely if anyone is to occupy one of those hallowed thrones, it should be an Umber?"

Silas was fascinated by her words about other families with Januses, but he could feel her pushing him. It was becoming clear that she expected something from him more than merely becoming Janus. *Let her go on revealing her hand one card at a time,* thought Silas. He would listen and be wary.

"So, I am going to have to read some old script to perform the rite? Is it said in Norse?" Silas was only half joking. He didn't like the idea of reading or saying words he didn't understand. Though he wondered what such a ritual would have looked like in ancient times. He wondered what the oldest version was that Maud might have seen.

"Maud, have you ever been at an original one? What's the oldest Door Doom you've witnessed?"

"I have only seen the rite performed in this house. But I have heard one of the old Dooms described by someone who saw it. Would you like to hear it? Let's see if I might call it up. Maud closed her eyes and lowered her head. Her form dimmed for a moment, but then she sat up, her eyes wide, as if she were looking upon a scene in some far distant place.

"Now . . . there was a man, Thorfinn was he named. He and several of his companions went fishing. A great storm fell upon them, and their ship, like a submissive dog, rolled over and showed its belly to the angry sky. All the men drowned and the bodies were not found. As was the custom, a funeral feast was held for them, and the mead that was being saved for midwinter was used. That first night of the feast, when all the guests had come and been welcomed and taken their seats, who should appear at the door but Thorfinn and his shipmates, water falling from them like dripping stones left behind by the tide. They walked into the house, heeded none, sat down at the fire, and began wringing out their clothes while they ate and drank. No one minded, for in those days, heathendom still held sway and people believed that when a drowned person showed up for the first night of his funeral feast, that was to be taken as a very good omen; it meant that their god of the sea had received their kin. At the end of the feast, when the cooking fires had all burned down to ash, the dead men left the house. Sadly, the story does not end there. Those restless men returned for every night of the feast, getting louder and rowdier with each homecoming. They got into the stores of dried fish being saved for deep winter. People thought, let us be done with this funeral feast, and then the dead shall depart. So the feast was ended. But the very next night, when the small cooking fire was lit for the regular evening meal, the door flew open and the dead came in again. Well, now, as you can imagine, everyone in the house was frightened by this. But no one wanted to upset the dead and so this bad business went on, right through the Yule season and into the early part of the year, even though the food was running out and people were getting sick—perhaps because of an epidemic, perhaps because of the presence of the dead. Who could say? Finally, the family had had enough. They sent word to the old men of the nearest village and the cry went out, up and down the fells, that the Door Doom would be held.

A short while later, men began arriving at the farm. The wise gathered at night in the house, standing in a partial circle about the door, and then they called out the names of the dead. When Thorfinn and his men came to the doorway, they stopped and listened and did not enter farther, for the power of the threshold is a mighty thing unto itself and the dead cannot resist it if it is held properly. The wise men convened the court, and charges were read, and then Thorfinn, seeing the strength of the house, spoke.

"I have sat in this house, while the sitting was good. I see now that, perhaps, the time has come to move on. Maybe in the spring." And though there had been a judgment against the dead, everyone could see the dead were still reluctant to leave. But then one of the wise stood forth and pronounced the Doom against Thorfinn and his men. Strong words, not to be ignored. Mighty words, that needed to be heeded.

Thorfinn spoke again.

"Even in my own house, there is no welcome. All right! All right! You have chanted at us enough. Come now, boys, let's all be gone!"And Thorfinn and his men departed and did not return. And that summer, the weather was fine and the fishing very good."

As she finished, Maud put her head down.

Fascinated, Silas asked, "But they were not destroyed in any way?"

"No."

"They were asked to leave."

"Yes."

"And they left."

"Yes."

"And that's all I am going to be asked to do? To say they're in the wrong and ask the dead to leave? I sort of do that all the time. Why all the fuss?"

"Well, as I said, the rite is always changing, bit by bit, and it has been over a thousand years since it was performed in the way of the story."

"But that's basically it, right?"

"Silas, if you will but wait until—"

"There he is!" said Jonas, entering the library. "I have been looking for you, Silas." Jonas seemed relieved to have entered when he did. He put himself between Silas and Maud and continued where she had stopped. "If I have heard you correctly, you are asking about the Door Doom and its development, no? The particulars of the rite *are* important, Silas. But it's the intention of the Janus that drives all. And, of course, certain words do hold considerable power. When the moment comes, I will tell you those words, you shall speak them with intention, and the work shall be done! But now, let us go to the hall and begin."

Silas hesitated, but Jonas spoke quickly. "I think the best way to answer all your questions is just to get to work. There is no teacher like experience, eh?"

"Right," answered Silas with a mix of excitement and trepidation in his voice. His stomach was a jumbled bag of anxieties, but he added, solemnly, "I am ready."

Maud, Jonas, and Silas made their way into the great hall.

"It is law that the Doom must be presided over by a living Janus, though in times of need, the family may do what is necessary to assist the rite. Until you came to Arvale, Silas, many spirits have been held awaiting judgment. Some of the deepest vaults are bursting. Now that you've taken the waters, we may at last properly enact the Doom again, and those souls may be settled, banished, dissolved, made to take the Waters of Lethe or subjected to the rites of dissolution. *Cedo nulli* shall be our watchword if any spirit proves difficult; then and only then will those words be spoken. The phrase is very old and carries a terrible power. If all goes well, it should be unnecessary. It must be used only when the dead refuse to comply. This is important, Silas. Are you listening?"

Silas nodded and repeated the phrase, "*Cedo nulli.*"

In the instant when those words were spoken by the Janus, they hung upon the air, and the very fabric of the house trembled as if it might itself dissolve. Jonas looked about nervously for a moment, then said, "It simply denies the ghost its place in the world, erases it, if you like. These words you say after pronouncing judgment if there is too much delay, or should *anything* go wrong, or should you feel threatened at any time. You speak these mighty words upon the dead and we'll sort out the rest after. Do you understand?

"I think so. What do the words mean?"

"It's an awkward translation. . . ."

"Do not coddle the boy, Jonas," said Maud.

Jonas nodded. "It means, roughly, *not being*. At the end of the Door Doom, particularly if the ghost refuses the Waters of Lethe, you will say these words. You must, Silas, for while the door is open during the Doom, we stand in some peril. But don't worry, we shall proceed slowly. We'll let this first be a practice."

"A practice?"

"Yes. We shall not even convene the judge's council. Just the three of us. Very cozy. We'll keep it simple. We three shall, with your permission, Silas, make a quorum. It used to be three, long ago, in any event. So if you prefer, a triumvirate. Once, the spirits of three ancient kings stood in judgment over the dead: Rhadamanthys, Aiakos, and Minos. Three judges of the dead, and behind them, Hades held the final word. Now, the Janus stands in the place of the king of dead, but who knows . . . who knows what may come now that you are with us?"

Maud looked hard at Jonas.

Silas was confused. From what he'd heard and read, it was the living that had to deal with the dead when they became a problem. This much was familiar to him. But ghosts—*ghosts*— were advising him on the fate of other ghosts! Had Jonas become so numb to his own condition that he could not see the awful irony of this? Perhaps Jonas was so entrenched in the work of his life that it was habitual, continuing in death. Silas realized that just because a ghost seemed aware, that didn't mean he wasn't also hindered in ways that might be difficult for him to see or understand. If the whole house was indeed a sort of prison, albeit a much larger version of the shadowlands he'd seen—an idea Silas was entertaining more and more the longer he remained—what was Jonas *in* for?

Oblivious to the concern on Silas's face, Jonas continued.

"Yes. Three is always best, so tonight, just us three. I know as Undertaker, you have for the most part done what we shall do tonight. It's the approach and your attitude now that are crucial, Silas. We shall follow the hallowed rite verbatim. No elaboration, all right? I have to tell you, once you start, we shall not be able to stop. We must finish once it's begun, for the safety of all."

"Stop frightening him, Jonas," said Maud.

"Okay. I understand," said Silas, putting his slightly shaking hands into his pockets.

Perhaps to distract him, Maud pointed out to Silas the covered chair he had previously asked about, and removed its dust cloth. Next to it, a table held a scepter, and a large tin goblet filled with water.

"This chair is a rather old thing, though rest assured, it is as solid as the foundations of the earth. This is the seat of the Lord of the Dead. In the world outside these walls, it has been lost for some time, but such objects cast long shadows. It appears here in Arvale because it was once kept by the Umbers long ago, so it is part of our ancestral holdings. Once, in ages past, several of our ancestors held the Ebony Throne themselves. What do you make of it?"

Silas walked back and forth before the dark wooden chair. The longer he looked, the more details stood out. There were carved heads of dogs at the ends of both armrests and a third hound's head that crested the top. The long, turned necks and heads of birds, perhaps swans, decorated the back. Looking at the table, his eye was caught by the scepter, and without thinking, Silas reached for it.

"Wait," Jonas said. "It is too much."

"There is no harm in letting the boy hold it," snapped Maud.

"While he is here he can do with any of these things as he wishes. You do not rule here, Jonas. Time to let him enjoy discovering who and what he is!"

"I am only interested in protecting him. Why do you press the matter so?"

But Maud ignored him. She was looking at Silas, who had picked up the scepter and was turning it over in his hands.

Silas could barely hear what the other two were saying. The black stone was ice cold, and electric to the touch. He felt his skin tighten and all the hairs on his arms stand up. He closed his eyes and, for an instant, he saw himself sitting on a throne, holding the scepter, and before him, a throng was singing a hymn in whose crescendo Silas thought he could discern the names of all the dead of the earth.

"Can I keep this?" Silas asked, not looking up.

"For a time if you like," said Jonas with resignation. "Everything in this house is yours, in one way or another."

Maud smiled.

"What does it do?" asked Silas.

Jonas looked down. "It enforces the dead to be complacent."

"Is that all?"

"No."

Silas held the scepter up closer to his eyes. Its surface was smooth and impenetrable. He could not look away.

"Yes, you can feel it, can't you? Like you, Silas, I was an Undertaker in life, eager for power and authority, but death can bring such perspective. From where I now stand, I can see that while some may reach very high for attainment and position, sometimes it is in doing merely what needs to be done that we achieve true honor. On this, if nothing else, I believe your father and I would have agreed."

Jonas gently guided Silas's hands down, never touching the scepter, as Silas released it.

"Tonight, *we* shall do what needs to be done. There is some unfinished business and it is important for you to see how essential it is to conclude matters, thoroughly, in the accustomed way. Shall we begin?"

Silas turned away from the scepter and the Ebony Throne and walked to the doors. Maud stood to his left, Jonas his right.

"Silas, now you shall open the threshold. It is traditional for you to say, 'I, Janus of the threshold, open wide the door!'"

Without hesitating, Silas repeated the words. "I, Janus of the threshold, open wide the door."

"Good. Now, you can go to the doors and open—"

But already, Silas was feeling different, like something a little less and lot more than himself. The light in his eyes had begun to change. He felt empowered, anticipation surging through him. His back straightened. He raised both his hands, clasped them briefly together, then quickly cast them apart. With a thunderous crash, the doors of Arvale threw themselves open. The doorway no longer looked out over the front of the estate. It was not the cobalt of night or the sable of cast shadow. The doorway now framed an impenetrable blackness kept over from the time before the stars were made.

"Fine," said Jonas quickly. "That's fine. Now call the name of Joseph Downing."

Silas nodded, but then paused. He knew that name.

"Silas, you cannot stop. This is important. Though others wait to be called, this name must be summoned for you to see the road you must take now, else you shall continue on in error. The way lies open and the house is in peril. Call the name. It's all right. But do it now."

Before he could think again, caught up in the propulsion of the ritual and the power he held, Silas called out, "Joseph Downing, stand before the door!"

Out of the murky darkness beyond the threshold, drawn by the force of his name being called by the Janus, the ghost of the lighthouse keeper, Joseph Downing, came to stand upon the Limbus Stone before the doors of Arvale. He looked confused and nearly blind, squinting toward the hall. He was soaked with seawater that dripped from his body onto the dark stone beneath him.

"Now say to the ghost: 'You stand guilty of wandering and of malfeasance against the living. I sentence you to your rest. Joseph Downing, will you take the waters I offer you?'"

"But as Undertaker, I already—?"

"The waters of Lethe were never administered. The ghost remained. Trapped beneath the sea. That is no proper end. Now is not the time for sentimental questions. He stands here because you were unable to effectively perform your obligations back in Lichport. Go on!"

"All right!" Silas snapped back, unsure what else to do but continue. "Joseph Downing, will you take these waters I offer you now? Will you go to your rest and wander no more?"

But the ghost looked lost. He stared up at the lintel on the door, his eyes pale as quartz. The ghost shook, then threw his head to one side, over and over, as though hitting it against a wall that wasn't there.

"Joseph Downing?" Silas entreated the ghost now. "Joseph Downing? Will you take the waters of Lethe? Will you forget and sink down?" Silas fumbled with his satchel, trying to find the flask of Lethe waters he'd refilled in the catacombs, but Jonas pointed to the tin goblet already on the table and nodded.

The ghost seemed to be entirely unaware of where he was, or

what was being asked of him. "No more water. No more water. Where . . . where is my son?" the ghost stammered. "Where is Daniel?" the ghost continued absently. He was falling back into his old confusion. He began to weep.

Silas looked pained, watching the ghost in its pitiful state. Jonas said, "Say the words, Silas. End his suffering. Do not fall into the trap of sentimentality that is this family's plague. Say the words, now, and let it be done! Have pity on this spirit and do for him what he cannot do for himself."

Silas could feel the pressure on him to act—the terror on the ghost's face, Jonas's words, Maud's expectant stare, the weight of it all, as though the entire mansion of Arvale had just been set down upon his shoulders. The stress awoke something very old in his blood. Sensing the pressure on Silas, Jonas began speaking the words of the ritual into Silas's ear, but a moment later, he stopped. Silas was saying them by himself, as though he'd known them all along, as though he had presided over the Door Doom a hundred times before. Silas's voice rose and the doors of Arvale began to shake. Silas raised his hand, pointing at the ghost.

"Now I speak my judgment against this ghost, Joseph Downing, against the walking one. Here and now, he shall depart, shall be as if he never was, and shall never again trouble the living or the dead!"

Joseph Downing hung speechless above the threshold. Below his feet, the surface of the Limbus Stone grew bright and transparent, but he still remained, arms moving up and down while his hands opened and closed desperately as if clawing to keep hold of the air.

Silas, lost wholly in the rite, pitched his voice into a thunder. "*Cedo nulli!*" he pronounced. At once the black stone under Joseph Downing swallowed him, and the room grew still. Silas's heart was racing. His words flowed with the force of command and his body shook with the power he held over the dead. Something in his world had shifted in that moment and whatever was to become of him, he knew he would not be able to turn back.

Jonas looked at Maud, as if to say, *You may have been right.* He moved to Silas's side.

"I hardly know what to say. I have stood before the Door Doom many times, but I have never seen it conducted so well, so efficiently. That was excellently done, Silas! Did you see, Maud? Silas, I am without words!" Something had altered in Jonas Umber's demeanor. Where once there was reticence and reluctance, now there was hope. Silas could see that Jonas was proud of him, but his limbs were still shaking and what he'd done to the ghost didn't feel right, now that he was returning to himself again.

Jonas couldn't stop. "Silas! Really! I must say—"

"Okay! Thank you!" Silas said louder than he'd meant. He needed to think and wanted to hold the silence a moment longer. "I'm sorry. I heard you. . . ." He felt nauseated and confused. For the last several moments, he had felt like he was locked away somewhere small inside himself, watching what transpired as though someone else had spoken the words, as though someone else had banished Joseph Downing. He knew, in every particle of his body, that his father would have wept to see him in that moment, and the tears would not be of pride.

"Shall we call another to the Door Doom?" asked Jonas calmly.

"Jonas, enough!" said Maud. "Leave him be. Can't you see he's spent?"

"Yes, all right. Just one for now. But Silas, tomorrow we shall proceed, yes?"

"All right. Tomorrow," Silas said wearily, not wanting to

discuss it any further. He was bone tired, his legs shaking.

"I know it's hard at first. The sad condition of the spirits of the dead can blur one's sense of responsibility, particularly when they are unable to take the waters. We will try again tomorrow with something where the lines between obligation and the so-called desires of the dead are more clearly delineated. It's better, more humane, when they can understand you as you speak to them. Most will take the waters. It is easier that way, I promise you. I'll take care of the preparations myself and will call for you tomorrow."

Jonas left the hall. Maud smiled encouragingly at Silas, and then followed Jonas out.

A few moments later, the mighty horn sounded far atop the house.

Lars came running into the great hall. He took one look at Silas, his face pale and hands shaking, and ran to his side. "Let's get you upstairs, eh? A little rest will put all to right."

Silas only nodded. He felt pulled in two, sick at the thought of doing it again, but also eager to hold the power in his hands once more. He knew that if he looked in a mirror, in that moment, he would not have recognized himself.

When they got back to Silas's rooms, Lars asked him to come up the stairs to the top of the tower. Exhausted, Silas protested, but Lars looked so pleased about whatever it was he wanted to show him, Silas relented.

Reaching the open air of the tower roof, his legs aching, Silas said, "So, cousin Lars, what is so important that it can't wait until tomorrow?"

Lars walked over to the wall and pointed down. Silas looked below and saw torches burning in the small field beyond the garden.

There were tents and banners that glistened in the torchlight and he could hear horses and the ringing of silver bridle bells. And there was music. The scene was enrapturing. And though he was becoming drowsy, Silas could not look away.

"What is it?" he asked Lars, putting his arm around his cousin's shoulder for affection as much as support.

"Both within the house and outside its walls, spirits such as these come and go as they will, but the spectacle below is rare and very fine, you must agree," said Lars without looking away from the night tournament.

"Yes. Very fine indeed," replied Silas. He was relieved by Lars's comment. And he was glad at the chance to eventually be able to share a little more with someone who asked nothing of him. Wanting to know more of what Lars believed, Silas pushed a bit further. "We find ourselves in strange circumstances, do we not? We are not like the folk here, are we?"

Lars made no answer.

"Lars?" said Silas as he turned toward him. "You know that though we are living men, we are residing in a house of the dead?"

Lars smiled wanly. "Cousin, I am a simple man, but I am no fool. I know how far we are from Lichport. That is partially why I remain here. Some nights, I think I can see Lichport from the battlements of this house, yet . . . I know the troubles I left behind are a great ways off. As strange as this place is, that odd distance is a kind of comfort to me, though my heart, every day, aches for home and what I left behind. Do you feel that way, Silas?"

"Yes. I miss Lichport. I'll be glad to get back. It feels as though I've been away for ages now."

Together they looked back over the battlement. Below, two knights with banded lances rode their horses slowly toward each other in a sort of mock joust. Lords and ladies watched from their tents, their clothes trimmed in ermine, laughing and singing below the moon, and the torchlight played on the armor of the knights and made them glow and waver in the air like living flames.

Silas glanced gratefully at Lars in thanks for the gift of the distraction, but when he looked back at the night tournament, it was gone. Shadows of every length and hue had fallen across the land, and the moon hid behind a wandering cloud. The tents and horses had vanished, and the music faded from the air like the song of some swift-departing night-bird.

Before they turned to go downstairs, Lars sighed and spoke again. "It is true that we have found ourselves in a very unusual place, Silas, an estate beyond my ken to understand, although I do know we are both very far from home. Still, cousin, you must admit, this house can afford some wondrous views."

That night, Silas dreamed of Bea again. She was calling out, her voice falling upon his ears like a bell ringing up from below the waves. Silas wasn't sure what she was saying and didn't hear her say his name, but he knew, needed to know, that she was looking for him. In the dream, he tried to yell back, but his jaw was locked and he couldn't speak or even move his arms to signal that he was there, wherever "there" was. He could sense her behind him. At last, the mist parted and he found himself standing before the mill pond. Thick ice and an old piece of Mrs. Bowe's lace tablecloth lay across the water. He leaned down over the frozen pond and saw her below. Beatrice was struggling. She beat furiously at the ice with blue hands. Silas struck the surface with his foot, but it was like iron and would not crack no matter how he stomped at it. Suddenly, Beatrice's face was very close to the clear crystal surface of the water, and he could see her mouthing his name over and over, forming sounds around the bubbles that poured from her throat and spread out against the underside of the ice.

When Silas awoke, the small fire Lars had set for him on the hearth had burned down to glowing embers, and in the dim light, little carved faces on his bedposts stared down at him with flat, dead eyes of wood, daring him to go back to sleep.

For those who die unshriven, or furious, or vengeful, or are too fond of their estates and wordlie fortunes, shalle surely walk again after death. Beware then, for these Restless folk will wander forth from their graves and other habitations, their breath bringinge plague and contagion upon where e'er they walk. And lo! How many goodlie folk have come to death by even idle conversation with a wand'ring corpse.

—FROM THE NOTES OF WILLIAM OF NEWBURGH (c.1190), TRANSCRIBED BY JONAS UMBER FOR AN UNPUBLISHED TRACT ENTITLED "THE UNDERTAKERS NEEDFUL NIGHT-WATCH AGAINST THE EVILS OF THE RESTLESS"

CHAPTER 20

RELATIVITY

As Silas lay between sleep and waking, a sound drifted down from the roof over his bed. There was a scratching, then the noise of something being dragged, or pulling itself across the floor above. There was a pause, then the latch of the trapdoor leading from his room to the tower roof rattled sharply. But as Silas rose from bed, the horns of Arvale sounded again, the shrill staccatos blasting out, blaring even through the thick stone of the walls: calling him *Attend! Attend! Attend! Return to the hall! Doom! Doom! Doom!* and banishing whatever had been trying to enter his chamber. *It's nothing,* he told himself. *The house is full of noises. It's nothing.* He knew the family was waiting. Yet his dream of Beatrice still clung at him, drawing his mind toward home, Lichport, his real home. Bea was trapped and he longed to go to her. But the straining chain of family obligation pulled the other way. It was the Doom more than anything that had taken hold of him. What had happened yesterday upset him, but hadn't Maud said that each new Janus may make changes in the rite? In time, he could make the Doom his own. When he stood at the door, he now knew, he wielded an extraordinary power he was only beginning to understand. If he could summon the dead by their names . . .

But the Doom brought other concerns.

How often must it be held? How frequently would he need to come back? Could he convene the Door Doom anyplace else?

How much of the ritual's force lay in him, or in the Limbus Stone, or in Arvale itself? There was still a lot he needed to know, yet the longer he remained at Arvale, the more it felt like, in the end, all his questions were becoming choices.

At Arvale, he was seeing and learning things about the spectral that he had not experienced at home, and his world was expanding very quickly. Each day brought some new vista of potential privileges. He was beginning to hope that some of his new authority might enable him to help Bea. So he would stay a little longer. He would conduct the Doom as he'd agreed and learn whatever else he could, but then he was going home.

The trumpet call became more shrill, more desperate. Silas pulled his great-grandfather's coat over his dad's jacket. When he opened the door leading into the corridor outside his room, Jonas was waiting for him.

In the great hall, the family had gathered, arrayed before the walls like figures in a faded tapestry. Candles were lit atop the long table and a fire blazed in the massive fireplace.

Three hooded figures, cowls drawn up, took their places by the closed doors. Jonas seemed to become more distinct as he entered the hall with Silas. One of the robed men raised his hand and another mighty horn sounded outside. The door shook on its titan hinges.

Cast in shadow, present but indistinct, members of the family whispered amongst themselves.

"Is this a public event?" Silas asked, uncomfortable with the idea of being watched and possibly evaluated.

"Not generally, no," Jonas replied. "But this is an important moment. The Door Doom proper has not been held for some time. It is well to share such a night with family."

"I think it has something more to do with spectacle being

the delight of the idle," said Maud. "Though I won't deny today's proceedings are of particular interest to *some*."

"Why?" asked Silas. He could see Maud was not pleased with whatever was about to happen. There was something they weren't telling him. But in her words he also sensed a shift in power between her and Jonas, as though now that the business at hand was the Door Doom and not merely welcoming Silas to the house, Jonas had reassumed an accustomed authority. He wanted to be needed and was eager for Silas to rely on him.

"Let us waste no more time. Shall we begin?" Jonas said, ignoring Maud completely.

There was a desperate edge to Jonas's voice. Silas was sure it wasn't fear. Jonas was smiling. Was he excited? Yes. He was eager for the Doom to begin. Even if Jonas derived a kind of pleasure from meeting family obligations, his excitement seemed to Silas to violate the solemn nature of the rite. The dead were to be called and judged. Where was the joy in that?

"Are you in a hurry, Jonas? Do you have someplace else to be?" Silas asked lightly.

"Silas Umber," Jonas laughed impatiently, "where else would I go? I am here because you are here. Without the Janus, what need would we have to assemble? I assure you, I am merely pleased that we can, together, put an old wrong to right. The indolence of our house has long preyed upon my mind. Indeed, but for that, I might have long ago gone to my rest. Ours is such important work, and I'll be honest, I was against your coming here. I thought it unwise to bring you to Arvale so soon. But now I see you are ready to embrace your obligations, and that you have a gift, yes, a true aptitude for this work. So I am pleased to continue, and to help you as I may, so long as I am needed."

Jonas was sincere, Silas could feel that. But there was

anxiousness beneath his words that still seemed out of proportion. Whatever was going to happen, Jonas desperately wanted it to occur. Silas looked hard at the ghost of his ancestor. Jonas seemed larger than yesterday, his form weighing more heavily on the air, his presence strong and intimidating. A brightness shone from his brow, and when he spoke, words filled the large hall from floor to rafter.

The quality of the atmosphere in the hall was changing. It was growing swiftly colder and sharper. The edges of objects in the room became hard, more distinct, and the dim light congealed, clinging to everything like tiny, bright droplets of water.

Outside the door, a great whirring could be heard. It was followed by a long, soft crunching, like something was being dragged across the ground toward the house.

"Jonas, what is coming?" Silas asked in a near whisper, moving closer to him.

"Prepare yourself. I have no desire to worry you, but some things that appear before the Doom are more . . . unnatural than others. More monstrous. But you shall overcome all who stand against the order of things. In times past, when one such as what you will see tonight appeared, it was quickly put down by the Undertaker, or the Janus, if it came to that. But this house, indeed Lichport, has long been without one capable of rising to the task, and so this evil has spread and endured for many, many years. These are no ordinary spirits, no mere ghosts, but an appalling horde, a plague. It must be this way. When the dead walk and their feet make impression upon the earth, the Door Doom must be convened to banish them. It has always been so. In the past, such folk as you shall face tonight have brought pestilence in their wake. They are often cognizant of their estate, and so may speak to you, even in pleasing words. You must ignore them."

"But they have to be allowed to speak, or I can't—"

"Silas, forgive me. I know this will be hard for you particularly. Human fear and primitive reverence might make this hard for anyone, but the Janus must serve both the living and dead by putting down these unnaturals, these monstrosities. Now, Silas, do you promise to do what's required? I will stand by you."

Silas's hands were shaking. But he tried to remind himself that this was no different from any other aspect of the Undertaking. In Lichport, he rarely knew in advance what form a troubled ghost might take, and so he had to be willing to face whatever came. *This is my job,* he told himself. *This is how it goes, how it always goes. This I have done before.* But it felt different. Something was coming and he knew he wasn't going to like it.

"All right. I promise," he said, straightening his back, trying to raise his courage. The sooner this was done, the sooner he could go home.

"Excellent," said Jonas. "The names have already been called and the great horn has sounded the summons. Let us take our places. They are almost here."

By the door, Silas saw the small table, with the ewer of water from the Lethe spring. The black stone scepter lay next to it. Beside the table, closer to the door, were several cords of dry wood. There were buckets of what smelled like pitch, and a few feet away, an iron brazier stood upon a tripod, its flames weaving together, sending black smoke twirling toward the ceiling.

Seeing Silas looking at the wood, Jonas said simply, "A necessary precaution."

More nervous now than before, Silas took his place in front of the door. His hands were shaking and something Jonas had said set a bell ringing in Silas's mind. He clenched his fists to still his hands.

Silas looked behind him, as though he might reach back and

pick up the black scepter, for fortitude. But Jonas said, trying to steady him, "The only power you need to govern the Door Doom already rests within your hands. You need no other."

The three robed spirits arrayed themselves along with Maud and Jonas in a semicircle before the doors of the great hall. Jonas looked at Silas and was about to speak, but Silas, determined not to be led along, spoke first with a loud voice that wavered only a little. "Now let the dead be called to the hall of judgment. I, Janus, Lord of the Threshold, open the door! Let the Doom commence."

The words tasted like ashes in his mouth, but Silas was determined not to be humiliated in front of his family by doing or saying something wrong. As on the previous night, he raised his hands and moved his arms apart, and slowly, in like manner, the doors opened.

At first the opening framed only darkness. But then Silas saw movement beyond the threshold, shadows lurched just outside the wedge of light cast outward from the torches and candles of the great hall. Shambling forms approached the door, some with dragging feet. Silas could hear heels being scraped across the ground as though they were being pulled roughly by invisible ropes. One figure stood ahead of the others and raised an arm. Was it in fear, an attempt to stop what was happening? Or was it a salute?

A voice leapt up, strong, deep, and sure of itself, from the figure at the front of the crowd.

"Hello, the house!"

Silas knew the voice. He instantly recognized its proud timbre, but he could also hear how the bravado was tinged with fear. Slowly, the awkward human shapes approached, and as they stepped upon the Limbus Stone, they froze, and the light from the hall fell upon them all.

Augustus Howesman stood upon the Limbus Stone with

the other Restless from Lichport. Despite his predicament, he carried himself nobly. Next to him, expressionless, was the old woman from Fort Street, the lady from the garden, her hat still alive with weeds growing from the band and brim. Flanking them were others, perhaps ten or twelve in all. Men and women. Some bore an absent expression, their jaws hanging slack. Most seemed aware that something was happening to them. All of their eyes pierced the doorway questioningly. Only the entropy cast upon them by their long years of existence slowed their facial reactions. But all their mouths had begun to move as they whispered desperately among themselves.

Silas stared in disbelief. He told himself it was a play of the light, or his nerves, that had called up the image of his great-grandfather out of desire to be with someone he could trust absolutely. But it was no illusion. The corpse of Augustus Howesman stood before him, and Silas could feel his presence, the bond of love between them. He was struck dumb. Of all the dead to call to the Doom. *Them?* They hadn't hurt anyone. They haunted no one. They lived in their own houses. The irony of someone like Jonas Umber, a ghost in his own house, judging these people, made Silas feel sick.

Silas tried to speak, but no words came. His face was flushed. Shock and anger tightened his jaw.

Jonas glanced at Silas's face. He leaned over quickly and said, his mouth close to Silas's ear, "I know, family is difficult. We shall walk through this together. I can say the words for you. So long as you're present and approve, that will suffice to make the Doom binding on the deceased. The Restless are much easier. They rarely fight. Especially if someone they know is consigning them to oblivion. All you need to do is be sure they are on the Limbus Stone, then say the words, and I will—"

"You tricked me!" shouted Silas.

"No, Silas, I am trying to help you."

"You are trying to turn me against my family! My father has offended you in some way, and now you are punishing me for it because you can't get at him anymore."

"Silas," Maud interjected, trying to calm him, "*we* are your family."

"Family is more than blood and bloodline," Silas railed at her, "more than a name!" He could see now why she had been against this happening. She knew he'd be furious. This was not Maud's doing or a part of her plans. He turned back to Jonas and shouted, "How could you expect I would go along with this? What were you thinking?"

"There is no need to lose your composure. Do not take the work personally. We did not cause the condition that afflicts the corpse that stands before you. We merely seek to cure it of this curse."

"He is not an *it*!"

Jonas looked wounded. "I see you and your father indeed share more than a name. Silas, listen to me. What you see before you is corruption. It is an abomination of nature. We need not become hysterical. It is merely our job to restore order, and we can absolutely do that. I have done it many, many times. Do what must be done. I promise you, it will get easier and easier. In time, you will come to take satisfaction from your work. I swear."

"Enough!" Silas snapped. "That was your life! This is mine! I refuse to bring the Doom down upon these people. Can't you see how incredibly stupid it is for you to claim any moral high ground here? You are a ghost! You are dead like them!"

"I most certainly am not dead like them. You speak as if you think I am some unnatural thing."

"That's not what I said."

"Let me assure you, I am nonesuch!" said Jonas, the flames in the brazier rising higher behind him. "Even before incarnation in the act of birth, spirit is present. When death comes, spirit remains though the body decays, dissolves. Those you see in this house, the ghosts of your family, we are not like the putrid corpses you see before you, neither are we like those poor shades who grow quiet too soon, who give up so easily in death and consign themselves to an eternity of silence. We are the enduring essence of life itself. Pure souls who—"

Silas waved his hands in the air as if to dispel Jonas's words.

"No more philosophy. You have asked me to do something. You have the right to ask. I refuse. That is my right. Now I am going home, as is also my right. If you continue to argue with me, to coerce me, or try to stop me in any way, when I leave this house, I will shut these doors so that they shall never open again," Silas proclaimed coldly, though he was unsure whether or not he could actually seal the doors of Arvale.

Jonas's face fell. The air around him soured as he stared at the floor. "Always and always it is to be the same. As with the father, so with the son." He looked up. "Silas, there is no need to threaten us with imprisonment. It is merely redundant." Jonas closed his eyes. He looked at Silas miserably, as if the words he was speaking were diminishing him.

Jonas gestured with his hand and many of the spirits in the room fell away, through wall, through floor, passing beyond the candlelight. When the hall had become absolutely silent, Jonas spoke softly to Silas alone.

"Silas, in you now is the blood of all your kin—"

"Please, I want no more lectures."

"Hear me out, I beg you. Then I will be silent on the matter and you can do as you please."

Silas nodded, his breathing slowing slightly.

"In your veins is the blood of many extraordinary people. Some noble, some kind, some loving, a few wretches, to be sure. There are certain tendencies, particular gifts. Again, some are a boon, others . . . less so. From your mother's side, from your great-grandfather's line, comes the potential of something very unpleasant. You see it before you now. You must fight such inclinations, both in the dead and in *yourself.* To indulge such tendencies could . . . complicate your ongoing work. You would become something very terrible, something infinitely worse than a mere walking corpse."

"Are you saying I am going to be like him when I die? That I will *continue*?"

All the color went from Silas's face. He loved his great-grandfather, as much as he had ever loved anyone, but he wasn't at all sure he wanted to be *like* him.

"I cannot see the future. I am saying it is *possible*. After making a life's study of the *ataphoi*, of the Restless, I believe that there may be a choice involved. I am saying that if you are dedicated to eradicating those who suffer from this illness, you may be less likely to share their fate."

Silas stood unsure of what to say. In the heavy silence, Augustus Howesman peered inside and spoke up in a kind and encouraging tone. "Silas, it's all right. I don't want you to come to any harm, son, and I don't want you to worry. You can let these folks have their way. If *you* need this to happen, it's all right. If it will help you to become what you want to become, I'll step down. Hell, you know it's only mere curiosity that keeps me going . . . that, and my love for you. Stand tall if you must. If need be, I'll call it a day. And if my spool's about to run out, well, son, I'd just as soon it be you who cuts the thread."

Silas couldn't feel his limbs. He would never do anything that would bring harm to his great-grandfather. Love and instinct drove him on.

He stepped toward the doorway and said, "Great-grandfather, is it your wish to take the waters and forget and pass on beyond?"

"Not particularly, no. But I will, if it will help you."

A hopeful smile crept across Jonas's face.

Silas's eyes were sodden with tears.

"Augustus Howesman, great-grandfather, step back from the threshold into the world again. Return with your neighbors and friends to your true homes and never again heed the call of this house, unless it is your express wish to do so."

Silas raised his hand and the door began to close. "I, the Janus of the doorway and Undertaker of Lichport rel—" but Jonas rushed forward cutting off his words.

"Stop!" he shouted at Augustus Howesman. "You are not released. You are bound to the threshold and must remain. Do not stir a step from this place, Augustus Howesman! In the absence of the required words, I shall pronounce the Doom upon you!"

Maud ran forward, crying desperately. "Jonas, you must not! It is not your place. Please! You'll drive the boy from the house! He will leave us! Let these others go for the boy's sake!"

Without thinking, Silas grabbed the black scepter from the table, and ran to stand between Jonas and his great-grandfather. As he held it up, he felt all the muscles in his arms pull taught as though a current had been put through them. The heat ran from his hand up his arms and into his torso, radiating through his body like a spreading fever.

"Silas, what do you think you're going to do with that? Shoo him from the porch? Shatter the Limbus Stone?" said Jonas incredulously.

Silas looked at Jonas coldly. "It's not for him. I was just wondering, Jonas, what would happen if I struck you with it."

At the threat, Jonas moved swiftly backward through the air, retreating as far away from Silas as he could while remaining in the hall.

Maud joined Jonas at the back wall. Seeing Silas wield the scepter clearly frightened them. Now Silas knew they would not stand against him.

Much of the anger had left Jonas Umber's face and was replaced with a mask of desolation. Silas stared at Jonas, daring him to speak. *Good,* Silas thought, *now I will finish this my way.* He turned back toward the door in preparation to release his great-grandfather and the other Restless. Suddenly, Silas heard a sound from outside that was both awful and familiar, a cry, somewhere near the outer wall of the house, just beyond the door. It was that moaning, the soft, pitiful crying Silas had heard in the sealed cell down in the catacombs. It swiftly rose in pitch, shattered the cold quiet of the night outside, and tore through the walls as though the stones and bricks of Arvale were made of cloth.

As the cry became a shriek, most of the remaining spirits in the hall fled. Something struck the roof of the house and howled along the battlements. A wail of pure anguish reverberated through the walls. One of the enormous oak corbels, covered with intricate carvings of birds, fell from its nest among the ceiling beams of the hall and broke to pieces as it struck the floor.

Maud seemed to assume the noise had started because of something Jonas had done. She turned upon him, shouting, "Jonas Umber! Your days of governance are long since finished. You may *not* preside over the Doom, nor command the dead in any way. In death we are all made equals. This is out of all proportion, and will bring harsh judgment down upon this house and everything we have built here. The Janus is present! You must not take upon yourself the—"

But Jonas rallied. "If the house is besieged by one such as him," Jonas said, pointing accusingly at Augustus Howesman, "I shall do what is required! Besides, Silas has yet to discharge the duty that would remedy all!"

The scream came again, and in that instant, with the harrowing shriek rending the fabric of the air, Silas knew the sound had nothing to do with the corpses standing silently in the doorway, some of whom had now turned to look above and behind them. Something was moving in the sky outside. Confusion grew on Jonas's face. But as Silas stared at the stone arch in the wall and its small door leading down to the catacombs, he knew in his gut exactly where the screaming spirit had come from.

Silas strode to the far side of the Limbus Stone, still holding the black scepter. As he walked past his great-grandfather, he touched the corpse's hand while holding the scepter as far away from the corpse as possible, unsure of what would happen if it touched him.

Feeling the confidence it gave him, Silas held aloft the scepter and called out into the night, making up the words as he went along.

"Spirit of the crypt, ghost of the catacombs, the Janus of the Threshold commands you to appear upon this stone and stand in judgment!"

The screaming continued, circling the chimneys above, and bricks came plummeting down into the clearing in front of the house. Silas looked up and saw the ghost hanging in the air. At first the spirit looked like a comet, wreathed in flame, slowly falling toward the earth. Then, as he stared, Silas began to discern the form of a young woman within the fire. As she flew closer to the house, flames trailed behind her like a serpent formed of smoke and ember. When she screamed, Silas clapped his hands over his ears, watching in fear as the flames flew from her mouth and scourged the battlements of the house.

Staying as far from the Restless as possible, Jonas came a little closer to the door and said to Silas, "Whatever, whoever she is, she is very old and will not be compelled merely by the force of your words. You must call her by her name to bring her to the stone."

Silas stood before the threshold.

"I do not know her name," he admitted in a near whisper.

Remembering Maud's visit to the library, how she pored over the family's genealogical records, Silas called back into the house, "Maud, do you know the name of this spirit?" There was only a resigned silence. Silas looked frantically from Maud to Jonas while above, the sound of the attack upon the house continued with mounting fury.

"How could anyone here know her name?" asked Jonas, angrily. "We have not seen her face. Silas Umber, you obviously know something of this matter! What has happened?"

Silas came back inside the house. "I saw initials on the door where she was imprisoned below."

Jonas's countenance went dark. He turned to Silas with accusation bristling in his voice. "What are you telling me? That *you* have done this? *You* have released something down in the catacombs, and set it free to wreak its malice upon this house? That *you*, whose particular work in the world is to *constrain* and *banish* the dead have, on a whim, *released* a spirit who had been deliberately imprisoned?"

"I didn't mean to. It was an accident. I only put my hand to the door. I will make it right."

"Which part of the Janus's authority did you not understand? As Janus, no door can withstand you. Ever."

"I didn't know you meant it literally. I didn't think you meant *any* door." Silas looked at the floor, embarrassed, shame reddening his face. He'd screwed everything up. Why couldn't people speak more plainly to him about what he could and couldn't do? *Because,* he told himself, *you aren't interested in taking instruction from anyone. Because you don't trust people and you don't inspire trust in them. Because, just beneath the Undertaker's mantle, lurks a child. A lost child.*

He looked up at Maud and Jonas, trying to sound confident. "I will find out her name." The tables had utterly turned. A moment ago, he commanded these spirits with force and conviction. Now he was the initiate again and he was apologizing, and he hated himself for it.

"Tell me the letters on the door," Jonas demanded.

"*D* and *M*."

Maud let out a gasp. Jonas closed his eyes and shook his head. "We are lost," he said.

"Why?" Silas asked desperately. "Those might be her initials. We'll consult the lineages in the library. We can figure it out."

"Those letters are not her initials, I assure you," said Maud.

"What are they, then?"

"A curse," said Jonas.

"Darkness without ending," said Maud.

"Horrible. Most horrible." Jonas shook his head in defeat. "She will not heed your call, Janus of the Threshold," he said coldly. "Indeed, the very house has been forbidden her or why else would she not be, this very moment, inside here with us bent on some act of destruction? Even the very bricks and mortar of this place are anathema to her."

"I don't understand," Silas said, trying to follow what Jonas was implying.

"*Damnatio Memoriae,*" whispered Jonas.

"What does it mean?" asked Silas.

"That her name has been erased from the world," said Maud.

Jonas walked up to the throne. "This task is too difficult, and we are cursed. Whoever did this to her had a hateful heart and a terrible power, perhaps even a Janus's authority or something stronger. That person was the last to know her name, and is the only one who would still know her name. This is beyond you, Silas Umber, because if her name has been torn from this world, she cannot be compelled. She will not heed you. We are accursed."

Jonas turned to the door where Augustus Howesman and his fellow revenants still stood, awaiting their Doom. "But at the very least, Silas, you can finish what was begun here today. Pronounce the Doom over the walking corpses. You cannot leave another door gaping wide. Do what is required, finish what you've begun, and close the threshold once more."

"I will not," said Silas forcefully, wanting to take back some authority.

"Silas, we have had enough—"

"I will renounce my role as Janus and leave this house. Now."

Jonas smiled thinly to himself as though he had heard this entire conversation before, as though everything Silas said was a mere echo of a speech that had bubbled up again out of the long-ago bog of the past.

"Hear me out," said Silas. "Here is what I propose: Augustus Howesman will return to Lichport with the others immediately, and will never again be called to the Door Doom. And then I will bring this furious spirit to peace even if it requires my own death to do so."

"Very well," Jonas said to Maud in resignation, "and at least if he dies in the attempt, then we shall all reside in this house on equal terms." Despite his wry words, Jonas's expression was downcast and hopeless. It was easy to see that Silas's resolution, his disobedience, so like something his father might have said in the past, together with the presence of the unbanished corpses on the threshold of his home, had broken Jonas Umber utterly.

"Silas," said Maud, "you have no need to ask our permission. You are Janus of this house. Do as you will and we shall abide." And as she spoke, she held up her hand before Jonas's face to ensure he'd say no more. But Jonas spoke again, very softly, words of care and sorrow both.

"Silas Umber, I am sorry I have failed you so. It was my wish to stand by you as you rose to your office and your destiny. I wished only to advise you upon the many perils that attend one of your position and talents. I had hoped, perhaps, you might even have helped those here whom you father has consigned to . . . well, it is of no consequence now. I am sorry to be of so little use to you."

Without another word, Jonas Umber left the great hall.

For an instant, Silas thought to call after him, to try to explain that things had changed, that not all the old ways needed to be adhered to and that prejudices of the past could be undone.

But then Silas looked outside where the revenants still waited nervously, and he couldn't bear to think of them having to remain at Arvale another moment. He walked outside onto the Limbus Stone and hugged his great-grandfather. "I didn't know this would happen . . . ," he began as he pulled the old man close, smelling the familiar tang of honey and pitch as it smudged from the corpse's coat onto his own.

Silas took a step back, steadied his voice, and said, "Augustus Howesman, you and your neighbors are free to go. You will never be called to this house again, not so long as I'm alive." He put his hand on the corpse's dark, taut-skinned cheek. "I love you, great-grandfather, but you're a lot of trouble for an old man. Now go. Do not look back and do not stop until you pass the gates. I will see you at home as soon as I can."

His great-grandfather's face was wrought with worry.

"Son, I hope so, I truly do." The corpse took his hand and squeezed it. "You be careful, Silas. Have eyes in the back of your head!"

"I will. I promise. Now go. Hurry!"

Augustus Howesman turned slowly around on the Limbus Stone as though his feet had been glued down. But as he strained, his feet came away. When he stepped off the stone, he moved more quickly, and strode away from the house, down the road leading toward the gate. The other Restless followed him. The trees beyond the clearing in front of the house suddenly cast out their tenants, and the skies filled with black shapes as crows flapped and cawed over the heads of the corpses, heralding their way back to Lichport.

Suddenly, words both strange and familiar formed in Silas's mouth and without meaning to, he began speaking out into the night.

"Let them pass from this place without harm or care. Let them return whence they came. Let nothing afright them or halt their progress in any way. Let no gate enclose them. May the words of the Janus hold fast, through night, through day, over water, in this world and in all others!"

Upset at the position he'd been put in, embarrassed by his stupidity in the catacombs, and exhausted at even the thought of the task now before him, Silas crossed the Limbus Stone and came back into the hall, as the screaming began again. The burning ghost had flown close to the tree line where the departing revenants had just passed. As she cried, her dreadful wail appeared to shake the air and loosen it, and the path leading back to the gates unraveled into shreds of darkness and fell away from the land. The road home had vanished. The pitiful condition of the burning ghost was now Silas's condition too: banished, homeless, lost.

The ghost flew back toward Arvale, and resumed rending portions of the masonry from the high walls as she wailed.

"Shut up!" Silas yelled back over his shoulder at the tempestuous air, and though the shrieking continued, the great doors, obeying the Janus's words, slammed shut and locked behind him.

Within the abyss of the underworld, Lethe flows and meanders gently on, and draws away our cares. So we may have no way to retrace our steps, it onward glides with windings many, its vagrant stream falling back upon itself, then pressing onward, always turning one way, then another, thus we are never sure whether we seek the sea or its source.

—FROM SENECA, *HERCULES FURENS*, TRANSLATED BY JONAS UMBER

CHAPTER 21

STEPPING DOWN

JONAS UMBER STOOD at the back of the hall watching Silas release the abominations standing on Arvale's threshold, his heart breaking. He'd wanted only to help the boy. Long ago, he'd nearly given up hope of seeing a new Janus rise to hold the Door Doom. Then Silas Umber came to Arvale, and Jonas allowed himself to imagine things changing, even that Silas might open the doors to those imprisoned in Arvale by his father, Amos. But almost as soon as he'd arrived, it was over before it truly started. Silas would go the way of the father. A dark road. The boy's life had begun in shadow and lament, and it would now end the same way. Jonas knew that now as surely as he knew his own name.

Jonas could not wait and watch what was coming. He wasn't strong enough. It would shatter him and then what would be left? Ahead lay terrible mysteries he did not wish to see enacted. Now he only wanted to be gone from Arvale. But the doors were closed to him. No way forward. No way back. Amos Umber had left the ghosts of the house only one choice.

Jonas passed through the small door and descended the long stairs into the catacombs below Arvale. He had come this way before in life, as Undertaker, as Janus. He had never walked this path in death, but he could feel his own presence from long ago. Retracing his steps moved him deeply. He was going back to the beginning, back to the source.

He arrived in the chamber where the two springs flowed up from deep in the cold earth. The guardians who stood before the spring of memory did not move. There was no welcome. No fanfare. It was over. His life was far, far behind him. Now his death would be set aside as well.

He knelt down by the spring whose origins were that distant river of forgetfulness called Lethe. Jonas leaned over, put his mouth to the waters, and was Jonas Umber no more. He felt the cold enter him, the beautiful cold, like the night, like the distant stars.

A stream flowed away from the spring, and the spirit followed it without haste or intention. It wandered through forest and beyond the low sand hills that run their way to the sea. The spirit wandered on in joy, bearing no weight, no memory of its life or what came after. And in the twilight fields where Death and Sleep join hands and all worldly cares are no more, the spirit lay down among golden flowers and slept and did not dream.

CHAPTER 22

LOST CHILD

AFTER THE DOORS OF ARVALE SHUT, Silas could hear Maud calling him from the fire at the far end of the room, gesturing for him to follow her. She led him through a passage lined with bronze mirrors, past a door of polished amber, and into the familiar library. She walked to the arched window, peering out through the stone tracery at what was left of the night. In the distance, the screaming of the furious spirit could still be heard like a challenge to the coming dawn.

"Why do you think she's so angry, Silas? I thought I caught a glimpse of her through the window. She is young; she died little more than a child. What did you see below in the catacombs?"

It's to be twenty questions, then, Silas thought wearily. For a moment, he had allowed himself to hope that Maud was taking him aside to tell him something that might help him.

"I saw only the door and the prison that once held her. There was a tiny doll. When I first saw it, I thought it was a baby, but its head was carved of wood. It was a toy."

"A little doll, you say?" Maud's face came alive with interest.

"Yes, and there were bones too. She was indeed young, I think maybe in her early teens. I'm not sure."

"But no bones of the baby?"

"It wasn't a baby. It was a doll—"

"Yes, yes, of course. A doll," she said, correcting herself, but her tone was knowing.

"It was a girl who had been locked in there. The door was sealed. She must have done something very awful. Yet, when I touched the door, I could sense something of the mind of whoever imprisoned her. Someone hated her."

"Yes. Whatever the reason she was put away, it is distressing to think of her remains, let alone her mind, down below, souring, hardening over, hate and fear burning her heart. So much of her is still present in her wrath and fury. You can feel it, can't you? She'll never know peace in such a state. And she has grown very strong in the fullness of time and her imprisonment. To come against the house like that . . . she is *powerful*. You've heard her wailing. The sound unhinges my mind. Indeed, I can barely remember my own name when she's screaming out there. How it pierces the walls . . ."

"Why is she damaging the house? Bricks were falling outside—what is she doing, prying them loose? Throwing herself against the battlements? Why?"

"I suspect it is her condition, in close proximity to the house. The very mortar of this place *is* memory, and when she draws near to the stones, they crumble before her. That is what's causing the damage. Her very nature is forgetting and loss, the curse of no name, of having been deliberately forgotten. She causes dissolution wherever she appears now. It may be that some spirits of this house have already suffered in the wake of her siren's cry. The house is not immune to her power. Neither are you."

"The land, or the road home . . ."

"Indeed. Even the topography of the estate is assaulted and changed by her condition. She cannot find her way home, or toward whatever it is she is seeking. Neither shall anyone else find their way so long as her cry is heard at Arvale. Your great-grandfather was fortunate; I suspect the revenants shall be the last folk to leave Arvale until this matter is settled. Without laying her to rest, I think you would not be able to leave this place, even if you wanted to. And if you remain, and do not restore order, she will bring the place down about our heads a brick at a time. Given long enough, Arvale shall be no more. She must be brought to the threshold so the Doom may be settled upon her. This is no punishment. She is beyond helping herself. She cannot let go of her hate. You must make her take the waters and forget what has happened to her. That is the only way. Do what you can, and if it means the end of this house, well, you will have tried your best and we shall all perish together. I shall be content."

Silas walked closer to her chair. He could almost bring himself to admire her detachment, her distance. "Maud, you have been here longer than most. What is this place, really? This house? Where are we?"

She waited a moment before answering, making Silas wonder if she was trying to come up with a safer explanation. "Arvale is present here, as you find it. But it is also present for me in my own time. There is no 'we'. You and I are not of the same moment. All my moments were long ago."

"Are you saying we are in different houses?"

"In a sense."

"But you are still here."

"Am I?"

"Well," Silas said, laughing uncomfortably, "I think so. I am talking to you."

"Silas, for all you know, you are talking to some part of yourself. What if everything and everyone in this house were merely a portion of your own mind given shape and voice and presence?"

Silas didn't like the way the conversation was turning. The more he considered Maud's words, the more schizophrenic he felt.

"How can that be? I don't know what you know, and you've told me lots of things I know nothing about."

"How do you know you don't know them?"

"I—I just know."

"Well, then! Silas, I'm not saying I am right about any of this."

"Do you mean my being here is all an accident? Just happenstance?"

"No. Because I called you here."

"*You* called me?"

Maud quickly corrected herself. "I mean *we* called you here, the family called you so that you might be Janus."

"I think we both know there is more to it than that now," said Silas, hoping to draw her out.

"Silas, perhaps I will just leave it at this: We are who we were. You carry this house, and indeed, the entire family, in your blood. You are here because you are an Umber, and all Umbers find their way to this house, eventually. Family does not end. It endures. Through life, beyond death. We are all here now together, for good or ill. The world outside is changing, winding down to its inevitable end. Yet, this house remains, a bulwark against time. Such places endure because they are remembered, in the blood and in the imaginations of their dependents. You carry this house in your blood and in your name. So here we are."

Silas looked up at Maud and smiled, though he did so halfheartedly. He could feel the sincerity of her words. The Undertaking every day confirmed it. Yet that didn't mean everyone he was related to was good, or didn't have their own agendas, which he knew, just *knew*, Maud did.

Maud looked away from Silas and out the window over the estate, saying, "I don't know who this girl is you've let out of the catacombs. But, I know you can find her name and help her. I know this because I know something about you. You were a lost child, Silas. You have never been at peace in the world. You wander from place to place, settling the accounts of others, and only recently have you found your own home. That home comes from helping those who are, like you, lost. And because of your youth, you are especially predisposed to find what you are yourself. Lost children are your speciality." As she as spoke, her face hardened. A desperate gleam shone from her face, like the flash of ember before it either leaps again to flame or goes out.

Silas had not forgotten the Bowers of the Night Herons, could never forget the ghosts of the playground. Maud's words were true and he knew it, and he was beginning to believe she might even know something about his own past experiences. Yet her words came so easily, as though she was speaking a well-practiced script. A daily prayer. She'd been waiting to say these words since he arrived at Arvale. Silas also suspected she knew more about the anonymous ghost than she was letting on.

"Maud, if this nameless spirit is an actual child of this family, a lost child, where do you think I should begin to look to find her name?"

Maud continued to gaze absently out the window, her voice became low, and she put one hand on the stone casement to steady herself. "Silas, you are the expert on such matters, not I." She put an arm up to cover her eyes as if she were planning to weep. "Indeed, I lost a child once, and the topic is very hurtful to me."

Her voice wavered, yet her tone hinted at her anxiousness to keep speaking. She was purposefully trying to draw him in.

"I'm so sorry, Aunt Maud," Silas said, going along. He was beginning to guess what she wanted from him. "Where is your child now?"

"Limbo," she said in a whisper. "The Limbo of the Innocents."

"But isn't this house a kind of limbo? Is your child lost somewhere in this house?"

"This house shares many qualities with Limbo. But it is not *the* Limbo, the one I learned about in life. That is a very particular place where children go. Or, rather, where they once went. Long ago, before I came to better knowledge of my estate, I thought I would come across him, my son, somewhere. If I waited long enough, one day, I would open a small door in some corridor and there he'd be, wrapped in a swaddling cloth, waiting to be picked up like a Moses child. That day has never come, and all these years he has been lost to me. He is in Limbo and cannot come out. Not until the breaking of the world, or until he is *brought* forth. I have prayed for him."

"Is there nothing you could do to get him out yourself?"

She was clearly trying to hold back her rising grief, but she bent forward and started to shake softly. The edges of her gown's hem seemed to unravel and pool about her like falling water. Her words were muffled by the long woolen sleeve that she'd drawn up to catch her tears.

"Even at the time of his death, I tried to help him. I traveled to the shrine at Avioth, in Lorraine. Perhaps it still stands. A miraculous statue of the Virgin had been found there long, long ago upon a bush of thorns and called *The Welcoming One* . . . or by some, *The Receiveress*. Many grieving mothers went to Avioth with the corpses of their babies, for it was known that if a child had been stillborn or had likewise died without rite of baptism, he could be brought there and the power of the shrine might briefly return the child to life. So many lost children. So many parents desperate to have them back."

"What was the purpose of restoring the baby's life for just a few minutes?"

"A corpse cannot be baptized, Silas. It was revived so that the priest might then baptize the living child, and when life fled the infant again, its soul might enter Paradise and not be sent to Limbo."

"Did it work?" Silas asked, feeling Maud's desperation, his voice beginning to catch in his throat at the thought of those parents holding their unmoving children in their arms.

"For many, yes. I myself watched a tiny stillborn infant . . . saw her skin flush, the blood turning from black to red . . . the hands moving this way and that. I witnessed the miracle. But there was nonesuch for me and mine. I shall never forget the sight of my baby upon that cold stone, still and lifeless. A wind rose and blew out the candles of the shrine and I knew there would be no beneficence. I left that place and buried my child on the north side of a small church. The *north side*, Silas, oh! The burial ground of the lost!" Maud sobbed freely for several moments, but opening her eyes once more, she breathed in deeply and said, "Oh, Silas, this was so long ago. Each age of the world has its own beliefs and which are true and binding in their time. When this happened, children who died without having been baptized went to Limbo. This was not an opinion, or a guess. It was fact. At that time, Priest, not Peller, held authority. The priest told me my child was in Limbo, and so that is where he was and where he remains. It was explained to me very plainly, and I shall never forget those words, such as they were then, burned into my heart, each one:

> Yf a chylde be deade bore—
> Thogh it were qwyk in womb before—
> And receive not the baptime,
> Of Hevene may yt never claime;
> With-oute doute, beleve ye thys,
> Tht yt shal never come to blys.

"And, so I am bound, in this earthly purgatory, until I might hold a loving child in my own arms. You yourself can attest to the power of a child's love. Let us recall, a woman once ascended to the throne of Heaven, all for the love of a child. Even though mine is trapped in Limbo, I have tried to see my child at peace, to imagine his contentment. The accounts in my day were numerous, and there was much disputation by the church fathers about Limbo. I have tried to imagine a place filled with children, quietly waiting, together."

"There are such places still. I have seen one," said Silas, softly.

Maud lifted her head and stared intensely at Silas.

"Were the children there happy? Were they at peace?"

Silas held back, not wanting to hurt her further, but Maud looked at him with such sharpness, such desperation, that he could not turn away or refuse her, as though the weight of her sorrow exerted a kind of gravity.

"I think most would have been happier elsewhere. None were in pain. But I think they understood their condition was one of loss and isolation. They understood they were incomplete. They knew they were not home and not among their kin."

Maud looked back toward the window and began to weep again, choking out her words through her soft sobs. "He passed so quickly, perhaps even before he came forth from me, and there was not time for a priest. I never had even a moment to hold him while he lived. He is the reason . . . oh, Silas. But this breaks my heart. And it pains me to ask this—"

Here it comes at last, Silas thought with pity and apprehension both.

"Perhaps there is something you could do?"

Silas stood and could not speak. He didn't know what to say, or what exactly she was asking of him. She wanted him to restore her child's spirit to her? He wasn't sure how to answer, though he could see his silence was upsetting her. He now understood that she had been waiting to ask him this since they'd met. Maybe this was why Maud wanted him here in the first place. She was shaking as she waited for a reply.

"Maud, I'm not—"

Anticipating refusal, she turned on him, crying loudly.

"Go on, Silas! If you will not help me, leave me here to my grief and be gone! But think on this: We are kin. Does this not obligate you to help me if you can?" Her face began to twist with frustration and tears of fire flowed from her eyes. "You have helped others! Strangers! Brought their children back to them. Out upon the marshes! You brought those mothers children to love. Even when the children were not their own, they were set free of their sorrows! How could you help them and not me? Why will you not do for me what you have done for them?"

So she knows something of my work in Lichport, Silas realized, his nerves pulling taut.

Her voice rose into a scream. She was becoming hysterical. As if in answering chorus, the nameless spirit beyond the walls howled from the battlements. A wind rose up outside and sent its blast down the chimney, blowing a shower of sparks from the fireplace into the room.

"Maud, I don't know how much you've seen of my work in the marshes back in Lichport, or how you've come to know about it. But most of those children's mothers had long ago passed on— those women in the marshes were content to hold the spirits of children not their own."

"I would be likewise content, I promise you!" she begged.

Silas was at a loss. This made no sense to him. "Are you asking me to bring you the ghost of a child? Some lost child from somewhere? Wouldn't that merely be consigning the child to another kind of perdition? Why would you desire such a thing?"

"You have not a mother's heart," she whispered. Then, raising her voice in accusation, cried, "So you think me so poor a mother, then? Say it, Silas Umber, and be done!" She had risen off the floor and a bleak, miserable light emanated from her body.

"No. Maud, I'm sure you would have been a great mother, would still be a great mother," Silas said, trying to calm her, "but where would I find such a ghost? How would I get it here? In a tin? Do you want me to force it here to Arvale? This is too much, really! Are you asking me to summon a child's spirit to the Limbus Stone? Just look up any name of a dead baby in these scrolls and summon it? It would be terrified. What kind of mother would subject a child to such treatment?"

She gave no answer to his questions, but only posed questions of her own.

"Are you not the Undertaker? Do you mean to say that in all the misthomes between heaven and hell there is not some child in need of keeping? Have you not already walked the lychways? Is this not your own especial work?"

"Yes, but this feels different. In those other cases, I knew where I was going. Some of them I could enter only because my own experience was linked to the nature of the shadowland itself. But maybe I could try to—"

"Or in this house? You can feel the pain of children. How else could you have heard that spirit down below? You might search the chambers of this house. Who knows what you, with your particular gifts, might find? My misery has closed many doors to me. Will you not try? Let the lost call out to the lost!"

"I am not lost," Silas said, his voice unsteady.

"As you please," Maud replied in a terse whisper as she turned away.

"Maud, please, you are not hearing me. I do not think—"

But she'd had enough excuses. She tore at her hair and wailed as Silas looked on, unsure how to calm her. He wanted to tell her that his work at the marshes had been based on guesses, that he hadn't known then if anything he did would work.

"Maud! Maud!" Silas couldn't think of anything to do but call her name. She would not answer. She sobbed frantically, casting aside the reins of self-control, her words an unintelligible mix of misery and Latin. Silas stood there, unsure what to say or do. Maud looked down from where she hung on the air and spoke through her tears once more.

"Go! Find *your* lost little girl! Leave me now to recover myself. Perhaps when you have settled your own mistakes you might again consider your obligation to your own kin. Until, then, leave me to my grief. Silas, go!

In her face, Silas saw pain and betrayal, but something else. Was it revelation or resolve? She had learned something from him, or figured out something for herself. He didn't like not knowing what had she had gained from their exchange.

She drew her hand over her eyes to dry them.

Before Silas could speak again to comfort her, she rang her small bell furiously and Lars came running to the doorway. When Silas turned back to Maud to say good night, to tell her to be easy, that he would try to help her, she was gone.

As she departed the library, Maud Umber's shoulders grew heavy, for she wore both sorrow and shame about her like a shawl of iron. She had shown her hand too soon. Silas knew what she wanted and how desperately she wanted it. She had pushed too hard and he had refused to help her.

Maud retreated to her private chapel. She lit no candles. Her tears were quickly drying. *What to do now?* she considered. *Perhaps Silas is truly unable to help me. Perhaps I brought him here too soon.* Yet, it might still all be for the good.

She thought she knew who had been released in the catacombs: perhaps the lost daughter of the one imprisoned in the sunken mansion. Yes. That seemed more than likely. Who else would have called out like that to Silas? What other spirit could sense so particularly Silas's gifts? It must be the lost daughter. What a miserable time in the house that had been. Now her mind was turning, striving to call up the events of six hundred years ago. The girl's name was stricken from the world. The *Damnatio Memoriae* had done its awful work, but the threadbare events of the past still hung in Maud's memory. The father had punished the daughter. Why was that? Had there been a child? *Yes.* The girl had a baby, in secret, and the father had *put her away*, but not before there had been terrible curses all around and the threat of worse. But what had become of the baby? How in wrath the father had scoured the house and the forest for it! If Silas found the girl, he might find the baby, too . . . and then . . . the girl might be put back in the catacombs, the poor immoral thing. Or, she might take the waters and the baby could remain . . . *in the house. With me. Like the spirits of the mothers of the marshes, another child could bring me peace. And then . . . would I then ascend to some higher seat?* she wondered. If she was right about what and who the girl might be, why, there was already a bond. Had she been quicker to help, things might have gone another way long ago, the baby might even have come to her then. *Yes,* she thought, *this could be the ending of my many sorrows. Perhaps Silas's settling of that terrible and ancient spirit could, in its way, serve to bring me peace.* Silas would find the ghost's lost name.

Already, Maud could feel the house changing around her, passages and halls long sealed, now throwing wide their doors for the new Janus; old spirits stepping forth from the very stones of the walls, eager to speak to the one who might one day command them all. All she needed to do now was wait. *Abide, abide,* she told herself, *and all shall come to joy.*

In her mind, like the dawning of the midwinter sun, there rose a small bright vision of the child. Only a child. Nothing more. She closed her eyes and could almost feel it in her arms. Silas would find the name of the lost girl, and bring her to the Limbus Stone. He would. He promised. Maud prayed that it might be so.

"O Holy Mother, Lady who is the defense of all, Glorious Queen of Heaven, preserve me now when my eyes are heavy with shadow and the darkness of death, and the light of the world is hidden from me. Oh, most gentle Lady, who was borne through the mist and into the midst of the angels and archangels and stood singing to thy glorious child, succor and preserve me in this dread hour when my heart's ease waits close at hand . . . ," she began, her words falling away into desperate repetitious whispers. "Let him find the name he seeks. Let him bring home the child, and bring it to me, and all will be well and all will be well and every good thing shall be well."

Maud grew quiet. She lit a candle and sat in her chair within the glow, imagining the weight of a child, any child, in her arms. She looked with longing and jealousy both at the statue of the heavenly mother and the baby seated on her lap. When she'd lost her child she lost herself, her place as Undertaker, and any status she'd once held in the family. Her death had not improved matters, but only brought her grief into terrible focus. She knew this, she'd always known it, but she could not see beyond it. Only a child could bring her peace. She reached out for the statue. The carving was smooth with a patina of devotion and desperation. She took it from the altar and cradled the statue in her arms, rocking her body back and forth. She closed her eyes and began to sing so softly that her breath did not disturb the candle flame.

> Lully, lullay, thou little tiny child,
> by, by, lully lullay.
>
> O sisters too, how may we do,
> for to preserve this day,
> this poor youngling for whom we sing,
> by, by lully lullay.
>
> Herod the king in his raging,
> charged he hath this day,
> his men of might, in his own sight,
> all young children to slay.
>
> Then woe is me, poor child, for thee!
> And every morn and day,
> for Thy parting not say nor sing
> my, my, lully lullay.
>
> Lully, lullay, thou little tiny child,
> *now mine*, lully lullay . . .

CHAPTER 23

SOLAR

LARS WAS STANDING OVER SILAS, shaking him.

"Let go of the dream and wake!" Lars shouted, clutching Silas's shoulders.

Silas threw his head from side to side. His hair and face were soaking wet, as if water had been poured over him in his sleep. He was sitting upright in the bed. His eyes were wide open, and he was staring in terror at something not in the world of the room. Lars looked frantically over his shoulder to be sure. The chamber was empty but for the two of them.

"Silas Umber, wake!" said Lars, striking him with an open palm across the cheek.

Silas's head fell back, then rolled to the side, his eyes fluttering, but a moment later, he spoke.

"Lars?" he asked hoarsely.

"I am here," Lars answered.

Silas looked up, his breathing labored. He was gasping as though there had been no air in the room. He could see the real worry on Lars's face.

"It's okay," said Silas finally. "I'm okay."

"What did you see?" asked Lars.

Silas shook his head, not wanting to answer.

"Silas—"

"Nothing more than I deserve," was all Silas replied.

There was only the sound of their breathing in the bed chamber.

Outside the window, the howling had stopped. A sallow light crawled in through the casement. *Perhaps the furious spirit only comes at night?* Silas thought as he rose from the bed. It might be morning.

Woven throughout the twisted bedclothes, books and scrolls were strewn across the bed. Silas had brought them from the library and he'd fallen asleep looking for a name or a clue to the identity of the spirit from the catacombs, all to no avail.

His plan was to return to the library and spend the day there, continuing to search through the enormous volumes of family genealogies. Then, when darkness fell, if the ghost returned, he would ascend the tower to see if he could speak with the spirit, or call her into any state of conscious presence. Silas thought that if he could get her to talk, there might be a chance of calming her, and hopefully bringing her Peace. It would be better, he thought, to try this without Maud or anyone else about. He found little comfort in the simplicity of his plan or the desperateness of the situation, but he knew nothing of the spirit or its past, and so would have to go gather shards and join them together as best he could.

He dressed quickly. Before leaving, he looked out of his window toward the front of the estate. Everything was as it had been before he'd slept: Bricks lay scattered on the earth below the walls, and the path home was still nowhere to be seen. The trees remained woven together as if the road to Lichport had never been.

Opening the door of his rooms, Silas could hear music drifting through the corridor.

Somewhere, a violin played an elder tune, all in a minor key, all filled with longing. The music seemed to be coming from the stones of the wall, or emanating from a lower room, below the thick wooden boards and carpet, or perhaps drifting down from above, sifting past the beams. It rose and fell, and Silas imagined it was the house, singing to itself. The tune, a reminder of some age long gone, hung upon the air like smoke as they made their way toward the library of Arvale.

"Where does all the family stay?" Silas asked Lars, who walked a few steps ahead of him, leading the way.

"I really cannot tell you. I have wandered the longest corridors, visited rooms on every side of Arvale, and have found only empty chambers. Truly, Silas, they must reside within the very bricks themselves."

When they entered the library, a fire was already burning upon the great hearth. Someone else had been there through the night. Without waiting, Silas began to explore the shelves, pulling out books and scrolls and piling them on the long table. Lars pretended to share an interest in the books for a few moments, but then took a pair of dice from his pockets and sat down on the floor and began to play with them idly.

Soon Silas was engrossed in reading, poring over pages, not entirely sure of what he was looking for, but hoping some hint of the spirit's identity would rise from the words before him. Lars sat upon the carpet, playing with the ivory dice. Lars rolled a nine and then tried to hand the dice to Silas. "Your turn, cousin."

Silas shook his head. "No, no. You roll for me."

"How do you know I won't cheat you?" Lars asked, raising an eyebrow.

Silas smiled but did not look up from the table. He reached down from his seat and put his hand briefly on Lars's shoulder, saying distractedly, "Go on, I trust you."

"So be it," said Lars.

Lars shook the dice vigorously in his hands. When he threw them to the carpet, they immediately fell and did not roll. He tried again, and again.

"Threes thrice. Silas, I think this does not bode well for you," Lars said, picking up the dice.

"Wait!" insisted Silas. "How many times was that?"

"You mean the threes? Two threes, three times in a row. What are the odds of such a thing, eh?"

The room was very still. The spectral music had stopped and the house drew in its breath and held it. Even the floating motes of dust appeared to pause upon the air. The three were not accident but omen. Silas remembered that the ladies of the Sewing Circle said they might see him in Arvale. They had helped in the past. They were more than ghosts, and he knew that they were not always bound to a place—for, once, hadn't one of them wandered with him upon the marshes? Strange as they were, the three had been helpful to him in their way. Many of his journeys about town, or beyond town, had required a visit with them. They stood watch over many thresholds. Now he was Janus. Maybe it made them all colleagues? And wasn't he setting out on a new path? Despite how nervous they made him, he realized he wanted to see them.

The air of the library grew warm and portentous.

Silas had made little progress with the books of pedigree and heraldry. No name had yet stood out. Maybe the little dice were showing him the way. Maybe the three were close and this is how they might signal to him. He looked to the fire, burning low on the hearth, and was sure he could discern a blue, preternatural hue in the three small flames dancing above the embers.

But where would they be in the vast expanse of Arvale? Silas had seen many tapestries in the house, here and there among the rooms and halls. None had ever stood out to him as worthy of their particular talents.

A thought occurred to him and he turned to Lars.

"Cousin, is there a place in the house where needlework is done, or was once done?"

"Indeed, there is a place that might have served in that way. The light is very good there. It is always empty though. Several times, it seemed that I might have just missed someone, because a piece of needlework was left there, unfinished. Needles still pierced the tapestry as though its maker had just a moment before fled the room. I go there sometimes for a bit of quiet. It's a very pleasant place, with the sun coming in through the rippled glass. It makes interesting designs on the floor."

"Can you take me there?"

"I shall try."

Lars threw the dice one last time. "Lucky seven! I win again."

"Lars," said Silas suspiciously, "I think the dice are rigged."

"Cousin Silas," said Lars with a face of purest innocence, "the game is always rigged. Or how else might a simple man find his fortune in this wretched world?"

They passed through gallery after gallery filled with the most extraordinary carvings Silas had ever seen: wildmen carrying staves of oak, satyrs dancing upon cloven feet, columns crowned in acanthus. Such excess implied that this part of the house could only have been made in the early seventeenth century. The next rooms and corridors showed still more masonry and were clearly much older, their surfaces worn smooth with the passage of time. Silas suspected they were moving closer to the outer walls of the house; the light was getting better and the stonework was more delicate with high arched windows. Lars suddenly laughed softly in relief.

"Here we are, Silas!" he said. "This is the solar."

The two young men came through a stone archway and into a high, bright gallery with windows lining the left-hand wall. In front of the windows, a wooden frame held an enormous tapestry that stretched from one end of the long gallery to the other. The tapestry's length was divided by the shadows cast by the portions of the outer walls between the windows. As he walked farther down its length, Silas could see that those shadows divided the tapestry's myriad subjects. Various ages of the mansion were depicted. At the far end of the gallery, there was a cave stitched in dun- and lichen-colored threads, thick and homespun with strands of . . . was it sinew? As the tapestry wove toward the far end, the images of the house grew larger and more elaborate, as if the house itself was moving, stitch by stitch, through time.

"Lars, I am sure of it. We are not alone here." An idea struck him. If the tapestry showed successive representations of the house as it progressed, there should be a panel of the house, now, as it was standing at this moment. Silas ran down the gallery. He stopped at a place far down the room where a warm, wide beam of light fell through the window onto the tapestry. He studied it closely.

"Lars! Come here!"

His boots slapped the wooden floors and echoed as he ran. Lars leaned over and looked where Silas was pointing. They gazed at a small portion of the embroidery depicting the house cut in half like an anatomical drawing. There, in a long gallery stitched in hastily worked brown and golden flax, stood two figures.

"That's you and me, just there," Silas said.

"You're mad . . . ," said Lars in a whisper as he looked closer, trying to identify something of himself in the tiny sewn figure.

Silas looked farther down. He couldn't make out anything

specific as the stitching moved away from him into the future. He wondered if he could follow his own story along. Silas stood up, and very nonchalantly began walking the rest of the tapestry's length. *Maybe just a little farther,* he thought. *Just another panel or two, to see if there might be a hint of how I might find out something more about our furious ghost. . . .*

"Oh, Silas!" chided a familiar voice right in front of him. "You know the rules. No peeking ahead!" It was the first of the three.

"And what have we here?" said the third. She looked closely at Lars and then down at the needlework. "This is a rather old thread, though I see now it was never bound off properly."

"I think it's lovely that Silas has found a friend," said the second very sincerely.

"Indeed!" said the first, leaning in so only Silas could hear. "Lovely Long Lost Lawrence Umber. How strange that handsome Lars should enter your story here and now."

Lars blushed in awkward embarrassment and looked down at the floor.

The third began to laugh.

"I wonder if it isn't because he and Silas have shared so much in common?" said the second with a sharp ironic tone.

"Enough," said the first, cutting in. "There is more there to see, if Silas would share with us his recent news."

"Reverend Ladies . . . ," Silas began, and, very carefully, with much attention to detail, outlined the recent events relating to the ghost released from the catacombs.

"Yes," said the first, "I can see by your looks you've had a hard time of this business. Shame can be an awful burden, especially for the young."

"And this is not the first time you've helped a troubled little maidy into the world, is it? What a gallant you are," added the third.

"Well," continued the first, "who can say why she has sat so quietly down below in the catty-combs and why she rose up in wrath? In some ways, she has been fortunate to only have been imprisoned, for some first-born children come to more devilish ends. But my sister is not wrong. What a knack you have for attracting women with issues, Silas. Truly. I wonder, might it have been your arrival that has annoyed her for some reason? Or perhaps the sounds of revelry from the upper halls? Music and good company are hateful to those not invited to the feast. Makes even the kindest soul go all Grendle-ish.

"It may be only partly to do with you. Perhaps her blood has been simmering all this time and has only just, with her release, rolled over into a boil. That seems unlikely, though. Most things fade in the lands of the dead, but not loss and not wrath. Those can remain a very long time, as you know. The forgotten condition of her life, the darkness and dampness of her prison-tomb, the taking away of her name—for that was stolen from her—see here?" the first of the three said, pointing to where the ghost was stitched in flame silk, but with gray binding cord about her chest. "We cannot discern even a hint of the face; that means something very special has been lost. A way. A name. A child. Hope. Yes. All her losses have left her little grace. Even should you find her name, she may not heed you. Even with your new title and lovely commanding stage voice."

"And see here, Silas," the second of the three said, pointing at the woven door of the underground cell. "These letters. Can you read them?"

"*D* and *M*. I saw them down there. I thought at first they might be initials of her name, but then—"

"Oh, no," said the first with steely certainty in her voice. "This we know very well, for it is part of a terrible rite going back to

Roman times. We know about that. We do indeed. That is very old, very awful magic, Silas. Whoever hated her, hated her very much. All die. But all may be remembered and so live. Except when *those* words are invoked. Crueler than death are *those* words."

Silas looked at the thickly stitched letters again on the tapestry and he said, wanting to sound knowledgeable, "Yes. *Damnatio Memoriae . . .*"

As he spoke, the three, for the first time since he'd known them, looked frightened and stepped back from him.

"Do not speak those words in our presence! Do not even whisper them."

"I'm sorry," said Silas. "I didn't know."

"*Qui non intelligit, aut taceat, aut discat*, Silas Umber!"

He looked back at them blankly.

The second of the three stared at him sternly, and said, "Those who do not know, must learn—"

"Or be silent!" spat the third.

The three took another step away from Silas and composed themselves.

"Silas Umber, you have come upon us very late here at Arvale. We have been waiting so long for you, and would have delighted in coming upon you sooner so we might have advised you to take greater care when traveling beneath the earth. But, there it is. We shall return to Lichport and await you, for the last act promises to be very fine and will require some preparation," said the third of the three.

"Oh, dear, yes," added the first. "You should not tarry too long in this place either, for look here." She pointed at a gray figure, sewn down horizontally against a blurry scene in rough wool yarn, newly begun on the tapestry. "Your mother . . . has looked better."

Silas quickly leaned over, trying to make sense of the stitches.

"What is going on?" he demanded. "What's happened to her?"

"Nothing," said the first.

"Yet," said the third.

"Only," continued the second, "she may be in for a bit of trouble. Hard to say. It's still too soon. But don't worry, Silas. If something befalls her, she may come to—"

"Enough!" snapped the first of the three. "There is no point speculating. There are many threads yet to be sewn down. They may not hold, and then who can say what will be? Let us be gone." But the first looked at Silas, who was now intensely worried, and her face softened in pity. She whispered with the other two and then spoke to Silas again.

"One more thing we will tell you, for since we are all met here at this time, it must be because you have great need of us. Look here at the tapestry, Silas. You require a respite from all this oppressive architecture. Fresh air! An attitude of recline. Seek the house of summer, if you wish to settle these family accounts and get home quickly. The folks who dwell in that place know something about this nameless ghost of yours, I warrant you. They have been here a *very* long time. Longer than even we can reckon. Look here!"

And the three showed him on the tapestry a spot where, a little away from Arvale's walls, there was a small summer house past the garden. Figures in white and green thread were stitched down and studded with little resplendent jewels. Beyond them, thin white silk trees grew from the top of a round, green hill.

"Yes, this is a family matter, Silas. Go and meet your cousins. They may know something of the beginnings of this, for they are often at their leisure and have seen much of the comings and goings upon this estate. They are not bound to the house, and so enjoy a . . . wider perspective."

"Now you should go, and be swift. Time runs through its glass for us all," said the first. "And as I've said, you've looked better."

"I'm fine," said Silas, shifting his weight from foot to foot.

"For the moment. Take care, Silas Umber."

Wanting to ask more about his mom, but knowing it was pointless to press them, Silas said, "Most reverend ladies of the cloth, I thank you." He bowed low, encouraging Lars to do likewise as they exited, walking backward out of the long gallery.

"Such polite young men," said the first and second as one as they returned to embroidering the image of a bull-headed man in bronze-colored thread.

"They just don't make them like that anymore," replied the third as she ripped some stitches from the tapestry a little farther along its length.

CHAPTER 24

GARDEN PARTY

SILAS BARELY GESTURED WITH HIS HAND and the great doors of Arvale opened, groaning upon their massive ornate hinges but obedient. He and Lars walked quickly out into the courtyard. The gray light afforded a better view of the surroundings, but the path to Lichport was still indiscernible. The trees had woven their branches into an impregnable thicket, and about the ground at their trunks, briars twisted in thorny spirals. Beyond the trees, there was only darkness. Until he settled this business, there would be no going home.

Lars led Silas to the north, staying close to the sheltering walls of the house. As they walked beneath scorched and blackened portions of the battlements, they had to pick their way around chunks of masonry, broken bricks, and shards of glass, all cast down by the assault of the nameless spirit the night before. Passing under an arch covered with roses, they soon came to a gravel path. On both sides, wild topiaries suggested the forms of animals now grown feral, subsumed below the unattended vegetation. Somewhere beyond, Silas could just hear the soft, distant roaring of the sea.

"It gets nicer just up there," Lars said, walking faster. He led Silas to the top of the path, but then refused to go any farther. Below them, the garden spread out in surprising beauty. Silas had expected something more overgrown, but this part of the estate seemed well-kept and thriving. Everywhere Silas looked, bright flowers spattered the plots with color. Running along the far side of the beds, between it and the forest, a wide green field lay, opulent with tall, swaying asphodel. Lars eyed the landscape nervously.

"Why so spooked?" Silas asked him.

"Do you see that field?" asked Lars.

Silas nodded.

"There have been great battles there, or so I've heard. Just below the sod, there is a deep layer of bones."

"So all it takes is an old battlefield to scare you?"

"No. *They* scare me."

"Lars, you expect me to believe that you wander around Arvale all day long and never bat an eye, but a little visit to the summer house in the garden and you're quaking? You're not seriously staying behind?" Silas asked.

"They frighten me, Silas. I said I'm not going and I'm not." Lars paused; he was breathing hard. "You remember when we spoke about the folk of the house, and how we're not like them?"

"Yeah?"

"Well, we are not like these people either. We are *really* not like them. They are not ghosts. They are . . . I don't know, Silas. . . . They are something else, something *older*."

"They are my cousins, Lars. Our cousins. Everyone says they're lovely."

"Then everyone is being polite. I've seen them hunting. They are not lovely, they're terrifying."

"If they're so terrible, why are you letting me go?"

Lars looked guilty, but said, "You'll be fine. They'll receive *you*. They're gentry. Act like a gentleman and you'll be all right. Do not be rude. About anything. You're one of them after all, a man of the manor. You'll fit in. You're *someone*. I will wait for you here."

Silas wasn't sure whether he'd been complimented or insulted. But he hugged Lars quickly, said he'd see him later, and continued down through the garden, passing fountains and shaped hedges. Silas realized to his surprise that the farther he went, the warmer the day became. When he'd left Lichport, it was the bitter cold of February. And Arvale's rooms were cold at any time of day unless a fire was lit. Here, flowers bloomed as though it were early summer.

He arrived at the bottom of the garden, where a tall ornamental stone arch stood, overgrown with wild roses, their petals red as blood. The smell was intoxicating, and Silas breathed in heavily. Somewhere before him, the sound of chimes softly drifted on the air.

Beyond the arch in front of him rose a low hill crowned with gray-skinned, ancient beech trees. All about the base of the hill, primroses thrived. Among the flowers was bright green lawn, and in the midst of that stood the summer house, its many shining windows and front door wide open. An old victrola was playing, the words floating gaily over the grass. . . .

> Hold your hand out, naughty boy!
> Hold your hand out, naughty boy!
> Last night in the pale moonlight,
> I saw you! I saw you!
> With a nice girl in the park,
> You were strollin', full of joy,
> And you told her you'd never kissed a girl before!
> Hold your hand out, naughty boy!

On the lawn, some of the cousins were playing badminton. Small tables bearing refreshments of the daintiest sort were scattered across the grass. Wooden and wicker chairs were placed here and there, all filled with smartly dressed people.

"What-ho!" cried a tall woman, throwing up her hand and waving. She wore a long velvet dress with a great swinging strand of garnet beads that glowed bloodred against her pale skin as they caught the light. Her enormous hat was tied to her head by what looked like a silk bandage wrapped over the hat and under her chin. She wore a lengthy diaphanous scarf that flowed like two gauzy pennants behind her as she walked. "This is never cousin Silas! I didn't believe it when I heard you'd come . . . and didn't you take your time to come and pay a call. Shame on you! But, my! How handsome you are. Lord! He's done the family proud, hasn't he? Come here immediately and embrace me, silly Silas! I'm your cousin Ottoline, quite the best person you know, I am sure of it!"

She waltzed across the lawn and took Silas in her arms and whispered in his ear, "You're not really dressed for a lawn party, you know. But we shall forgive you, just this once." She pulled Silas along behind her and called out to the rest of the party.

"Aggie! Monty! Rupert! Percy! Freddie! Vita! Puffy! Fruity! Ricky! Tipton! Mustard! LuLu! Can you guess who's here? Cousin Silas!"

Everyone set down their drinks and rackets and welcomed Silas to the party. They were the handsomest people Silas had ever seen. They all greeted him warmly but distantly. Ottoline pulled him away, wanting to keep him to herself, for a little family gossip.

Her skin was flawless and bore not a single wrinkle or any evidence of the passage of time.

"Goodness, but you look tired. How dreadful! Is it the awful screaming we've heard up at the house? What *is* all that commotion? There's been no word from the manor and all the servants are off, and here we are with only poor old Nursey to keep us in line. Isn't that so?" she shouted toward an elderly woman dressed all in white who was standing by a perambulator. Nursey was reaching down to give the baby inside a little toy, but looked up wearily at the sound of Ottoline's voice.

"Isn't that right, Nursey?" Ottoline's voice rose to a shout. "Only you here to keep us in line?"

The old woman rolled her eyes.

Ottoline leaned over and whispered to Silas, "She must hate us. Still, the child adores her and it's so hard to find good help in the country. The household staff are positively useless."

Silas followed Ottoline over to the chairs and sat down with her to watch the badminton. "Woodhouse?" she called. "Do be a darling and bring Silas a G and T, will you? There's a dear!"

A man in a long-tailed coat covered in gold braid, and with a back so straight it seemed he had never once bent over in his life, walked briskly back into the summer house. When he returned a few moments later, he was holding a neat little silver tray of glasses that all clinked together like bells.

When they had their drinks, the badminton resumed. Never taking her eyes off the game, Ottoline said to Silas, "Now, little cousin, perhaps you can tell me what all the noise is about. It's quite shattering my poor nerves every time that air-siren goes off over Arvale."

"It's no air-siren—"

"Yes. I *know*," Ottoline said, drawing out the last syllable. "The screaming, dear. Where is it coming from?"

Silas told her the story of his time in the catacombs and the nameless spirit's attack upon the house. With every word, Ottoline nodded, then began to look more and more impatient and increasingly annoyed. Her face seemed to come under a shadow, and she lifted one dark eyebrow up as if she was about to ask a question to which she already knew the answer.

"Silas, dear," she said, "why don't you simply ask her father to tell her to close her little mouth? Goodness, give the child a glass of milk or something. A spanking. A new doll. Whatever it takes to quiet the brat."

"I don't know who her father is."

"Don't you? I'd be happy to tell you if you promise to do something about the noise. I don't recommend spending much time with *those* sorts, however. We don't care for the father very much, I can tell you. But, if her own father doesn't remember her name, no one does."

"How do you know him?"

"We once shared an interest."

"May I ask . . . ?"

"Hunting. We used to come across him on the deer paths of the forest. In his day, he was more centaur than man, always on a horse, charging after boar, or deer, or whatever he could spear or shoot or catch. And never a word of thanks. Never. That did not sit well. Not tickety-boo. So, as he took from *us*, we took from *him*."

"Do you mean—"

"The daughter? The loud one? Silas, do follow along!" Ottoline pointed up toward the chimneys of the house in the distance. "Really, it was an honor, she never would have married well with a father like that. So one of our own little princes paid her court. Where's Robby?" she shouted back toward the summer house.

In front of the hill, the two badminton players—perhaps arguing over which side of the line the bird had fallen—had thrown aside their rackets and drawn thin, wicked-looking swords. They fought with such grace and speed that Silas could barely see the blades cutting this way and that through the air. "Ha!" one of the men shouted, taking a step back as the other raised his fingers to touch a thin, bloody line now running across his cheek. He smiled, and the onlookers all began to laugh.

"Well, I doubt he'd remember anyway," Ottoline continued. ". . . So many parties, so many paramours. And she loved him. Oh, my, didn't she? And he was so very amused, for a time. Little came of it in the end. Well, summer romance-arinos never last, do they? But the father was furious, and truly, we enjoyed goading him. How he would charge through the forest screaming for her. And she, with her paramour, holed up in some green bower beyond his reach, laughing through soft kisses and . . . more. I adore a good *chanson d'amour*! How strange to even remember such a thing. Still, it was good sport, back in the day."

"Do you remember her name?"

"Certainly not. I am sure no one knew her name even then. She was 'that sweet little thing from the house.' She was a darling, though. Anyway, if you want to know more, you should make enquiries with the father. It will be little trouble to find him, for he lived in a very great tower; there's only one place like it among all the halls and manses of Arvale. But like the man, the tower is a little . . . unfashionable."

"You mean old? Another part of the house?"

"No, I mean to say, it's cursed. He was a terrible chap and grew ever so much worse. Well, what could you expect? His hobbies had turned decidedly dark. Who knows what awful names he summoned by? Certainly by the end of his days he had not been himself for some time. And now, well, whatever state you find him in, I assure you he will be much more and much worse than he seems, so do have a care, little cousin."

"How was the tower cursed, cousin Ottoline? Did he bring it

down on himself? Was it put upon him by someone else? How did it happen?"

She looked back at Silas, smiled, and twirled her beads about her fingers.

"Why, it was the simplest thing imaginable. We just rallied up all our annoyance, which was considerable at the time, and then we spoke the curse to the tower, sent our stern words into the stones and foundations. We may have cursed the father too, I can't recall. No, no. I believe, at the time, the *daughter* cursed him. Yes, most vehemently. But it *was* two curses, so the old man must still be in quite a pickle . . . bound up down there with whatever malefaction he had conjured to himself in those final days. That's it! He offended us, then he put the daughter away, then we cursed him, then the daughter cursed him . . . or did she curse him before he sent her down? Oh, dear! What a muddle it's become."

She lowered her voice as the subject was, perhaps, a little impolite. "Of course it might be, that through the fault of the many evils of its owner, that tower might have simply attracted too much bad luck. Anyway, this wretched tower of his *sunk*. So I'd still call it cursed, whatever the circumstances. But if curses make you queasy, little cousin, you may simply say the tower has seen better days, and leave it at that. The curse shouldn't bother you, in any event."

"What do you mean 'sunk'?"

"Dear silly-Silas, I mean, It Hath Sunk. Into the earth. Put low. Made subterranean. Rendered deep. So unfashionable, subterranean dwelling. . . . It's so . . . *tres Mésolithique*. I assure you it's quite awful. Just try to open a window, you'll see. I am sure the father of the sweet thing is still there, moldering among his losses. He'll be thrilled for company, as it's been only him and his devil down there for so long. You be sure to give him our best, won't you?"

But before Silas could ask where the sunken mansion was or

what Ottoline meant by "his devil," someone with a drink in his hand seemed to tell a joke and the entire company of the summer house, even Ottoline, erupted in laughter and could barely be brought back to any sensible conversation. It was as if he weren't there at all anymore. So he turned to go. After a few moments he heard Ottoline shouting his name and he turned around and walked back toward her.

"Oh, dear, Silas! We can be so tiresome! Do come back soon and we'll try to be more useful."

"All right, I will."

"When dear?"

"What?"

"When will you come back? Evening? Twilight? Easter? When?"

"I don't know. Perhaps tomorrow."

"*Tomorrow?* Oh, now who's being tiresome?" moaned Ottoline. "Silly Silas, Tomorrow has already been, and yesterday sits here among us on the lawn laughing at the stars. What good is time at a party? We change with the season but only for the sake of fashion. Why not just stay with us? What care we for tomorrow and tomorrow and tomorrow?"

"Oh, I can't. I must get back. But that was lovely," Silas said, a little enchanted at Ottoline's turn of phrase.

"What's lovely?"

"What you just said."

"Who?"

"You," Silas said, the enchantment broken.

"Did I say something cleverino?"

"Yes . . . it was quite lovely."

"Well, there it is. Aren't soliloquies a bother!"

"Could you say it again?" he asked.

"Oh, silly Silas! I'm sure I already have!"

If thy daughter is wanton, keep her in straitly, lest she cause thine enemies to laugh thee to scorn. If thy daughter be not shamefast, bind her down straitly, lest she abuse herself or the name of her family, or ought else through too much liberty. Here you see in what cases the parents may seek the death of the children: namely, if they be riotous and disobediently refuse to hear the admonition of the parents. . . . If the daughter curse the father, they must have no pity. They must be stoned with stones, put away in a small place, unto death, or else sacrificed if it can be compassed. Then, in death as in life, bind her straitly that she walketh not and bring neither harm nor disturbance to thine house or domains. But if the profit of her disobedience be born, if the Mistle Child be made and brought into the world, it must be hunted, found, and sacrificed. Yea, and even though you must hunt for it all the rest of your days. And thus, only when the Mistle Child be offered up in fire, shall you have power and peace, and restore dignity and all due authority to thy name.

—FROM THE BOOK *A Rule of Discipline*, 1432, BY CABEL UMBER

MOREOVER, THOU HAST TAKEN THY
SONS AND THY DAUGHTERS WHOM THOU
HAST BORNE UNTO ME, AND THESE
HAST THOU SACRIFICED UNTO THEM TO
BE DEVOURED.

—BOOK OF EZEKIEL, 16:20. MARGINALIA OF AMOS
UMBER

CHAPTER 25

OLD FLAME

WHEN SILAS APPROACHED THE TOP of the garden, he found it empty. Lars wasn't waiting for him as promised. Perhaps he'd returned to Arvale when the weather turned. A chill wind had risen and the earlier warmth he'd felt had vanished from the air. The once bright flowers of the garden had closed their buds against the coming night. The farther Silas walked from the summer house, the colder it got. Thick, ashen clouds covered the sky. Silas wondered if it was going to rain in Lichport, too.

He was eager to be gone from Arvale now. Every time he heard the spirit cry out over the house he felt ashamed, and the desire to run home made the muscles of his legs twitch. He could also understand why his father had turned his back on this place: the reliance on blind tradition, the fact that even members of the family seemed, in their own ways, lost. Arvale was a hiding place. He'd met his obligation to ancestry by returning when summoned, taking the waters of memory, and presiding over the Door Doom. That would have to be enough. Even though he knew there were other challenges waiting at home, he wanted to be *there*, not *here*. He wanted to wrap the Narrows around him like a blanket. He could see himself sitting in front of the fire at Mother Peale's. There would be warm soup and good people filling the room with gossip. That world felt a thousand miles away now. He had to find the spirit's name and bring her Peace. Even though she was dangerous—she had cursed her father in life and who knows who else—Silas could not turn away. One way or another, she must be put down. Until that happened, the path home was lost to him.

He pulled up his collar against the wind. Night was coming on.

As if in answer to the dimming of the day, somewhere above him the low wail began again, rising, quickly growing louder. Silas's mind clouded. The miserable sound tore at his nerves. It was the screaming of a girl and it was full of fury and vengeance. Silas wished he was anywhere else. His mind flew to the edge of the millpond in Lichport. Down below, another was crying and waiting for him. A moan crawled up from his throat. "I'm sorry . . . ," he said. "Bea, I am so sorry." The crying grew louder and it seared the air around him. He put his palm to the back of his neck and could feel the burning heat on his hand. It was like an oven door had just been opened directly behind him. Silas turned around, confused, and in pain.

The nameless girl was there.

Hanging in the air before him was a spectral conflagration, as though a small bonfire had been lifted up off the ground. The flames flowed around a human form that seemed sculpted all of glowing embers. The heat coming off her was so intense that Silas raised an arm to cover his face.

The ghost screamed and Silas looked again in horror.

Within the writhing flames, her mouth open and wailing, was a face. Now Silas could make out more detail, could see how young she was. She couldn't have been more than fourteen or fifteen.

"Please," Silas cried. "Let me help you. Tell me your name."

The ghost opened her mouth again, but only a molten keen poured forth. His ears were going to burst. He stumbled backward trying to cover his eyes.

Suddenly someone was pulling him by the arm.

"Silas, come away! Come away!"

Lars was dragging him toward the house. Silas caught his balance, Lars let go of his arm, and the two of them ran.

Behind them, the ghost ascended to somewhere up along the roofline, her wailing weaving itself among the chimneys and high towers. Bricks and chunks of mortar began to rain down into the courtyard.

Silas opened the front doors of Arvale, and they moved quickly into the hall. They closed the doors behind them, and stood catching their breath.

"Did you see her?" Silas asked, gasping.

Lars nodded, terrified.

"She must be brought to peace, or sent back below. The longer she remains, the more danger we're in. We have to hurry."

"Hurry? You're one to talk of haste. Where have you been? I thought you'd gone home to Lichport!"

"What are you talking about? I saw you just a couple of hours ago."

Lars stared at him. "Silas, I left you in the garden three days ago. . . ."

Silas shivered. He'd only been with the cousins for an hour, or so he'd thought. Now everything was out of joint. He could feel it: a sickening displaced feeling in his stomach like the moment when, after falling asleep on a train, you awake to find you've slept past your stop and now have no idea where you are. He said quietly, "I am sorry, Lars. I didn't mean to frighten you."

"They throw quite a party, eh?"

"Lars, we have to move fast. I think I have stayed here too long and I want to go home. I know what we need to do."

"Whatever it is, you know I'll help if I can," said Lars.

"Listen," Silas said, looking up at a hole recently torn in the roof of the hall, "she's coming back."

The screaming outside picked up with renewed fury, and stones and roof tiles could be heard shattering on the ground just beyond the door. From the darkness at the back of the hall, a voice near the cold fireplace spoke.

"I see you learned gentleman have not yet completed your task. I am not sure what will become of us if she pulls down one of the outside walls."

"We are making progress, Aunt Maud. I promise you."

"Truly?" she said, her voice rising in interest. "You have found her name?"

"No," Silas admitted. "But I know who to ask."

"Well, that is something, then," she said, her tone going flat.

"We are, even now, on our way to the sunken mansion."

Lars looked at him questioningly. "Silas, do you know where that is? For I don't. I have never heard of such a place."

Maud rose from her chair and crossed the distance of the floor in an instant. She was smiling. This news pleased her. There was not a hint of surprise on her face.

"This is well," she said, drawing very close to them. "It seems at last I may be of some use to you. I know where the sunken mansion lies, and I will take you there at once so you may conclude this matter and fulfill the rest of your duties to this house."

Even though he needed her help, Maud's eagerness gave Silas pause. There had been harsh words between them. But it was possible she was trying to be helpful now in order to mend her earlier display of anger? And Lars didn't know where the tower was. Silas knew he had no choice but to put his trust in Maud.

A crashing sound above them brought Silas's attention back to the moment. One of the roof beams shook as though someone was striking it with a great hammer, and a large carved corbel in the shape of a chimera plummeted to the floor a few feet away.

"Shall we make our way?" Maud said.

Silas and Lars followed her out of the hall and up the stairs.

From the wide landing, she led them down a long-unused corridor of the east wing. The thick glass in the windows was nearly black with dirt, and the tapestries along the walls were filled with holes, which was just as well because their woven themes, when they could be discerned, were grim. The tapestries appeared to depict episodes from a medieval *Danse Macabre* and showed images of capering skeletons pulling the crowns off the heads of kings, playing instruments as people died in piles from the plague, and generally bringing death to one and all, rich and poor, pope and peasant, young and old. The tattered weavings shivered as they passed.

At the end of the corridor stood a heavy door, studded and bound with thick iron bands.

"Beyond this door you will find what you seek," Maud told them.

"You are not coming?"

"I cannot go this way, no. In any event, you shall have no need of me where you are going. Be strong, Silas Umber. Do not waver from your appointed task, no matter what you find."

Silas could hear that her words held expectation.

Maud turned and walked away, her long wimple flowing behind her. She blurred upon the air, became indiscernible from the shadows and dusky colors of the corridor around her, and was gone.

The door appeared to have been closed for a very long time. It was covered in thick dust, its keyhole at first completely hidden. Lars brushed at its surface. "I have no key," he said.

Silas stepped forward and put his hand upon the wood. The lock turned, and the door opened partially into the darkness beyond. He took a step toward the threshold and lurched forward. Before Silas could even cry out, Lars grabbed his collar, and then his arms, pulling him back.

The two stood in a doorway that opened into the night. There was no room or hallway beyond. Only cold and insubstantial air. Whatever building had once stood beyond the door, it wasn't there anymore.

"I don't understand . . . ," Silas said, confused.

Lars pointed down. "It is truly sunken. The tower has broken away from the house. The battlements of its roof are there, see? Below. Why didn't Maud direct us to the tower from the outside?"

"Because," said Silas, "the tower is now beneath the ground. The only way in now must be through the chimney, and it stands too high to get at from down there. And because, despite what she's told me, I don't believe she can leave this house."

Silas looked beyond the door. A few feet away and to the left, he could see a large rectangular hole, a little blacker than the night, framed in brick. One long step from where he stood and he'd be on the edge of the chimney.

"Lars, you wait here for me, okay?"

"No. I am going with you. It is clear from your earlier adventure that you just get into trouble on your own."

Silas shook his head. "I'm not precisely sure what's down there, but I can tell you that I have seen places like this—misthomes for the dead—that are very dangerous. The way this place presents itself is a kind of warning. Whatever dwells in this tower was put here against its will and I suspect it won't be very pleased to greet us."

"Thank you. Now, Silas, let me be clear. You are not the only one in the family who can be brave. I let you go alone to the summer house, and you lost track of time and were gone for three days. I should have gone with you. It weighs heavily on me. Now we must try to keep together. Let us go and waste no more time. The sooner we go down there, the sooner we may return."

Silas took Lars's hand. "All right, then. But you must trust me, especially if anything . . . happens. I know something of who awaits us, but I have no idea what form this spirit might take. If he is truly the father of our nameless ghost, then he is also very old. You may see things down there that will upset you. Listen only to my voice. Nothing else. Do you understand? And if I ask you to do something, you must do it without hesitation."

Lars was shaking.

"Are you sure you still want to come?"

"I am."

"Then, cousin Lars, let's make our way down."

LEDGER

The manner in which the lord
rules the hells may also be
briefly explained. . . .
All the inhabitants of hell are
ruled by fear. . . . Punishments
in hell are manifold. . . . It
is to be noted that the fear of
punishment is the only means of
restraining the violence and fury
of those who are in the hells.
There are no other means.

—From Swedenborg, *Heaven and Hell*,
transcribed by Amos Umber

First, Moloch, horrid king,
besmeared with blood

Of human sacrifice, and parents
tears;

Though, for the noise of drums
and timbrels loud,

Their children's cries unheard that
passed through fire

To his grim idol. Him the Ammonite

Worshiped in Rabba and her watery
plain,

In Argob and in Basan, to the
stream

Of utmost Arnon. Nor content
with such

Audacious neighbourhood, the wisest
heart

Of Solomon he led by fraud to
build

His temple right against the
temple of God

On that opprobrious hill, and made
his grove

The pleasant valley of Hinnom,
Tophet thence

And black Gehenna called, the
type of Hell.

—from John Milton, *Paradise Lost*, transcribed by
Amos Umber

CHAPTER 26

DOWN

SILAS AND LARS DESCENDED THROUGH A COLUMN of soot and ash. The stones of the chimney were close in about them, and though Lars had a small lantern, the blackness of the walls absorbed the light.

They made their way slowly down the chimney, a bit of rope and one foothold at a time. When at last they emerged from the fireplace, they were covered in soot and had become just two more dark forms in a room hung thick with shadows.

Silas could tell immediately that the quality of this building was different from that of the main house. Whatever this tower had once been, it was now a prison. Even the far wall of the room seemed to press in on him. The tower also felt less present somehow. He was sure that if he were to look out the arched windows, Arvale would be gone.

Curious, he went to a window. When the shutter opened, Silas could see nothing but earth. Rocks, roots, and soil. They were now below the ground.

Claustrophobic and uneasy, Silas spoke the words and tiny ghost lights appeared about them, lighting their way. The little candles floated on the air before and behind him, and Silas felt his courage returning.

Lars looked at Silas briefly, but only nodded as if to say, *Little surprises me anymore.*

They made their way down rough stone steps, following the curve of the wall, toward what was once the ground floor of the tower. Each chamber they passed was filled with artifacts of necromantic obsession: bones, circles, and strange glyphs traced in chalk upon the floor, candles inscribed with ancient runes, parchment scrolls, books with faded sigils and spines broken from lying open over the centuries. Many of the objects were burned, as though fire had once scourged these rooms. Silas and Lars did not pause long to look.

When they reached the far side of the bottom chamber, there was another locked door. The air was fetid and foul, and Silas could feel the presence of something old and mighty beyond. He turned and looked at Lars, worried that his cousin might come to harm.

"Lars, here's the plan. You must wait for me here."

"No, Silas, I'm going with you."

"You *have* come with me. Now I am asking you to stay here, so if I need help, you will be close at hand. I can it feel it now. It's waiting for me, has been for some time, I think. I need to go in there by myself. It gives me strength to know you're right here if anything happens. Okay, Lars?"

"I will abide. Call out if you need me and I will come."

"I promise."

Silas took a step forward and placed his hand upon the locks. The bolts slid open before he could move them. He took hold of the handle and pulled opened the heavy door. From within the chamber beyond, Silas heard an awful sound: the gnashing of teeth, back and forth. Someone there, in the dark, was slowly, endlessly, grinding his teeth together. The lights about Silas's head flickered but remained alight, casting a pale glow over only the closest things in the room. Silas closed his eyes and thought of the sun, torchlight, the warmth of the hearth in Mother Peale's house. The lights once more leaped up to make a bright corona about his head. Then he could see more of the room, and what resided there. But as he entered, his heart called out in its rapidly rising beat: *Get out! Leave this place and never return!*

The chamber was a museum, its shelves and floor covered with inscribed tablets from Babylon, frightening statues of obscure Near Eastern gods and monsters, and the remains of candles. Several tripods, perhaps once used as braziers, lay fallen over about the room. Dominating the far side of the chamber was an enormous bronze statue of something like a minotaur. The bottom of the statue was bell-shaped. Its thick human body, arms up with palms facing away, was surmounted by the massive head of a bull whose long horns nearly touched the roof beams. In the belly of the idol was a scorched hole, like a large bread oven. Above that, several rectangular niches might have once held smaller offerings. Next to the idol were stacks of rotten wood suggesting that whoever brought the idol here was no mere collector; the sacrificial oven had once been intended for use.

Horse skulls and bones were scattered throughout the room along with pieces of smashed furniture. In the center of the chamber was a seated human form. On the floor beneath him was a circle made in chalk, and within it danced glyphs and sigils of elder power. Silas could feel that the seated figure was not here by choice, and so took care not to step on or drag his foot through the chalk lines on the floor, in case they were part of the spell holding him here.

The head of the seated figure was partially skeletal, a bare patch of white bone showing through along the side of the skull. The rest of his face was emaciated, skin drawn tight and blackened with age. A small coronet of silver had slipped from his brow and hung awkwardly about his neck like a slave's collar. His hair was dark and pressed down and flat against the skull as though it had been spun of tar. The remains of a short beard curled and stuck out slightly away from his head. Silas was reminded of one of those sacrificial corpses taken from the Danish bogs, sodden right through with blackness as though it had been carved from pitch.

The figure turned his head toward his guest. Silas did not wait for him to speak.

"Ancestor, I am Silas Umber."

There was a long pause and a deep intake of air as though the figure were trying to smell something.

"Oh, yes? I would walk over to welcome you, but you see I am encumbered by the pettiness of my relations and no longer enjoy the privilege of freedom. I cannot leave this circle. But I know who you are, son of Amos Umber. I have heard your name rise in sulphur from the abyss. I wondered if you would come. And now, here you are. How fortuitous. Do you like my collections?" asked the figure, gesturing to the idol. "Who would have thought the Holy Land could hold such wonders?"

Silas remained focused. "What is your name, sir?"

"In life, I was Cabel Umber, onetime lord of this demesne. Janus of the house. Lord of the Dead who sat upon the throne of ebony. And a pilgrim. Now I am . . . as you see me: a mere dependent on this enduring estate, though I once was heir to a greater one." The spirit held his gaze upon the massive bronze idol, then closed his eyes and may have smiled.

Silas struggled to understand what he'd heard. Surely this was bravado, some display meant to impress or frighten or belittle him.

Fairly certain he could discern the rising lie in Cabel Umber's voice, Silas said, "*You* once sat on the Ebony Throne?"

Cabel turned to look at Silas. "I did, Silas Umber, that

selfsame chair which, I suspect, you yourself are inclined to take."

"I have no such aspirations," said Silas, not giving too much away.

"Not yet . . ." Cabel Umber laughed in a low, unsettling gurgle. "Do you think 'Janus' is the last title you'll bear? Your path has been trod out for you since before you fell into the world. There are great things in store for you, little Janus. Very great things. The first born of our family are so very useful. Of course, should you decide you'd rather bestow those honors upon *another*, I am sure *someone* would gladly oblige."

"I'm not up to any more tests or initiations just at the moment."

"Pointless relics, I call such rites. You can be whatever you wish to be. Summon what you want by name and it shall come to you. Thinking makes it so."

"So you mean if I had said 'I am Janus,' when I first arrived at Arvale, I would have been, even without the rituals?"

"Most certainly. But why stop there? Say you are Lord of the Dead, and watch what happens next."

Silas paused, his voice trapped in his throat. How much did Cabel Umber know about him, about his vision on the Limbus Stone? After a moment of silence, Silas asked, "Is that who used to sit on the Ebony Throne? The Lord of the Dead?"

"They haven't told you?" Cabel Umber's voice rose, excited. He gibbered.

"No, not really. I'm not sure anyone up there really wants to say much about it."

"I am sure you are right. But I can tell you this, if that chair is offered to you, think twice before taking it."

"Why?"

"Because it carries with it a very great responsibility. You might wish to enjoy the pleasures of life and youth a little longer," Cabel Umber said, softening his voice very deliberately.

"I see. It is still yours, then?"

"No, no. Long ago I sat there briefly, and it seemed likely I might hold that seat more permanently, but my allegiances eventually fell elsewhere," he said looking again to the idol, as if for approval. "You should leave the throne be."

"I thought you just told me I could proclaim myself anything I wanted to."

"And so you can, but then you may find yourself in an awkward position. I am not talking about being a mere porter at the door, Silas Umber. No. I am referring to a more ancient post than that, one with a little more authority. One in which you might keep better company."

"There is no need for you to worry about me, or indeed, for what you might have been. Your life has ended and the days of aspiration for you and for your immediate relations are long gone. Now, why not tell me what brought one so important as you to such an awful fate as this?" Silas said, trying to play to his ancestor's easily discernible ego.

Cabel Umber's face briefly contorted in anger, but then he closed his eyes and regained his composure.

"I did not *come* here. I was imprisoned here, Silas Umber. Do you think I placed this curse upon myself? I was *put* here. . . . Do you understand? I am a victim of a most terrible curse. A victim bound by blood! I long only for justice. For freedom. And now, here you are. I call that timely."

As terrible as Cabel's condition was to behold, Silas almost pitied him. All those years in the darkness below the earth. Who could bear such a fate? Still, it was clear that Cabel Umber was not speaking the whole truth of the matter.

"You are Janus now, are you not?" Cabel Umber asked.

"Yes."

"Then allow me to congratulate you. Of course you are Janus. How easy it would be for you to free me. You, who can now command the dead at will. I do not suppose the others have told you about the extent of your authority, have they? That lot upstairs are so afraid of the Old Powers and Dominions they try desperately to forget them. Silas Umber, if you so desired, you could, with a word, command me from this place, or conjure me by name from this place unto some other. Try . . ."

"I must decline," Silas said flatly, although inwardly intrigued. "But, if you don't mind, let me tell you why I have come."

"There is no need. I know why you are here. Very well. Cast your damning waters on me and let me forget at last!"

"That's not it at all. I need your help."

Cabel Umber began gnashing his teeth again. For several moments he did not speak, perhaps deep in thought, perhaps listening to something far away. "Silas Umber, I understand. This explains all the noise above, that adolescent screaming so familiar to me. You have become Janus. You have opened doors long sealed. I see what has happened. You have committed terrible errors in your exuberance and now seek to redress them."

"Yes," Silas responded, embarrassed. Pushing past his shame, he answered with directness. "I would like to set matters to rights, but before there is peace, the dead, like the living, must remember. Tell me, did you have any children? What were their names?" he asked.

"Oh, Silas Umber, little cousin, I know you wish more from me than mere biography. Oh, son, if I were free, I would put her back in the earth myself!"

The room went cold and fear took Silas in its teeth at the sound of those words. Cabel's anger filled the chamber like acrid smoke, and Silas could feel the spirit's desperate hate—how much he wanted to put his own child back down into that tiny vault of deep, unbreakable rock.

"Tell me your daughter's name."

"Impossible. I have no daughter."

"You did have a daughter and you have one still. You locked her in a cell in the catacombs below this house and left her there to die. Whatever else she has become because of your actions, she remains your daughter. Even now, she assails this house."

"I have no daughter," Cabel Umber said softly, though light from a long-banished past now lit his eyes. "No loving daughter would do to her father what that one did . . . ," he cried.

"If you could just tell me her name—"

The thing threw back his skull and wailed to the vault, "I HAVE NO DAUGHTER!"

Silas took a step back.

Cabel Umber quickly composed himself. He remained silent for several moments, then said, "I am sorry, Silas. Sorry you have been drawn into this awful business." But his eyes brightened and his lip curled up, perhaps with inspiration or remembrance, or expectation. "Silas, I cannot tell you her name because I struck that name from the world. Even if I wanted to speak it now, I could not. It is gone. At that time, I was not without pouissance."

Silas looked intensely at Cabel's face. He wanted to believe his words, but the arrogant expression worn by the spirit told him that everything Cabel said was at best a partial truth.

"Silas, you have tried to call her to the stone?"

"I have. She will not come."

"No. She was always willful, even in life. I can see this matter pains you."

"I want to fix things. That's all."

"I see more sorrow than that in your eyes. There is grief born of your own losses. So we share something in common, more than merely a name. You have yourself lost a daughter? No. Not a daughter. There is a father once lost, that is easy to see. But such loss is common; there is one more particular. Someone young. A wife? A lover?" Silas could feel Cabel Umber looking at him, sifting *through* him for the knowledge he sought. It felt like fingernails being lightly drawn over his skull.

Silas couldn't answer. He looked away.

"Yes. A lover. Tragic to lose a maiden in her blush. Trust me. I know."

"I don't know what you—"

"No need to hide it from me. Perhaps I can help you. I have endured so many losses, it would ease my heart to be able to help another. What is lost can almost always be found. I promise you, calling up the dead poses no real challenge. In my time, I summoned forth much greater personages than mere village ghosts. There are certain rites . . . I might gift you with a few references, some texts to look for, a few words to commit to memory, then you can bring her back as you see fit. You have the look of a scholar about you. Such arts, dark as they are, exist to be used by the wise."

Bring. Her. Back.

The words burned into Silas's heart like a glowing brand.

"It is not so difficult as most would have you believe. It is your especial right. In your way, I expect you have done it already. Of course, if you are Janus, you have taken first footing on this path. Have you not called a name to the black stone? Do not let some false morality cloud your mind. The common dead are cattle. We are their lords. But I digress. We are kin, after all, no? It is right that we should help each other. Let me help you," said Cabel, leaning into the words as they left him.

Though his mind churned with discomfort at whatever kind of deal was being subtly worked out, he could not push from his heart the image of Bea standing by his side again. Silas said, barely a whisper, "What would I have to do?"

Cabel Umber spoke softly then, continuing in an unctious and ingratiating tone.

"It's not hard, Silas. There are many ways to raise the dead. But, I wonder if I might ask you for a little heart's ease? Oh, dear Silas . . . just a little comfort. Some forgiveness. I know I must remain here, but the weight of my sins is terrible. If just someone would put their hand upon me and say 'thou art forgiven.' Please. You could do it, as Janus. Let me serve out my term here, not as sinner but instead pardoned, by your leave. I would remain a prisoner, but with a lighter heart."

Cabel Umber began to writhe and turn as if a fire had been lit below him. "Merely a little sympathy . . ."

Despite his many misgivings, the words touched Silas, for wasn't this almost always the case with the dead? Didn't they all require some kind of absolution, the simple acknowledgment from the living that their words had been heard? Even the most horrific ghost needed to be heard and helped. *How could I withhold that, even from one like him?* Silas thought.

Silas reached out to put his hand upon Cabel Umber's head, but something flashed suddenly, deep in the sockets of Cabel's skull, and a low sound rose in his throat. Silas quickly drew back his hand and merely said aloud, "For all the troubles of your past, whatsoever they might be, and for what it's worth, as I cannot free you, I do forgive you."

The sound Cabel Umber made then was truly pitiful and

it seemed, when he spoke again, that his words were pushed through tears.

"Even you, Silas, cannot bring yourself to touch me. Wretched I must be then if one so familiar with the horrors of death cannot bring himself to even lay his hand upon my shoulder."

Guiltily, Silas stretched out his hand again, then paused. Was the partially revealed skull beginning to grin, were the thin tendrils of his sinewy jaw drawing tighter? No. He thought of his great-grandfather, and how he must have, so many times, appreciated the simple kindness of a touch.

Silas put his hand on Cabel Umber's shoulder and said with more sincerity, "Cabel Umber, I forgive you." Cabel let out a long breath, half sigh, half laugh. Though he was still bound by his curse, he looked as though the light of salvation had been cast upon him. He stood up from his chair, a garishly carved mockery of the throne in the hall of Arvale, and walked in a circle just inside the chalk line. He paced back and forth in front of Silas like an animal circumventing the bounds of its captivity.

The moment the words left him, Silas knew that while he had acted in kindness, it was also in ignorance. Something had changed. Now he was following someone else's plan. Still, what if both of them might benefit? Was that wrong? Cabel's daughter had cursed him. Silas knew that. Maybe, if they could bring her to the stone, she could be made to take the water. That was appropriate in any situation. He wouldn't need to judge the father or the daughter guilty or innocent. Silas could just do his job.

Cabel inclined his head. "Ah. You are kindness personified. I could not ask for more beneficence, no, not even from Amos Umber himself. Now, Silas son of Amos, let me help you with your lost love, and then I shall tell you what we are going to do to resolve our mutual problem.

"There are rites. Some simple words, thankfully recorded in antiquity. It's your right to study and use them. Had any of the family a little more decency, they would have taken care with your education. You can, if you wish, call her to you, and there will be little under heaven that can keep her from your side. Would you like to know the names of these books, the words of these spells? Ask, and they are yours."

Silas's heart was beating fast. All his good sense drowned out by the pounding rhythm of his desire and the chance at a solution to the nameless spirit's release that might get him back to Lichport quickly. "Tell me."

"Then lean a little closer. Such words should not hang upon the open air. Come closer and I'll tell you."

Silas leaned in until he was a foot away from the skull. Cabel had begun to shake in anticipation.

"Closer, I prithee."

Silas inclined his head another inch.

"Clo-ser."

Silas took another step and stood just the merest inch away from Cabel's body on the other side of the pale chalk line inscribed on the floor.

"Let me put my mouth to your ear, son."

Silas bent his head until he could almost feel the teeth of the skull scrape against his earlobe.

"Yessss . . . that's better. Now," said Cabel, hissing, "here are some words that you will find . . . efficacious."

Cabel Umber whispered, and the words were like maggots crawling into Silas's ear. Names of certain necromantic books of elder rites . . . *The Spells of Ezekiel, The Dark Call*, certain chapters of the *Virgilian Heresies*. Cabel Umber shared words and shards of advice, telling Silas what rites to find and which spells were best for summoning. The information swam in Silas's mind, eddies and whirlpools of frightening invocations and grim phrases. He'd never be able to remember it all, though some words were familiar, the titles of rare volumes he might have seen in his uncle's private library.

"Now," said Cabel as he looked down at his empty hands, "I need you to bring me something, and with it, we shall put all to rights at Arvale. This is a very small thing. Long and long ago I hunted for it, but couldn't find it. It's mine by right and I still want it. We all bear our obligations, and I have made promises in life I have yet to fulfill. You see how they weigh upon me."

"Name it," said Silas. He had no other idea for how to silence the nameless spirit. If there was something that could help, he was willing to try it, even it meant he would have to negotiate with and possibly anger Cabel Umber later if they did not agree on the particulars. Besides, maybe whatever it was he needed to find was something Silas could use himself. Either way, Silas felt he had no choice but to finish what he'd started.

Perhaps sensing Silas's hesitation, Cabel said, "Every parent must bear a portion of his children's sins. That portion has been withheld from me. The right to restore honor to my house has been hidden from me."

"I don't believe in the sins of children."

"You are fortunate in that, but you must allow me to remain a man of my own time. It is a father's job to keep his family safe from sin. For sin is death, and death must be held at bay until the terrible day comes. The child sinned, and then she stole from me, and then she cursed me. I am a hunting man by nature, and I do not allow my quarry to escape. Until you released her, she had been well repaid for the shame she brought upon this house. She is nameless and lost and should have remained so. But the *thing* she carried with her out of this house, the *thing* that should have come to me . . . how I searched the vales and dells of the forest. How my dogs dug among the roots for its hiding place. I will not have the dignity of our name remain lost."

Silas could see Cabel was becoming increasingly agitated. "I don't take your meaning. She stole money, or something valuable? What could you possibly want with it now? I don't understand. . . ."

Cabel Umber threw back his skull and wailed, "Bring unto me what is mine! The Mistle Child! Bring it to me and both our sorrows shall be ended!"

Silas had no idea what he meant. Perhaps some relic, a valuable carving, or a gold icon. What was a "Mistle Child"? He waited until Cabel had regained his calm. "If I can find such a thing, I will give it to you. And then you will show me how to settle the ghost of your daughter, right?"

Cabel sucked air through his teeth at the word "daughter," as though it had been an arrow that struck him, but said, "Yes. Cousin Silas, you are indeed fortunate to have met me. Yes. Bring me the Mistle Child and all shall be well with this matter. You may kill two little birds with one stone. When you find the Mistle Child, my daugh—the other will be no more trouble, I promise you. One is the key to the other. Bring me the Mistle Child, and all shall be well done. We are agreed?"

"Yes."

"Good," said Cabel as he sat back down in his chair.

The air of the room stilled and grew heavy. A bargain had been struck. Silas already felt he'd done something wrong, but his desire was now all toward Beatrice and how quickly he could settle matters here and then get home to her. He turned to leave.

"What is this, no farewell for your ancestor?"

"Good-bye, Cabel Umber," said Silas he left the room, eager to be away.

"All right, then," Cabel began to shout through the closing door, "but hold to your promise, Silas Umber, or I shall know why not. We have made a bargain. So you will bring me what is mine. If you do not do this, I shall have something else in return. Promises have now been made and accounts must be paid. We are yoked together in obligation, Silas Umber. If you break with me, we shall speak again on this matter. Indeed we shall. And if it comes to that, I fear we shall never be friends. Never. Never. Never."

Also beware that you do not lye too long under dust, nor in olde chambres whiche be not occupied or kept clene, specyally such chambres as spyders, myse, rattes, and snayles resortheth unto. For the howse is the verie mynd of man, and if it be allowed to become untidy, so shalle then owre verie thowts become lykwyse and no goode shalle come of it.

—FROM *A COMPENDIOUS REGIMENT OF HOWSEHOLD HELTH*, 1562

SILAS AND LARS SAT ON THE CARPET by the fire in Silas's room, brushing the soot from their clothes. Silas had spoken very little since they'd returned from the sunken mansion. His mind turned with distraction, trying to sift through everything he'd heard there. He realized he might have asked Cabel Umber what a Mistle Child was. Cabel obviously assumed Silas knew or could figure it out. But something in Silas suspected that if Cabel had wanted to say more about it, he would have. Maybe, as with his daughter's name, specificity regarding the Mistle Child was forbidden him.

"Lars, who is the oldest person you've met here?"

"Maud, by far."

"No one else?"

"Why do you ask?"

"Because I have a question that needs answering and I don't want to ask Maud, even though I suspect she knows the answer."

"Why not?"

"Let's just say she has a hard time being objective where children are involved. Everyone here wants something from me. There is work I must do, but I don't want to tie it to anyone's expectations. Is there no one else you can think of who might be reliable, trustworthy? Someone discreet?"

"Well, it's generally understood, if you want to know something about what's happened in any house, ask a servant. They know *everything*. There's a very old woman I've seen once or twice wandering up and down the long corridors. A spider-brusher."

"A what?"

"A web-maid. She dusts. You know. Little stick with a mop on the end, you wipe it over things to make them clean. Goodness, Silas! What a life you've lived. So what do you want to ask her?"

"If she knows what a 'Mistle Child' is. I think it's an old term. Maybe someone who's been part of the household for a long time would know it. It's connected to the nameless spirit. Cabel Umber said if I found it and brought it to him, it would make her listen, in some way."

"I don't think I've ever heard of such a thing. Are you sure he can be trusted?"

"No. I'm not sure at all, but I don't think I have any other options. So I need to talk to someone who knows anything about that phrase. If we can find out what it is, I think we'll be able to make some progress with the ghost before she brings the house down."

"That all sounds fine, but how will we find the spider-brusher? I've seen her only once or twice. I can show you where, but it's more than likely that she will not be present. I have no idea where she resides in the house, and if you are unwilling to ask Maud, who might know—"

"I think it will be simpler than that. Lars, take me to where you saw her, and be sure we pass by a few untidy corners on the way there, please."

"Untidy corners? Silas, the whole house could use a good dusting."

"Indeed. I will a do a bit of dusting myself."

Silas had begun to understand that traversing the house was

a lot like his previous experiences in the shadowlands. Much depended upon the traveler's ability to hold a name in his mind, think particularly about where he wants to go, and then walk with intention. Although Silas did not know the spider-brusher's name, he knew her occupation and suspected that because she was a servant of the house, she would be amenable to speaking with him, as an Umber, as a descendant of people from Arvale.

As Lars and Silas walked up stone corkscrew stairs and down corridors lit with dripping candles in branching sconces, Silas drew his fingers across the wall, catching as many cobwebs and as much dust as he could. Soon he had a handful of debris.

They climbed several more staircases and came to the end of a long, high-ceilinged gallery. The walls were covered with portraits, and marble busts stood on carved pediments.

Lars said, "This is it, Silas. This is where I saw her."

Silas walked down the gallery, taking pinches of dust from his hand and sprinkling it over some of the sculptures. He took wads of cobwebs and pressed them to the portraits. Then, in a kind but sure voice, he spoke.

"Here's a fine thing! Dust over all! Cobwebs gathering! Mother of the Gallery, Mistress of Motes and Webs, come now, for good work awaits your good hand!"

At the far end of the gallery, something moved.

"There!" Lars said, impressed. "Look!"

An ancient woman moved slowly in a sort of dance. Dozens of small mops and brushes and whisks hung from her belt, and they clicked as they moved about her when she swung this way and that. She wore a long pale apron over a plain black dress. Down its front was a chatelaine's chain holding hundreds of keys. Her back was bent, yet she went neatly about her dusting, sometimes standing on her toes and reaching far up the wall to brush away a cobweb. Wherever she saw a web or a clot of dust, she would draw forth a particular brush, and with a slow, graceful up-and-down motion of her wrist, the web would be caught up in the brush and removed. Then, on to the next. Whether the web was hung between two objects, or from a corner, or veiled one of the carved busts, with each brushing, she said, "My busy little dears, I am sorry. So sorry. Oh, my busy little attercops, ho, ho!"

She hummed absently to herself, broken shards of lost tunes, the sweet, soft ramblings of a mind too much on its own.

"Hello, ma'am!" Lars called from a distance, not wanting to get any closer and startle the old woman. The spider-brusher turned slowly, and made a sort of bow, then, still bent forward, she smiled and looked up at them, her head turned to one side.

"And who's that you've got with you, Little Mercury?"

Lars pushed Silas forward. "This is my friend, ma'am, my cousin, Silas Umber."

"Oh, oh! What's this? The doorman come a-wandering the upper halls? The world is topsy-turvy, hey! Look here, my children, what comes flying into our webs!"

"My cousin would like to ask you a question, if that would be all right, ma'am."

"What's that, Little Mercury? A question? For me? For me? What would old Jane know that would be of interest to you, hey?" She looked up at the dark rafters where tiny shapes scuttled, and said, "Did you hear that, my dearie-o's? Proper folk come askin' old Janey questions! Of course they do, for what haven't I heard in my many years of tending these long hallways and corridors, eh?"

Silas approached her. "I am very pleased to meet you, ma'am."

The spider-brusher nodded quickly, but cast her eyes down. Silas continued.

"You must know every object in this house, every portrait and sculpture. Every treasure. And perhaps, over the years, you may have heard this and that about the family of the house?"

"Indeed I have, sir. For don't my naughty little children like to make their messes, spinning their webs over finery as well as the coarsest beams? And don't folk like to talk and talk in a big house? Aye, they do. . . ."

"Ma'am, have you ever heard of a Mistle Child? Perhaps some valuable thing that's called by that name?"

The spider-brusher lowered her voice to a whisper. "'Tis no bauble, young sir. Mistle Child be a secret thing. Who has said those words to you? I have not heard tell of a Mistle Child, in, oh . . . many a long year. It was once just an old sayin', a sort of custom, and even long ago 'twas something of a mystery. Sometimes, it was a word a young woman might use, or a nurse who knew a secret. Now, 'tis just an old thing old Jane sings to herself when she comes to a lonely room or passage, for it's always the lonely place that brings it to mind, in'it?"

"Can you please tell me what it is, this Mistle Child? Is there more than one?"

"Oh, there be countless numbers of 'em! For as long as boys be boys and girls be girls, there shall always be a Mistle Child somewheres. Poor little innocents. No. I don't believe there be a Mistle Child in the house," said the spider-brusher, winking at Silas. "Well, they don't usually come in, for isn't that the whole point of the very trouble? They don't come in for they are *left out*. Maybe this will put a candle on it for you. Here are the first strange words about them, from the old days, just a little ditty now from old dotty Jane."

The spider-brusher sat down suddenly on the floor and closed her eyes. All about her, the brushes, sticks and floppy-headed mops attached to her belt splayed like spokes upon a cartwheel. She lifted her head, opened her eyes, and softly sang:

> Sit ye upon some high place, on hill or tower
> And late in an evening, near a wood
> A firedrake will appear; mark where it lighteth
> And there ye shalle finde an oake
> With mistletoe thereon,
> At the roots whereof
> Be the Mistle Childe hid
> Whereof many lost things
> May be learned and set right.

Silas tried to read between the lines. Was it an actual child? Some kind of lost child? Had the nameless spirit lost a baby? Is that what it was looking for? Silas remembered the little doll in the spirit's prison in the catacombs. Is that what Cabel Umber wanted? Silas ran the words of the song over in his head. . . . They seemed to be a kind of instruction, almost a map, but from where to where, and what to what? "I'm still not sure I understand."

"Old words say 'follow the firedrake,' for ain't that a lost thing too, just a summat, a little flame fallen from the stars and into earth. Way leads on to way, eh? Like to like. And aren't you nowt but a little lost thing yourself, my Silas?" said the spider-brusher, brushing a dusty hand softly past his cheek.

"Are you saying the firedrake comes from the sky? Is it some kind of light in the sky I need to follow?"

The spider-brusher stood up again, smiled kindly, and straightening her skirts and brushes said, "Oh, sir, how fine the woods will be at this time, why, the forest will be a very Flora's paradise, I reckon! And the robins and wrens about, such wise creatures do attend the woods, eh?

And little birds know about high places, do they not?"

"Madam, thank you," said Silas, making a small bow in gratitude for her good words. He was beginning to understand what he might be looking for and felt she was showing him how to find it.

"Now please, sirs, let me be about my work. The towers of the north range are nearly grown full up with the endless toils of my little spinners." She looked up suddenly and laughed. "Eh! My naughty children! Eh? Oh! Some of those towers are very high, so many stairs. So many little webs. But one can get a fine view from a tower, eh, Master Umber? Out over the woods? Under the fiery stars and the burning globes of night, eh?" She swatted Silas playfully on the bottom with a brush as she walked by him.

Realizing they had just been given an invitation, Silas said, "Ma'am, it is late and you should not go alone. May we accompany you there?"

"Oh, sirs," replied the spider-brusher. "Old Jane thought you'd never ask. Come along, then, and we'll see if we can find your little lost missel-thrush."

Silas looked at Lars, who smiled back, and the two of them followed the spider-brusher down the hall, her dust-mops swaying this way and that, back and forth like little pendulums on a dozen clocks.

CHAPTER 28

ANCIENT LIGHT

SILAS AND LARS HAD BEEN FOLLOWING the spider-brusher for what seemed like many hours, passing through rooms that looked older, more occupied than other parts of the house. They walked down long corridors lit by small candles burning in windows, melting low, waiting for folks who might never be guided home by their light. They passed through a wood-paneled chamber with a fire glowing in its hearth. Some stools were drawn in close to the fire, and while Silas saw no one in the room, he could hear voices murmuring in quiet conversation.

"End of a long day," said one voice.

"Morning's a long way off yet," said another.

"Put more wood on," one said. "I'm cold right through."

The spider-brusher put her finger to her lips and said, "Leave 'em to their eventide," as she led Silas and Lars through the door opposite the fireplace.

Silas saw no more windows as they continued deeper into the interior of the house, and he could no longer hear the wailing of the nameless ghost. Through the evenings at Arvale, her wail had come and gone; sometimes loud as a storm against the walls, other times drifting about the house, a soft but invasive crying from some distant, half-remembered place. The presence of the nameless ghost had almost become a background noise, a sound you could talk over and sometimes almost ignore but for knowing the awful source of it. Now Silas couldn't hear it all. Perhaps her cries were muffled by the insulating walls of interior stone, dense wood, and thick beams.

On and on they walked. They entered a small hall, very like a chapel, with high ceilings and carvings along the wall depicting the exploits of dozens of past ancestors. There were images of warfare and the taking of captives, as well as scenes of more domestic accomplishments: a midwife at work, a carpenter completing a cupboard, a young man returning home from a successful hunt in the forest. The hall was filled with music. The more Silas tried to focus on a particular sound, the more complex it became. A chorus of ancient voices rose, singing verses of memorial praise, and ending in long melancholic notes that fell upon the ear like the last breath of the dying. To this was added the soul-deep sound of the viol de gamba that stirred the very air into a rich hymn of longing and loss. Then flutes, from the rafters; high notes, like birdcall, flitted across the hall.

"We must not stop," said the spider-brusher.

"Why not?" asked Silas dreamily, the music lulling him.

"We will lose the path."

"How can that be?" said Silas.

"There are many ways to get where we're going. But upon all paths in this house, it is the same. We must keep our minds upon our destination, young masters. That we must. We are passing through the very heart of the house and must press on, or we shall find ourselves lost, just another thing in an old room in need of dusting. Press on, young sirs! Press on! Old Jane knows the way. . . ."

Silas understood her completely. In her way, she knew, as he did, how to find your path among the shadowlands. In all worlds, the work was the same: Stay focused or become just another shadow among the shadows.

But Silas found it hard to walk. Lars had sat down in a chair near the wall with his eyes closed, listening to the music. Silas leaned against him, and looked up as a new tune rose to fill the room. It was a lullaby and so familiar. He closed his eyes and heard the sound of birds.

"No! No! Sirs, come away!" the spider-brusher called to them. Suddenly, something tickled Silas under his chin, at his ear, crawling on his skin. He slapped at it, hitting himself in the face. Lars was also waving his arms as if swatting at a fly.

The spider-brusher stood in front of them, a brush in each hand, laughing. "Come now, my lads! We have many stairs to climb and no time for hymns and tunes and tickles!" She raised the brushes again, poking them toward Silas and Lars in mock threat.

The three left the hall. Before them rose a spiral stair, climbing upward and through the ceiling. As they ascended, the spider-brusher drew her little mops and brushes across the risers and over the rails, and anywhere she saw a web.

They emerged at the top of a high tower in Arvale's northern range. Three old men in dark velvet robes stood gazing at the sky. They were surrounded by astronomical instruments of every kind: compasses, astrolabes, sextants, primitive telescopes, and orreries of various sizes and complexities with their metal miniature planets and moons circling around and around one another to hypnotic effect.

"These young masters do come to see the firedrake," said the spider-brusher.

"Oh. Oh," said one of the old men. "Too late, I am afeard."

"Why too late?" Silas asked desperately.

The two other men drew back their sleeves and consulted a large, brass astrolabe, pointing at certain lines engraved upon it.

"See here," said the man who was by far the oldest of the three. "The firedrake has long since past. I cannot recall how long ago it was, but oh, oh, many a-long year it must be now."

Lars was distracted, looking out over the battlements.

"Pardon, sirs, but are those the lights of Lichport?"

"Aye, master. That is Lichport town."

In the distance, a carpet of jewels across the land and ended at the sea. Stars blinked over the water.

"That bright one there." Lars pointed, trying to figure out the town's layout. "Is that Gormlet house? Silas, is it?"

"I can't tell from here," Silas lied. Gormlet house had burned down more than a hundred years ago. But an instant later Silas felt unsure. They might be looking down upon a Lichport far older than he knew.

"Oh, my little poppets," said the spider-brusher, "Old Jane is sorry to have brought you so far for nowt. All those stairs, and nothing to see . . ."

One of the old men put down a sextant and looked at Silas.

"You come to see the firedrake, but I tell you it flew past long ago. But look up, young sir, look up! Everything we see in the heavens is but a fire out of the past. The flames of those high candles were lit long ago. The sky is a great vault of ancient wisdom, another door into the past that may be opened if we wish. The star's light lives on long after its living fire has been extinguished. So who can say when a thing begins and ends, eh? Our night is lit by very old light. And the light remembers. You know what I say is true, for you have a constellated look about you. Very well connected . . . indeed you are. Look to the heavens and see what you will, young sir."

In the past, when Silas used the death watch, he always thought of its mechanism like a heartbeat. When the clock's heart ticked, the world was as it was. When Silas stopped the dial, time stopped as well. He understood that the firedrake was some kind of brief light passing overhead, its illumination soon lost from sight. For an instant, it had once been a presence. Now it was only a memory; its light extinguished. Silas guessed that, like seeing ghosts, he could see that celestial fire if he wanted to. A comet was not a spirit, but hadn't the death watch also showed him other things? Old rooms. Fallen buildings. Images of the past of a place. Moments out of time. Why not a celestial event from long ago? *Show me the firedrake,* he thought. *Show me. . . .*

Silas could hear his own heartbeat. *Show me the firedrake,* he said over and over to himself. As he did, his heartbeat began to slow. He looked up and closed his eyes, then opened them. Nothing. But slower and slower his heartbeat became and as it stilled for just an instant in his chest, he looked up and saw that the stars had grown brighter, younger. Far beyond the battlements, a tiny gem of brilliance flew toward him. A comet. A dragon-tail flame of blue and red passed over him and streaked south, where it vanished beyond the summer house, above the woods, over an enormous oak that loomed above the other trees. Silas set the image of the firedrake and the tree in his memory and then closed his eyes again.

When Silas sat up, the night was cold, and he and Lars were alone on the tower.

"They've all gone," Lars said quietly. He was still looking out over the battlements toward where the town lights had been, but now, Lichport and the land were dark.

From the other side of Arvale, the peace of evening was broken by a familiar scream. Without fear or haste, Silas stood and said, "Lars, let's go back. I'm tired and we're not safe out here at night, especially so high up."

"Where are we going?"

"Back to my rooms. I need to rest. Tomorrow I will try to find the Mistle Child. I've seen in which direction it lies. And after I find it, I'm going home to Lichport."

Silas was deep in thought as they made their way back. He was sure his heart had stopped in that instant when he had seen the firedrake, a comet that had flown and died upon the air hundreds of years ago. He knew then, with absolute certainty, that to see the past meant releasing the present. The idea of stopping his heart to achieve this frightened him, but he wondered if this was how his great-grandfather had his visions. His heart had stopped beating long ago.

As they approached the door of his rooms, Silas tried to put from his mind the question of what kind of power might be wielded by an Undertaker if he were dead.

CHAPTER 29

FALLEN

THE WALLS AND PARAPETS OF ARVALE played host to a riot of carvings. Gargoyles. Grotesques. Noble busts. Triumphal Urns. Foliate Heads. Each one, an individual vision or memory fashioned in stone. Heroic events and past lives were memorialized by such sculptures. Leaf-faced men recalled the forest that once flourished where the house now sprawled. Demonic faces and chimeric creatures endured as testaments to the nightmares and terror-dreams of their carvers.

Far above the great doors of Arvale, perched on a ledge, was a small sculpture of a seated lion. It could barely be seen from the ground. The lion was a minor work, an apprentice piece, and indeed, its rough finish evidenced the talents of a young artist's hand. That apprentice's name was Will. When he completed the lion, his master looked it over and smiled. It was not perfect, not nearly, but in the curl of the mane and depth of the eyes, there were hints of the artist that might yet be. The master told Will to make his mark upon the stone. A bold *W* was carved on its base and the lion was set upon the high wall to look down over the courtyard. Three days later, the young apprentice fell from one of the parapets and died. He was buried in the village of Lichport in a small grave, but no gravestone remains. Only on the walls of Arvale did he leave his mark.

◆ ◆ ◆

The furious ghost was moving again, the very air shaking with her long cries.

As the nameless spirit careened over Arvale, her wailing fractured the mortar between the bricks and shook loose the slate shingles. Portions of the house crumbled before her as she flew, engulfed in flames. From the walls high above the courtyard, she reached out and tore a small stone lion from its long-held seat, and hurled it to the unyielding ground below. When the lion struck the earth, it burst into fragments and dust, and the maker's mark of Will the apprentice was shattered, and his name went forever out of the world.

Silas sat by the hearth in his room and pulled off his shoes. Outside, he could hear distant crashes and wails as the nameless ghost went about her mindless destruction.

He was exhausted but intent on investigating what he'd seen in his vision of the comet. Tomorrow he would go to the place in the forest where the "firedrake" fell. The cold air in the tower had cleared his mind, and brought him to another decision as well.

"Lars, when I leave, I'd very much like you to come with me."

"Silas, I don't think—"

"I know you don't really want to stay here, Lars, and why would you? You are as out of place here as I am. We should be back home in Lichport. I couldn't bear the idea of leaving you behind in this house."

"You make it all sound so easy, Silas."

"It is easy. I leave. You leave. We do this at the same time. Simple."

"I'm not sure I can face it, Silas. I left in a bad way."

"I'm telling you, whatever it is, I can help," said Silas, reassuringly. The truth was, though, Silas wasn't really sure what he'd be able to do for him. Lars had stepped out of his life into the otherworld. Where would he find himself if he returned? Silas knew when they got back, much time and care would be needed to help Lars adjust. But now, he would tell him anything to bring him some comfort and convince him to come back.

"What do you mean 'in a bad way'? Tell me what happened, Lars. It's okay. Whatever happened, it's all in the past now. "

But instead of beginning his own story, Lars asked Silas a question.

"Has it been hard, being away from Lichport?"

"Yes. But like you, I left things . . . unfinished, unsaid. I left in anger, and hurt a good friend. If I had it to do over again, I would do it differently. I might have waited a little longer to come here."

"You must have lots of friends there," Lars said.

"No, not really. I mean, I have some friends in Lichport, but not really anybody my age. I had a friend back in Saltsbridge, when I was younger, but he's gone now."

"Saltsbridge. I don't know that place. Is it up past Kingsport?"

Of course he doesn't know that name, Silas thought suddenly, *it had not yet been founded when he was last in Lichport.*

"Silas, come on now, not even a girl? Really? A fine fellow like yourself?"

"There was a girl, but I lost her. All I want now is to get her back."

Lars looked into the fire. His face softened, going wistful.

"I had a girl in Lichport. How alike we are, cousin. I've lost my girl too."

"Well, I suspect we're both rogues at heart, that's why," Silas said, trying to lighten the mood. Lars didn't look up. "What did she look like?" asked Silas.

"Oh, she was pretty. We used to meet often at night, for her father did not know about us. And in the moonlight . . . her pale skin . . . and her arms about me so tight—" Lars broke off his description, tears flooding his eyes. "Lord, Silas, I cannot speak of her. I'm such a coward. I've ruined everything."

Silas ached a little to hear the description. To feel Bea's arms about him, to feel her pressed against him, he would have given anything.

"Lars, you haven't ruined everything. Most problems can be mended. Tell me what happened."

Slowly, Lars began.

"We had been meeting at night, by the millpond. For weeks we made our assignations there. I'd leave her a little white stone, on her windowsill, and that way she'd know to meet me that night. It was perfect. I would come to the millpond and she'd be there, drawn out in moonlight and starlight against the reeds. But one evening, I left my white stone, yet when I arrived at the millpond she was not there. So I waited. Soon I heard footsteps and thought she was approaching, but as I watched, her seven brothers appeared on the path and saw me there. Fear took me, and I couldn't run. They grabbed hold of my arms and held me fast, and one pushed my head down into the water. Before my sunken eyes was blackness and I knew my life would end there, below the cold water. But then they roughly pulled me up and asked me what I was doing there, at the millpond, at night, as if they didn't know.

"Coughing up green water, I said I'd come to walk by night. I'd come for the quiet.

"'We'll show you quiet,' one said, and they thrust my head underwater again.

"I choked on weeds and frogspawn, and just when I thought I would succumb, I was pulled out again and jerked to my feet.

"'Leave this place, or die here,' they said.

"'I will leave,' I promised.

"'Leave here, and never come back.'

"'I will leave,' I said again.

"'Go from Lichport and never return,' they yelled. 'Never return.'

"And their words were a curse, for I ran into the woods along the marsh and lost my way, and came here to this house. But as I ran, I heard her voice and her brothers' shouts. There was a scream and all was silent, but still I ran and did not return."

Some of the details from Lars's story were uncomfortably familiar. But similar scenes must have played out in Lichport dozens of times over its long history. And the millpond, Silas knew all too well, was a traditional spot for secret lovers' assignations. But could it be that Lars was describing the story of Beatrice's own death? What was the lover's name in her story? No. Silas couldn't accept it. He refused to accept it. But far in the back of his thoughts, somewhere beyond his quickly silenced fears, a wiser part of Silas whispered: *Denial is easy when you don't want to know.*

Lars was sobbing.

Silas put his arms about Lars to comfort him and darkened his mind to anything other than calming his friend. "Those days are long past. Maybe, when we go back, things will be better. Maybe her brothers will be gone, or maybe there will be another girl," Silas said. Those things were certainly true. Her brothers, whoever they were, would now be in their graves. All the people he knew would be gone. Silas wanted to get Lars to think about a new life, but he needed to be careful and not say too much at once. Lars was from a Lichport that was no longer there. Still, let him come home and see his place and accept his lot. Then Silas would try to help. Lars could stay with him. *Roommates,* Silas thought, warming to the idea of having someone his own age in his life back home. And clearly, the dead did not terrify Lars. Maybe Lars could even help him with the undertaking. A friend *and* an assistant.

He lifted up Lars's face. "I promise you, it's going to be okay.

I'll help you, one way or another. You will come back to Lichport, and you'll live in my house. We shall be gentlemen bachelors, and all will be well," Silas said, trying to smile, trying to get Lars to smile.

"All right, Silas," said Lars, resigned. "All right. When you leave this house, I shall go with you, if I may."

"Good. That's settled then. We will not let the past haunt us." Silas took Lars's hand in his and shook it.

He poured two glasses from the decanter on the table and handed one to Lars. He raised his cup and encouraged Lars to do the same. "Come on! Let's drink to the past that was, and the future yet to come. Whatever is waiting for us back home, we can get through it together!"

They both emptied their glasses in one gulp. The liquor went down like fire, but Silas poured another round.

"And to Lichport. May our homecomings be happy ones."

Lars quickly wiped his eyes and then drained his glass. He took the bottle from Silas and filled their cups again.

"And to Beatrice," Lars said softly, "my dearest love."

Silas stopped breathing and set down his glass. The brief spell of self-delusion was shattered the second he heard Lars say her name.

"Do you know her, Silas? Do you know Beatrice, or her family? Is she still in Lichport?"

At hearing the words spoken out loud a second time, Silas felt like someone had hit him in the back of his head. Nauseated and dizzy, he knew it was his Bea whom Lars meant. He'd known already. There was no hiding from it. In that instant Silas realized he could never tell Lars the truth about her. Everything was ruined now. When he found Bea, she would see Lars and forget about Silas. Blackness rose like a veil before his eyes, and all he could think to do was speak the lie and get it out of the way. "No, Lars. I've never heard that name before. But if it's possible, I'll help you find her and you can be happy again."

Lars raised his glass to Silas's words, and drank once more. He smiled as he rose and went to the door, saying he would gather his things and see Silas the next day. Silas only nodded in response, and then bent over as if scratching his foot. After Lars left the chamber, Silas sat down on the carpet and put his face in his hands. He could command the dead, and bring them peace, but there was never going to be any joy left for him.

The weight of his promises was crushing him. As Silas considered that he had just agreed to help reunite his girlfriend with another guy, a small sob pushed his shoulders up and down, and he began to cry quietly into his hands.

CHAPTER 31

WAKE UP

THAT NIGHT, SILAS DREAMED OF BEA AGAIN, but he could not see her face. He jumped from one side of her to another, but always she turned her head away. In one hand, she held a piece of cloth. In the other, a needle and thread. She was stitching two letters in gold flax: *B* and *L*. As she put down the last small, careful stitches she said, "Gold is always best. What is stitched in gold shall last forever and cannot be undone. Beatrice and Lars."

"Say *my* name," said Silas. "Remember me, please."

But Bea only laughed and turned her head away from him again.

When Silas awoke, he found that his thigh was bleeding where he had clutched it during sleep. His nails had broken the skin. He wiped it with a cloth and dressed quickly.

The water in the basin was cold. He splashed his face, pulled on his shoes, and left his rooms, moving quietly through the house, not wanting to meet anyone, especially not Lars. It wasn't Lars's fault, but he couldn't look at him. Silas only wanted to finish what he'd started. He could at least try to do that. He would go alone and do whatever needed to be done to restore peace to the prison-house that Arvale had become to him.

Then he could go home with his girlfriend's lover and his heartbreak in tow and once again, make everything right for everyone but himself.

CHAPTER 32

IN THE WOODS

SILAS WALKED QUICKLY THROUGH THE GARDEN and toward the summer house. He barely noticed the change in the weather. It was not as warm as it had been when he last visited; a chill breeze nipped at the edges of the air, trying to chase the summer away. There were other small differences in the land. The roses were all blown now, petals gone, their thorns grown long and threatening. The topiaries that lined the garden path, previously wild and shapeless in exuberant growth, had now each taken on the same spare, discernible shape; green heads of boxwood wolves watched Silas as he passed.

As he emerged onto the lawn in the front of the summer house, Ottoline's voice greeted him.

"It's been AGES, Silas! How dare you keep yourself away! It is lovely of you to come to our little soirée! But as you see, you come upon us unawares. We weren't expecting you until this evening. Why, Cook hasn't even finished making the canapés!" Still, it's better you've come now. Yesterday was an utter miserino. Teddy lost all the shuttlecocks and then the rain came, completely spoiling the hunt. I was so looking forward to it," she said, drawing her finger gently back and forth across her lips. "It has been so long since I've gotten any blood on my hands. . . ."

"The weather is much better today, if not a bit colder," Silas said absently, wanting to keep moving.

"I am glad for it. I thought the season was going to be over early. I think tonight it should be very clear, the last of the good weather. Perfect! Now, you must have something to eat, you look famished. And goodness! Wherever have you been! Your unfashionable coat is covered in soot! Silas, really, your man should have seen to it!"

"I am sorry, dear cousin Ottoline, but I fear I can't tarry here with you today. My path lies a little farther on."

"Are you going hunting yourself? You look ever so determined. I like well that gleam in your eye. The weather is brisk and fine, as you say. If you can wait a tick, I'll go change into my hunts and we shall ride together."

"Oh, I would love to hunt with you, but today I haven't time."

For the briefest instant, Ottoline's exaggerated frown became something else. She tilted her head slightly and her eyes grew small and dark as she looked at Silas. He took a step back, suddenly afraid she was going to strike him for disappointing her. But then the moment passed, the smile returned to her face, and she swatted Silas's shoulder with her gloves.

"Silas, how tiresome you are! Very well. Wherever are you off to that you can't even stop for a small G and T with your cousins?"

"I am following the path of the firedrake into the woods to find the Mistle Child. I don't suppose you've seen it?"

"Oh, Silas, what a question. Don't *you* know where it is? I thought you were the scholar of the family. Didn't you speak to the father in his wretched basement?"

"I did. He did not elaborate much more on the matter. But he said that if I wanted to stop all the screaming, I would need the Mistle Child—"

"Yes, he would still want it, I suspect . . . ," mused Ottoline, looking down at her sharp, immaculate, and translucent fingernails.

"I've learned that it's in the forest—"

Ottoline smiled and held up a hand. She closed her eyes and, with the other hand, fondled a long strand of polished amber and jet beads. The mere mention of the forest set her into a little private reverie.

"Oh, Silas, the forest is lovely, simply divine. How we used to adore our romps in the greenwood," she said in a bit of a swoon. "Once, long ago, our country house was deeper in the woods. We favored privacy then, and didn't much receive company. Still, you could meet the most curious folks upon the forest paths. Such sights we saw within the wild places, when we hunted so regularly, and what good sport! And I can't lie, the trysts we all had were absolutely the choicest . . . but it was so long ago and everyone was so handsome and delicious. The long green days . . . yes, you must go to the woods and see what's still there to find. Cupid's victims always leave a little something behind, no?"

She opened her eyes and looked at Silas. "And when you come back, we'll have a little party for you. Won't that be nice?" She looked up at the sapphire sky. "See, it's going to be a lovely night to be out of doors. Positively perfect."

"Later, then," said Silas, as he began walking toward the forest.

"We will light the lamps for you, so you may return by way of the summer house," Ottoline said as he left. "What a time we'll have! It will just like the old days . . . with carpets on the grass!"

At the end of the lawn, there was a long, low mound, and behind it the edge of the forest rose up like a rippling green curtain. From the summer house, Silas had just been able to catch sight of the tall oak he'd spied from the tower. He thought that if he kept to a fairly straight line as he walked, he should run into it.

His optimism was ill-founded.

Soon after entering the forest, he became confused as to which way the tree lay. After walking for several minutes, he looked back over his shoulder, and realized that he was now surrounded by nearly identical trees and couldn't even discern the path back to the summer house. Indeed, there was no path at all. Before him, thick beams of sunlight pierced the canopy, making little glowing islands on the forest floor. Far away and deeper into the woods, he thought he heard the sound of horns.

He wandered for a time, unsure of how long it had been since he'd entered the forest. As the light began to gray, he looked up. Very little of the sky could be seen through the emerald canopy. He had no idea which way to go.

His mind drifted back to Beatrice again and what he was going to do when he got home with Lars. Maybe, he hoped, faced with the choice, she'd actually choose him. His gut told him she never would. Why would she? Lars was from her world, a lost fragment of her life. Lars was probably the reason she never went to her rest. Maybe if the two of them were reunited, then all the bad things that had happened to her would be mended somehow. Anyway, he'd made a promise to Lars to help him and he wasn't going to break it. But what would happen when he found her, when he broke whatever binding held her to the millpond, and brought her back from the waters? What then? How would he feel when he saw Bea's face again? Would he come to hate Lars for it? Or himself for making a promise before knowing the particulars?

The sound of birdcall sifted down from the branches, drawing his mind back to his search. Before him, a little robin jumped about, gathering leaves. It would take a few in its beak and fly off, then come back, pick up more, and fly off again. On one of its returns, it hopped just in front of him. Silas stood very still and the robin landed on his shoe, then flew off once more.

Silas followed the bird as it darted farther into the forest and finally toward a large oak tree, its branches hanging thick with mistletoe. *For the Mistle Child,* Silas thought.

The robin flew to the other side of the tree and disappeared. When Silas came around the wide trunk, he saw a great hole in the tree, an old deep hollow, its edges worn and rounded with age. The robin sat there, with two leaves in its mouth, then darted into the tree. Silas peered inside and saw the bird gently place the leaves on a small pile of other leaves at the bottom. The size of the tree allowed more than enough room to accommodate a person, so slowly and carefully, Silas climbed inside.

The rich smell of mold and earth was in his nose and mouth at once. A familiar smell. A grave smell. The floor of the hollow was deep with soft soil, and in the center was the robin's little mound of leaves. It looked to Silas like a small burial. Without hesitating, acting purely on instinct, he gently pushed his hands down through leaf and loam. Tiny pebbles, acorns, and cool dirt pressed against his skin. He probed a little farther. Perhaps eight or ten inches below the surface, Silas felt something not-earth scrape his hands. He drew it forth.

It was a small parcel, perhaps twenty inches long, made from thin oilcloth or perhaps from a sheet of uncut vellum. It was slightly rounded and a little open at one end, very stiff. Inside it, Silas heard a soft rattling. He climbed out of the tree with the parcel, careful not to spill its contents. He could sense the presence of remains, and in that instant, he understood what, or rather who, the Mistle Child might be.

Sitting on the ground in the fading light, surrounded by the snaking roots of the great tree, Silas opened the parcel.

Within were tiny bones and a small book. He opened the book briefly, and knew he'd found what he was looking for. His eyes welled with tears, for there, within the tree, was a place where hope had been hidden, but only sorrows had grown. He closed his eyes, feeling for the presence of this lost child. He sat for many moments, but no ghost appeared and he knew whatever else the tree had been long ago, it was now only a quiet grave.

He put the bones and the book back inside their vellum coffin and came away, carrying the Mistle Child in his arms. Silas followed the robin through the trees toward the lights now flickering in the distance.

As Silas approached the summer house, the robin departed. Night had fallen. The trees and hedges all about were strung with little fairy lights. Persian carpets covered the lawn and large tapestry cushions were strewn in all directions. Cousins lounged everywhere, laughing softly. Great lanterns dotted the lawn, and on low tables, drinks awaited their drinkers in cut crystal glasses and decanters that caught the light of constellation and candle both.

In the midst of the resplendent setting, Ottoline silently held out her arms to Silas, welcoming him back. She gestured to a place among some large pillows near a lantern. Silas sat down and opened the little parcel as if in a trance. The bones rattled softly as he took out the book. Its cover and pages were very thick, and when he held it in his hands, he could sense love and sorrow and fear pressed into it. He gazed over the small, hand-bound volume. On its cover were written the words *Booke of Erth*. Silas turned the pages and touched its inscriptions with his finger. He could feel the presence of the author. There were brief entries that seemed to be her own personal thoughts. Then there were lines of verse, perhaps hers, perhaps merely scraps of song from her time that held her heart and framed her own life's sad tale. Silas breathed in, smelling the loam still clinging to the parchment. His heartbeat slowed and the words rose up in him, filled him, until there was nothing else but what the nameless girl had written hundreds of years before.

Silas did not realize that he had begun to read aloud. The jeweled lantern lit his face, and in his eyes shone the glow of memory. His voice rose, and some of the lines spilled forth like a song, as though Silas had lived through those long-ago days himself. The words of the girl who'd written the *Booke of Erth* became his words and it sounded like two voices spoke as one as the story ascended into the evening air. The chatty cousins were spell-stopped, there upon the rich carpets lit by lantern and star.

One of the cousins silently rose from the carpet and, drawing her shawl over her head, took on the character of the girl in the story, not in mockery, but with absolute solemnity, as though she were miming events she once saw herself. A young man joined her—the fellow Ottoline had once called the girl's "paramour"— and as Silas read, he knew that here, before him, moving in pantomime, was the same youth who had been the girl's undoing in some ancient past. The young man was unchanged, handsome and lithe, timeless, a young lord of a thousand summers, barely able to remember, until now, his former lover . . . one little bird from so many that once flew across the forest where he had hunted long ago.

CHAPTER 33

THE BOOK OF EARTH

He cometh to my house and below my
window singeth sweetely to me. Each
night, these wordes from him to me he
calleth so faire. And in the light of
the moone he stands and with his songs
putteth me to swoone. . . .

> Between March and April
> when spring beginneth to spring
> The little bird hath all her will
> On her branch to singe.
> I live in love longinge
> For the fairest of all things—
> She may my bliss bringe;
> I am bound to her will.
> A fortunate gift I have received
> From heaven it is to me sent.
> From all other women my love rent
> And lighteth on Alysoun.

And I do meet him in the wood so wild
and he singeth to me in wordes milde.

Where be they that before us were,
Who hunted hawk and hound so long ago
And owned all the field and all the woode?
We are yet here, my lover telleth me plain.
And I know he speaketh well.
For in this wood we ride
And lo! my belly swells
All fulle with his pride.

My father sayeth women flaunt their
pride

and spring becomes them ill.
If I cannot hide my sin
then lost to fortune, I shall flee
and dwell in the wilde wood.
And tho winter cometh in, we warmed
shall be
All by the flames of my lover's love,
My little child and me.

All our Summer tyme now
endeth
Where to my love his love
sendeth?

Merry it is while summer lasts,
With birds in song;
Oh, now threatens north winds blasts
And storms so strong.
Oh, oh! But this night is long

And I do bear such wretched wrong,
In sorrow and mourn and fast.
For his love in sleep I slake,
For his love all night I wake,
For his love mourning I make
More than any maid.
Blow northern wind!
Send thou me my sweeting!
Blow northern wind! Blow, blow, blow!

Thoughe deepest winter now lay all
about,

My father cometh hunting in wilde rout.
No more songs my lover maketh me

I sing only winter that blighteth ev'ry
branch on ev'ry tree.

Winter wakeneth all my care;
Now the leaves waxeth bare;
Oft I mourn and in despair
Sigh when he cometh in my thought
How this world's joy
It goeth all to nought. . . .

My child,

Once I did come here and put my back
against this great oak tree.
Now I place you inside and pray my

father shall not find you, ever.
May your own sweet father soon come
here!
May his people hold and keep you dear!
Oh, folk of skin moste bright
gather ye up this innocent wight.
My child, I pray you shall go
Free from all my cares and worldly woe.
Now, child, take my name for all your
own
Though my name be all covered o'er
with sin
On you, in death, may it be washed
clean again.
Alysoun, Alysoun, no longer named I
Alysoun, your name shalle be, when I do
die.

And now I put this child of earth in
earth.

> Earth take of earth, earth with woe
> Earth other earth, to the earth do go
> Earth laid earth in the earthen trough
> Then had earth of earth earth enough.

I am nameth Alysoun and do love well
my forest childe. Alysoun I nameth her
so she shall remember in what world is

next her mother dear who must needs
leaveth her where she were born. And
so her mother's name shall be upon her
always even though her mother's loving
hands may not.

CHAPTER 34

LULLABY

AT THE END OF THE LITTLE BOOK, there was a name almost scratched into the vellum of the final page, and Silas spoke it softly into the evening air.

Alysoun.

Alysoun.

Alysoun.

And when he looked up, Alysoun, the terrible spirit who had wrought her sorrows and losses furiously against the walls and very stones of Arvale, stood quietly before him, little more than a child, perhaps of fourteen, in her ruined and tattered raiment, her face hidden below her hair. Seeing her then, as she was, and knowing what had befallen her, Silas knew he would never let anyone harm her again.

By the doors to the summer house, the nurse sat by the cradle, rocking the child and singing. The baby was crying softly, almost in time with the nurse's song.

Lollay, lollay, little child, why weepest thou so sore?
Little child, little child, you have been kept since
days of yore.
Child, if it betideth that thou shalt thrive in joy
Remember only that you were fostered upon your
nurse's knee.

Ever hold in your heart these things three:
Whence you have come, what thou art, and what
shall come of thee.
Lollay, lollay, little child, child, lollay, lollay.
With sorrow thou came into this world,
but in joy may thou wend away.

The nurse looked up at Silas and slowly nodded. He knew then what child it was she'd kept and tended. For though the infant had died and been buried by its mother in the tree, the baby's father's people had taken up the child after all. The nurse leaned into the cradle and brought out the Mistle Child. She followed Silas back to the edge of the lawn, where Alysoun stood, her hands shaking. Looking back once at the company, who waited silently in approval, the nurse handed the baby to her young mother. Alysoun stood and wept, and the stars stopped their round, and the company went quiet. She clutched the child to her and held her tight and dear. Slowly, she lifted up her head and spoke to Silas.

"Is this heaven?"

"No. I cannot give you heaven, but I can give you home. Little sister," Silas said tenderly, "come home with me." As he spoke the invitation, Silas realized he had just broken his promise to Cabel Umber, the same monster who'd wrought such horrors upon his own child and grandchild. Silas couldn't care less about his promise now.

He led Alysoun away. As they reached the path at the edge of the lawn, Ottoline waved and said, "Farewell, Silas! We'll come later to see you off!"

Silas looked back, and said with regret, "I fear there won't be time."

"Oh! Little cousin," Ottoline called after him gaily as he and Alysoun walked away, the sound of all the cousins' laughter briefly bubbling up, "there's all the time in the world!"

And beneath the ever-living stars, the candles and all the ornate lanterns were suddenly extinguished. Arrayed in shadow and starlight, the cousins left the lawn in quiet reverence, and took away with them the bones and the little book. They walked into the summer house, and its doors closed silently behind them.

CHAPTER 35

HOMEWARD BOUND

Silas broke into a run as he approached Arvale. The ghosts of Alysoun and her child were right behind him.

As he came to the entrance he held up his hand and the doors swung open. He crossed over the Limbus Stone and turned around to see the ghosts waiting in the middle of the threshold, unable to come any farther.

At the long table, Maud Umber and Lars sat staring.

Lars ran to Silas's side, but Maud spoke first. "This is well done! Well done. But Silas, abide a moment. She has been bound from entering the house. She may not pass the stone. Have you given her the waters? Is she safe? Is she nameless still?"

Maud's voice was measured. She smiled. But her eyes were fixed on the baby.

Silas saw this. "She has a name."

"You have found that as well? Very impressive, Silas. Truly, you are Janus of this house. Still, as she is, she may not enter here."

"Maud, I would break this stone in two before I allow it to become a wall to keep out this mansion's kin. She has the right to come in; this house was once her home."

"Yes, but she was banished," Maud said, then added gently, like the merest afterthought, "I do not imagine the baby is likewise bound. Perhaps if you bring *her* in . . . take pity on the infant . . . then you could more easily give remedy to the mother. For her, the obsequies must be obeyed, Silas. The Doom must be pronounced upon her. She has wandered. She has embraced unrest. She has wrought vengeance against this house. A judgment must be made, Silas. Let her take the waters and find rest, or send her down, if you must. Give me the child."

Alysoun stood upon the threshold but did not speak. She rocked her child in her arms and Maud's head moved back and forth, following the baby's face as though it were a pendulum.

"Thank you, Maud, but that will not be necessary. Tradition must bend to necessity. I am the Janus and will stand for the dead and for the peace of the house. There has been a terrible wrong committed against this girl. We must acknowledge that, and concessions must be made to heal the sins of the past."

"How?" asked Maud, her face flushing with desperation.

"I will start as I mean to go on. I will bring peace to my ancient sister. She has been judged enough. I mean to help her. Let me show you."

Silas put one foot onto the Limbus Stone near where Alysoun stood with her child.

"Little sister, Alysoun, welcome home. Be welcome here, among your kin. Come in, come in, come in."

Silas reached across the threshold and brought her inside the house by his own hand.

Maud Umber began to shake as the mother of the child entered Arvale. Her lips moved furiously, as though the frantic workings of her mind were spilling senselessly into her mouth. She muttered beneath her breath, but then began to speak, rapidly, madly. "The cursed one is coming *inside*. See how she clings to the child! Mother of Heaven, see! The cursed one! No child needs two mothers. Where is my child? Bring home the child! Give me my child!"

Maud's form erupted in flames that swirled about her, obscuring her face. From within the spectral fire, a terrible cry was heard. Maud flew toward the doorway where Alysoun and her child were standing oblivious to all.

"Let the baby come to me! It's mine! It must come to me!" Maud cried.

Alysoun stood immovable, holding her child, as Maud circled before the door in a burning arc.

"Maud Umber! Stop!" Silas commanded. For a moment, Maud was still again. Her eyes were wild, and tears streamed down her face. Silas did not want to call her to the stone, but as she began to move again toward Alysoun, Silas acted without thinking. He reached into his front coat pocket, pulled out a handful of the grave earth Mother Peale had put there, and threw it at Maud. The crumbling clod of earth struck her in the back and the effect was immediate. Dust engulfed her, extinguishing her cloak of flames. Her face softened instantly as she descended to the floor of the hall. She stood quietly, her jaw hanging slack, tears spilling from her eyes.

Silas knew the effects of the grave earth were brief. He could see now there would be no rest for her. "Maud Umber, be still. Will you take the waters that may bring peace and rest?" Maud's eyes were closed as she barely moved her head from side to side.

"No?"

Maud did not speak, but slowly, she raised her arms toward the baby, her hands reaching and clutching desperately at the empty air.

"Very well." Silas drew in a breath and when he spoke again, his voice rose in the cadence of command. "Maud Umber, I bid you to return now to that sphere within this house where you abide in solitude, until such a time as you can return to your kin in peace." As Silas finished speaking, his words echoed through the hall. Maud Umber dissolved upon the air and was gone.

Lars stood by the door with his mouth open.

Silas turned to Alysoun. She would look only at her child. In her child's face was all the home she wanted. In that moment, he knew that Arvale could offer her no solace at all. Silas imagined mother and child, sitting in the empty hall and he knew there would be no real peace for her in merely enduring on in another, larger prison of stone.

"Little sister?" said Silas, taking the vial of the waters of Lethe from his satchel. "Here is Heaven for thee. Here is peace, if you will take it."

Alysoun looked up at Silas. "Heaven's peace for my child and me?"

"I pray so, yes." He held up the crystal vial. Did she understand him? Did she believe it was holy water? Did it matter?

Alysoun held out her child to Silas. He gently tipped the bottle toward the baby's tiny mouth, letting fall three drops of the water. He held the vial up to Alysoun who looked at him questioningly. Silas whispered, "And Heaven for thee," and Alysoun drank from the vial. Light rose up about Alysoun and her child and they closed their eyes in bliss. For an instant, brightness filled the hall and pushed all the shadows up beyond the rafters. When the light faded, mother and child were gone.

Silas walked to the small table by the door and took the scepter, sliding it into the deep inside pocket of the coat his great-grandfather had given him. He looked past the threshold and saw that the path back to Lichport had been revealed once more. Exhausted but determined, Silas looked at Lars and said, "We're leaving. Now."

LEDGER

When the infernal huntsman rests, the earth weeps to bear so great an evil deep within her bosom. When the infernal huntsman rides forth, the earth trembles to bear the weight of so great an evil. When the infernal huntsman chooses his quarry, the earth hides its eyes so that it may not see the evil one soul may wreak upon another.

—From *A Mirror of Penitence*, by Jacopo Passavanti, 1354, translated by Amos Umber

CHAPTER 36

A PROMISE BROKEN

HIS DAUGHTER HAD BEEN SENT OUT OF THE WORLD and taken the Mistle Child with her, and Cabel Umber knew it. He looked at the massive bronze statue of Moloch, its swollen belly-oven and empty sacrificial receptacles glowing red from the eager flames and hungry embers he'd set burning inside it. Now there would be no sacrifice. Long ago, the offering had likewise escaped him when his daughter had hid her filthy infant—the firstborn of his firstborn—in the forest. Now Silas, firstborn of his own family, had put the sacrifice beyond his reach. Cabel threw another log into Moloch's belly.

Amends would have to be made.

The bronze idol groaned as the fire inside it flew upward into the bull-shaped head. Its wide hollow eyes blazed and flashed.

Cabel stood in his deep chamber, his vengeful thoughts boiling in anticipation. It was true. Silas had not brought him the Mistle Child and would have to pay the price. All to the good, he now saw. With his daughter gone, her curse upon him had dissolved. And to seal it, Silas had broken his promise. The Undertaker, the Janus of Arvale, had deliberately cast aside his vow.

Cabel Umber was free to leave his prison house.

How long had it been since he'd moved in society? He was eager to hunt again, hungry to begin taking back his losses. And wasn't there a pretty little doe he might chase down for sport?

Hadn't he seen such a creature in the front of Silas's mind? Oh, indeed he had. Pale and lithe. Cabel Umber thought a visit to the village might be in order to settle accounts and seek out a little diversion.

He looked about him and began moving quickly and deliberately through the debris of the room, selecting a horse skull, certain bones, and crooked pieces of wood, weaving them into a mockery of a horse's frame. He went to the belly of the idol, and, drawing out two burning embers, set them in the eye sockets of the skull. He drew a sigil in soot upon the bony brow and spoke words as dark as the ashes on his hands. At once, the semblance of a horse threw back its skull and screamed, rearing up as Cabel leapt upon its back.

CHAPTER 37

A HUNTING I WILL GO

SILAS AND LARS CAME OUT OF THE FOREST and quickened their pace as they entered the long valley of ancient tombs. Behind them, in the distance, they could hear the sound of horses' hooves and the long cry of horns. They pressed on. Night noises rose and fell all about them. Disembodied voices whispered, drifting aimlessly from the mausoleums.

Side by side they made their way. Bright moonlight fell across the sarcophagi and monuments lining the path, making them glow.

The two walked in silence until the quiet between them became too much and Lars said, "Won't you say something, Silas? You're making me nervous."

Silas could barely hear Lars's voice. He was deep in thought, trying to anticipate the awfulness waiting for him beyond the gate. He was walking from one world of problems to another.

"I'm sorry if I said something wrong. I didn't mean to make you angry. Please, Silas, you're the only friend I have just at the moment. You'd said you'd help me."

Silas stopped and turned to Lars.

"I will help you, Lars. I'll keep my promise. It won't be easy, though, and I need you to understand that. Finding Beatrice might be particularly hard for me."

"Why?"

"Beatrice and I have a past."

"I thought you said you didn't know her."

"Well, I do know her. I mean, I did know her. Look, Lars, I said I'd help and I will, just—" Silas thought of how tenderly he felt about Lars. He did want to help him, it was just that to give Lars back his heart, Silas would have to break his own. That wasn't Lars's fault, though. No one had to be at fault. No one had to be blamed. It was a terrible situation, but taking it out on Lars wasn't going to help either of them.

"It's okay, Lars," Silas said. "We will work it all out later. Let's just get home."

Lars looked up, trying to smile. "Good. Home, then." But then he asked, "How long have I been away?"

"I don't know."

"Silas—"

"A long time. Leave it now."

The closed gates were just ahead and beyond them, Lichport waited.

"Come on, Lars," said Silas. "Almost home."

But their brief accord was shattered by the deafening sound of hooves, and, flying down the path toward them, a nightmarish horse and rider. His body was awash in black flames and his horse was formed from large bones and slabs of rotten wood. Splinters flew from the horse's body as its hooves struck the earth.

"Silas!" Lars cried desperately. "Open the gates!"

Last time he'd stood there, his great-grandfather had bellowed and the gates had opened. Now, Silas could do it for himself. He reached out his hand. The metal bars shuddered.

Silas took out his pendant, a reminder of what he was now, as if showing the Janus pendant to the gates would compel them to open more quickly.

It sounded like a train was roaring down the path in their

direction. Lars was terrified. "It's coming, Silas! That *thing* is coming!"

Silas was about to run up and put his hands on the gates to try again when a thunderous voice hurtled down among them. "Hold fast, ye gates!" screamed Cabel Umber. "Hold fast!"

"Maybe it's because I'm here . . . ," Lars said, shaking.

"No. It's me. I owe him something and now he's never going to get it. He wants to challenge me." Silas began to intone, "I am the Janus. I am the Lord of Gates and none other. I am the living heir of Arvale! Open!"

There was only the moonlight glinting off the heavy iron scrollwork.

Silas conjured an image of his great-grandfather into his mind and began to yell, his voice becoming the roar of a storm.

"I am the Janus!" Silas screamed, his eyes closed. The pendant burned against his skin, as, for an instant, his heart seized in his chest.

Deep from the earth came a groaning, as though some ancient mechanism had been engaged, and titanic wheels of stone started slowly turning. Before them, the gates began to open, the iron vibrating as though charged with current.

Behind them, Cabel Umber and his skeletal steed plunged down into the earth, and a second after, burst up again between them and the path home, blocking their way out. Before Silas could run or think of anything to do to protect himself, the spirit spoke.

"There is no need to fear me. I come only to settle accounts, then I shall be on my way."

Not pausing for even an instant, Silas roared, "Cabel Umber, I call you back to the Limbus Stone! Go back, Cabel Umber! Sink down into the Abyss!"

Silas's voice was electric with command, but Cabel sat upon

his mount, unaffected.

"You are standing on the wrong side of the stone to be giving orders. But more to the point, you cannot compel me to any action. I am still here, Silas Umber, because you may have no power over one to whom you are in debt. And you are in debt to me, are you not? Now I shall have my due. All debts must be paid, little man. One way or another. That is Old Law." The cruel features of Cabel Umber's skeletal face had sharpened in the air and contorted into a mask of unmitigated hatred and fury.

Lars tried to jump between Silas and Cabel Umber, but the spirit moved too quickly, and Lars was thrown out of the way.

Looming over Silas, Cabel said, "I will not haggle with you, Silas Umber, like a tinker at the gate. Here is my price!" And he leapt from his steed. From the churning shadow of his form, a gray hand with nails tipped like daggers flew down at Silas, passing through his clothes at the shoulder, and into his flesh. Swift and determined, they moved over his skin, tearing where they touched. Silas writhed in agony, but could not move from the spot. As Cabel cut the curse glyph into Silas's skin, his cruel voice rose in a crescendo on the cold air.

"Gods of the Inferno, take his breath! Bind his limbs. Nemesis, Queen of Vengeance, shorten his days, turn his blood cold. Dark Ones, by this sign I make in flesh and blood, know that Silas Umber is your victim!"

Silas's head fell back in pain and his ears throbbed and hummed as though Cabel's words were poison poured into them. He heard Lars shouting, but it sounded miles away. There was darkness before and behind him, and his limbs grew cold. He heard the horns again. They were closer, rising into an excited cacophony. As Silas opened his eyes, riders burst forth from the tree line and onto the path ahead of him. Cabel drew back his curse-tipped fingers, fearfully recoiling and remounting his horse in a swirl of coal-black shadow.

"Little cousin Silas!" cried Ottoline at the head of the company of riders. "It *is* kind of you to give us our sport this night!" She was a welcome sight, resplendent in her red coat and black boots.

Silas nearly passed out with joy at seeing his cousins from the summer house, here, upon the road home. He recognized many of them, but their aspects were darker, crueler. This was their natural element. Their features were sharp and they wore expressions of delight and exuberant bloodlust.

"I am so happy to see you, cousin Ottoline!" Silas said, clenching his teeth at the pain in his shoulder.

"But of course you are, Silas. Why wouldn't you be? Now, I see this shifty fox has fled his den; I'd hate to deprive you of your fun, but perhaps we might give chase for a bit?"

"Yes . . . please," said Silas.

"How kind of you! We'll see him back into his hole!" The bright coats of the riders and the silver bells on their horse's manes shone in the moonlight as the horses stamped impatiently on the earth. The riders drew their thin, sharp swords and bared their teeth. Their eyes burned with predatory zeal. One of the riders took up a golden horn and let loose its cry. Cabel Umber turned and fled, but the riders wheeled their steeds and rode hard upon him through the icy night and back up the road to Arvale.

The sound of hooves and horns faded in the distance. The gates leading home stood open.

Silas took a step and saw that Lars wasn't following him.

Silas turned and took Lars's hand in his.

"We're going home," Silas said, the words at first sticking in his throat.

"Silas, do you still promise to help me? I can't go back alone."

"You won't be alone. I swear."

Lars nodded, and they stepped together through the gates and back into Lichport. They had walked a few feet in, onto Fort Street, when Silas felt Lars slow his pace slightly, no doubt nervous about his homecoming. In Silas's front pocket, the death watch began ticking again, and Silas could feel the small rhythm of its mechanism leap into a whir. He took it out, comforted to know that time had returned to its forward motion. He was about to ask how it felt to be home when Lars's hand slipped from his. Silas turned around.

Lars stood a few paces away, frozen where his feet touched the ground of the town where he had been born nearly three hundred years before. His face was gray, as were his hair and clothes, and his skin looked dry and rough. Lars's eyes were closed and his mouth hung open in an unvoiced gasp. The air seemed to waver about him. Silas took another step toward Lars and went to take his hand again. But as Silas reached out and touched him, Lars broke apart, as though made of ash, and fell away to dust.

Silas stood there stunned, gazing at the empty air where, only an instant before, his friend had stood.

Then, without thinking, Silas bent over and took up a handful of the dust and put it in the outside pocket of his greatcoat. Sorrow clutched at him. But already another thought siezed his mind, though it filled him with shame. His heart began dividing. There was grief and guilt at his friend's death, and they were almost too much to bear. But somewhere deep inside him, from a place beyond his misery, another voice spoke, and said without a hint of sorrow: *She is yours again.*

If Silas could free her, he could have Bea back. It was easier to think only of this. What could he do about Lars now? Maybe it wasn't really his fault. Weren't there ancient stories about those who wandered into the otherworld only to come back and find their postponed deaths waiting for them? *Yes, Silas told himself, there are such stories, and so you should have known better.*

With his pockets filled with dust, Silas turned away from the gate and started walking back into Lichport. As he made his way down Fort Street, he looked up at the window of his great-grandfather's house. Nothing greeted his gaze. He looked down at the ring his great-grandfather had given him. In the deep blue of the stone, he could see the towers of Arvale looming. Below them, figures stirred in familiar scenes, as though the events there had all been stored within the bright gem. But now even the ring made him feel as though he were being watched. He didn't want to think about Arvale now. He slipped the ring from his finger and put it in his pocket, and instantly his memories of the house began to pale and blur. So this was the ring's gift, perhaps its gift to a living wearer: The stone granted memory of the otherworld. Silas took out the ring again and looked at it. His mind flooded with the names of necromantic texts and spells that Cabel Umber had told him. And in that moment as he put the ring back on, Silas was adamant about what he would do next.

He didn't trust anything about Cabel Umber, but some of the books he'd mentioned Silas knew were real because he'd seen them. While his father's library held a few general books on things like necromancy, Silas knew they were merely academic works. The subject would have been abhorrent to his dad. But there were other libraries in Lichport that held older, more practical texts.

So Silas would not go home. Not yet.

His shoulder blistered and burned. The place where Cabel had struck him and dragged his sharp nails through his skin was sore to the touch and burned like a hundred wasp stings. The pain went deeper into his bones. Silas rubbed his shoulder and sucked in air quickly through his teeth. Maybe Mrs. Bowe could help. No. He wouldn't go to her begging. When the night's work was done he'd go ask Mother Peale for help. He tried to push as much of the pain from his mind as he could, and, as if in response, the wound began to numb. He knew he should go home and rest, but his heart, rousing itself at the thought of Beatrice and the hope of seeing her, spoke and lied to him: *If you could only see her again, all might be well. When you look into her eyes, everything shall be restored. Call her back to you. Summon her. Bring her back and your joys shall banish everything else in the world. There shall be no more pain. No more pain. Only love.*

As he turned down Fairview Street, he glanced back toward the millpond and said softly, "I will come for you," before he started to run. With necromantic intentions burning at the edges of his mind, Silas ran down Fairview toward Temple Street and his mother's house, where his uncle's rarest and darkest books were still kept, locked away in the north wing.

As he ran, he briefly noticed the awkward weight of the scepter he'd taken from Arvale had vanished from his coat pocket. The scepter had not come with him beyond the gate. *Forget it,* he told himself, starting to run a bit faster. It was the smallest item on his growing list of losses.

CHAPTER 38

CURSES

WHEN DOLORES UMBER HEARD THE FRONT DOOR open, she knew it was her son. She was relieved he was back; part of her worried he was not ever going to come home. He'd been gone for a month.

As Silas walked into the parlor, Dolores could see by his face that he was in pain, and his clothes were torn at the shoulder and stained with blood.

"Christ, Si, what happened to you?"

"Nothing," he said distractedly, "I'm fine. I fell. I'll be okay."

But Dolores could see he was not okay. Her son's face showed it, and every time he moved his arm, he grimaced and squeezed his eyes closed tightly.

"Take off your coat, Silas."

"Mom, I said I'm fine. I just fell."

She walked over to him and started pulling off his coat.

"Mom! I said—"

"I don't care what you said, Silas. You show me, or by God . . ."

"All right, all right." Silas removed his coat and jacket and then, with difficulty, unbuttoned the top of his shirt and slid it down.

Dolores's heart nearly stopped at what she saw. "Jesus Christ! Silas, what the hell happened to you?"

"I told you, I fell and hurt my shoulder." He wasn't even trying to lie.

She couldn't take her eyes off the malicious glyph burned into her son. All about the lines torn through his flesh, the skin rose up red and angry. She didn't know what kind precisely, but she knew this was a cursing mark. Someone was trying to kill her son. Her face paled as she pulled his shirt back up over the wound.

"Silas, we need to see someone about this," she said, stumbling over her words. Who could help them? Mother Peale? Possibly, but this was no Narrows shanty spell.

Silas kept looking back at the stairs with an anxious look.

"Mom," he said, "I don't want you to get worried, but I need to go upstairs."

"Those doors are locked, Silas, and they are not going to be opened again."

He looked at her, all expression gone from his face and said, "It's important. Please."

"Silas! You know what went on up there. That's all in the past. We don't go into that wing."

"Mom, I just want to read and rest. I am not of afraid of this house or anything that happened in it. Please."

But then Dolores thought if he went upstairs and relaxed, it might give her a chance to go get help. Maybe, if Silas stayed put, she could run out without worrying he was off getting into more trouble. "All right, Silas, if it's important to you, you can go up there for a bit, but why not rest downstairs first." She didn't think he'd wait, but it was worth a try to buy her more time. "I was just about to go out. How about when I get back, I'll unlock the door for you? I won't be gone long, and when I get home, I'll dig up that key. How about that?" She could tell he wasn't listening to a word she said. *Fine*, she thought. *I'll go get help and fight with him later.*

"Silas, please wait for me. You look terrible. Sit down here and wait. Please say you will."

"I will."

His answer was cold, mechanical. A portion of light had left his eyes and he stared at her, unblinking.

Without another word, Dolores went into the hall and grabbed her coat, calling back over her shoulder, "I'll be back real soon, Si. Fix yourself something if you like. You just relax until I come home!"

As she went out the front door, she could already hear him on the staircase. Was he going to break down the door up there? On the sidewalk, she looked back and saw lights on now in the north wing. *How the hell . . . ?* She mustn't stop. She started to walk fast.

Dolores knew that her son was in bad trouble. She knew it. As she walked, her mind started to play out every horrible scenario it could imagine. She saw herself walking back into the house and finding Silas cold and dead on the carpet of the parlor. "Oh, Christ! Oh, Christ . . . ," she said, and before she could stop herself, she was sobbing. She knew she wasn't going to Mother Peale's.

There was only one place in Lichport where she might find the kind of help Silas needed.

"WELL, THIS IS QUITE THE SURPRISE," said the first of the three.

"Indeed," said the second, "especially considering what you said to us on your last visit. We thought you'd brought your baby to us for a blessing . . . because he'd gotten such an awkward start in life."

"But she called us meddlers," said the first.

"So long ago," whispered the third. "Hardly worth mentioning."

"We'd thought you'd forgotten about us," the first said.

"No. I have not forgotten you," said Dolores in a low voice, her eyes running wildly over the tapestry. There were hastily stitched depictions of a dark figure striking someone wearing a large coat. Was it Silas? There was the same youthful form, leaning over a desk covered with books. Several unknotted threads still hung from it, as though it had only recently been stitched down. In the scene, a menacing shadow of black wool was hanging from the ceiling of the room just above the figure's head.

Back and forth, Dolores's eyes scanned the tapestry for signs of her son.

"Can't you look upon us, even now?"

Dolores raised her head and looked at the three women. They were cloaked in tattered sackcloth and their faces were streaked with ashes. In their hands they held an unfinished winding sheet. While they stared at Dolores, their hands continued embroidering its edges.

"So, Dolores Umber, you have come to observe with us the ancient rites of passage? That is good. To have the mother of the Janus present as we weave and embroider his burial shroud is indeed an honor. Will you take up needle and thread and join our work at last?"

"No . . . I cannot. I have come to ask you—"

"She is here to sue for his life," the second of the three interrupted with disappointment weighing down her words, her needle pausing its work.

"Is this true, Dolores Umber?" the first asked. "Do you come here on behalf of your son, to beg? It is too late. The curse will hold. His spool has raveled down to thrums. A great pity, for we had such high hopes for him." And the first glanced at her sisters with a knowing look in her eyes and nodded slowly as if to say, *Almost there.*

"Besides," said the second, "you should be grateful. Had Amos not been so talented, Silas would never have lived even this long."

"Silas does not know I am here. I have come because I have failed him so many times and now I must . . . if I can . . . I must help him. You must help him!"

"Does she ask us or tell us?" said the third, raising an ash-encrusted eyebrow.

"She would do better to beg," the second said to the third, "for we find compulsion a most unsavory dish, even here, upon the eve of the funeral feast."

"I *am* begging you! Please!" Dolores cried, falling to her knees on the floor. She struck her breast with her fist and cast down her eyes. "I know you owe him something. He is important to you. I know that."

But the third corrected her. "That depends on where you're

standing. We might, however, agree to an exchange. We cannot annul the decree, that is not within our power. The curse is a terrible one, wrought by a powerful spirit, and its price must be paid . . . one way or another."

"But," said the second, relishing the words, "if there were another sacrifice who was willing . . . a worthy sacrifice . . ."

The aspects of the three were growing darker as they spoke. Older, wilder. A fire leapt up in the cold hearth at the center of the room.

"Only fair," said the third.

"A life for a life," added the second.

Her heart almost stopped when she heard those words. Still, something in Dolores had known that it would come to this, that an Umber man would be the death of her one way or another. It was for her son. She was ready to do whatever was required. She opened her mouth as if to argue, but then thought, *For my child, anything, anything.*

"You realize," said the first, "we would do this only for a woman, and a mother, someone with strength. You know this seals it?"

"I'm not going anywhere," Dolores said, resigned. "I've always known that."

"Then it's a bargain?" the first of the three asked, leaning in close to her.

"Yes." Dolores nodded slowly in assent, but quietly thought to herself, *We shall see.*

"You know there must be blood," stated the third. It was not a question.

"I understand."

The first of the three bent down and pulled a long thread from the hem of Dolores's dress. She cut it in half with small silver shears and handed one part to the second of the three who held it briefly while she began to pull out the stitches depicting Silas in the tapestry. Then the second drew up another spool from the floor, black flax, and used it to stitch down the piece of thread from Dolores's dress, quickly covering it over, embroidering the shape of a woman upon a bier.

The first examined the new stitches on the tapestry. Tiny particles of ash fell from her face as she pulled a thread from the now ripped-out embroidered form of Silas that hung loosely from the weaving. Turning back, the first then plucked a hair from Dolores's head. These she twisted together with the piece from Dolores's dress into a tight, thin thread. She drew a tiny bone needle from her gown and stood next to Dolores.

"Dolores Umber, do you come here of your own free will?"

"I do."

"And do you make this sacrifice willingly?"

"I do."

The first of the three smiled, threaded the needle, and then took up Dolores's arm.

"This will only hurt a little. . . ."

Almost instantly, the thread was stitched through her flesh in the shape of the curse-glyph. Dolores's skin rose up in a red sore all about it, as though the thread were being absorbed into her body. A moment later, the thread was gone, but a bloody scar stood upon her skin in the shape of the same sigil she'd seen on her son.

"It is done," the three said as one.

"Do you promise? Is he safe?"

The three spoke together. "He will never be safe, but he will live tonight. The curse is no longer upon him. Who knows what tomorrow may hold for him?"

"It is broken, then?" Dolores asked, already knowing the answer.

"No. The curse is not broken, but has been lifted from *him*. Now you must leave us. Travel well, sister. And return to us when you can."

Dolores Umber made her way slowly down the stairs.

After Dolores had gone, the three spoke among themselves.

"Well, that's something," said the second of three.

"Indeed," said the first, "only two more to go and then perhaps we may walk a little and be free of our troubles."

"May it be so!" the three said in chorus.

"And what of the other two?" asked the second. "The Bowe woman and the Mother of the Narrows? Will she bring them?"

"They would be fine choices, but who can say?"

"There must always be three," said the third.

"Indeed," said the first. "That is law."

"They are all moved by their love of the boy . . . ," suggested the second.

"This has not escaped my notice," replied the first of the three.

"But enough! We'll keep on until the others come. They are close. Very close. None are so very young, and they keep dangerous company. Patience. Patience. Even now, the scene is changing."

And the three took up their needles and returned to the tapestry.

CHAPTER 40

MOONLIGHT BECOMES YOU

As Dolores left the mansion of the Sewing Circle, the wind was coming in from the east, carrying the smell of the sea. She looked at the marking on her arm. It no longer hurt, but the rest of her body ached with chill.

She just wanted to get home.

It was almost over.

She was nearly to the end of Prince Street. Not much farther.

Dolores looked up as she walked. She wanted to see the stars, but the moon's light outshone them. There was only the moon. Ahead, she thought she saw someone, maybe Silas, go running up Fairview Street and swiftly pass out of sight again. Dolores called out to him, but the words fell back in her tightening throat. Had it even been Silas?

The moon seemed too bright now, as though it had swung too close to the earth, as though it were stooping to crush her. Her chest pulled tight and her teeth crashed together as the pain shot through her like a dozen barbed arrows. She knew where Silas was going eventually. To the millpond. He was always going to *her.* She put her head down. *But my son is still alive,* she thought. No matter what followed, at least he was alive. Dolores began to sob. The millpond. Christ. She had saved and failed him both at once.

The pain pulled her down to the sidewalk. She closed her eyes and saw her son's face. In her mind's eye, he was kneeling next to her. She held the vision for as long as she could, but the curse knotted her body with anguish and poison. The moonlight spilled across Dolores Umber's form, and her cooling skin appeared to glow against the dark stones of the street. She shook her head slowly in self-reproach. She wished she'd worn her pearls. With her last remaining strength, she tried to move her limbs to her sides so she wouldn't appear so pathetic when someone found her body.

LEDGER

Every night and every morn
Some to misery are born.
Every morn and every night
Some are born to sweet delight.
Some are born to sweet delight,
Some are born to endless night.

—FROM WILLIAM BLAKE, *AUGURIES OF INNOCENCE*,
TRANSCRIBED BY AMOS UMBER

CHAPTER 41

HOMECOMING

AUGUSTUS HOWESMAN HAD LEFT HIS HOUSE to find Silas. He had seen his great-grandson pass by his house on his return from Arvale. Why hadn't he come in? He'd wanted to follow, but he was moving slowly again, and knew he wouldn't be able to catch up. Yet the more Augustus thought about Silas, tried to see him in his mind, the more his limbs eased, allowing him to move more quickly.

It was a bad night. There was a bite in the freezing air, and something worse. They were all bad nights now. What had happened up at Arvale since Silas had set him free from the Doom? He'd make sure Silas was safe with his mother and then make his way back to Fort Street and wait this night out. He stood still, and his eyes paled to white stones. He could see Silas in this way. Ease his own mind.

The vision came rising up behind his rheumy eyes.

First he saw Silas sitting in a room lit only by a candle. Old books lay open on a table before him, and he was furiously writing on a notepad. Then the vision turned, and Augustus could see only ice, but the angle of sight pulled back suddenly. He saw his great-grandson not at Delores's house on Temple Street, but standing by the edge of the millpond. Silas was speaking into the air, on and on. Then Silas leaned over, put his hand on the ice, tilted his head back, and shouted again into the night. The ice covering the pond cracked.

Beyond the vision, in his mortal hearing, Augustus heard a clap like thunder break the air. Before the vision dissolved, he saw a shadow rise up in front of his great-grandson, a familiar form coming up from below the waters, taking shape upon the rising vapor. In his vision, through their shared blood, he could feel Silas's heart and hear his voice crying out a terrible spell, dark with words of summoning, and command, and a love from which no good comes. Words to break the binding of the dead. Words to summon shades up from the murk places of the earth. Words of love and longing to call the dead back into the circle of the sun. And something else, rising above all the others. A name. *Beatrice*. But was the vision showing him the present or the future? He couldn't be sure, but he prayed none of it had happened yet.

Either way, Augustus Howesman knew he had to go to Silas, to warn his great-grandson, or, if it had already begun, to cover the boy's mouth with his hand, to make him swallow those awful words, and hold him back from that grim path that led to perdition.

He was about to begin walking again when he heard a loud howl, maybe over on the Beacon. *A black-dog night to be sure,* he thought. Augustus turned his head slowly toward the sea, toward the sound of the night-cry, and saw something on the sidewalk farther down Prince Street. He stared for many moments and finally, realizing what he was seeing, choked around the lump in his throat, and tightened his hands. Silas would have to wait.

Augustus Howesman walked slowly toward the corpse of his granddaughter.

He leaned down, careful to keep his balance, and stroked the side of her face with his large hand.

"Child, child . . . ," he said, the dry skin of his lips and throat straining the words into a low rasp. He put his hand under Dolores's head and began to lift her as though she weighed nothing. He put his other arm under her knees and stood up, cradling her against his large chest. ". . . Child, come away with me. Blessed child of the people of the barrow, be easy within your limbs. Child of the dawn and the twilight, may you rest in the shade of the cedar. May you be content until you wake again, at home and forever in the house of your eternity. Little daughter, how I love you, now and always. Look, I shall carry you home."

And as dry sobs wracked his body, Augustus Howesman carried his granddaughter back to her house on Temple Street, hoping that Silas would be there.

ARI BERK is an award-winning writer who works in a library filled to the ceiling with thousands of arcane books and more than a few wondrous artifacts. When not writing, he moonlights as professor of mythology and folklore at Central Michigan University. He lives in Michigan with his wife and son. Visit him at ariberk.com.